Particular
Attachments

L.L. Diamond

Particular Intentions

By L.L. Diamond
Published by L.L. Diamond and White Soup Press
Copyright ©2017 LL Diamond

Cover and internal design © 2017 L.L. Diamond
Cover design by L.L. Diamond/Diamondback Covers
Front and back cover: Catharine Gray, Lady Manners by Thomas Lawrence
Back cover: The Recital by Vittorio Reggianini
Source: Wikimedia Commons.

ISBN 13: 978-0-9967891-5-8
ISBN 10: 0-9967891-5-4

Facebook: https://www.facebook.com/LLDiamond
Instagram: @l.l.diamond
Twitter: @LLDiamond2
Blog: http://lldiamondwrites.com/
Austen Variations: http://austenvariations.com/

Other works by L.L. Diamond include:
Rain and Retribution
A Matter of Chance
An Unwavering Trust
The Earl's Conquest
Particular Intentions

To those who give me the highest compliments by saying you have re-read
one of my books, to those who comment on every chapter when I post a story,
and to those who have loved one of my books enough to buy another.
You are the one of the biggest reasons I continue to write.
I wouldn't enjoy it nearly as much without your lovely words.
Thank you for your love and support these last five years.

Chapter 1

One more daisy! With a gentle tug, the lush stem gave way to her small fingers, and she added it to the cluster she was holding in her other hand. Georgiana Darcy studied the bouquet, giving a decisive nod. Mother would adore them.

She glanced about her, peering around the tall green grass near the pond. Now, where had she left Matilda? After several steps in the direction of the house, she spied a bit of her favourite doll's painted golden hair peeking from behind the row the lavender she had plundered before the daisies.

"There you are!"

Once Matilda was again clutched in her free arm, she skipped in the direction of an enormous rug set out beside the pond. Her mother reclined on a chaise near the edge, her eyes following a pair of swans gliding gracefully along the glassy surface of the water.

She walked the last few feet and held the bouquet before her mother. "I picked them for you."

Her mother's pale face broke into a brilliant smile. "Oh, Georgiana, they are lovely." She took them and pressed her nose into the blossoms as she inhaled. "You know how much I adore the scent of lavender. Thank you."

She waved a footman closer. "Have these put in some water and have Claire set them upon my dressing table."

Georgiana grinned as she warmed at her mother's pleased countenance. She knew she would like them!

Her mother held her arms outstretched, and Georgiana fell into her embrace. Despite her frail appearance, her mother pulled her tightly to her. "I love you, my sweet girl."

"I love you, too."

"Oh, a picnic! What a wonderful idea!"

Georgiana lifted from her mother with care and turned. Why were Lord and Lady Lindsey paying a call?

A weary smile greeted the newcomers. "Amelia, I am in your debt!" Her mother's voice was weak and breathy. She had been ill for so long. When would she again be well?

Lady Lindsey rushed forward and took her mother's hands. "Nonsense!

You would do the same if I urgently required Nathaniel brought to me." Tears flooded her mother's eyes as her friend knelt beside her.

"How is Fitzwilliam?" asked her mother.

Fitzwilliam? He was supposed to be in school. Why would he return before summer?

Lady Lindsey removed a handkerchief from her reticule and dabbed the damp from her mother's cheeks. "He is refreshing himself and will join us in a moment."

Movement in the corner of her eye drew Georgiana's attention to the Lindseys' son standing slightly behind his father. Oh no! Why had they brought him? Was he not supposed to be at Eton? Well, if he was not, they could have left him at Totford Abbey. Why was he to impose himself upon them?

Her mother gave a slight squeeze of her hand. "Georgiana, if you could take Nathaniel to have some punch or tea, and some food. I am certain he is thirsty and hungry after their lengthy trip."

Why could Fitzwilliam not do so? Lady Lindsey did say her brother would join them soon. Nathaniel was always such a pest! He pulled her curls and tormented her. He was no gentleman! "Must I?"

A feeble gasp came from her mother and Georgiana's body sagged. Her mother was disappointed. "Yes, you must. You know you should not be so ill-mannered to our guests."

"Yes, Mother." Her shoulders were heavy as she stood. She approached the older boy with his tousled, dark chestnut hair and dark eyes and curtseyed to him and his father. "Lord Lindsey, welcome to Pemberley."

The gentleman's lip curved to one side while he bowed. "Miss Darcy. We are pleased to be here."

She turned to Lord and Lady Lindsey's son. Did he not have a title of some sort? Oh bother! Her mother called him Nathaniel and so would she. After all, boys who were a terrible nuisance did not deserve titles. "Would you care for some tea?"

He gave a slight bow. "I would, thank you."

As they stepped away from their parents, whispers from behind filled her ears, drowning the happy sound of the birds chirping in the trees and the cool breeze rippling the pond. Why were people always whispering? As of late, Mrs. Reynolds often spoke in hushed tones. Her father and the doctor, who was at Pemberley nearly every day, closed themselves in her father's study, though not a soul would tell her why.

A maid helped Nathaniel with a plate of food and a cup of tea while she watched her father stride in determined steps across the grass. He shook Lord Lindsey's hand and moved behind her mother, placing his palms upon her shoulders. *Her father always touched her mother in some fashion, particularly in the last month or so.*

"Will you not sit with me?"

She started at the voice before staring at him. *Did he actually think himself a welcome guest?* "I suppose I must."

The maid placed his meal upon the table as he turned with a grin. "You may as well stop pretending."

"I beg your pardon?" *Good! She had intended to sound as intimidating as Lady Catherine!*

He laughed. *Her aunt terrified her. Why would he find her impression humorous?*

"I said, you may as well stop pretending. I know you think well of me."

Pretending? Think well of him? What was he about? "I am not fond of any boys—except Fitzwilliam and my father, of course. I am not playing you false."

His irritating smile became wider. "You like me."

"Do not."

"Do too."

"Do not!"

"One day, Georgiana Darcy, you are going to marry me!"

December 1816

Georgiana inhaled sharply and shot forward from the squabs of the carriage.

"Georgiana? Are you well?"

She squeezed her eyes shut to clear her vision, opened them, and nodded. "Forgive me if I frightened you. I was dreaming."

"Do you need to speak of it?"

Lizzy was too good. How many dreams or nightmares had she recounted to her sister over the last four years? The number was too many to count.

"No, it was just a memory I had long forgotten. I honestly do not know why it suddenly came to mind." Little William turned his head and nestled back against Lizzy's chest. "If you are tired, I can hold him for a time."

Lizzy's fingers brushed through her son's curly locks and she kissed his crown. "I appreciate the offer, but I have no intention of sharing him at the moment. He has grown so much in the last two years. I dread the day I cannot cuddle him to me any longer."

"You will always have me to cuddle." The sleepy voice of Fitzwilliam made them both turn their heads.

"I hope we did not wake you," whispered Lizzy.

"No, I was enjoying the quiet. We have not had much of it since William was born."

A soft laugh came from Lizzy. "We certainly have not."

Though in looks he resembled Fitzwilliam more than Lizzy, her nephew was certainly a mischievous, stubborn, and exceedingly talkative child. Mr. Bennet, during his last visit to Pemberley three months prior, indicated the boy was as Lizzy was at his age. Between themselves and little William's nursemaid, they were forever chasing him about Pemberley without a moment's rest.

"What did you remember?"

Her eyes met her brother's. "The day we spent at the pond with Lord and Lady Lindsey."

A line formed between his eyebrows. "We picnicked often with Lord and Lady Lindsey, as well as their son."

"The week before Mother passed." Her voice cracked and her eyes burned. Speaking of her mother was always difficult. The pain had dulled some but never truly left her heart.

"Ah, I remember. When Father had Lord Lindsey fetch me from Cambridge and bring me to Pemberley." Her brother's lips curved upwards on one side. "Father had to punish you that day as I recall."

"What did you do?" Lizzy's voice was incredulous, as though it were inconceivable Georgiana would ever misbehave.

"It was nothing."

Her brother laughed and nudged his wife with his elbow. "I am sure Sele would disagree."

"Sele?" asked Lizzy.

"Nathaniel Howard, Viscount Sele. You made the acquaintance of his parents, Lord and Lady Lindsey, at Almack's last year. After Sele completed his studies at Oxford, he travelled to Ireland to oversee mining on Lindsey lands. Once gold was discovered, with the exception of a fortnight or so during the Christmas season every year, he remained."

Lizzy tightened her hold on her son. "His parents must miss him."

Lord and Lady Lindsey were certain to miss him dreadfully. Nathaniel was their sole child and heir, and his parents had managed to raise him using a fine balance between doting on an only child and rearing a gentleman, unlike most of the spoiled young men inhabiting society. Of course, Georgiana had not laid eyes upon him since her father died. She had never met the man, only the insufferable boy.

Rumours of his return for Christmas reached Georgiana's ears on several occasions over the last two years. He usually attended several parties in London during the holiday season as well as the theatre while she remained at Pemberley with Fitzwilliam and Lizzy.

"When will we arrive in Meryton, do you think?" Better to change the subject before Lizzy remembered to ask what had happened that day by the pond!

With a sly bit of a smile, Lizzy glanced through the window. "We passed through St. Albans a half-hour before you awoke. We are not far."

"I am glad we found that less congested coaching inn just outside of Northampton for our stops rather than the one we had used on our previous journeys," commented her brother. "Not being forced to wait for nearly an hour for a change of horses at a busier establishment certainly helped ease our journey."

"The stop would have awakened William as well. Without the interruption, he will have a better nap before we arrive at Longbourn."

Fitzwilliam checked his watch and returned it to his pocket. "What time is the wedding?"

"Half ten." Lizzy shook her head. "I still find it difficult to believe Papa is to be married—again. I thought that upon Mama's death, he would have retreated to his book room until he one day passed in his favourite chair. I expected Mrs. Hill to discover him when she brought him his morning pot of tea."

"I hope you are pleased for him." Fitzwilliam's fingers trailed along the top of her arm. "Your father seems to have found contentment with Miss Talbot."

"His letters are so different to what I am accustomed. He writes more of her than of books and inanities, but I am pleased he will not be lonely. Since Kitty wed Josiah Lucas and Mary wed Samuel Audley, I worried for him being alone with Lydia at Longbourn."

A giggle escaped Georgiana's lips, and she pressed them together. "Forgive me. I just remembered your mother's reaction to Kitty's and Mary's engagements."

Lizzy rolled her eyes. "Mama was not a woman of sense. She assumed after I married Fitzwilliam that all of her daughters would be part of the first circles. With Mr. Bingley betrothed to Anne de Bourgh, she was adamant Jane would marry Milton, Lydia would attract a duke, and Lord only knows whom she planned for Kitty and Mary. Samuel is brother to a baronet—even if he is a vicar—and well situated, and Kitty will be mistress of Lucas Lodge one day. While Sir William started with very little land, he has added to his property during his lifetime. I am certain Josiah will do the same."

"Your father describes Miss Talbot as possessing a great deal of good sense," observed Fitzwilliam. "He may have found her refreshing."

A sigh came from Lizzy as she leaned her head against the cushioned back of the seat. "He always did describe Mary, Kitty, and Lydia as three of the silliest girls in all of England."

"But Mary and Kitty are not silly," cried Georgiana. Why would Lizzy's father say such things?

"You did no more than make their acquaintance when your brother and I married. Prior to our wedding, Mary played the pianoforte very ill indeed and enjoyed reading and quoting theology. Her favourite book was Fordyce's sermons. Mr. Collins' mutual fondness for the same subject, however, gave her pause, and she began to read more of the contents of Papa's library.

"Kitty improved after your brother's warning against Mr. Wickham, when my father kept a tighter rein on both her and Lydia. Lydia fought him tooth and nail, but Kitty was not as stubborn."

Fitzwilliam pointed out the window. "I can see Netherfield."

The house was in the distance, but its appearance meant Longbourn was not far, and London was a mere afternoon's drive from Meryton. Georgiana swallowed hard. Her fears of venturing to the theatre and Bond Street had been conquered some time ago, but deflecting the barbs and titters of so-called polished society still disturbed her. After all, they were bound to gossip of the reason she was not yet out.

She was jolted from her thoughts when the equipage halted before Longbourn. Her eyes scanned the small columned portico when Mr. Bennet, Miss Lydia Bennet, and an unfamiliar woman, who could only be Miss Talbot, stepped from the door.

Fitzwilliam exited first, took William, and then helped Lizzy. Georgiana stepped down with the help of her brother's hand as Lizzy rushed forward to greet her father.

She pressed a kiss to his cheek. "Papa, you look well."

"I am quite well, and pleased to see this little one again." After shaking Fitzwilliam's hand, he tousled a fidgety William's curls, then stepped beside the unknown lady and placed her hand upon his arm.

"Miss Sarah Talbot, may I present my daughter, Elizabeth, her husband, Mr. Fitzwilliam Darcy, their son William, and Miss Georgiana Darcy."

Miss Talbot curtseyed, her smile tight and nervous. "I am pleased to make your acquaintance. I anticipate coming to know all of you better."

"We look forward to the same." Lizzy's eye held a familiar twinkle. Her sister was amused.

"'Tis good to see you, Lizzy."

Lizzy startled and stepped forward to hug her youngest sister. When she withdrew, she held Lydia's arms out to her side. "What a becoming shade! Is the gown new?"

Miss Bennet brushed her palms down the front. "Papa bought fabric and took me to the seamstress for my birthday. I have another new gown in my bedchamber for the wedding. Would you care to see it?"

A grin lit Lizzy's face. "Perhaps once we have refreshed ourselves and had some tea."

Lydia's enthusiastic nod was reminiscent of the Lydia of four years ago. Fortunately, her governess, now companion, and Mr. Bennet proved themselves more stubborn. Lydia was not to be declared out until her behaviour was no longer so wild and unrestrained. The death of Mrs. Bennet two years prior allowed for Lydia to mature for another year while she was in mourning. Yet, if one looked closely, the eyes of the sixteen-year old girl still lurked behind those of the twenty-year old before them.

"Miss Darcy, I hope you are well."

Georgiana returned Miss Bennet's curtsey. "I thought we agreed to address one another by our given names?"

"We did, but I was afraid you might have forgotten." Lydia responded with a reserve she only exhibited when she was uncertain. They had become better acquainted at Pemberley, but had not been in company since.

"I have not."

A dry laugh from Mr. Bennet interrupted. "Shall we take this reunion into the parlour? Mrs. Hill muttered about starting tea when your carriage arrived. We shall be drinking it cold if we continue here."

As they were about to take their seats, William's nursemaid fetched her whining charge, and Mrs. Hill bustled in with tea. She set out the service and exited with haste.

No one commented as Lydia prepared cups for the family, speaking little as she worked. She was so altered. Even prior to her mother's death, Lydia had become better behaved, but still lacked a certain amount of decorum. The most striking transformation was noticed when Mr. Bennet journeyed to Pemberley that autumn and brought a proper young lady rather than the barely restrained Lydia they expected. No one was aware of what occurred during the year of mourning, but the youngest Bennet sister was certainly changed for the better.

As the conversation flowed around her, Georgiana listened while she attempted to surreptitiously examine Miss Talbot. The lady could not have been more than five and thirty. She had ginger hair and a pale complexion, yet she was not terribly freckled. Her colouring suited her. She was, in fact, quite pretty.

"Miss Talbot, you are from Hertfordshire, I believe?" Lizzy cocked her head to the side. The pose was one Georgiana saw often: Lizzy was sketching Miss Talbot's character.

"My sister is the wife of Mr. Henry Newell of Leabrook."

Lizzy's eyes widened a hair before she smiled. "Your resemblance to your sister is remarkable. I thought you familiar, but now that you mention Mrs. Newell, I know why.

"I understand from my father you were a companion for a time."

A small line formed on Miss Talbot's forehead. "My sister was newly married when my father passed. I had no wish to intrude, though she offered me a place to live, so I took a position with an elderly widow. Mrs. Stanton was kind, but her eyesight was poor. I spent my days helping her pay calls and my evenings reading aloud and playing the pianoforte. I was quite fortunate. My brother was acquainted with Mrs. Stanton's grandson and knew the family to be respectable."

"Mrs. Stanton could have said she was fortunate in her choice of companion as well." Mr. Bennet's lips had a slight curve at each end as he complimented his betrothed. How peculiar! Who would have expected to see Mr. Bennet besotted!

Georgiana's eyes met Lizzy's as her sister bit her bottom lip. They had wondered at Mr. Bennet's marrying again, but the consensus among the family was perhaps a need for companionship. Loneliness might have been a factor, yet the adoring gaze he was bestowing upon Miss Talbot could not be misinterpreted. Stodgy, reclusive, never leave his book room Mr. Bennet was in love!

When she turned back to Miss Talbot, the lady's pink cheeks left no doubt of her mutual affection for Mr. Bennet. How lovely! He had not had an easy time between Lydia and Mrs. Bennet these last few years.

They chatted long after their teacups were empty, and likewise, their plates contained only crumbs. At a pause in the conversation, Lydia stood. "If you have finished your tea, I shall show you to your rooms, so you can remove the dust from your travels and rest. I am sure your journey was taxing."

When the entire party stood, Lydia led them up the stairs where she opened the first room along the corridor. "This bedchamber is yours, Georgiana."

Lizzy leaned to catch a glimpse of the room. "It has not changed since Jane wed."

"I have not altered much." Lydia scanned the walls and furniture. "Jane's preferences were simple and very fine. As long as the wall coverings or draperies do not fall into disrepair, they will not be replaced. Sarah felt much the same when I took her through the house a fortnight ago."

"Do you like her?" asked Lizzy.

"I do. She is kind and cares about Papa. He has been unhappy for so long, but now, he smiles and even hums as he tends to Longbourn's business. He is a different man."

"Perhaps some of that change could be attributed to you as well?" Fitzwilliam's eyebrows were raised. No doubt he was correct. Lydia's improved disposition was certain to lessen Mr. Bennet's displeasure.

Lydia's forehead creased, she cleared her throat, and turned to Georgiana. "If you require anything, your maid need only request it of Mrs. Hill."

"Thank you."

A small smile was upon her brother's lips. "My sister is usually as quiet as a mouse. You will hear little from her this evening, I assure you." He placed a hand to Lizzy's back. "We will only be a few rooms away."

"Oh, yes! They will be two doors down on the left should you need them."

She nodded to Lydia, whose hands were clasped before her. "Thank you. When do I need to be dressed for dinner?"

"Hill will serve at seven. Papa thought you would be fatigued this evening and wished for a quiet, family meal. I hope that is acceptable?"

"A quiet, family meal at Longbourn?" Lizzy laughed. "I have never attended one as such."

The youngest Miss Bennet had appeared in good cheer since they arrived, but she gave a brief giggle and glanced between her guests. "I should let you have your privacy."

Georgiana gave a slight bob of the head. "Thank you."

When she closed the door, Georgiana took in the room. Bright floral papers adorned the walls with pale blue window coverings. Jane's tastes were similar to this day, though now that she was married to Sir James Audley, she had the funds for richer materials.

By the open lid of her trunk, her maid had unpacked what she would require for this evening and the wedding on the morrow. Georgiana's journal lay upon the escritoire in the corner. Lucy knew her well.

She sat in the dainty chair and dipped her pen in the ink well.

December 16th 1816

I dreamt of Mother as we journeyed to Longbourn today. How long has it been since I have done so? Seems an age ago! She visited my sleep often when I was young, but she has not ventured into my mind like she did this afternoon for several years. I have missed her presence as much in my dreams as I have in my waking hours. Moments in which I long for the safe haven of her embrace have lessened, but never fully waned. Lizzy has helped in that I can speak to her of those matters one confides in a mother, yet the experience could never be the same.

I remember once waking in tears and Father holding me while I cried. How miserable I was to awaken and find my mother gone once again! Today's experience, however, was different than those that preceded it. Rather than my mother holding me or speaking to me, I experienced once more our last picnic before her death. Fitzwilliam and I rarely speak of that time, but through my dream, I have come to realize that she knew her time was near. Her countenance was sombre, and she clung to me so when I brought her the bouquet of lavender and daisies. She was as despaired at the knowledge of leaving us as I was when she left this earth. How could I have forgotten?

Fitzwilliam returned to Pemberley from Cambridge that day. Lord and Lady Lindsey brought him as a favour to my parents. My mother must have wished for time with him before her passing. She was not like most ladies of fashion. Her days were passed tending to household duties, yet she never failed to spend as much time as she could spare with us.

Lord and Lady Lindsey! We have not enjoyed their society for so long. They were such great friends of my parents and came to Pemberley often until Lord Lindsey fell ill almost three years ago. His recovery, according to rumour, was slow, so two years passed before Fitzwilliam and Lizzy happened upon Lord and Lady Lindsey at Almack's. I have been seldom to London so I have not had the opportunity to be in their company. My parents would be upset their closest friends should be estranged from us now. I should call on them while we are in London. No, I will call on them while in London! My parents would expect no less than the utmost consideration for their closest friends.

She read back through the latest entry while she stood and stepped over to the bed. When she finished, she sat and fell back upon the pillow.

"As long as I am not forced into the company of Nathaniel."

Chapter 2

The household retired early that evening, and Georgiana, who had been engrossed in a novel since her return to her room, startled at a light knock. After placing a piece of ribbon to mark her page, she stood and opened the door to find Lydia standing upon the threshold in her dressing gown.

"I hope I am not disturbing you. I thought we might talk." Lydia's fingers grasped and released each other and she shifted on her feet. "When we were younger, Kitty and I would stay up and chat and giggle. Those nights were ever so much fun. With all my sisters married and residing elsewhere, I have come to miss those evenings immensely. Since I am to journey to London and stay with Lizzy and Fitzwilliam, I hoped we might become better acquainted . . . if that is acceptable to you, that is."

She pushed the door further open. "Lizzy and I have had similar talks, but she has been much occupied by William since he was born. I would be pleased to know you better." With a wide grin, Lydia crept into the room and climbed to sit upon the foot of the bed.

Georgiana moved her book and resumed her place under the warm coverlet. What should she say? They had conversed when Lydia visited Pemberley, but they had become no more than friendly with each other. Most young ladies their age thought of nothing more than marriage. Perhaps such a subject was a good beginning? "Have you had any suitors since your return to Meryton?"

Lydia's eyes rolled to the ceiling for a moment. "La! 'Tis always the same young men, and they are such a bore. I have no interest in any of them."

"None?"

She exhaled a heavy breath. "Amongst our neighbours, three gentlemen are of interest to those ladies of a marriageable age. The youngest son of the Gouldings is but five years older than me, yet he has no property or profession and speaks of naught but himself. He is so dull! I should sooner dance with Papa than with him.

"The master of Haverhill, Mr. Standage, is widowed, one and forty, and positively ancient." Lydia gave a dramatic shudder. "I have danced with him thrice in the last year. I promise not to be exaggerating when I say he stepped upon my toes during each set." She swallowed. "The last of the unwed gentlemen of Meryton is Mr. Gibb, who is five and thirty as well as forever in his cups. Papa would never give his consent—not that I would want it. The last time Mr. Gibb asked me to dance, I thought I would become tipsy from the smell of his breath alone."

Georgiana's hand clung to the base of her neck. How vile!

"All of them are wanting in some manner. I have no wish to be courted by any of them." Lydia leaned forward upon her knees with bright and eager eyes. "What of you? Do you fancy some young man? Is he handsome?"

She could not help but smile at Lydia's current manner, which was reminiscent to when she was younger and more unfettered. "No, I am not yet out."

Her eyes bulged. "Truly? Why?"

"When I was but fifteen, a young man tried to convince me to elope with him. I did not love him and refused, but the experience was . . . unpleasant to say the least. I have yet to feel equal to such a conversation again. I do not plan to ever marry."

Lydia's gaze became unfocussed. "Never marry?" Her words were faint. Why was the notion such a strange concept?

"Really, Lydia! I shall not be a poor old maid! A single woman, of good fortune, is always respectable. I am not an oddity and plan to have a full life. Lizzy and Fitzwilliam will allow me to live with them at Pemberley, and I shall see their children born and grow to adulthood. I consider myself fortunate since I shall not be forced to seek employment. I can remain in my home for my lifetime."

Her hands were taken into Lydia's quick grasp. "Forgive me. I have never considered a life without a husband nor have I met a lady with such an inclination—until now." Lydia's teeth wore at her lips for a moment. "I just hope I find a worthy suitor while we are in London for the Season."

"Do Lizzy and Fitzwilliam know of your plans?"

Lydia drew her knees to her chest and wrapped her arms around them. "I have not told them, but I do not think they will object. Do you? Like you, I am twenty, but too many people in Meryton remember how I once was. I must leave Longbourn and find my future elsewhere."

"Do you truly feel your past behaviour prevents you from making a suitable match here in Hertfordshire?"

She stared at her fingers and picked at a piece of dry skin near her fingernail. "A few local gentlemen have married in the last two years, and while the mourning period for Mama prevented me from being courted for part of that time, I *know* I remain a poor prospect for a wife."

"Has someone said as much or are you making assumptions? Your manner is so altered from when we first met, which one might attribute to maturity and experience. Your mother's death also changed you a great deal."

"'Twas not so much Mama's death as it was the ladies of the neighbourhood in the months following."

Georgiana leaned against the pillows and headboard behind her. "Which ladies?"

A beleaguered breath was noisily blown from Lydia's mouth. "The day after Mama passed, Mrs. Simms, my former companion, and I walked to town to purchase some black ribbon. I felt trapped within Longbourn and needed to escape, so I volunteered to go in Mrs. Hill's stead. When I entered the shop, Mrs. Goulding, Lady Lucas, and Mrs. Long were speaking of Mama and her lack of decorum. They had no compunction about gossiping with Mama when she lived, but once she was dead, their true opinions of her were no longer suppressed. Upon taking note of me in the doorway, the shopkeeper cleared his throat, but not before I heard what was said."

The poor girl! "What did they say?"

Lydia gave a one-shouldered shrug. "They belittled Mama. They described her as silly, vain, and shallow before Mrs. Goulding said, 'Her youngest is just like her, and the last girl in the world my George will marry. I will not have that little strumpet for my daughter.' I know naught of what Mrs. Long or Lady Lucas would have said because they blanched and ceased their conversation when they became aware of my presence."

"Were you not friends with Lady Lucas' daughter? Forgive me, but I do not recall her name."

"Maria. Yes, I was, but she did not call as much after Charlotte married Mr. Collins and Mrs. Simms became my companion. Once word spread into town that Mama passed in her sleep, Lady Lucas had no reason to call at Longbourn. Maria then married George Goulding." One side of her lip turned up in a pathetic attempt to feign unhurt feelings. "We greet one another at church on Sunday."

"Your changed manner must have had some effect on your friendships in Meryton. How can it not?"

"But I was not changed until Mama's death—not in essentials. I grew tired of fighting Papa and Mrs. Simms, so I pretended in the hopes they would give me some freedom. Instead, I learnt people's true opinion and found I did not like it."

Georgiana took Lydia's hand and gave a gentle squeeze. "No one can deny your improved temper. They are fools if they cling to the judgements they made almost five years ago."

"You are very kind, but I am no longer wilfully blind to how I behaved."

"Then, we must introduce you to new acquaintances. My aunt knows all of London. I am certain she could help."

Lydia giggled. "I do not require all of London. One nice young man from a good family would be sufficient. I do not require him to be a duke, despite what Mama once said. I also do not wish for a marriage such as she had with my father. I hope to marry a man who loves me like I do him." Her cheeks turned a little pinker as she glanced away for a moment and then back. "I have shown you my gown for tomorrow. I should dearly love to see yours. I am sure it is quite fine." With a jump from the bed, Lydia made for the wardrobe while Georgiana rose and followed at a more sedate pace. Georgiana opened the door, removed her sky blue silk, and held it by the shoulders.

"Look at the colour!" gushed Lydia. "I missed colour so when we were in mourning. I shall be well-pleased to never wear black again." Her eyes met Georgiana's for a moment and flickered back down as she fingered the small pearls along the edge of the bodice. "I hope I do not sound selfish. I know I shall be required to don that wretched shade more than once in my lifetime, yet I shall loathe every moment."

Georgiana hung the gown back on the peg. "The pale rose of yours complements the subtle glow in your cheeks. My aunt tends to choose fabrics she feels matches my eyes. Do not misunderstand me. I like blue, but I hope to purchase a few gowns of a different shade while in London. I would adore a day gown in a pretty sprigged muslin."

Lydia's eyes narrowed as she stared at Georgiana for a moment. "Rose or pink would suit you well, I think. Perhaps the right shade of silver?"

With a smile, Georgiana took Lydia's hand and tugged her back towards the bed. "Well, you shall help me decide. I hope you will not mind shopping with me on Bond Street."

Her friend placed the back of her hand to her forehead and dropped to the bed. "How shall I survive?"

They both dissolved into giggles as Georgiana settled back into her place, tilted her head, and appraised the young lady before her. "Do you have any particular wish for while we are in town? Fitzwilliam has taken me to the theatre and a few exhibitions. I have obviously not attended any balls thus far, but I—"

"Why ever not?" cried Lydia. "Despite what happened with that man, you cannot hide for the rest of your life. After hearing what was said about Mama and myself, a part of me never wanted to leave the security of Longbourn, but Mrs. Simms would not have it. She made me understand that I could not closet myself from the world. Instead, I could change and no longer provide fodder for them to criticise."

"Mrs. Simms sounds to be an intelligent and well-informed lady."

"She is. I was sorry to see her leave, but with you, your companion, Mrs. Annesley, and Lizzy for the next several months, her services were simply not required."

"Mrs. Annesley is with her relations for the next month, but we shall have Lizzy and my family. When you return, you will have the new Mrs. Bennet."

"Precisely! 'Tis a luxury my father does not need to continue. He should be saving those funds for a more worthy purpose, though I have no idea what." She gave a weary smile. "We are a sad lot, are we not?"

Georgiana crossed her arms over her chest. "Why would you say so?"

"Well, we have exhausted the subject of young men, discussed fashion and shopping, Mama's death, and my alteration. We shall never stay awake the rest of the night with naught to entertain ourselves." Lydia lifted herself to sit straight. "I know! We should creep down to the kitchen and make ourselves some tea and steal a few biscuits from Mrs. Hill's pantry."

Her eyes widened to the point that they hurt. "Would we not get into trouble? I cannot imagine doing such a thing at Pemberley."

Lydia waved away Georgiana's concern. "Mrs. Hill has not minded since it is just me who remains at home. When all five of us were young, her biscuits all disappeared on more than one occasion. She was furious when the ladies came to call and she had nothing to serve them."

"I cannot imagine Lizzy stealing from the kitchens."

With a grin, Lydia shook her head. "Who do you think taught me?" She took Georgiana's hand and pulled. "Put on your dressing gown! If we make haste, we can return before anyone is the wiser."

Lydia cracked the door. "No one is in the corridor. Quick, we must hurry."

At the sound of a loud noise, Georgiana's eyes shot open, she placed a hand to her forehead and shifted. Why were her sheets scratchy? Had someone put sand in the bed? With a groan, she wiped her cheek and studied the residue upon her fingers. Biscuit crumbs!

A deep, rattling snore sounded behind her. She rolled onto her back and propped herself on her elbows. Lydia was sprawled across the majority of the mattress as the most ungodly noise sounded as though it was being pulled raggedly from her when she breathed. Georgiana managed to smother a laugh. Lydia and her future husband would certainly have separate bedchambers! How did one sleep through such a racket? Thank goodness they would not be sharing a room at Darcy House!

With care, she lifted herself and sat upon the side as Lucy entered and silently closed the door behind her. Georgiana put a finger to her lips and Lucy grinned.

"I looked in on you earlier," whispered her maid. "I wondered at how you slept on such a small sliver of the bed."

"Not well at all." She brushed the sheet with her palm. "I am afraid we made a mess of the linens."

"Do not fret. I shall take them into the garden and give them a good shake. No doubt, Mrs. Hill will give the room a thorough cleaning once we have departed after the wedding breakfast anyhow." Lydia's next snore reverberated around the room, and the both of them watched to see if she would awaken herself. She did not. How did Kitty share a room with her for so many years? Lucy covered her mouth in an attempt to restrain her mirth.

As Georgiana crept from the bed, Lydia rolled to her side, murmured to herself, and tittered. They both halted in their steps to be sure she did not awaken.

Her maid hastened to grab Georgiana's brush and a few necessities before they crept through the adjoining door to what was once Mary's old bedchamber. "Mrs. Hill offered for us to use this as a dressing room should we require it, but at the time, I had no notion we would."

Georgiana peeked back at Lydia and began to giggle. "Did she say, 'La! I would adore a dance!' as we departed?"

"I heard 'La' and 'dance,' but I am unsure of the rest." She peered back through the doorway before she closed the door with care. "Who do you think she wanted to dance with?"

"I am uncertain, but I would wager on a handsome but mysterious gentleman." They both grinned while she removed her dressing gown and handed it to Lucy, who gestured towards the water and towelling.

"While you clean yourself up, I shall fetch your gown."

Lucy crept back into the bedchamber, but soon returned with the blue silk over her arm. She then styled Georgiana's hair in a trice and helped her dress. "As soon as Miss Bennet awakens, I shall pack your trunk and have it ready for when Mr. Clarke, Phoebe, and I depart. Phoebe has said she plans the same with Mrs. Darcy's trunks."

She caught Lucy's eye in the mirror. "It has been some time since we travelled, has it not?"

"Aye, it has." Her slight smile disappeared when she pinned the last curl into place. "I can't say as I blame you for wanting to remain at Pemberley, though. I hope you don't think me impertinent, but I am pleased to see you back to the young miss you were before Ramsgate."

Georgiana opened her mouth to speak, but had not the opportunity.

"I know you are forever altered in some ways, but you seem more content as you are, which is a good thing. If only I had not departed that evening—"

She grasped Lucy's arm and removed the brush from her fingers to join their hands. "I have told you before you are not to blame. Neither of us is."

"I heard the talk below stairs about Mr. Wickham at Pemberley and London. I knew what he was. I should have never left you alone with Mrs. Younge."

"No more! You were helping me to escape. You had no way of knowing Mr. Wickham would appear at the house and force himself upon me. Neither of us is responsible." She searched Lucy's eyes. "Do you understand?"

"You are too kind, miss."

She stood and clenched Lucy's hands in her own. "No, I simply refuse George Wickham the satisfaction of causing either of us further grief. He is dead and can no longer harm another soul."

A knock came from the adjoining room, causing them both to jump and hurry to return to the bedchamber Georgiana was sharing with Lydia. As Lucy opened the door, Lydia sat up in the bed and groaned.

"'Tis too early!" Lydia's eyes blinked hard, likely to adjust to the light from the window, and her brow furrowed as she glanced about the room. "Lord! I think I have biscuit crumbs in my shift."

Lizzy's merry laughter came from the door. "So, you have been initiated into the Bennet sisters' tradition of talking late into the night and stealing from Mrs. Hill's pantry?"

A huff came from behind her and Lydia stepped to her side. "Well, someone had to teach her, though she was positively scandalised by the idea of doing so at Pemberley or Darcy House. What sort of servants do you employ, Lizzy? If I had not been a guest of yours before, Georgiana's reaction would almost make me fear staying with you."

"I am glad to see you have not lost your talent for exaggeration," teased Lizzy.

Lydia stuck out her tongue and Lizzy's eyebrows rose upon her forehead.

"Oh, I am only teasing! Ask Papa. He makes his sarcastic remarks from time to time and I do the same to him. He finds it funny. I would never behave so in company."

Lizzy placed her hands upon her youngest sister's shoulders. "I am proud of the changes you have made, and I am pleased to find you have not lost all of your lively spirit. Otherwise, you would resemble Mary."

"I love Mary, but it would be dreadfully dull to read histories like she does day after day."

With a curve to one side of her lips, Lizzy raised an eyebrow. "Well, is no one hungry for breakfast? Fitzwilliam has been with Papa in his study for an hour at least, and I mean to eat before William finds me gone."

"I shall join you." Georgiana peered around Lydia. "Lucy? Would you be so kind as to help Miss Bennet prepare for the day?" Lydia's eyes widened and she bit her bottom lip.

"Of course, Miss Darcy." She gave a curtsey and turned to face Lydia. "Whenever you are ready, miss." Lydia giggled while Lucy followed her into the corridor.

"That leaves the two of us." Lizzy offered her arm. "Shall we?"

When they stepped to the top of the stairs, Georgiana glanced over her shoulder. Lizzy was a wonderful sister, but she was going to enjoy Lydia's company for the next few months. She had not had a friend her age since school, and a part of her never trusted those acquaintances. Too many girls were merely interested in status or finding their way into the society of another girl's unmarried brother. Of course, her brother was no longer eligible, so she had few young ladies approaching her these last four years.

Lydia, on the other hand, desired nothing but friendship. Perhaps London would not be so bad after all.

Chapter 3

December 17th 1816

Despite the innermost portion of my soul crying to return to Pemberley, we arrived in London a short time ago. Lydia immediately declared herself fagged and retired to her bedchamber, Lizzy disappeared with William into the nursery, Fitzwilliam ventured to his study, and while I write, Lucy is in my dressing room tending to my trunks.

Dinner is in less than an hour, and I am certain today's wedding will continue to dominate our conversation as it did during our journey. I believe we were all overcome by the sincere attachment of the couple exchanging their vows as well as the expressions of pure love and joy upon their countenances. Despite its simplicity, today's was one of the loveliest ceremonies I have witnessed. I do believe the new Mr. and Mrs. Bennet will be the happiest of couples—behind Fitzwilliam and Lizzy, of course.

Lydia continues to open my eyes to her improvements since our first acquaintance. Despite the open manner and lively spirit she displays in private, she is reserved and circumspect in company; the only hint of her true self displayed in the smile upon her countenance, which hints of the, no doubt, irreverent turn of her mind.

Unfortunately, the ladies of Meryton continue to be unkind. Today, Mrs. Long, as though I had never before met Lydia, proceeded to inform me of her former behaviour and the ills of associating with such a creature. Of course, Mrs. Long could only speak of Lydia's brash statements and impulsive nature, yet I now understand better Lydia's eagerness to depart Meryton. My sentiments upon returning to London would, no doubt, mirror hers upon the threat of a swift return to Hertfordshire. I am pleased she is with us for now. She will have a respite from the shrews of Meryton, and Mr. and Mrs. Bennet will have some privacy for the first months of their new marriage. I am pleased she had the Gardiners at Netherfield as they were as lovely and accepting of her as they have always been of me. I was glad to be in their company again.

A knock made her start. "Come in!"

Lizzy stepped through and closed the door behind her. "I was surprised to hear you did not spend the last hour on the pianoforte. I wanted to be certain you were merely tired after your late night with Lydia and not that you were ill."

"I am fatigued, but my main reason for delaying my practise is my journal. I had some thoughts I wished to pen before I forgot them." She placed her pen back upon its stand, avoiding Lizzy's steady gaze.

"You have been quiet since you decided to spend the Season in London. Why do you not tell me what has you at sixes and sevens?"

Georgiana stepped to the window and watched the people walk along the pavement. They all bustled here and there. None appeared ill at ease or anxious, so why did the mere thought of London create such a nervous flutter within her? She had not travelled to Ramsgate for goodness' sakes!

"Are you or Fitzwilliam concerned about the gossip from my lack of début?"

After Lizzy sat in a chair near the fire, she shrugged one shoulder. "We have told you we would support your decisions for your future—whatever they may be. You never need marry unless you find a man whom you love and who loves you in return, and if you are uncomfortable among the ton, you need never take part." Lizzy's head tilted as she studied her. "Have you reason to think people are speaking ill of you?"

Georgiana brought her hands up and then dropped them back to her skirts. "Oh, no. I have heard nothing in particular. I am just certain there is some rumour. After all, a lady not coming out when she is either seventeen or eighteen is uncommon. How many ladies do not seek a husband? Even Lydia was shocked at my resolve." She put her hand upon her forehead. How it did not pain her with the worry was a mystery. "I am certain there has been gossip and conjecture and when it is bandied about that I am in town, there shall be talk again. What if it never abates? I would not want it to affect your children when they come of age."

"We cannot dwell on what may or may not happen so far into the future. Thankfully, William has many years before he must worry about a wife, and only God knows if we will be blessed with more children. I do hope we will, but a year lapsed before we found I was with child. Two years have passed since. I hope and pray for another, yet I have no say in the matter." Lizzy's forehead crinkled and she shook her head. "I cannot imagine your shunning marriage will still be the tittle tattle among the ladies when our children come of age. We can consult your aunt if that would relieve your anxiety on the matter."

"Aunt has no doubt my uncle's position will prevent any permanent damage to the family's name while gossip must have circulated as to why or how I am wanting to warrant such a delay."

"Your brother and myself, as well as your aunt and uncle, have made it clear we care naught for the rumours. Your happiness is first in our minds. Should you wish to have a Season, we will be pleased to arrange matters for you, but do not make yourself uneasy. When William is old enough to wed, you will be above forty years and likely be considered eccentric. People may wonder at why you never married, but I doubt you or William will suffer for it."

"Must I decide straight away?"

"Decide?" she asked.

"I suppose whether I want an event of some sort. I admit the thought causes me a great deal of anxiety, but I believe I would prefer the nerves to the stares and the gossip. As far as I am concerned, I am out. I want to attend the theatre and perhaps a tea or two, depending upon who is the host. I just do not know if I want the frenzy of a ball."

Lizzy brought her legs up into the seat and curled her feet under her. "You have no set time to choose one way or the other. Should you resolve to have a début at the end of the Season, your aunt and I shall make arrangements for a ball before those we would invite depart for the country. The affair would be considerably smaller at that time as well. A number of large events to close the Season are held in those last few weeks."

Georgiana could not help but give a weak smile. "And I am certain all believe theirs to be the affair to end the Season."

"Of course. I do believe Viscount Turnbridge is by far the worst in regards to such an attitude."

She crinkled her nose. "His daughter attended school with me. I have no doubt what you say is true."

With a grin, Lizzy brushed her lap as though she had fluff or some such bit of nothing upon her gown. "I have met her. She wed the Earl of Rochford last Season if I recall correctly from the papers. Your aunt was amusing in her commentary on that match. She dislikes both parties most heartily."

"Aunt Charlotte is rather discerning when it comes to true friends and those she tolerates for Uncle Henry's position." She took the seat across from Lizzy. "You have surely taken note of the difference in her manner between the two."

"I have, but I do believe only those who know your aunt well could see the change."

She nodded as she picked at her fingernail. "When do you plan to visit Madame Guiard's?"

"I sent a request for an appointment upon our arrival. I hope to hear back before long. Madame does not often keep myself or your aunt waiting."

"I was hoping to purchase several new gowns. I appreciate my aunt's efforts, but . . ."

Lizzy's eyes danced with amusement. "You wish for a colour other than blue?"

"Yes," she exhaled. "I hope Aunt Charlotte does not take offence, but I have considered asking Lucy to dye several of them."

"Do not fret. Lydia, though she does not know it yet, will have several pieces made, I require a few new gowns as well, and you shall have a good number. 'Tis a shame you are so much taller than me. I would be happy to give you a few of mine. This notion of a new gown for each event is preposterous. Such a waste of money!"

"Did Phoebe not remake some of your gowns over the summer?"

"She did, and did a beautiful job of it. I am thankful for her experience working for Madame Guiard. Phoebe's skill with a needle by far surpasses mine. I anticipate wearing my pearl silk gown with the sheer crimson overlay. The embroidery she added is exquisite."

"Oh! Lucy spoke of it. You must show me when we have the opportunity."

The door opened with a slam. "Mama?" Little feet ran further into the room and stopped when William was just behind and to one side of Lizzy's chair. A big grin lit his face when he set eyes upon Georgiana, and her heart swelled in her chest. "Gee!"

Before she could blink he had climbed upon her lap and held a book to her face. "I want book!"

"Pray?" she prompted. He was speaking in short sentences but always required reminding of his manners.

"Pway read book."

She bit back a giggle as she looked to Lizzy. William followed her lead. "Mama!" he cried and wiggled to the floor. With two jumps, he was before Lizzy, climbed upon her lap, and wrapped his arms about her neck.

Her sister's eyes closed as she savoured the moment with William. He was an affectionate child, but never failed to be swift at moving to the next activity of interest. True to form, he pulled back and gave his mother a loud kiss on the cheek.

"Did you want Aunt Georgiana to read to you?"

"Yes, I want Gee to read me book." He leaned against Lizzy's shoulder with his eyes upon Georgiana. "Pway?"

A laugh came unbidden. He had all the appearance of her brother, but his personality was definitely Lizzy's. Neither of the Darcy siblings had been outgoing as young children, but William would hug and kiss a stranger if he had the inclination.

"I would be pleased to read to you." She held out her arms as he slid off the chair and ran back over to her. Once he was comfortable and settled, she opened the book as Lizzy stood.

"I am going to see what became of Mrs. Wynn."

When Lizzy turned, the harried face of William's nursemaid peeked into the doorway. "Thank God! I put him in his cot, read him several stories, and he closed his eyes. When I rang to the kitchen for a cup of tea, I was certain he was sound asleep. All I did was go to my room for a moment to retrieve my book, and he disappeared. The door to the corridor was open. I must have forgotten to lock it. I am so sorry, Mrs. Darcy."

"I do understand, Mrs. Wynn. He has escaped from us all at one time or another."

Poor Mrs. Wynn! Mrs. Reynolds' younger sister had a brood of children in her youth, who were now all grown with little ones of their own, but she was unaccustomed to William's propensity for eluding even the most vigilant of caregivers. Lizzy smiled as she reassured William's nursemaid.

William tugged on her sleeve. "Gee!" He pointed to the book. "Read!"

After placing a kiss to his temple, she hugged him closer and began to recite the words upon the page. This was all she would ever require—a little one to cuddle and those who loved her. She could never want for more.

"You should have allowed me to purchase the blue silk this morning, Georgiana. That particular shade would have been lovely with the white overlay. Why you insisted on that pale green?" Her Aunt Charlotte huffed as she fingered the light tea green coloured fabric on the table before them.

Lydia's lips all but disappeared as she attempted to restrain her giggles. Instead, Lydia indicated a preference for her aunt's choice of material; she had already selected her pattern and been measured as well—much to Georgiana's relief.

"You have been so kind as to give me several gowns in a similar colour, and I do not want people to believe I am wearing the same clothing to every event or call."

With a sniff, Aunt Charlotte relaxed back onto the sofa. "Most ladies are discerning enough to recognise the slightest variations in patterns."

"Unless they are looking to find fault, Aunt."

Lydia leaned forward to pull another bit of fabric from under the offending length of material. "The green suits you, as does the blush-coloured silk. The sprigged muslins are quite pretty as well, and I just adore the pattern for the ball gown."

Despite her hesitance towards an official Season, her aunt, Lady Fitzwilliam, insisted she would attend their annual ball. The year after Fitzwilliam and Lizzy's marriage, the ball's date was changed to occur during Twelfth Night and had remained as such ever since.

A part of her anticipated the event with curiosity since she had never before attended, yet a part of her dreaded it.

Lizzy entered the room and exhaled. "Have we made plans for all we bought at the draper's yesterday?"

The fabric upon the table was now sorted into four piles and had various notes pinned to each. With a nod, Georgiana stood. "I believe so. Has Madame taken the measurements she requires?"

"Yes, thank goodness. I do long for a new gown from time to time, but the process never fails to make me wonder why." Lizzy retrieved her reticule from the midst of the silks and muslins and turned to Aunt Charlotte. "Shall we to Gunter's then? I could use a cup of tea."

Her shoulders dropped. "Is there not another tea shop?" Her aunt, Lizzy, and Lydia all stopped to stare. "I do enjoy Gunter's, but they never lack for a crowd. I am also in no mood for an ice."

"Gunter's has pastries and tea," placated Lizzy. "Besides, Lydia has never been."

Lydia shook her head. "We can go another time. I have no plans to depart on the morrow."

"Once the Season truly begins, Gunter's will be a constant crush. Their establishment is too popular." Her aunt tilted her head and gave her that look— the one that silently requested her compliance. "Now, before the remaining families journey to town, is the best time."

"'Tis not necessary—"

Georgiana placed her hand on Lydia's forearm. "No, my aunt is correct. We shall go."

Lydia's eyes held hers. "You are certain."

"Yes. I am positive. I am merely being moody when I should not. Forgive me."

A giggle came from Lydia before she wrapped her hand around Georgiana's elbow. "There is nothing to forgive. I do understand about whims and moods as I am not immune to them."

The four ladies made their way from the back rooms to where the Darcy carriage awaited them in front of the shop. Once they were aboard and the equipage was moving through the streets towards Berkeley Square, Aunt Charlotte took Lizzy's hand.

"I sent a letter to Sir James and Lady Audley along with the invitation to the ball. I thought they might like to have their children at the house in order to be more at ease."

Lizzy smiled. "Jane indicated they would arrive on Boxing Day. They are spending Christmas at the small estate he recently inherited from his cousin. The location was so close to London, they felt it was ideal. He could meet the steward and assess the situation without a great delay arriving in town."

"I am so pleased they came to Pemberley when Papa and I journeyed from Hertfordshire." Lydia gave a slight tug to her kid gloves as though they were slipping from her hands. "Unless they came to Longbourn on their way to and from London, we never saw them. They would only come on the return when Mama was alive."

"I am afraid Mama never accepted Sir James as Jane's husband. He spoke to Fitzwilliam on several occasions about Mama's rude comments."

Lydia's head lifted with haste. "Do not misunderstand. I do not blame him at all. Mama was intolerable. She belittled him and his title on more than one occasion. Her criticisms and barbs were unfair. He was a splendid match for Jane in that he adores her."

"Yes, he is," agreed Lizzy.

They lapsed into silence as Georgiana re-situated the ribbons of her reticule on her wrist. The Bennet sisters were all fortunate in their marriages. The shame lay in Mrs. Bennet's dogged reluctance to see the advantages to each of her daughter's suitors.

The slowing of the carriage drew her from her thoughts as they pulled before Gunter's. After a short wait, they were able to procure a table and ordered.

Lydia's wide eyes studied everything and everyone around them while Lizzy and Aunt Charlotte discussed the upcoming ball. As Georgiana looked about the room, one young lady caught her eye. This woman watched Georgiana unabashedly, and leaned forward to whisper to a young lady sitting beside her, who then turned to look in their direction. Georgiana's head dropped and she studied the tassel on the bottom of her reticule.

"Oh, he is handsome."

Georgiana glanced up at Lydia's whisper and leaned towards her shoulder. "Who?"

"He just stood across the room."

She shifted forward and gasped. The dark, tousled ash brown hair and smile were the same on the grown man as they were on the impertinent boy she had known so long ago. His eyes looked up, and she jolted back in her seat. Was Lydia tall enough to hide her sufficiently?

Lydia glanced to her with her eyebrows drawn. "Do you know him?"

"Yes, our parents were friends. He is . . . insufferable to say the least." She opened her reticule and made a point of searching for any object. If she kept her head down, perhaps he would not notice her.

"I believe I could bear with insufferable to gaze into those eyes." Lydia opened her fan and gave a slight wicked grin as she pretended to cool herself.

She bit her lip to keep from laughing. "You are incorrigible."

"What of you?" Lydia's eyebrow rose in a look eerily similar to her sister's.

"What of me?"

The bell on the door jingled and Georgiana exhaled as her entire body relaxed. He tipped his hat to a lady when she passed and began to walk in front of the window. His head turned, their eyes met, and her face heated feverishly. Had he recognised her? A slight curve to one side of his lips would indicate he had. No, no, no!

"For a lady who never hopes to marry, you certainly have an interesting reaction to that gentleman. I had no idea your face could turn the precise shade of a ripe cherry." Lydia's voice was soft but amused.

"I know not of what you speak."

Lydia giggled. "I think you do, and I do expect you to tell me tonight. I have a suspicion it will be worth the effort to convince you to talk."

"Lydia—"

"Oh no! I told you of my dismal prospects in Hertfordshire and why I was determined to leave Meryton behind. Since that night at Longbourn, you have heard a great number of my secrets, but shared none of your own. You will tell me your history with that man. I insist upon it."

She held Lydia's amused gaze. "I have nothing to tell."

Any and all amusement disappeared from Lydia's countenance. "While I may snore, you, my dear, talk in your sleep."

Georgiana's heart pounded furiously against her sternum as she peered around them. Lizzy was still speaking to Aunt Charlotte. She looked behind her. No one could hear them, could they?

"Do not fret. I shall not tell your secrets here, and I shall not force you to speak of your nightmares. But, should you confide in me, I swear to never tell a soul."

"Georgiana?" Her head jerked to Lizzy who reached across the table to take her hand. "You are pale. Are you well?"

She cleared her throat. "I am."

"I am afraid I gave Georgiana a shock a moment ago." Lydia rolled her eyes. "Forgive me. While I try to do better, I forget at times and do not think before I speak."

Georgiana's eyes moved between her sister and her aunt. Both watched her as though she was fragile china that might shatter into tiny slivers at any moment. "Lydia is being kind. I thought I noticed a familiar face, but I was incorrect."

Her aunt peered about the room. "Who could have disturbed you to such an extent?"

"No one of importance. I assure you."

Aunt Charlotte stared at her a moment longer than Lizzy, her gaze lingering as she turned her head. When she was once again conversing with Lizzy, Lydia nudged her in the ribs. Georgiana turned and lifted her eyebrows.

"You owe me," mouthed Lydia.

Chapter 4

December 26th 1816

The Yule log was still burning in the grate and the candle's flame still shone in the dining room when I retired last night. Uncle Henry and Aunt Charlotte, as well as my cousin Milton and his wife, Amelia, joined us for Christmas services and shared the delicious dinner Cook prepared. The day was a wonderful time for our family, though I do wish Milton and Amelia had brought Hugh and baby Cecilia with them as William would have much preferred a playmate his own age to the familiar company of Lydia and myself. Richard arrived in time for the meal and engaged in his usual antics, teasing us all and indulging in Fitzwilliam's supply of brandy.

Lizzy, Lydia, and I drank wassail and played cards with Aunt Charlotte. After dinner, Lizzy, Amelia, and I all played the pianoforte and Lydia sang. I never knew she had such a clear, strong voice hidden behind her girlish giggles. I shall have to tempt her to sing in company when I have the first opportunity. She has hidden her talent in Meryton, which was a grave mistake. Those awful harpies need to see Lydia's accomplishments have expanded and are no longer limited to flirting!

Thus far, I have been able to avoid Lydia's inquisition over what occurred in Gunter's, but I know she will not relent for long. I enjoy having a sister closer to my age in which to confide, yet I am appalled to have had nightmares and spoken in my sleep while in her company. I confess I had hoped the dreams that began more in earnest when I made the decision to come to London would be held at bay by the presence of another. I was wrong.

How much does she know? When I first made the acquaintance of Lydia Bennet, I would not have confided in her unless I desired all of England to hear my secrets, but I believe her now to be sincere. She has assured me of her silence, and has, thus far, kept her word.

She placed the ribbon along the binding, but left the journal open so the words might dry. With a sigh, she again read through the entry. Careful of the wet ink, she then turned back two pages.

I could scarce believe my eyes when I searched for the gentleman Lydia found so handsome and discovered Nathaniel. Indeed, his tall frame was difficult to miss as he stood across the room. I find myself amazed at how little he has changed. He has grown taller and has acquired other attributes which distinguish him from the boy he once was, yet I could see the boy I knew in the eyes of the man—particularly when he smiled.

Could his manner be much the same as it was? I dread meeting him face to face because of his antics when we were children. Why do irrational fears seem to be my lot in life? He would not be respected among his peers if he persisted in stealing the dolls of young girls, pulling curls, and proclaiming himself betrothed to them all.

Despite my twenty years, I remain a silly girl!

She was a silly girl. At the slam of her bedchamber door, she jumped and shut the book with a snap.

"You have avoided me thus far, but I shall not allow it to continue." Lydia dropped ungracefully onto the bed and pulled a pillow beneath her chin. "I wish to know of the young man at Gunter's."

Georgiana rubbed an ink smudge on her fingers, yet regardless of how she scrubbed, the mark would not disappear. "He is no one of consequence. His parents were friends with my own. We were often in company together as children."

"Name."

She licked her finger and began to wipe the offending black mark with more vigour. "Pardon?"

"His name, Georgiana."

Her hands dropped to her lap. "Nathaniel Howard, Viscount Sele."

Lydia grinned as she lifted to a sitting position, still holding the pillow to her chest. "That was not so difficult, was it?"

Shaking her head, she stood and moved to the window. "You well know that you will not stop with his name. You merely requested the simplest information first."

"Oh, very well!" Lydia shifted to sit as primly as one could on a bed. "Is he a sensible young man, a man of information?"

An improper noise escaped as Georgiana, who fought to stifle a laugh, began to chuckle through her nose. "I have not been in company with him since I was twelve or thirteen. I could not tell you."

"Well, what was he like when you knew him?"

She leaned against the window seat. "Insufferable."

"You are insufferable, Georgiana Darcy! One word is not a sufficient response! No, I want a description. I want to know why your complexion is scarlet when you lay eyes upon him, and why, when he took notice of you, he gave you such a lively grin?"

She threw her hands into the air before they dropped to her sides. "He teased me, he pulled my curls, he hid my favourite doll—I still do not know where. He always insisted upon his way, he swore he would marry me, he put a frog in my reticule, and he claimed no girl could ride a horse as well as a boy."

Both of Lydia's hands were palm out in front of her. "Wait a moment. Go back two complaints. Did you say he swore he would marry you?"

Heat radiated from her body as though she was standing before a roaring fire instead of a cool window on a misty December day. If Lydia heard her dreams, she knew far worse incriminating information, so how could trusting her with more be a problem?

"Yes," she grumbled, watching her slipper clad toe trace the ivy pattern on the carpet below.

"Georgiana! He is so handsome! All of those complaints you listed were attempts to gain your attention. What if he meant what he said?" Her eyes glazed and her voice held a faint, dreamy quality Georgiana had never heard. "What if he has been waiting all this time for you to come out?"

"I am certain he was never truly enamoured of me." Lydia opened her mouth and Georgiana rushed forward to cover it with her palm. "Even if he was, that was a long time ago. With the exception of a Christmas here and there, he has been in Ireland since he completed Oxford. I am certain he has long since forgotten me." She removed her hand and sat upon the edge of the mattress.

"What if he still loves you?"

"He does not love me, and if he once did, 'tis a good thing he came to his senses. If you will remember, I do not plan to marry."

"You cannot allow one bad experience to dictate your life."

Georgiana glared into Lydia's eyes. "I would never expect you to understand what occurred or how it has affected me since."

Lydia took her hands. "I have heard your nightmares. I am assuming it was the man who proposed who hurt you so dreadfully." She paused, but Georgiana would not meet her eyes. Instead, she studied the fire as each tendril of flame curled upwards, changed colour, and wavered before it tapered to a curved point. How much did Lydia know? "If you continue to shun the world, you allow him influence over your future—he is still a part of your life. He deserves no such attention."

Her stomach tightened and churned. How could flighty, immature Lydia have proven to be so discerning?

"Do not stare at me so. I learnt a great deal while I sat in solitude and observed those around me. I can now understand why Lizzy is so often occupied by the activity. I also have little to do but think when I am awakened due to your dreams."

She swallowed the sick that had risen in her throat. "You could have removed to your own bedchamber." Her voice was weak and shaky. Lord, but she hated when she was feeble-minded!

"I considered doing as much, yet you were so terrified, I could not leave your side. Instead, I remained and held your hand."

Her vision blurred, and she blinked hard, looking anywhere but at Lydia. She would not cry! "What do you believe happened?" whispered Georgiana.

"I am not certain, but I hope one day you might trust me enough to tell me." Lydia's head tilted. "I want to know more about Lord Sele."

Georgiana groaned. "Nathaniel. Fitzwilliam calls him Sele since we have grown, but when we were children, he was Nathaniel."

"Was he handsome?" Lydia bit her lip with a smile.

"He looked much the same as he does now."

She rolled her eyes. "Tosh! He is sure to be taller than he was then, and I doubt his shoulders were so broad or that he could grow a beard."

Her lips tugged upwards on each end. "Well, of course not, but whether he was handsome or not was irrelevant because he was the most infuriating boy. I was once so irritated by his presumption I kicked him in the shin."

Lydia rolled back onto the bed in a fit of giggles. "Why?"

"As I mentioned before, he insisted he would marry me."

"If he made such a proclamation to me, I would not argue one jot!"

A light knock made them both turn towards the door. "Yes?"

A maid entered. "I beg your pardon, miss, but Mrs. Darcy asked me to tell you of Colonel Fitzwilliam's arrival."

"Thank you."

They rose from the bed, straightened their appearance before the mirror, and hastened to the drawing room where Lizzy stood near the fire speaking with Richard and an unknown lady. Georgiana made an abrupt halt.

Richard held out his arm. "Georgiana, I would like you to meet my betrothed." Her eyes pained her they bulged so. Richard was marrying? Why had he not said as much yesterday when they were a small family party rather than shock her with the information in company? She put a tentative foot forward, but a hand grabbed her elbow and hauled her in their direction.

She shook herself free. "Lydia, I can walk on my own."

When she approached, Richard steered the lady to step closer. "Miss Julia Raeburn, I would like you to meet my cousin, Miss Georgiana Darcy." He gestured towards Lydia. "And this young lady is Lizzy's sister, Miss Lydia Bennet."

Once the ladies all curtseyed, Miss Raeburn glanced to Richard and back to them. "I am pleased to meet the both of you. I have heard much of you, Miss Darcy, and I anticipate knowing you better."

A painful jab to her ribs prompted her to jump. "Yes, congratulations, Richard." She stepped forward and kissed him upon the cheek. "Forgive me. My cousin has been quite circumspect. I had no idea he was planning to marry."

Richard's expression softened as he smiled at Miss Raeburn. "I hope you will forgive me, but we have been betrothed for nigh on two months. I wished to tell you in person, so I requested your brother not say a word. I thought the announcement would be better with Julia present, so I delayed until today. We set the date for when we knew you could be in attendance, so we marry in a fortnight."

A fortnight! "Is it to be a grand wedding?"

A light appeared in Miss Raeburn's eyes, and she hugged Richard's arm a bit tighter. "I hoped for a small affair, but my father could not be stopped. He insisted he invite his business associates as they might be offended should they be excluded. I am afraid Lord and Lady Fitzwilliam took that as permission to include the entire House of Lords. Their ball in but two days' time has been turned into a celebration of our marriage and might prove to be a greater crush than the past events Richard has described."

Lizzy sighed. "Oh, Fitzwilliam will be miserable if your prediction is true."

Richard covered Miss Raeburn's hand upon his arm with his own. "Some might sneer at Mr. Raeburn as a tradesman, but I find it doubtful they would offend my father by snubbing the evening."

As Lydia looped her arm through Georgiana's, Lydia leaned forward a hairsbreadth. "How did the two of you meet?"

Richard's cheeks became slightly reddened. "I happened upon Julia walking with her nephews and their nurse in the park. She was distraught over the disappearance of one of the boys, so I, being the dashing gentleman that I am, could not rest until the child was located."

Georgiana observed Miss Raeburn while Richard spoke. Miss Raeburn appeared to be several years older than she—perhaps six or seven and twenty? Her countenance was open and happy. She looked upon Richard with fondness and blushed when their eyes met. Georgiana's utmost concern was Richard's long-standing claim of requiring a wife with a fortune. She did not want him to wed without affection, but her concerns appeared to be for naught. The colour in their cheeks and the looks they were bestowing upon one another were proof enough of their mutual attachment.

"I did not know the gratitude I would receive for my part in discovering him."

Miss Raeburn peered upwards and gave a playful scoff. "You always tell the tale as though I made an improper overture. I merely invited you to dinner."

Lizzy's shoulders shook as she held back her amusement. Lydia wore a happy expression despite her slight acquaintance with Richard and his betrothed. Was she the lone surprised party here?

"Sir James Audley and Lady Audley." Jobbins gave a short bow and departed.

"Jane!" exclaimed Lizzy while she rushed forward to embrace her elder sister. "I had not expected you until tomorrow."

Sir James shook Richard's hand before he kissed Lizzy on the cheek. "Huntleigh is but a two hour carriage ride from London. We left as the sun rose, and have settled the children at Audley House. Jane simply could not wait until the morrow to be with all of you."

Georgiana kissed Jane on the cheek as Fitzwilliam entered and greeted the newcomers before taking his usual place at Lizzy's side.

"I have missed them." Jane's voice was exasperated, yet her happy countenance was proof she was anything but upset. "I cannot wait to see William. If he has grown as much as Jamie and Clara, I fear I shall not recognise him."

Lizzy retained her hold on her sister's hands. "You are not one to be so dramatic."

"Little Jamie has taken after his father. He has grown several inches at least since we returned from Pemberley, and Clara is walking! Their growth has been so swift! Jamie is not the baby he once was, and Clara is so fiercely independent. She reminds me of you, Lizzy."

"Why are all the headstrong children in our family compared to me?"

With his hand to her shoulder, Fitzwilliam pulled her close. "Because you are the most stubborn and wilful woman we know."

Georgiana inhaled sharply at her brother's tease while Lizzy elbowed him in the side. "I should take great offence to such a statement," she cried.

"You shall only prove me correct."

A small growl came from Lizzy as she crossed her arms over her chest. "Very well, I shall know how to act."

A bark of laughter erupted from Richard. "Poor Darcy! I believe you have spent too much time in the company of Lady Catherine."

Lizzy paled. "Heaven forbid!"

"Do not fret." Her brother gave a slight tug to Lizzy's elbow and ran his hand down her forearm and entwined his fingers with hers. "Lady Catherine shall remain at Rosings until Anne and Bingley come in late January since they cannot travel without her advice and supervision."

"Poor Bingley was well aware of Lady Catherine's disposition before he asked Anne to marry him." Richard grinned like he was plotting some great revenge. "He cannot claim ignorance."

"No," responded Georgiana, "but no amount of foresight could have told him she would become more overprotective of her grandchildren than of her daughter."

"As long as she has no thoughts of pairing William with her granddaughter, Catherine, as she did with Anne and Fitzwilliam." Lizzy tugged the nearby bell pull. "I have no wish for rumours to abound of my son's arranged marriage."

A maid bustled through the door and curtseyed. "Yes, ma'am?"

"Have tea and refreshments served as soon as they can be arranged."

With one last bob, the maid departed and Lizzy gestured around the room while Richard introduced Miss Raeburn to Jane and Sir James. "Let us sit while we can. Once William wakes from his nap, I shall have Mrs. Wynn bring him to join us."

When they were seated, Richard glanced to Lizzy and then to Lydia. "Miss Bennet, you have been rather quiet. Are you enjoying London thus far?"

Georgiana looked to her hands and awaited Lydia's recitation of their last few days. She had not ceased speaking of Gunter's and the modiste's, and it was possible she would repeat the entirety of her week without pausing for breath. You had no way of knowing with Lydia.

"I have seen little since our arrival: a few shops, Gunter's, and the modiste. Yet, I have taken great pleasure in what we have done. We have fittings tomorrow at Madame Guiard's, and Lizzy indicated we would shop for bonnets and hats afterward."

Lizzy straightened in her seat. "Miss Raeburn, we would be pleased if you could join us tomorrow. We could all become better acquainted."

"I would love to join you. Oh! And I would be pleased if you would call me Julia."

A twinkle lit Lizzy's eye. She looked to Georgiana and Fitzwilliam as though she was requesting their permission. "Well, then you should call us all by our given names as well. I am Lizzy to my family and sisters, only Fitzwilliam calls me Elizabeth, but you are welcome to call me as such."

Richard chuckled. "You are allowed, my dear, but I am not. My staid, stingy cousin will not allow it."

Why could Richard not leave well enough alone? He loved baiting Fitzwilliam with that nonsense!

After a pinch to his arm, Julia frowned in his direction. "Mr. Darcy is allowed to have an endearing name for his wife. Need I remind you your preference for the nickname my brother gave me when we were children? Would you care to have your cousin refer to me in such a familiar manner?" Fitzwilliam's low, muffled chuckle was heard in the pause.

"You know I am teasing him," complained Richard with a pout. "Why must you spoil the fun?"

"Because you have a similar habit, and I see nothing to mock in the manner in which a man loves his wife. Too many people wed for concerns other than the heart. 'Tis refreshing to see so many marriages based on affection in one family."

His shoulders dropped. "Forgive me." He held his hand palm up, which Julia took in hers. "I had not thought of how unforgiving some of my parents' acquaintances have been. I know you have been upset by their attitudes, but remember their prejudices and talk will lessen over time."

"When I first married Fitzwilliam, the disdain of some ladies was written upon their expressions." Julia's eyes never left Lizzy while the latter spoke. With this similarity, they were bound to become good friends. Their likeness in temper would also facilitate their relationship. "Over time, those disappeared and a few even deign to speak with me. I care naught for those who place money and class over other considerations. They cannot comprehend what they lack. Do know that Lady Fitzwilliam will not allow her guests to abuse you."

"My aunt does not abide the cattiness of some ladies," interjected Georgiana. "Lizzy is correct. My aunt once had a viscount removed from one of her balls because he snubbed one of her dearest friends. If nothing else, no one will cut you for fear of losing their invitation to next year's ball."

"Mother and I have told her as much," added Richard. "Though, I wish she did not worry. Besides, I shall be a gentleman once my commission is sold and Julia will be a gentleman's wife. When we are at home in the country, her background will matter less than in town."

"He is correct, you know," said Lizzy. Julia looked back to her without blinking. "My mother's father was a solicitor and her brother a tradesman, an importer, yet no one in Meryton derided her roots."

Wait! Her head shot back in her cousin's direction. Richard was selling his commission? "Richard, you are leaving the military?"

With a huge grin, he glanced to his betrothed and back. "I am, Georgiana. Between my allowance from Father, my investments, and my salary, I saved enough to purchase a small estate in Nottinghamshire. The house is not terribly large, but it is sufficient. Julia's fortune is also such that I can buy a parcel of land adjoining mine since the owners changed their mind about retaining it."

"I am so pleased for you." How fortunate! Richard had always despised being subject to the whim of his superiors, and now, he would be free of those strictures.

"Thank you. We do hope you will join us for a stay once we are settled." Richard's brows rose to his forehead. "I know how you adore Pemberley, but I promise you will not be away from Derbyshire for long."

Georgiana scanned the faces of her family. She was truly fortunate to have such relations. Even Julia gave a slight lean forward in her seat while she awaited the answer. Georgiana inhaled in order to quash the turning of her stomach. Richard would never wed someone who was not genuine. Julia would be much like Lizzy, and how could she reject another sister? The answer was simple, she could not. "When you are prepared for guests, then I shall come."

Chapter 5

The merry tinkle of the bell rang from the door, and Aunt Charlotte leaned against Georgiana's side.

"Why do we always happen upon those we would rather avoid in this shop?"

She peeked over her shoulder. Two ladies had entered and now scanned the interior. The first was one with whom she had attended school and was certainly not one whose company she would seek. The second was unfamiliar, but her association with the first was not in her favour.

She fingered the finely woven silk ribbon attached to the bonnet in her other hand. "I am acquainted with Miss Thorpe, but I do not know the second."

"Lady Harriet Neville. Do not be fooled by her manner. She is a tremendous gossip. I doubt she would care if the scandal was related to her own mother. She would call on all of her acquaintance to ensure its dissemination."

"The details and the colour are lovely." Julia fingered the rosette where the ribbon attached. "Do you have a spencer or pelisse in a similar shade?"

With a start, Georgiana turned back to the hat. "I do, though I already have more bonnets than I require."

"Mrs. Darcy!" exclaimed Lady Harriet. "I was just telling Miss Thorpe that I had yet to hear of your arrival in London. I would have called had I known you were in town."

Georgiana, Julia, Lydia, and her aunt all turned to watch the exchange.

"You are too kind, but we have not yet begun to receive callers. We have spent our days shopping or spending time with family."

If only she could be as adept in such an awkward situation! To someone who knew her well, Lizzy's reserved politeness was obvious. To those who were not her sister's intimates, her manners were all that was proper and bore no signs of artifice.

"Lady Fitzwilliam, how pleasant to see you again," exclaimed Miss Thorpe when she took note of Aunt Charlotte. "My mother and I enjoyed speaking with you Monday last."

Her aunt nodded. "It was good of you to call."

With a look around the shop, Lady Harriet grinned. "Miss Thorpe has been invited to a house party held by the Earl of Sussex, and though her mother was unwell today, we are procuring a few items for the occasion."

Georgiana did her best to keep her expression neutral. Everyone in London knew the deplorable reputation of the Earl! Even with the presence of a chaperon, what sort of parent would allow their unmarried daughter to reside under his roof?

"I hope you have an agreeable time." Aunt Charlotte gestured to Julia. "We were shopping for my son's betrothed, Miss Julia Raeburn, as well as my niece, Miss Darcy, and Mrs. Darcy's youngest sister, Miss Bennet."

Lady Harriet's attention was drawn behind Lizzy and she pointed to a ruby-coloured velvet bonnet. "Oh! Do look, Isabella. Is that not a similar shade to your new cape?"

Lady Harriet bobbed a quick curtsey to Lizzy. "I beg you excuse us. We have so much to do before Mrs. Thorpe requires Isabella's return for tea." The two ladies bustled to the rear of the shop.

A sigh caused them to turn to Julia, who shook her head. "I suppose her snub was better than a cut direct."

"Do not let them disturb you, dear," soothed Aunt Charlotte with a dismissive wave of her hand. "They are not worth your time or injured sensibilities. Now, you mentioned desiring a new fan and a pair of gloves for the ball. I know of a quaint little place two shops down."

Lizzy's head lifted from where she searched in her reticule. "I require a new pair of gloves as well. Georgiana? Lydia? Do you wish to remain here or will you depart with us?"

Lydia scanned the room and her shoulders dropped. "I have yet to find a new bonnet. When I think I have found the perfect one, I find another I adore just as much. 'Tis a hopeless situation."

One corner of Georgiana's lips tugged upwards. The drama and exaggeration in Lydia's words never failed to amuse her. "I shall remain with Lydia. I have yet to wear the gloves I received from you on my birthday. I have no need of more."

"I thought not," replied Lizzy. "I will have a quick word with the proprietor before we depart."

Lydia and Georgiana perused the displays side-by-side. The bell on the door sounded, signalling the remainder of their party's departure.

As Lydia removed a pink silk confection, she giggled. "At one time, I would have thought this quite pretty." She placed it upon her head and batted her eyelashes. "I would have added more lace and ribbons as well."

Georgiana removed the yards of lace and silk from Lydia's head. "I believe I had a similar one for my doll when I was young. I thought it quite handsome." They both burst into quiet laughs.

"Lord Sele!" Lady Harriet's voice was loud enough to reverberate around the room. "Lady Lindsey mentioned you were to return for the season this year. It must be of great comfort to her after so long a separation."

Her entire body stiffened. Perhaps he would not notice them tucked away in the corner. The likelihood was small, was it not?

"I prefer to believe she is pleased to see me. She appears gratified, nonetheless. I hope your family is in good health, Lady Harriet, as well as yours, Miss Thorpe."

"They are all very well. Thank you, my lord." The enthusiasm in Miss Thorpe's voice was ridiculous, and reminiscent of Miss Bingley. Nathaniel would not care for such affected attentions, would he?

When he spoke to the two ladies, the timbre of his voice carried around the shop. The tone was much deeper than when they were children. Of course, he was no longer a child, but a grown man. She was ridiculous not to consider him so. Lydia had even suggested he was now capable of growing a beard. He was certainly taller. A sharp pain in her ribs caused her to suck in a hard breath.

"Would you cease with the infernal elbow to my side?"

"Why would he enter an establishment for ladies' hats?" whispered Lydia.

She shrugged. "Perhaps a gift for his mother?" She mouthed the words. The last thing she wanted was to be overheard—she would prefer not to be discovered either.

Lydia's eyebrow rose on one side. Obviously, she was doubtful as well. Then, Lady Harriet's too loud whisper reached her ears.

"She is not yet out, did you know? All of the ton has speculated as to why she has not had her début, but the Darcys and the Fitzwilliams have been exceedingly tight-lipped. 'Tis most vexing."

"I heard she had a scandalous affair with a servant's son. She is sure to be ruined."

"Oh no, Isabella, I have it on good authority that she has a deficiency of the mind. These last years of seclusion at Pemberley were due to her infirmity, though I heard she was present at Mrs. Darcy's lying in. Can you imagine? How improper!"

Her back and shoulders went rigid. How dare they!

A tight squeeze brought her attention to her hand. When had Lydia taken it? The gesture, however, did nothing to alleviate the tension now plaguing her. She was so stiff, Lydia was certain to feel it.

"Ladies, I would beg you importune me no longer with your unfounded gossip. My family has been on intimate terms with the Darcys since before I was born. I spent a great deal of time with both of the Darcys when I was young, and I can tell you in no uncertain terms, Miss Darcy is not deficient in the mind, nor is she likely to have been intimate with a hired hand. Now, if you will excuse me."

A small squeak came from Lydia. A jerky movement could be seen from the corner of her eye. Was Lydia bouncing?

The bell rang. Nathaniel, no doubt, stormed through the door in his anger, and Georgiana turned to watch him through the window, but rather than seeing the street through the glass, she stepped forward into a hard mixture of fine lawn and scratchy wool. When she drew back, amused dark eyes and a lop-sided mischievous grin were the first attributes she noted.

"Nathan—Lord Sele! I—" Her heart thudded in her chest and her palm rested upon her stomach.

"Forgive me if I frightened you, Miss Darcy." He bowed as a painful pinch was delivered to the sensitive flesh of her side.

She curtseyed, clasping her hands tight before her. "I had not expected . . ."

He glanced to her side. "Would you do me the honour of introducing me to your friend?"

Her head whipped around to . . . Lydia? He wanted to meet Lydia? This was mortifying! Could she not run back to Darcy House directly and hide between her bedcovers?

"Lord Sele, this lady is Miss Lydia Bennet, the youngest sister of Mrs. Darcy. Miss Bennet, this is Nathaniel Howard, Viscount Sele."

Lydia curtseyed. "A pleasure, my lord."

"Are you enjoying the Christmas season in London?" His eyes had returned to her. He was speaking to her?

"Very much. In the past, I have missed my brother, Lizzy, and their son while I remained behind at Pemberley. I am pleased to have joined them this year."

His head tilted just a fraction. "I have yet to make the acquaintance of Mrs. Darcy. Perhaps on the morrow at the Fitzwilliams' ball? I have not attended in several years, but I anticipate this year's event. The Fitzwilliams have much to celebrate, it seems."

"Yes, my aunt and uncle were thrilled when their eldest and his wife welcomed a son in June. My cousin Richard's betrothal and retirement from the military is a blessing as well. They will be glad to see him safe from harm's way."

His lips curved a mite on one side. "If you are attending, I hope I am not too late in requesting a set—perhaps the supper dance?"

Her eyes hurt, they widened so. A dance? With her? No!

"I—"

"She would be honoured, Lord Sele."

Georgiana's head jerked to the side where Lydia stood wearing an enormous grin. Was there a tooth in her mouth that could not be seen?

"I—"

"I shall also mention making your acquaintance to my sister," continued Lydia. "I am certain she will want to add you to the invitation list for Miss Darcy's ball. I believe the date is in early March—just at the beginning of the season."

Her head was beginning to spin. What was Lydia doing? Her pulse pounded against her eardrums and her breath was coming in short pants. She was going to swoon! How horrifying!

Nathaniel's smile lit his face and his eyes. "I would be pleased to join your family for such an auspicious occasion. Pray have Mrs. Darcy send 'round the invitation. Thank you."

He leaned forward and caught her gaze. "However, I would like to hear your acceptance of my request for a dance in your own voice."

She swallowed the lump in her throat. What choice did she have? "Yes, of course." Why was her voice so weak and shaky? "I would be glad to reserve the supper dance for you."

"Excellent!"

Look at his smug, self-satisfied grin! She should tell him she changed her mind, but Lydia already made her appear ridiculous. How would it look if she then refused him? Lydia was well meaning, but this notion of a ball was nothing short of terrible. What had possessed her? When they returned to Darcy House, she was going to lock Lydia in the cellar!

"Nathaniel?" He stepped back as he turned to where Lady Lindsey stood just within the door.

"Look who I have happened upon, Mother."

Recognition flashed in Lady Lindsey's eyes, her arms stretched out, and she strode forward. "Georgiana Darcy, I cannot remember the last time we were in company."

Before Georgiana knew what had happened, Lady Lindsey held her in a warm hug. Her eyes closed as she savoured an embrace that brought back memories and sensations of her mother. A similar calm and sense of security overtook her in Lady Lindsey's arms.

"Forgive me, but I have missed you, my dear." She held out Georgiana's arms and took her measure. "You have grown into a handsome young lady—so like your mother. Your hair might be chestnut where hers was golden, yet your eyes and your features are hers."

As Lady Lindsey continued to hold her hands, she glanced towards Lydia. "I have been rude not to request an introduction. Would you?"

Georgiana cleared her throat. "Lady Amelia Howard, Countess Lindsey, this is Miss Lydia Bennet, Mrs. Darcy's youngest sister."

The lady's smile became wider and her eyes glowed. "I have met Mrs. Darcy. Unfortunately, I have not been in her company enough to call her a great friend, yet I like her very much. Fitzwilliam's happiness is evident in his manner and looks when they are together. Anne wanted nothing less for both of her children. I am pleased to see him make such a match."

"Both my sister and brother are content in their situation," interjected Lydia. "They are indeed well-matched."

Lady Lindsey sighed with a smile. "Marriages based on love are rare in our sphere and to be valued. I hope you both are as attentive to such matters when a young man attempts to court you."

"I—" What was wrong with her? Why could she not utter a coherent sentence other than an introduction? "What I meant to say was I had not—" A pain shot through Georgiana's upper arm at Lydia's relentless grip.

"Neither of us would consider less, Lady Lindsey. How could we settle when we have such an example of felicity set by my sister and her husband?" Lydia exuded such confidence and poise. Who was this girl and where was the friend with the bubbly giggle? This Lydia was not as much to her liking. She accepted dance requests in her stead, squeezed her arm painfully, responded to questions for her, and the pinch! How could she forget the pinch?

Nathaniel cupped his mother's elbow in his palm. "I am loath to interrupt, but we promised my father we would return by two."

While she checked her son's open pocket watch, Lady Lindsey rubbed her thumbs over Georgiana's knuckles. "You must come 'round for tea. I shall send an invitation for the two of you and Mrs. Darcy. Perhaps we can arrange a dinner in a few weeks' time?"

"I shall let Mrs. Darcy know." Her voice was so faint. She wanted to call upon Lady Lindsey and become acquainted with her mother's good friend once again. Why was she behaving with such timidity?

"Excellent." She leaned forward to kiss Georgiana's cheek. Could Lady Lindsey feel her tremble? "I look forward to your call."

When his mother released her, Nathaniel shifted so he was directly before her and took her hand. "Until tomorrow evening." He kissed her knuckles, released her hand, and bowed to Lydia. "A pleasure to make your acquaintance, Miss Bennet."

"Lord Sele."

Once Lord Sele and his mother departed the shop, he grinned through the glass when he passed, much like he had at Gunter's a week prior, but all she could do was stare. Could she even make a peep?

Georgiana closed her eyes and took a deep breath, filling her chest as full of air as she could. Her entire body shook. She needed to calm. She took another long inhale. She was going to string Lydia up in the attics by her toes!

"Georgiana?"

She reached over and pinched the flesh over Lydia's ribs.

"Ow!"

Without turning to the friend who betrayed her, she strode from the building, pausing when her boot hit the pavement. The chill air was a shock after the warmth of the shop and prompted a shudder.

She pivoted in both directions and peered across the busy street. In which direction did Lizzy say they would go?

She made an abrupt halt in the midst of her next turn. That hat! She narrowed her eyes and squinted, but the lady's face was still unclear. It could not be, could it? But who would own the same headpiece?

"Have you completed your purchases?" She whipped around. When had Lizzy crept up behind her?

"I wish to return home."

The bell behind her rang, and Lydia stepped beside her.

A crease formed between Lizzy's eyebrows while she looked back and forth between them. "What has happened?"

When the remainder of their party joined them, Aunt Charlotte stroked her cheek. "You are pale, dearest. Perhaps we should return you to Darcy House before you take ill. The weather does have a bite to it today."

Fortunately, the carriage awaited them nearby, and they were soon all settled for the return to Mayfair. Georgiana had no desire to be near Lydia as she had on the trip to Bond Street, so she seated herself across the carriage and stared through the window.

Lizzy leaned forward where she could see them both. "Neither of you have indicated what occurred to upset you so. I expect an explanation now."

Lydia opened her mouth, but Georgiana threw her arm up and pointed. "Lydia has decided I am to have a ball in early March, and she has taken it upon herself to invite Nathaniel Howard."

An incredulous chirp came from Lizzy, and all the ladies in the carriage stared at Lydia.

"Nathaniel Howard?" asked Aunt Charlotte. "Viscount Sele?"

Lydia's hands lifted palm up in a sort of shrug and then dropped to her lap. "Yes, and he fancies her. He noticed her in Gunter's a week ago, he approached her in the hat shop today, and he defended her to those nasty harpies who had entered before you left. He also requested a dance at tomorrow's ball."

Why was her voice so exasperated? She was not the injured party! "Which you accepted for me!"

"Lydia!" Her sister's head shook. "I knew you had curbed the worst of your impetuous nature, but to force Georgiana as you have . . ."

"Why do you coddle her and protect her?" asked Lydia in an exasperated tone. "No other lady would wait until she was twenty to début. She lives in the world, yet she does not live."

Why was any of this Lydia's concern? She would one day marry and Georgiana would be perfectly content to remain with her brother's family. "I have managed myself quite well before your officious interference!" Georgiana argued. "I take pleasure in a full life and have no intention of changing!"

Lydia rolled her eyes. "Oh, you enjoy time with your nephew and shopping excursions, but you do not venture from the safe, secluded world of your creation. You are like a caterpillar in a cocoon who refuses to break free."

A strange, strangled noise came from Lizzy's nose before she broke into giggles. Georgiana bit her bottom lip and managed to stifle a laugh.

"What amuses you?" Lydia's wide eyes and serious mien only made Lizzy fall against the side of the carriage trying to restrain her laughter. The youngest Bennet could do naught but cross her arms over her chest with a huff. Aunt Charlotte's lip twitched as she paid rapt attention to the buildings passing while Julia's shoulders shook but no sound emerged.

"Forgive me," pleaded Lizzy. "I am not accustomed to such statements from you. Your behaviour since Mama's death, while proper, still surprises me at times. Do not mistake me. I am proud of the changes you have wrought, yet what you said was so unexpected. I could not help myself."

Lizzy sank back into the squabs and pressed her lips into a fine line. "Today, you were quite brazen to speak for Georgiana. Her brother and I promised to abide by her decisions and your interference could force her into unwanted situations."

"I have not pushed her from a precipice or put her in an improper position. She is attending the ball tomorrow night, so what is one more in her honour? Besides, Miss Georgiana Darcy," chided Lydia as she wagged a finger in her face. "You were as red as beetroot when he approached you. Your face when he kissed your hand . . ."

Lizzy's favourite brow lifted. "He kissed your hand?"

Was that Gunter's they were passing? She stared through the window at the people walking the pavement. Why was a kiss to the hand so important?

"Georgiana!" The tone of Lizzy's voice was one she had heard before. She would not allow the argument to lie. Georgiana rotated in her place so she faced the interior of the carriage and Lizzy's admonishment. "Will you have a ball or shall we call upon Lady Lindsey and correct Lydia's misinformation?"

"Lady Lindsey did say we should call soon." She cleared her throat in an effort to make her voice louder. "She mentioned tea or inviting us to dinner."

Aunt Charlotte pivoted in her seat and cradled Georgiana's cheeks in her palms. "I remember your mother and father speaking of your frequent arguments with Nathaniel. He could ruffle your feathers with little to no effort. Lady Lindsey and your mother were certain he sought your attention."

That frustrating finger was again waving in the corner of her sight. "I told you!"

A gloved hand pushed Lydia's to her lap. "Lydia, this is hardly helpful." Bless Julia!

"We still have one unexplained item from Lydia's list." All eyes turned to Julia. "Why did Lord Sele feel the inclination to defend you? What did those two ladies say or do once we departed?"

Lydia huffed. "Georgiana and I were laughing at a ridiculous pink frilled bonnet when Lord Sele entered. Those two ladies greeted and fawned over him before they began telling him of the rumours surrounding Georgiana."

Aunt Charlotte placed a hand over Georgiana's and leaned forward. "What did they say?"

"The ladies argued over which rumour was correct. One said Georgiana had a scandalous affair with a servant and was ruined. The other claimed Georgiana had a mental infirmity, which was why she remained at Pemberley the last few years. Her presence at your lying in, Lizzy, was another bit they found shocking."

"I plan to never use that midwife again," growled Lizzy. "Did she tell all of Derbyshire, who then spread it to all and sundry? I shall never understand why an unmarried lady cannot witness childbirth. The process is a natural one and I daresay, after witnessing a birth, many a young lady may give more thought before behaving in an improper or imprudent fashion with a man!"

With a wince at Lizzy's loud defence, her aunt sat back. "Nevertheless, the gossip is about. Her presence in London will soon be known as well. A ball is a prudent idea. No one can claim Georgiana has some deficiency of the mind once she has been presented, but the talk of her potential ruin could prove more persistent as a result."

"By proving one incorrect," queried Julia, "the other would be fixed as truth?"

"The possibility exists." Aunt Charlotte lifted her eyebrows. "You must decide, Georgiana. Would you prefer to remain as you are or eliminate a good portion of the talk surrounding your seclusion? For all intents and purposes, you are out, should anyone enquire, and a ball held at the beginning of March in honour of your first London season would do well to quell most of the rumours.

"If Lydia is correct and Lord Sele has carried a tendre for you all of these years," continued her aunt, "he may attempt to pursue you. He is known as a respectable gentleman. He would be a wonderful match for you."

The carriage came to a halt in front of the house, and before the footman approached, Georgiana threw the door open and hastened into the hall. She stripped her gloves and tugged at the ribbons of her bonnet, handing them to the maid with little care.

"Georgiana?"

She pulled her pelisse from her shoulders and dispensed with it in the same fashion as her other outdoor garments. "Perhaps I never sought his attention, and perhaps I do not wish for it now!"

Her eyes stung and her breath caught in her lungs. She hiked her skirts and sprinted up the stairs to her room, slammed the door, and dropped into the chair at her escritoire.

December 28ᵗʰ 1816

Why do accomplished ladies and gentlemen require lies to find entertainment? It seems I must have a ball else people will talk, but the gossip may change to a tale just as heinous. I hate this! I hate George Wickham!

Besides, Nathaniel never sought my notice! He was an annoying, headstrong young man and is, no doubt, much the same as an adult. His defence of me to Lady Harriet and Miss Thorpe was out of loyalty to my parents and caring for his mother's dearest friend. Naught but those reasons exist. The notion he could have feelings for me is preposterous! He does not know me! I appreciate his defence of me, and for that reason alone, I shall dance the supper set with him, but no more!

I would have been out without much fanfare had Lydia's statements not forced me into a more formal début into society. Despite the circumstances, my resolution will not waver. I will never marry!

A bubble of ink caused a black stain at the end of her entry. "Blast!"

"Georgiana?" Lizzy peeked through a crack in the door before she entered. "Your aunt means well, but you were rude. I agree Lydia overstepped, yet she had the best of intentions, which is a phrase I never thought I would utter in my lifetime."

Her body sagged. She had been frustrated when they departed the shop, but she had not meant to be impolite to Aunt Charlotte. "I shall apologise to my aunt, but Lydia should not have—" Her voice cracked.

"No, she should have remained silent, and I will discuss her behaviour with her once I know you are well." Her sister's hands rested upon her shoulders. "Do remember there was a time when Lydia thought of no one but herself, and today, she thought of nothing but your future happiness. She has made remarkable progress in the last few years. Do not ruin the bond between you over such a trifling incident—and when you consider what has occurred in your life, it is a mere trifle."

Lizzy kissed her forehead. "As your aunt said, you must decide, but do not take too long. We will need time to plan." She turned to leave, but before she could close the bedchamber door, Georgiana stood.

"Lizzy?"

She turned. "Yes?"

"Would you and aunt plan the ball?" Her thumbnail scratched an imperfection in the wood of the table. "I worry so about the repercussions of not adhering to the ton's expectations, and this course would eliminate those fears."

With a smile, Lizzy nodded. "Very well. I shall inform your aunt. We can discuss it more on the morrow when you are rested."

"Lizzy?" Her sister stepped back. "Allow Lydia to believe I am vexed with her for a while longer."

After a grin, Lizzy nodded. "I shall not say a word."

Chapter 6

From the edge of the ballroom, Georgiana sipped her punch while Lydia chatted merrily with her current dance partner. Her behaviour had been similar with all of her partners thus far: open and gregarious. She was definitely enjoying the ball.

Georgiana peered a short distance away where Lizzy and Fitzwilliam were deep in conversation with a good friend of her brother's. Lizzy tilted her head as she regarded Georgiana. Lizzy was ensuring she was well, so she lifted a corner of her lips to set her sister's mind at ease.

In contrast to Lydia, Georgiana's card this evening had been dominated by her male relations, who all made certain she was not forced to endure awkward conversation with a stranger during her first ball. Uncle Henry, her brother, Richard, and Milton had each partnered her for a dance and now, she struggled not to fidget while she awaited Nathaniel for the next set.

Lady Lindsey had greeted her after the second set, and they spoke amiably until Richard claimed her hand before the music could begin again. She had even espied Lord Lindsey taking a turn with his wife, but thus far, Nathaniel was missing.

After another sip of her drink, she rose to her tiptoes to scan the room. Lydia could no longer claim Nathaniel held a tendre for her if he failed to even make an appearance at the ball. Ha! She would not be forced to uphold her side of a polite discourse on the weather, the state of the roads, or—

"Miss Darcy, I hope you are well this evening."

She dropped ungracefully from her toes as she attempted to whirl around. A palm supported her elbow while she steadied, her punch splashing precariously around the edge of her cup. Did it spill? A glance down the pale blush silk revealed her gown was unblemished. Thank heavens!

"I believe we have escaped catastrophe."

Her eyes rose from her cup to the cheerful, deep mahogany eyes she had just been seeking. "You startled me."

His hand left her arm as he bowed. "I wholeheartedly apologise. I had no reason to believe you would take such a fright in a room crowded with people."

One side of his lip twitched, and it took all her strength to withhold a frustrated growl. "I was by no means frightened. You merely caught me

54

unawares."

"As I said, I humbly beg your forgiveness." His voice was tinged with humour.

Good heavens! He was still as impossible as when they were young!

With a grin, he offered his arm. "We should move closer to the dancers. I would not want to miss our set. Should I be so careless, you might not see fit to grant me one in its stead, and your brother would tease me mercilessly after I sought his permission."

"You did?" Fitzwilliam would have allowed the privilege with the close relationship of their families, but he was correct. Her brother would enjoy pestering Nathaniel if she refused to dance with him now.

She placed her punch on a passing servant's tray and rested her hand upon the heavy wool of his sleeve. Better to have this portion of the evening concluded than to prolong the agony.

"I anticipate an enlightening conversation at dinner. We have not spoken in years, so I hope to learn of your adventures since we were last in company."

Dinner! Custom dictated they be seated together during the meal following, and he actually expected it of her. Could she not sit with Lydia and Lizzy?

"I had not thought . . ." What was she to say? Would he consider her rude if she claimed she had no desire to dine with him?

"Miss Darcy." His voice lowered as he faced her. "I requested the supper set for the pleasure of dancing with you as well as conversing with you during the meal. I do hope you are not considering abandoning me to the whims of the other ladies present."

Her eyebrows rose. "They might expect the enjoyment of your company after you prove yourself a willing and able partner. I may not have the ability to protect you as you seem to think."

"Nathaniel!" called Lady Lindsey, strolling forward on her husband's arm. "I am glad to see you have arrived. I sent the carriage back as you requested." A mischievous glint lit the lady's countenance and Nathaniel's face coloured.

"Yes, Mother. I arrived a few moments ago."

Georgiana flinched. He arrived a few moments ago? He avoided the beginning of the ball and made an appearance merely for their set and dinner?

Lady Lindsey grasped her free hand. "Miss Darcy, I do hope you remember my husband?"

She gave a quick curtsey. "Yes, I do. I am glad to see you hale, my lord."

With a slight bow, the earl smiled. "Not as glad as I am to be well again, I assure you."

The music ended, the dancers dispersed to find their next partners, and

Nathaniel dipped his head to his parents. "I was promised a dance by Miss Darcy. If you will excuse us."

His steady and sure stride brought them to the top of the set near Lydia. The impertinent hussy glanced over and bit her bottom lip with a grin. Oh no! Lydia would not embarrass her again, would she?

A few moments after he took his place across from her, the music began and Nathaniel bowed as she curtseyed. They both stepped forward and joined hands.

"How are you enjoying London?"

Her gaze met his, but she could not hold it. Instead, she looked over his shoulder. "We have only been in town a short time. Other than preparing for the ball and making several calls, we have not ventured much further than Bond Street."

"If you are at all like my mother, nothing exists beyond Bond Street."

Her head whipped back in his direction with a huff. "In the past, I have taken great enjoyment in a few small recitals and performances as well as several plays at Covent Garden."

Their turn completed, they retreated to their original positions and awaited the other members of their group to take their turn. Nathaniel's curved lips and the crinkles at the corners of his eyes betrayed his amusement. How could he prick every last nerve she possessed?

As the pattern shifted them together once more, he stepped a hairsbreadth closer than necessary. "I beg your pardon if I caused offence. You will forgive me, will you not?" His bottom lip protruded into a slight pout. He appeared ridiculous with such a childish expression. A laugh burst from her, and she pressed her lips together in an effort to quash the sound.

She gave an affected sigh. "I suppose I must, though I do so begrudgingly."

"Oh ho!" he cried. "The Georgiana Darcy I remember still exists beneath the layers of silk and bejewelled pins in her hair. Should I be concerned you might care for retribution should I speak without thought?" He bent slightly towards her ear. "You will not kick me in the shin, will you?"

A wisp of his breath caught her ear and a frisson travelled down her spine, causing her to start. "I might. If you behave as you did at twelve." Good! Her voice did not tremble!

"'Tis tempting, but I believe I should prefer you to know me as I am now." He watched her from the corner of his eye. "However, you must allow me to prove myself."

They parted to take their places in the line once more.

Their eyes met and she held his gaze. Why would he need to prove himself? "To what purpose?"

His brow drew down. "Will you ask the same of any man who requests to call this Season? You cannot expect to débute without gentlemen taking notice."

She stiffened, filled her chest with air, and drew herself as tall as she could. "I cannot prevent their interest, but I can dissuade them. I have no reason to torment a respectable man."

They bowed and curtseyed when the first song ended.

With a tilt of the head, he stared at her while the music for the second dance began. They again honoured their partners and Georgiana stepped inside to turn with the neighbouring gentleman. When she returned to the line, Nathaniel did the same with the lady beside her. When they joined hands, he drew her closer.

"Pray tell, how would you torment a respectable man?"

The muscles in her back tensed. "I have no intention of marrying."

"Never?"

"No, never." They parted at the top of the set while she struggled to contain the words threatening to burst forth from her lips. Why was it such a strange concept? Perhaps she preferred a solitary life. Rather than allow the words that itched the back of her throat to escape, she pressed her lips together once more.

Neither spoke again until he offered his arm to lead her to the supper rooms.

"Perhaps some fortunate gentleman might persuade you to change your mind."

"'Tis unlikely."

"Then I suppose I shall have to settle for your friendship. If you will allow me."

She searched the room for her brother and Lizzy. Where were they?

"Miss Darcy?"

"Hmm?"

"Georgiana," he whispered close to her ear. She flinched from the warmth of his breath and gave a slight shudder.

"Sir—"

"Forgive me for my familiarity, but I lost your attention for a moment. You did not answer my question."

Her free hand clenched and released. Thank goodness for her gloves! How did he have the power to discompose her so? Her palms were sure to be damp with her nerves. "We can make the attempt, though I am not sure why you wish to try. As children, we never failed to be at odds. We always disagreed."

She opened her mouth to continue, but Lydia hurried before her on a man's arm. "Do you mind if we join you? I know so few people here, and I would prefer to sit with someone known to me. Mr. Grantley has been kind to allow me this indulgence, has he not?" She looked back and forth between her partner and Georgiana. "Oh! How forgetful of me. I had not considered that you were not acquainted.

"Lord Sele, Miss Darcy, may I present Mr. Grantley of Salehurst in Sussex."

"Miss Darcy? *The* Miss Darcy."

As Georgiana rose from her curtsey, the gaping mouth of Mr. Grantley was similar to that of a trout. Would he begin moving his bottom lip up and down like a trout would breathe as well? Regardless of how absurd he appeared, her spine stiffened.

"To my knowledge, she is, indeed, the one and only Miss Darcy." Nathaniel's tone was unfriendly. He glared at Mr. Grantley.

"I meant no disrespect. I have heard ladies mention Mr. Darcy's sister, but I see you are *by no means—*"

Lydia raised her eyebrow and crossed her arms over her chest. "I am afraid I am at a loss, Mr. Grantley. What did you expect of Miss Darcy?"

Mr. Grantley shook his head as if clearing his befuddled mind and grinned. "'Twas nothing more than a rumour. I see no reason to spoil the brilliance of this evening with idle conjecture." He glanced between Georgiana and Lydia. "Perhaps I may make amends? I have yet to request the final dance of a lady tonight. I would be pleased if you would do me the honour, Miss Darcy."

What nerve! Georgiana gripped Nathaniel's arm beneath her fingers. "I am sorry to disappoint you, but I am quite fatigued and do not plan to dance again tonight." Mr. Grantley's mouth opened and her knuckle made a cracking noise when she curled her free hand into a fist. "As this is my first ball, my brother limited my dance partners to family. Lord and Lady Lindsey were great friends of my parents, so he allowed Lord Sele the privilege of a family member."

The gentleman's lips thinned. He was displeased, but she would certainly not dance with him. She had no reason to stand up with any man, really.

Mr. Grantley gestured to Georgiana's side. "Ah! I see Mr. and Mrs. Seymour at the table near the fire. Their society is by far more entertaining than many of my acquaintance. May I introduce you, Miss Bennet?"

Lydia's cheeks held a slight tinge of red, but her countenance made it clear, her heightened colour was not due to a blush. Her set jaw and narrowed eyes projected a different feeling altogether. "If you will excuse me, Mr. Grantley. I believe I shall have dinner with my sister."

With a swish of silk, Lydia passed, but not before squeezing Georgiana's free hand. Not a word came from Mr. Grantley's mouth, despite the now all too common occurrence of his gaping jaw.

"If you will excuse us." Nathaniel's unyielding glare pinned Mr. Grantley where he stood. Georgiana began to shift her foot back to curtsey, but Nathaniel's decided step away from the offending gentleman tugged her in the opposite direction. He had not even bowed.

"Addle pate! Why some men thrive on gossip and the presumption of idiots, I shall never understand!"

"By remaining at Pemberley for so long, I have given them reason."

He came to an abrupt halt, and turned to face her. "Why? Because you had no desire to be auctioned off at seventeen or eighteen?" He combed his fingers roughly through his hair. "No, you have a home and a brother who cares for your happiness. He would not part with you to a man unless he was worthy, and he would not force you to take part in the ton's marriage block." His eyes met hers and the insistent tone in his voice was echoed by the resolution in his unwavering gaze.

"No, you are correct. From the age of fifteen, he ensured I knew I was welcome to spend my life at Pemberley. Lizzy has accepted me as Fitzwilliam does. She would be no dearer to me if she were my sister by blood. I am fortunate—quite fortunate." She blinked away a slight sting.

"Would you prefer to be seated near them?"

His expression was different—softer. The tension in his arm had dissipated, but it was the look in his eyes—she had to avert hers at the uncomfortable tug it conjured within her chest.

Lord and Lady Lindsey were seated at a table nearby. "We could share the table with your parents?"

He bent forward as he studied her. "If that is your wish."

She had hoped to be in company with Lady Lindsey while in London. This was an ideal opportunity, so she nodded.

When they entered, the supper rooms were not as crowded as the ballroom, but soon, every chair at their table was occupied and conversation abounded. Lady Lindsey's accomplishments included the pianoforte as well as a lovely voice, so music proved to be an agreeable topic. The two ladies spoke of composers as well as their favourite pieces while the men interjected a fact or compliment when the occasion arose.

The instrument was opened near the end of the meal, and Lady Lindsey gave a wide smile. "I should dearly love to hear you play."

Georgiana's eyes swept the room and her stomach dropped like lead to her feet. Her? Play? "Before all of these people?" Her voice shook and her fingers trembled. How could she play when all control of her fingers was lost? "I could not."

Lady Lindsey's hand covered hers. "I remember well my first exhibition and the nerves it occasioned. Perhaps when you call, we could practice a duet.

Then, we can play together when we are next in company."

She swallowed hard and exhaled through her mouth in a rush of air. "I believe I would prefer such an arrangement, thank you. Lizzy and I practice duets, but she avoids exhibiting as well."

"I have never heard Mrs. Darcy play," commented Lady Lindsey. "Is she accomplished at the art?"

"If you ask Lizzy, she would say she plays very ill indeed," laughed Georgiana, "but after a few lessons with a master, her technique improved a great deal. Her expression is where she excels. If she took more time to practice, no one could find fault with her performance."

"She does not care for practicing or she has not the time?" Nathaniel's deep timbre pulled her head to his direction.

"When I first met her, she preferred books and walking to sitting idly—as she described it—before the pianoforte. Now, she could find a half-hour or so most days if she did not prefer the company of Fitzwilliam and Little William."

A low chuckle joined his wide smile. "My mother combined the activity with her family by teaching me when I was young."

Something drew her back a bit straighter as though a string was attached to the nape of her neck and drawn toward the ornate Jacobean ceiling. "I do not remember your ever playing while at Pemberley."

"I never forced him to perform, but Nathaniel plays beautifully." Lady Lindsey's pride in her son radiated from her face.

Georgiana pivoted in her seat to once again face Nathaniel. His countenance was the colour of a cherry, and he could not meet her eye. "I should enjoy hearing you play."

He took a large gulp of his wine and cleared his throat. "The day we convince you to perform for us, I shall embarrass myself by allowing you to select the piece."

"I do not wish to hear a work you have never before seen. I desire a true display of your talent."

His fingernail wore at a slight catch in the tablecloth until his mother coughed. "If you wish." After a glance about the room, he stood and offered his hand. "The dancing should begin again soon. We could watch from the side. I could help you criticise sleeve-lengths and unfortunate colour choices should you wish it."

The tinkling laugh of his mother came from beside her, but she ignored the sound as she struggled to prevent her lip from betraying her amusement. "You desire a discussion on fashion—ladies' fashion?"

"Desire is perhaps too strong a word. I should merely be content to converse on those topics if you so choose."

As he helped her rise from her chair, she searched the room for Fitzwilliam or Lizzy, but they were missing. "I should find my brother and Lizzy."

He offered his arm. "Then allow me to be of aid. Your brother would not be much for the card room, so we should try the ballroom."

The next set was lining up as they entered. Lizzy and Fitzwilliam were in the midst of the dancers while Lydia and her partner were several places down the line. Lydia's posture and appearance caused Georgiana to keep her head turned and her attention fixed upon her. As opposed to her usual disposition, Lydia was no longer smiling or even composed. She was stiff and her eyes were bright as though she was holding back tears.

Nathaniel came to a stop and faced the dancers. "Does this suit?" he whispered near her ear.

Her eyes still on Lydia, she gave a distracted nod.

"Are you well?"

"Yes, I am quite well, thank you." But what was amiss with Lydia? While Georgiana could boast of good company—well, decent at least—and a comfortable place to watch the dancing, Lydia was for some unknown reason, not as fortunate.

Chapter 7

December 30ᵗʰ 1816

I am thrilled last night is behind me! I must admit I dreaded the ball, yet the evening proved to be more entertaining than I planned. The dance with Nathaniel even passed better than I had imagined. He is still a thorn in my side, yet at times he can be amusing—kind, even.

I was the envy of a number of ladies at the ball who attempted to garner his attention. Oh, I noticed the flirtatious looks and the bumps to his arm. He conversed with people when the situation necessitated it, yet he remained near my side for the last half of the evening. I cannot account for his behaviour except that of a brotherly need to ensure my comfort since the men of my family were engaged with their wives or betrothed. I came to London fearful of my reception but became more comfortable in last night's crush than I expected.

After dinner, Lydia danced with one gentleman and became subdued. Her cheerful, lively nature was hidden, though in such a crowded circumstance, I could not enquire as to her reasons. Upon our return home, she rushed to her rooms claiming fatigue. As it is still early, I doubt she is yet awake. I hope she will confide in me once we have the opportunity to speak.

While he and I have agreed to a friendship, I confess Nathaniel confuses me. I suppose I should say my reaction to him confuses me. I blush, I have difficulty with words at times, and I tremble. His glances in my direction cause my insides to roil and my head to become light, nearly senseless, as though I do not possess the least bit of intelligence. I hope I am not becoming one of those fainting ladies who will swoon at the slightest provocation. While I have been weak, I have never been so addle-brained in my life!

Georgiana placed her pen upon the stand, sprinkled some sand upon the page, and then, returned the coarse grit to its bowl. Bright light filtered in through the window, so she stood and stepped over to enjoy the view. The sun had already begun its path across the sky and a breeze rattled the limbs on the trees in the square. It was a brilliant blue day for December. If she were at Pemberley, she would saddle Phaethon and ride around the peaks. In weather such as this, Phae was always in high spirits, snorting and prancing about. How she adored riding on a crisp, cool day!

Well, if she could not ride, perhaps she could convince Lizzy to walk—if she was awake.

She arrived in the drawing room to no one about, but a humming reached her ears and she pivoted back and forth. Where had it come from? She followed the sound to the dining room where Mrs. Rowley ran a finger across the sideboard, looking for dust.

"Mrs. Rowley?"

"Oh!" The older lady's hand pressed to her chest. "You gave me quite a fright, Miss Darcy. I was not aware you had left your chambers."

"Forgive me. I had not meant to alarm you." She glanced about the room. "I was wondering if my sister, brother, or Miss Bennet were awake?"

"Mr. and Mrs. Darcy requested trays a little over an hour ago. I believe they were to spend the morning with young Master William once they breakfasted. Miss Bennet's maid has yet to be called to the lady's rooms."

Georgiana nodded. "Thank you. I shall be practicing my pianoforte should I be needed."

"Of course, miss."

She exited to the hall and was about to turn into the music room when a rap sounded at the door. Jobbins appeared from the servants' corridor and with his usual calm, slow manner opened it.

"Miss Darcy!" Before Jobbins could speak, Nathaniel strode forward, took her hand, and pressed a kiss to her knuckles. "I hope you will forgive my early call, but the weather begged for a canter down Rotten Row and I hoped you would join me."

She blinked. Nathaniel was in her home. She glanced at the clock—at half nine, and he wanted to ride—with her? "I had not—I—That is, I have no mount in town. My mare remained at Pemberley and Fitzwilliam does not keep a horse for me in London since I have stayed in Derbyshire the past several years."

"I hope you will not think me presumptuous, but I considered just such a circumstance. My mother keeps a horse in town for days like today, though after the late night at the ball, she preferred to keep London hours than ride." He grasped her hand, led her to the drawing room where the windows overlooked the street, and pulled back the draperies. "When I mentioned the possibility last night, she offered the use of her mare."

Her eyes darted to the street before the house where three horses stood with a girl holding the reins of each.

"Who is the girl?"

"Our stable master's daughter. She is as proficient a rider as the grooms, and you mentioned last night of your companion visiting her family for the holiday season. Since I was uncertain whether Miss Bennet would be awake and whether she even rode, I thought a chaperon might be a prudent idea."

"Prudent indeed." How she wanted to join him! Had she not just longed for Phae as she admired the pleasant weather? Not to mention, the closest of the mounts was the most beautiful dapple-grey she had ever laid eyes upon.

"Which is your mother's mare?" Her teeth scraped along her bottom lip. Be the grey! Be the grey!

His breath made the curls at her temple flutter and heated her face. "Which do you want her to be?"

She drew back and gasped. "What an impudent response!"

"You cannot deny you have a preference, else you would not think to ask," he taunted with an impish grin.

She crossed her arms over her chest. "Why will you not answer?"

He mirrored her stance, his riding crop still clutched in his hand. "Agree to accompany me, change into your habit, and I shall give you the information you seek."

She peered out the window one more time and back to Nathaniel. "Very well. I shall return as quickly as I can."

As she hurried up the stairs, she worried at her lip with her teeth. Was this wise? Nathaniel said they would just be friends, but was it a sensible expectation?

Lucy started when she strode into her dressing room and requested her habit, but complied with haste. With her usual efficiency, her abigail had Georgiana undressed and dressed again with her riding gloves in hand in under a quarter hour.

She stared at her reflection in the mirror. The timidity about London and being in town needed to cease! What did the opinions matter of those so wholly unconnected to her? The truth was they did not. She needed to do what she wished without regard to those who would disparage her for sport.

One last, large gulp of air was drawn into her lungs and released. If she and Nathaniel were to be friends, she would have to rid herself of this ridiculous aversion to his company. He was not the same as the boy she once knew. Of course, characteristics of the younger Nathaniel remained, but he was now an adult. He had also come to her defence in the hat shop, had he not?

When she returned to the hall, Nathaniel grinned and gave a bow. "I am pleased you would accept my invitation, milady." He held out his arm. "Shall we?"

A laugh escaped at his antics. "Lead the way, my lord."

As Jobbins appeared to open the door, she paused. "Should my brother or Mrs. Darcy enquire as to my whereabouts, inform them I am riding with Lord Sele."

"We will be in Hyde Park," offered Nathaniel.

The aged butler peered to the horses and the young lady who would accompany them. "Very good, miss."

After the door closed behind them, Nathaniel chuckled. "Did he ensure we had someone to accompany us?"

"More than likely. Since my companion Mrs. Annesley has been visiting her family, I am usually joined by Lizzy, Lydia, or my aunt when I leave the house. I am certain Jobbins found my departing on the arm of a young man singular and cause for concern."

"Jobbins was your butler before your mother's death. I remember I found him rather terrifying as a young boy."

"But he is kind and what I imagine a grandfather to be. When my governess would bring me to the kitchen for a biscuit, Jobbins would tell me the most wonderful stories. I believe he would create them as he said them aloud."

"Ah," replied Nathaniel, squinting a bit as a particularly gusty breeze blew in his face. "You have a perspective of him I lack. I remember the ever so tall, quiet, and imposing figure who answered the door. He also gave me a rather disapproving glare when I tried to chase after your brother on several occasions."

"There is no running in Darcy House, did you not know?"

Nathaniel studied her for a moment out of the corner of his eye. "You are different this morning."

"I hope the change is not unwelcome."

He faced her and their eyes held one another until she had to fight to remain still. How she needed to fidget about, but she could not. To wiggle like a worm would be mortifying!

She held out her hand and took a step in the direction of the dapple-grey, who stretched her neck and sniffed Georgiana's palm. Once she had deemed Georgiana worthy, she nickered and nuzzled Georgiana's glove with her velvety muzzle.

"Do you like her?"

Her cheek prickled from his steady gaze while she pressed her palm against the star between the mare's eyes and stroked down the length of her face. "She is stunning."

His shoulders relaxed as he smiled. "I am glad. She is your mount for the morning."

She gave a delighted gasp. "I had hoped. What is her name?"

"My mother named her Viola."

He laced his fingers and held them down and palms up to help her mount. Once they were both in their saddles, and walking towards Hyde Park, she lifted her face to feel the cool breeze as Viola blew noisily from her nose and tugged at the reins.

"She must enjoy *Twelfth Night* to name her horse for one of the characters."

"My parents attended a production of *Twelfth Night* for my mother's birthday the evening before Viola arrived as her gift. While she does take pleasure in that particular play, I believe the name is more as a remembrance."

When they entered the Grosvenor Gate and headed in the direction of Rotten Row, Viola began to stomp and prance about.

"She loves to run Rotten Row, and my mother tends to give her free rein. You will need to use a firm hand if you do not wish for the same."

"Phae knows the paths at Pemberley where I prefer to test her speed. She behaves much the same as Viola is now when we approach one."

Nathaniel's brows drew down in the middle. "Phae?"

"Phaethon is the immortal horse of the goddess of the dawn, Eos."

"Your brother's horse is named from the stories of the Greeks as well, is it not?"

"Boreas is the god of the north wind who assumed the shape of a horse to pull the chariot of Zeus."

He laughed and reined his horse back so they remained together. "While the story has Boreas pulling the King of the gods, the actual horse carries the Master of Pemberley."

One side of her lips curved upwards. "My father was still alive when my brother named his horse. He was not yet master. We have quite a few horses with names taken from the Greeks or the Romans."

After a peek in Nathaniel's direction, she cued Viola to a trot. The horse had a graceful gait. Her bottom would not be terribly sore on the morrow, thank goodness.

The rhythmic plodding of Nathaniel's horse from her side was a reminder of his presence—not that she required one. She was not far ahead of him as they neared the corner where the Route du Roi, also known as Rotten Row, began.

Despite this hour of the morning being a fashionable time to ride one's horse on Rotten Row, few men were out with their mounts and even fewer ladies.

"I hoped most of the ton would keep to their beds this morning. Between Lord and Lady Fitzwilliam's ball and Sir John Sutton's masquerade, most of London was occupied until the early hours."

She brought her mount to a canter and began riding down the path, ensuring she did not collide with the other riders. Nathaniel rode to her left, but his horse was just far enough to the rear that she could see nothing but his head if she peeked to that side. His horse stretched his neck and wore at the bit. Nathaniel was holding him back. Did he believe her to be a less than competent rider?

Without thought, she leaned forward and pressed her leg into Viola's flank. The horse did not throw her head or object, but accelerated forward with grace until the horse could not go faster without galloping.

An exclamation came from behind as she laughed and pushed forward until she neared the end where she pulled back and turned to ride along the edge of the Serpentine. She kept Viola at a trot until Nathaniel drew alongside and then slowed her to a walk.

"You do enjoy defying convention, Georgiana Darcy."

"I wanted to give her a good run." She lifted her chin just a bit. "Besides, I do not require you to rein in your horse. I have no doubt Viola and I can match your pace."

"Ladies do not typically race the gentlemen along the Row—not that I object. I enjoyed it immensely." His slight smile widened. "I wanted to be certain you were comfortable on my mother's horse, but I never expected my ensuring your safety from behind would wound your pride."

Her jaw dropped. "You did not wound my pride."

"Then why the need to prove yourself?" He trotted ahead with an altogether too smug expression on his face.

If only she could wipe it off as easily as a smudge of dirt!

"You have no response?" he taunted with his head turned back towards her. "The Miss Darcy I remember would not have allowed such a statement to go unanswered." He stopped his horse and pivoted in his seat as he awaited her.

She brought Viola to a trot once again and gave him what was hopefully her most disdainful expression. "The Miss Darcy you knew no longer exists. I do not seek your approbation. I need no one's approval."

She circled back around and cantered the length of Rotten Row again with Nathaniel at her side. When their mounts were blowing puffs of white from their nostrils and breathing hard from the exertion, Georgiana steered her mare in the direction of the Grosvenor Gate.

The ride to Darcy House was not far, so before long, they were dismounting in the same place they began their ride an hour or so earlier.

After Nathaniel helped her from Viola's back, he escorted her to the door where Jobbins allowed them inside. She passed her coat to a maid and went to the drawing room with Nathaniel following close behind.

"Would you care for some tea?"

"No, thank you. I promised my father I would return before luncheon. He desires my company at his club."

The burst she had gained from her indignation vanished as her stomach twisted into a knot. She glanced at the clock upon the mantel. "Of course.

Thank you for bringing Viola. I had found myself longing for a good ride across the countryside not a quarter-hour before you arrived. Not quite the Derbyshire peaks, but Hyde Park will do." His lips were pressed together and thin. Had she offended him?

He repeatedly turned his hat in his hand. "It sufficed."

Lydia strolled through the open door and came to an abrupt halt. "Lord Sele! I did not know you were here." She bobbed a quick curtsey as she glanced back and forth between them.

"Miss Bennet." He bowed.

With a tensed jaw, he dropped the hand holding his hat to his side in a heavy motion. He grasped Georgiana's hand and kissed her knuckles as he did when he arrived. This time, however, rather than releasing her, he maintained a firm hold upon her fingers. "I will agree to your assertion that you have changed, but I still see glimpses of the carefree young lady I remember. You hold yourself back, though I am unsure if it is merely with me or with everyone. I also do not believe you are as self-assured as you claim.

"Regardless, my desire is to know the woman before me—the entirety of her heart and what she adores, and I do hope you will one day allow me such an intimacy." His voice was low, barely more than a whisper. While his eyes held hers, a frisson ran from where his fingers touched hers, up her arm, and straight to the centre of her chest. She placed her free palm over her heart.

With a gentle swipe of his thumb over the tops of her fingers, he released her hand, turned on his heel, and departed.

Lydia watched Nathaniel leave, her jaw gaping. When the door closed behind him, she rushed forward and pointed after him. "Why did you not invite him to stay?"

Georgiana pulled at the fingertips of her riding gloves. "I asked if he would care for tea. He declined. His father is expecting him home."

After looking Georgiana up and down, Lydia placed a hand on her hip. "By your habit, I would say he took you riding. Lizzy and Fitzwilliam will have a fit if you were unaccompanied."

"In fact, his stable master's daughter is an accomplished rider. She joined us." She began to remove the second glove, watching her hands intently. "I rode his mother's horse several times down Rotten Row and back. It was an agreeable excursion."

Lydia ripped the gloves from her grasp and tossed them upon the settee. "It was agreeable? That man cares for you, Georgiana. You must have agreed to his request to call, else he would not have arrived so, but what occurred while you were riding or after your return? He appeared displeased."

"We talked as we rode through Hyde Park. We raced down the Row and then spoke some more. He wants the Georgiana Darcy he knew as a child, but I am no longer a child. Through age and circumstances, I am not the same. I can never resemble that girl again. He should relinquish any hopes he has of a future with me if that is his design. He professed a wish to be friends. I can promise him no more."

Georgiana retrieved her gloves from the settee and slapped them against her palm. "I would like to refresh myself. If you would excuse me."

As she made to shift around Lydia, a knock resonated from the hall. When Jobbins passed the open door, Lydia lunged forward, closed it, and pressed her ear to the crack. Jobbins muffled voice mixed with that of another man filtered through the small space.

Lydia flew around, grabbed Georgiana by the shoulders, and swallowed as though a brick were lodged in her throat. "He said he would call. I feared he would call! What do I do?"

"A maid can chaperon."

"No, you must remain." she whispered as her head jerked to the door and back. "'Tis complicated, but I trust you. If certain matters are divulged, I would prefer your presence to that of a maid."

"I do not understand." What could she mean?

Before Georgiana could enquire further, Jobbins entered. "A Mr. Hanson to see Miss Bennet."

Chapter 8

Lydia pivoted around in such an abrupt fashion she nearly landed on her rear, but a large step back saved her from complete mortification and brought her beside Georgiana. Lydia's arm wrapped around Georgiana's and held it tightly, as if she would never allow Georgiana to depart. What could this man have done to cause Lydia so much upset?

"Hurry!" she whispered, dragging Georgiana to the sofa. As they turned, a man entered the room and Lydia curtseyed, pulling Georgiana with her.

When he rose from his greeting, the man looked between them. "I have not made the acquaintance of your friend, Miss Bennet. May I have the honour?"

With a motion that was sure to have hurt, Lydia's head jerked to face Georgiana and then back to Mr. Hanson. "Mr. Hanson, may I present Miss Georgiana Darcy."

He stepped forward and took her free hand to bow over it. "I am pleased to make your acquaintance, Miss Darcy."

"And I yours." She held out her arm in the direction of the settee and chairs across from the sofa. "Do sit." She then looked to Jobbins. "Could we have tea brought up?"

"Of course, miss."

Once the door closed, Mr. Hanson backed to a chair near the fire while Lydia tugged Georgiana to sit directly beside her.

She peered back and forth between Lydia and the gentleman. "Were the two of you introduced last night?"

"Yes and no," he replied. "Viscount Milton made the introduction at dinner, but I first made the acquaintance of Miss Bennet in Hertfordshire, when I was with the militia quartered in Meryton."

Georgiana took her friend's hand, which gripped hers with a painful pressure. It was no wonder Lydia was at sixes and sevens. She had known this gentleman at the same time Lizzy and Fitzwilliam courted. How much of Lydia's former manners were familiar to him?

"I am afraid I took Miss Bennet by surprise, and she was startled by my presence. I apologise for that. I noticed you before supper, but had not the opportunity to approach you until later. The last thing I wished was to make you uncomfortable." He pulled at his cravat, tugging near the knot with a heavy swallow. "Perhaps more honesty than what is proper is required. I hope you will indulge me."

As she had no reason to object, Georgiana glanced to Lydia, who stared wide-eyed at Mr. Hanson without speaking. Since Lydia remained silent, Georgiana gave a dip of her chin. "I believe your idea has merit, Mr. Hanson. Pray continue."

He gulped again and rubbed his palms down his thighs. "When I completed Oxford, my father was displeased with me. My performance was not to his standards, though through no one's fault but my own. I never failed to overspend my allowance, I drank to excess, and I gambled more than I should. Through rumours and information from cousins of a similar age, who knew of my licentiousness, my father discovered my habits as well as my debts and demanded I behave with honour. I understood my father's dictates, but was young and reckless. I had no desire to be as boring as he. I was an ignorant and stupid young man."

One side of his lip gave an awkward curve. "When I did not act according to his wishes, he insisted I join the military or lose all hope of my inheritance. As it was, I had no recourse. My exploits were too well known. He would not pay for me to study the law and even should I be ordained, my reputation would prevent a good family from giving me a living.

"I, of course, agreed, so he paid my creditors, purchased my commission in the militia, and withdrew any support he had furnished in the past."

As he told more of his history, Lydia's grip began to slacken, but her attention never wavered from Mr. Hanson.

"I wish I could say the militia tempered my vices, but they did not. The men did little but drink and play cards when they were not training. I did not gamble as much as I once had due to my lack of funds, but I had not changed—not in essentials.

"When we were first quartered in Meryton, I remember Miss Bennet enjoyed the society of the officers until her father limited the exposure of his daughters to the men. Before last night, I had not had the pleasure of her company since the ball held at Netherfield in the year eleven."

He fiddled with his cuff and tugged the sleeve of his topcoat. His entire bearing screamed of his discomfiture, which had not eased. "When the militia moved to Brighton, I did not follow. My father discovered I had incurred further debts, mostly drinking with the officers, and insisted the militia had not given me enough discipline.

"My commission was sold, and he soon had me wearing the uniform of the Regulars. Fighting on the continent . . . Well, it cannot fail to alter a man. I shall not elaborate since much of what I witnessed is unfit for the ears of ladies, but needless to say I am not the same heedless, brash, young lieutenant you met in Meryton."

His eyes rested on Lydia and softened, but gazed at her intently. "I hope those who are my friends do not fear my judging them for their past behaviour. I look forward to knowing those of my acquaintance based on their current honourable manners and introducing them as such."

"Truly?" Lydia's voice cracked and held more than a touch of doubt while her hand tightened around Georgiana's once more.

A rap came from the door, causing them to start. Lydia gave a nervous giggle.

"Enter!"

A maid entered with the tea Georgiana had requested, placed it on the table before them, and departed with haste. Once Georgiana served their refreshments, she shifted back on the sofa.

Lydia took a sip from her cup and returned it to the tray. "But you attended the Netherfield ball."

"I admit that I did."

"Then, you must admit my behaviour was certainly not that of a proper lady."

Both of Lydia's hands now held Georgiana's one, and dear Lord, they were damp! What had she done at the Netherfield ball to cause such upset years later?

"It is not of any consequence, Miss Bennet. Since I left the army, I have struggled with people's recollections of my past. Last night, you were spoken of in relation to Mr. and Mrs. Darcy, but none referred to any past misdeeds. Your behaviour was also all that was proper. I would take no pleasure in seeing your efforts laid to waste."

A sniff came from beside her as Lydia sagged against Georgiana's arm. "Thank you. Thank you, sir." She dabbed a handkerchief under her eyes. "Forgive me. I was so worried."

"I had no intention of alarming you when I requested a dance, but I had no way of reassuring you in the crush without being overheard. I do not usually make calls the morning after a large event, but I wanted to resolve any upset or confusion. I could not leave you to worry."

Lydia released Georgiana's hand and retrieved her tea. "I appreciate your willingness to call and your candour. I did not sleep a wink after our return from Clarell House and fear I would have worn a hole in the carpet pacing the day away had you not called."

For the first time since her return from her ride, Georgiana looked at Lydia. How could she have missed the dark circles under her puffy eyes? She had been too caught up in her tiff with Nathaniel to notice. She was a terrible friend.

Lizzy would not have been so unobservant.

"Then I am glad I made an exception." His slight smile was not tight or forced, but more genuine.

"May I ask a question?" requested Lydia, resting her hands with her cup and saucer in her lap.

"I do not see why not."

She did not look Mr. Hanson in the eye, but stared at her finger, tracing the edge of the saucer. "Did your father appreciate the man you became?"

Mr. Hanson looked to his hands folded before him. "Unfortunately, my father died while I was at war. He never bore witness to the changes he wrought." He cleared his throat.

"I am sorry." She and Lydia said the words almost simultaneously.

With a glance at the clock, he set his tea upon the tray. "I have overstayed, but I hope you will indulge me once more?"

"I do not understand," answered Lydia.

He stood and stepped to the fire before turning to face them. "I would care to know you better, Miss Bennet. Would you permit me to call on you?"

She blinked hard and again grasped Georgiana's hand with an unrelenting grip. "Me?"

One side of his lips curved. "Yes, Miss Bennet. You."

Her mouth opened and closed twice before a sound emerged. "I think I would be pleased to accept your call."

A smile lit his face. "You can do no better than think?"

She made a soft growling noise. "Yes, I would be pleased and honoured to accept your call."

"Good. I shall request Mr. Darcy's permission when I have the first opportunity. I do appreciate your allowing my intrusion this morning to offer my explanation."

They rose, he took Lydia's hand, and bowed over it. "I shall call soon."

Lydia stared at her hand in his while her cheeks pinked. "I look forward to speaking with you again, sir."

With a final bow and a good day, he strode from the room. His voice could be heard in the hall, enquiring as to when he could meet with Fitzwilliam and leaving his card. When the sound of the door closing reached the drawing room, Lydia squealed and began to bounce up and down.

"I thought I was doomed when he stepped before me with Viscount Milton. He spoke to me during the set, but I could hardly utter a single word I was so terrified. I never expected a request to see me again." She ceased the infernal bouncing and placed her palms to her cheeks. "He is so handsome! Do you not think him handsome?" Her head darted to the door and back. "I think him handsome."

"Lydia, you are nonsensical."

She grasped Georgiana's hands and began to shift up and down on her toes again. "I am not."

Georgiana pulled away, closed the door, and dragged Lydia to the sofa where she pushed her to sit. "What on earth does Mr. Hanson know that had you so frightened?"

Her expression that was full of wonder a moment ago fell like a lead weight. "I cannot tell you!"

She gave an incredulous laugh. "Why ever not? I shall not tell."

Lydia's head shook back and forth. "My behaviour was shameful." Her head stopped its violent movement and she covered her face with her hands. "I was shameless." The sound of Lydia's voice was muffled by her hands.

"Lydia! I promise I will not think less of you."

Her shoulders slumped and she frowned. "You will continue to pester me until I tell. I know you will."

"I doubt I am as relentless as you seem to think."

Lydia dropped back into the corner of the cushions. "As Mr. Hanson said, I met him at the ball Mr. Bingley held at Netherfield in eleven. Papa *was* relentless that evening. He ensured our dance partners returned us to him directly after each set, and we were not allowed to leave his side when we were not dancing."

"We?"

"Kitty and I," she clarified. "Kitty behaved because she desired the freedom to do as she liked. I, on the other hand, fought Papa tooth and nail. I even tried to escape the ballroom with Mr. Denny, but Papa prevented us.

"I was so frustrated. During supper, I attempted to start an argument between Mama and Papa, but Papa held fast and did not allow Mama's complaints to sway his resolve." She sighed. "A few sets after supper, my father allowed Mr. Hanson a dance with me. When Papa was watching Kitty, I managed to sneak us outside to a copse of trees near the edge of the rose garden."

"Lydia!"

Lydia's pointed finger took aim at Georgiana's nose. "Do not 'Lydia!' me! I know what I did was very wrong, but I cannot change it. You are the one who asked for the story!"

She pushed Lydia's finger to her lap. "Oh, very well."

"Where was I? Oh, yes. I will not go into detail, but when Papa discovered us, we were kissing, and I brazenly requested Mr. Hanson touch me."

Georgiana's face burned in embarrassment for Lydia. "Where did you wish to be touched?"

"I do not know," confessed Lydia. They both stared at one another for a moment before bursting into gales of laughter.

"You do not know?"

"Well, I was not specific. I had no particular part of my body in mind."

"Oh." She tapped her fingernail on the arm of the sofa for a moment. "Is it possible another young man you kissed could turn up in London?"

Lydia picked a piece of fluff from her gown. "No, I only kissed two or three boys other than him, and they were all from Meryton. The Goulding's precious little boy was one." Her voice dripped with contempt. "The Lucas's youngest son, who is my age, and the butcher's son."

"Lydia!"

She threw up her hands and let them fall. "Well, I was curious. I never gave any of them my virtue."

"Thank God for that."

Lydia's expression suddenly changed to a wicked grin as she scooted closer, leaned against the back of the seat, and tucked her legs under her. "I have told you my secret, so you owe me."

Oh no! What had she done?

"I want to know why you never wish to marry. You have not told me all."

Her spine went rigid. "What do you wish to know?"

"Why do we not start with the name of the man who proposed marriage when you were but fifteen years old?"

She closed her eyes and she swallowed hard. She had not uttered his name in so long. What if her voice betrayed her? "George Wickham." Good! She said his name without her voice cracking or becoming emotional.

Lydia's chin whipped back a bit. "George Wickham? But I knew a George Wickham. He was in the militia at the same time as Mr. Hanson."

"Yes, 'tis the same man." Her voice was odd and hoarse. She cleared her throat.

"I believe Denny said Wickham was the son of a steward to a grand estate. I thought you referred to a gentleman."

"Wickham was the son of a respectable man who was my father's steward, though I am afraid the son turned out quite wild. His motive in requesting my hand was nothing more than my fortune, and he was willing to force a marriage if need be. I was fortunate to escape a life shackled to him." The last was spit out with a good deal of venom to her tone.

A warmth covered her wrist where Lydia's palm now rested. When Georgiana lifted her eyes from her lap, her friend leaned in her direction.

"Did you love him?"

She gulped the lump in her throat back down. "No, I told him as much, but he argued tenaciously for his suit. The situation . . . I cannot endure such an interview again. Do not request more of me."

Lydia's arms wrapped Georgiana in an embrace. "If you love the gentleman and he loves you, the proposal would not be dreaded but celebrated. Fitzwilliam would not allow a private audience unless you desired it."

"I know, but I am not a suitable wife for any man." She withdrew and wiped her eyes, which were damp. "If you will excuse me, I would like to refresh myself from the ride."

"Georgiana," chided Lydia. "There is more to the story than you are telling me."

She rose, but paused before Lydia. "I cannot speak of what has not been said. I also have no wish to recount it again, and I beg of you to allow me my privacy on this matter. I do trust you as much as anyone, but the knowledge would only give you pain."

Without waiting for Lydia to speak, Georgiana hurried to her suite where Lucy put her to rights in a swift fashion. When she returned downstairs on her way to the music room, voices came from Fitzwilliam's study. The door was open, so she moved into the entry and rapped softly upon the frame. Footsteps and the soft click of a door latch followed. Someone exited through the servant's entrance.

"Good afternoon, Georgiana. I hope you enjoyed the ball last night."

She stepped inside to stand behind one of the chairs. "I suppose it was agreeable. I enjoyed speaking with Lady Lindsey during supper. Will Lizzy be down soon?"

"Elizabeth is in her sitting room preparing the menus for the week." He gave a chuckle. "You enjoyed Lady Lindsey but not Sele?" He held her eyes for a moment before lifting a card from his desk. "Jobbins said you and Sele rode in Hyde Park this morning."

"Yes, he brought his mother's mare and a chaperon. I saw nothing amiss in going. Should I have refused his offer?"

He sat back in his seat, the card he held forgotten. "Sele observed the proprieties. He would not have made the invitation without ensuring your reputation. I am certain of that."

Nathaniel had been quite attentive to such matters. "I would not have gone without female companionship."

Fitzwilliam studied her for a moment. "No, I do not imagine you would." He placed the item in his hand back upon the work surface, rose, and closed the door. "I am concerned about you and so is Elizabeth. You wished to return to London after all this time. You have been excessively anxious about rumour and gossip, and you must admit, you have fretted about the worthless opinions of others more than in years past."

"Whether you or Lizzy acknowledge it, people have wondered about my lack of début," she explained. "I knew enough girls from school for them to question why no marriage announcement or ball has been held in my honour."

"Regardless of any talk, you need not make yourself miserable for William's sake." She opened her mouth, but had no opportunity to even make a sound. "Elizabeth also feels Sele might be favourably inclined towards you." Why had Lydia made claim of a tendre carried by Nathaniel? He had a brotherly affection for her, surely that was all.

"No doubt, she believes Lydia's assumptions." Her voice was tinged with bitterness.

"Lydia cares, Georgiana. You would do well to remember how much of a friend she has become. You have isolated yourself to merely family for so long, and while Lydia is a relation, she is another person in whom you can confide." He gave a disbelieving humph. "At one time, I would have never imagined myself describing Lydia thus, but she has proven herself a worthy friend else you would not have taken to her as you have."

He placed his hands upon her shoulders. "I also worry of you allowing the past more than is its due. You once said you would never marry. At the time, I had no notion of whom I could trust with your future, so I never pressed the issue. Sele is an honourable man and if you were to give a gentleman a chance, I can think of no better candidate for your husband."

"And how would we explain Ramsgate? If I were to wed, I would wish to do so for love, and I will not lie to my partner in life. What if I had a nightmare and screamed? What if I shrank from his touch?"

Fitzwilliam reddened and coughed.

"I did not mean marital intimacy, Brother, yet such a situation is also a consideration."

"Sele is a good man, and he knew Wickham. He would—"

She removed his hands from her shoulders and held them. "I am attempting not to be uneasy with the gossip which abounds in London. I hope to find some success with the endeavour, but ignoring the petty tittle-tattle is never simple. As for Nathaniel, we are like chalk and cheese. We argue more often than not." Her brother's low chuckle helped relieve the weight pressing upon her chest.

"You forget that I have witnessed your arguments."

She gasped. "What do you mean?"

He rolled his eyes and returned to his desk, picking up the card as he took his seat. "Now, who is Mr. David Hanson?"

"Fitzwilliam! I insist on knowing your meaning."

"Answer my question first."

She crossed her arms over her chest. "He was once a member of the militia quartered in Meryton and attended our aunt and uncle's ball last night. He called on Lydia after my ride with Nathaniel."

"Lord Sele," he corrected.

"Fine. Lord Sele."

He frowned and glared at the card. "Is he still in the militia?"

"No, I believe he is a gentleman. We did not discuss his situation or his income. He was amiable and requested Lydia's permission to call."

"He knew Lydia in Meryton five years ago and wishes to call again?" Fitzwilliam's voice was full of wonder. "Is he sane?"

"I believe his reasoning is sufficient for Lydia and should you wish an explanation, I am certain he would provide one. 'Tis his story to tell, after all."

He rubbed his hands on his face. "Yes, you are correct. Forgive me, I simply had not expected her to find a suitor within the first se'nnight." A piece of paper was pulled from his top drawer, and he retrieved his pen from its stand. "I shall enquire of our aunt. If he was invited to the ball, perhaps she is aware of his situation."

"You are a good brother."

His eyes sparkled as his lips turned into a tender smile. "I am pleased you believe me to be. I hope I shall always continue to be so in your eyes."

She hastened around his desk and kissed his cheek. "I could never see you any other way."

Chapter 9

"Good evening, Miss Darcy. I hope you have been well since our ride."

Georgiana held her breath while Nathaniel bowed over her hand. Why had Lizzy planned this dinner party? "I have been very well, thank you. I trust your parents are in good health?"

A wide smile adorned his face as he straightened. "They are well. Thank you." He looked to Lizzy who was standing beside her. "They asked I convey their apologies for sending their regrets, but they had previously accepted an invitation for the evening." He leaned a little closer to Lizzy. "My mother did confide that she would have much preferred to attend your dinner than Lady Granville's card party."

A bubbling laugh came from Lizzy. "Your mother is too kind. Lord and Lady Fitzwilliam were prevented from attending for the same reason. While I am certain the card party will have its own merits, I shall be sending out invitations for a more formal dinner party for Fitzwilliam's birthday next month. Hopefully, your parents can attend then."

"I am certain she will be pleased to send her acceptance. She was truly disappointed to miss this evening."

"I planned this at the last moment and most of the guests are family. Your mother and father will be missed, but we understand the late notice meant a few of our friends might be unavailable for the evening."

As Lizzy gestured towards the drawing room, the knocker sounded and Jobbins, who was posted nearby, opened the door to reveal Richard and Julia, accompanied by a maid, who disappeared into the servants' corridor. Her cousin noticed them at the end of the hall while he passed Jobbins his coat.

"Lizzy! What possessed you to have a party on such a foggy evening?"

"You were welcome to cancel," called her brother as he entered. "Though, we would have still expected Julia's company."

Richard feigned shock with a gaping jaw and a hand to his chest. "Now, I know my true worth to my family. I am tolerated simply for the charming company of my betrothed."

Her brother offered a hand to Nathaniel. "Sele, I apologise for my tardiness. My son was insistent I read to him before he fell asleep. I could not refuse."

"As it should be," responded Nathaniel. "I remember many a time where

79

my mother or father indulged my whims for a tale until one night my father told me a story that quite frightened me."

Georgiana turned to better see his face. "What happened?"

He grinned. "I had a nightmare soon after falling asleep and did not sleep a wink the rest of the evening. Mother was furious."

Lizzy kissed Richard's and Julia's cheeks. "I cannot blame her." She took Julia's hands. "How are the wedding preparations? You have but a few days."

A beaming expression lit Julia's countenance. "My mother is adamant nothing has been overlooked, but whether she is prepared or not, I will wed Richard in three days."

"I am pleased someone still cares for me." Richard offered his arm, which she took with a shy smile and blush.

At the sound of footfalls on the stairs, all assembled turned as Lydia neared the bottom. "Forgive me for my absence when you arrived. I was late already when I discovered William running from the nursery and in the direction of Georgiana's rooms. I wager the little imp thought he could manage another story before Mrs. Wynn put him to bed. I scooped him up, returned him to Mrs. Wynn's arms, and here I am."

At the next rap of the knocker, Jobbins opened the door to reveal Mr. Hanson, and like the day he requested to call, Lydia's hand grasped Georgiana's in a dreadful grip. Once he was introduced, Lizzy invited their party to move to the drawing room.

Mr. Hanson offered Lydia his arm, which she took with a reddened complexion, as a different black wool-clad elbow presented itself before Georgiana. "Will you do me the honour?"

"To the drawing room?"

"To the drawing room, to dinner in a short while, to the drawing room once more after if the ladies do not separate from the men. Will you indulge me?"

Her stomach was aflutter and Nathaniel's open, earnest expression held her attention captive. "But you might find yourself bored with my company before dinner is even served." Her voice was not right. Why was the tone a mite breathless? "If I accept your request, you are obligated."

"I do not mind being obligated as I have never failed to enjoy your society."

She placed her hand upon his sleeve. "Even when we were children?"

"Perhaps not when you kicked me in the shin, but otherwise, yes."

They were becoming too personal. "Why have you not brought Viola for a ride?" What? If only she could slap herself! Of all the things to say. Why did she imply she wished for another outing with him?

He steered her to the settee where he took the place beside her. "I was not sure you would agree to join me for another trip down Rotten Row, but I would be pleased for your company one morning this week. Will we again require a chaperon?"

"My companion returns soon from her holiday, but she has no mount in London either."

"I can make arrangements as I did last week."

She rubbed her palm roughly with the thumb of her opposite hand. "I fear I have been too forward. I should not have asked such a question."

"We have known one another since you were in your cradle. I care nothing for polite and proper discourse with you. I do not find your question offensive in the least. I wish you to speak plainly with me."

A soft hiccup of a laugh escaped her. "Be careful. I have a bad habit of speaking as I find, and at times, in quite improper terms for a lady."

To avoid meeting his eye, she looked the opposite direction where Lydia and Mr. Hanson were engaged in a quiet conversation of their own. The gentleman had called twice in the past week. On the first visit, he spoke to Fitzwilliam for some time before her brother granted Mr. Hanson's request, and the gentleman was allowed to speak to Lydia.

As a result, their sisterly talks of late had centred more on her conversations with Mr. Hanson, but that was not unexpected. Georgiana was pleased for her. If matters concluded as they ought, Lydia would wed a man who knew her as she was four years ago and the lady she became. No uncomfortable conversation would be needed to enlighten her suitor on why people whispered about her in Meryton because no secret needed to be withheld. A dull ache settled in part of her heart.

"Sele, what say you to a trip to the theatre? I assume you still enjoy the diversion?" Georgiana's head turned in the direction of her brother's voice.

"I do, though I prefer to attend with a large party of friends."

"My wife and I plan to use our box once or twice before London becomes more crowded for the season. Sir James and Lady Audley should join us as well since they could not attend tonight. We could remain for the main performance and then, return here for dinner."

"I think it sounds ideal," gushed Lydia. "I have not yet attended the theatre. My aunt and uncle spend more time in the country than they do in town these days, so I have yet to have the opportunity."

The flesh of her temple prickled. Was Nathaniel watching her again?

"I believe I should enjoy such an outing. I heard the most recent performances have been excellent, and I cannot find fault with the company." Nathaniel's voice was free and easy. He did not sound discomfited by her reticence.

She lifted her eyes enough to find he was indeed attempting to garner her attention. Good Lord! What did his expression mean? Was he conveying a message? Did he seek her approval? She could not make heads or tails of him!

"What say you, Hanson? Would you care to attend?"

Lydia clasped her hands before her, opened her mouth, and then, clamped it shut.

Mr. Hanson's lips curved at the very ends. "Say what you will, Miss Bennet."

After a fidgeting glance at those assembled, Lydia stared at her gloves as she adjusted them around her fingers. "I thought to persuade you to attend, sir. Nothing more."

His smile grew as she spoke. "If Miss Bennet wishes me a part of your party, then I am at her disposal. Name the day, Darcy, and I shall be there."

"Will you attend, Miss Darcy?" asked Nathaniel.

"I am certain I shall. I have always adored a play. I have missed little of London the past few years, but I did feel the absence of the theatre. At one time, my brother never failed to take me on my birthday each year."

"If you have enough room in your box after inviting half of town," teased Richard. "Then, Julia and I would enjoy accompanying you."

Her brother looked askance at Richard. "Miss Raeburn is welcome to join our party, but since you so rarely behave in public—"

"*I* do not behave in public?"

"Yes, you." A twitch appeared at the corner of Fitzwilliam's mouth. He was having difficulty maintaining a straight face. "You say what you will without regard to whom you are speaking, you laugh, and you gossip worse than most women. What you said to Elizabeth at your parents' ball?"

Julia attempted to cover her mirth with her hand, but the little noises from her nose as well as her shaking shoulders gave her away.

"Do you mean the evening you proposed?" guffawed Richard. "That was four years ago! You had been moping for weeks when Miss Elizabeth Bennet appears before my very eyes. You cannot fault me for saying more than I should in shock. I was also attempting to be of service to the both of you."

A glint appeared in Julia's eye. "You likely saw an opportunity to make mischief."

Richard leaned away from his betrothed and regarded her with his arms crossed over his chest. "Most unfair to agree with their poor attempts at humour, my dear."

Julia's eyes darted back and forth at the pair and she bit her bottom lip in an attempt not to laugh. Before she could respond, Mrs. Rowley announced dinner. Georgiana pressed her lips together to prevent a giggle and rose. When she stood, her eyes followed an arm before her to a set of broad shoulders and finally, to Nathaniel's lifted brows.

Her hand trembled as she placed it upon his sleeve. Where was her mettle? While she had never been outgoing and had been shy of strangers, Nathaniel was no stranger. She had known him since she was a young girl.

"Miss Raeburn appears well-matched to your cousin." His tone was gentle. He was speaking only to her.

"They are indeed well-matched. I believe she cares for him very much."

"Then, he is a fortunate man. While not every gentleman aspires to such a union, I could settle for no less with my parents' marriage as my example."

Her eyes met his. "All you need is the lady, then?"

His arm tugged her closer. "I have chosen the lady, but it appears I must garner her trust as well as her heart."

Unable to hold his steady gaze, she averted her eyes to the carpet. He had indicated a wish for friendship, yet his looks and his words never failed to hint towards a desire for more. Lydia thought her a fool for not allowing him to pay court to her, and Fitzwilliam thought Nathaniel the one man she could trust.

If he knew of her past, would he think her ruined? The papers and the ton would not hesitate to label her worthless were they to know the events of Ramsgate. A chair shifting beside her startled her. "Thank you."

She sat, but as she set her hands in her lap to await the remainder of the guests, Nathaniel seated himself in the chair to her right. "I hoped we would be partnered for dinner." His voice was low and her breath stuttered as she inhaled.

The chair to her left was withdrawn and she turned to find Richard taking his place at her left. "But did you hope to be his partner?" he whispered with a chuckle.

Nathaniel leaned in front of her. "Perhaps your betrothed would care to hear of the disagreement you had with Lord Weymouth two years ago."

Her cousin's countenance reddened considerably. "He was mistaken in his information. The culprit was Hastings, as you well know!"

A mischievous but devilishly handsome grin appeared upon Nathaniel's face. "I do know, but I am certain the ensuing discussion would keep you busy for the entirety of the meal."

Richard peered at her for a moment before he narrowed his eyes at Nathaniel. "Do what you will. I am not afraid of you."

"Really?"

"Boys, if you wish to be dining partners, I can sit beside Julia. I would much prefer to enjoy her society than have the two of you bickering with one another across my lap." Her voice had not wavered and she hopefully wore her most implacable expression. The problem was Nathaniel. He had turned, and by doing so, was impossibly close, his nose almost touching her own.

She could not breathe. Her flesh from the roots of her hair to the edge of her gown became heated. Why could she not control this . . . this . . . effect he had upon her?

When he made to move, he took her glass of wine and held it before her. "A sip of this will be of aid."

"How do I know that you will not attempt to put me in my cups?"

"He had best not unless he wants to be laid out dead on a field of honour," mumbled Richard, who then winced as Julia's elbow made a swift movement towards his ribs. Richard whispered to his betrothed, "He is too close!"

Before she could tip the deep red wine into her mouth, she pulled the glass back. Between Richard's remarks and Julia's response, she would need to be careful lest she spit wine on the pristine white tablecloth.

Nathaniel did not smile and his entreating gaze never left her. "I would not be much of a gentleman if I gave you too much to drink. I hope you know I would never do such a thing."

The footman placed the first course before her, and she was given a much-needed reprieve from Nathaniel's closeness. But when the footman's arm moved, Nathaniel's attention was still focussed upon her.

When she peered around the table, Lydia and Mr. Hanson were having a discussion while Fitzwilliam and Lizzy were speaking with Richard and Julia.

His arm brushed hers as he leaned closer. "Miss Darcy, all I ask is for your faith, as well as your honest words and actions."

She could not look at him, so instead, she closed her eyes as the warmth of his breath fanned across her ear. Why did he have this disturbing effect on her? She was so conflicted! He spoke as though trust was the simplest of requests, but he could not understand!

If all he desired was friendship, trust was easy and absolute, but if he wished for more, how could she have confidence that he would not flee once he knew all?

January 6ᵗʰ 1817

How do I discourage a man who refuses to be anything but encouraged? I have agreed to friendship, yet I do not understand why I agree to spend more time with him. When he assisted me from my chair as the ladies withdrew, I felt his touch through the lace of my gloves. With the feather light brush of his breath upon my skin, I cannot prevent the gooseflesh and the flutters inside my belly. My body betrays me at every turn, yet I have no power to cease my vulnerability to him. This will end badly, and I am beginning to think I can do nothing to prevent it.

Will Nathaniel be kind? If he discovers my secrets, I know he will not divulge the confidences to a soul, yet I am still terrified of his reaction. Why is that? I care for him as one would any long-time acquaintance, but I do not love him. I confess I feel an attraction—for that must be what this is, yet I cannot allow myself to succumb!

Dinner tonight was pleasant. Cook's meal was prepared to perfection, as always. During the meal, we decided on the twenty-fourth of January for our trip to the theatre. Lizzy informed the group that the celebration of Fitzwilliam's birthday is to be held on the seventh of February. Hopefully, with the notice, Lord and Lady Lindsey will be free to attend.

I see I am avoiding Nathaniel even within the pages of my own journal! Truth be told, if matters were different—if Ramsgate had not happened—then I could imagine myself falling hopelessly in love with him. He was a most attentive partner for the evening. I confess to being inexperienced in these matters, but his conversation was interesting, and he ensured I wanted for nothing.

I will see him at Richard's wedding, and I have an engagement to, once again, ride with him in Hyde Park. I must attend Richard and Julia's nuptials, so perhaps I can find an excuse to avoid our ride. I must do what I can. I cannot afford to develop deeper feelings for him than I already possess.

Chapter 10

The wedding itself had been just family and close friends and all that was proper, but the wedding breakfast! Georgiana turned sideways to slip between two rotund gentlemen as she searched the guests for Lydia or Lizzy. The Raeburns' house was large and in Belgravia, however, the number of guests at the moment rendered it tiny.

Where was Lydia? She had been beside her a moment ago. Where had she gone?

She tried a different direction until a finely tailored suit and an intricately knotted cravat blocked her path. "Miss Darcy, you appear lost?" For once, the deep, yet teasing voice of Nathaniel was a welcome one.

"I am searching for Lydia or Lizzy, but I cannot seem to find them."

He surveyed the room. "I do not see them either, but they might be in the ballroom or perhaps the hall?" He offered his arm. "Perhaps I can be of aid, and if not, we could join my parents. I hope you would not object to their society."

"Of course not. I would enjoy greeting your parents regardless. I took great pleasure in their company at the ball."

His expression warmed and his lips curved into a slight smile. "My mother and father have carried a great deal of guilt since your parents' deaths. They swore to help guide you and see that you were happy, but when my father became so ill, time escaped them. The letters received from your brother were read with fondness and sadness. In their eyes, they missed a prodigious amount of precious time."

She placed her hand just before the bend of his elbow. "I was unaware they exchanged correspondence these last few years."

"Darcy was not a faithful correspondent, but he tried. My mother rarely found the opportunity to pen a letter in return."

"My brother did indicate your father was quite ill."

As they began to walk in the direction of the ballroom, his head was down as though he was watching his shoes. "I returned home until I knew the danger of his death had passed, but he was so weak. I believe he is still alive simply because my mother would not allow him to die." He gestured towards his father. "He carried a walking stick before for the purpose of fashion, but now, he requires one. His gait is much improved, though he shall always require a certain amount of support."

"He is fortunate."

"Our family is fortunate. I know I must lose him one day, but I was not prepared for the eventuality at the time—I remain ill-prepared, for that matter." His voice was faint by the time he finished speaking.

"Forgive me. I should not continue to remind you of such a painful time."

"Do not make yourself uneasy. I am not averse to speaking of it, but I cannot recount his illness without becoming emotional. I should think you understand more than most."

She gave a squeeze to his arm. "I do."

When they entered the ballroom, Richard and Julia stood to the opposite side. Her cousin wore a rakish grin as he leaned towards his new wife, whispered a few words, and kissed her hand. Georgiana smiled. Her cousin's secret served to render his bride's complexion as scarlet as his former uniform. Though her heart was content with Richard's joy, a hollowness pervaded as she witnessed their felicity.

"Do you not envy their happiness?"

Her gaze met his. "I have no reason for envy. I am satisfied with my lot."

"Satisfied is not necessarily content, nor is it pleased."

She averted her eyes. "Do not."

His lead brought them around the edge of the room where tall windows shone the cloudy, grey skies as opposed to the brilliance of the candlelight reflecting in the glass and mirrors within.

A slightly forced exhale reached her ears, and she closed her eyes. She had no wish to hurt him, but why did he persist in discomposing her with thinly veiled hints of his wishes. A strange sound caused her to turn, but not before a hand wrapped around her wrist and pulled her into the chill January air. The jolt of fear that pierced her chest had no basis whatsoever, except in the past, and prompted her to rip herself from his hold once the door closed behind them.

"What are you doing? I insist on returning at once!" she exclaimed. She made to step around him, but he blocked her path.

"I want to speak with you, but we are never alone."

She hugged herself, rubbing her upper arms to help with the chill that prickled her skin. "There is an excellent reason for that."

With some difficulty, he released the buttons on his topcoat, draped it over her shoulders, and took her hand. After a moment of examining their surroundings, he pulled her around the back of the house until they found another door. Where were they going? Why could they not simply return to the ballroom and enjoy the occasion?

By some odd twist of fate, the latch gave way with ease and they stepped inside. The smell of dust and books overwhelmed her as much as the floor to ceiling shelves of musty tomes before her. The remnants of a fire smouldered in the grate. At least the room was warmer than the outdoors.

Georgiana made an immediate move towards the corridor to return to the breakfast. "I cannot believe you!"

He grasped her arm, preventing her escape. Without thought, she flinched and jumped back from him.

"Do not touch me." Her voice was harsh, even to her own ears. Why did she react so? While his actions were officious, she was convinced he would never harm her.

Both hands lifted, palms facing her. "Forgive me. I just wish to talk to you."

"We could have spoken where we were. If we are caught thus, my brother will be furious and my reputation could be called into question. Enough rumours circulate without adding fuel to that fire."

"Georgiana."

"Do not be so informal with me!" The words were forced through her teeth. How dare he! He had no right!

He veered into her path. "Once upon a time, I was Nathaniel and you were Georgiana. Do you not remember?"

"We were children, and when I became old enough to understand I should address you as Lord Sele, I abhorred the idea of calling you lord."

He gave a frustrated chuckle and clenched his hands at his sides. "Regardless of the reasons, we were never so formal. I have tried to speak with you, but when I attempt to further our acquaintance, you push me away. I hope to be open with you, but increasingly, I find I tread on eggs, worried I will offend."

She shook her head, gripping her skirts in her fists. "You do not offend me, but if I have interpreted your less than subtle intimations correctly, you desire more from me than I can give."

He gave an incredulous bark. "I wish for your friendship and a chance at your heart, but when the subject is broached, even with caution, you become recalcitrant."

"Because I cannot give you what you want."

"How do you know?"

"I—" She covered her face with her hands and then, dropped them to her sides. "One does not decide whom they will marry as a child. Have you never thought of another?"

"Never." He took a step closer. She stepped back, and he raked his fingers through his hair. "I cannot explain why, but my heart was yours from the time we were children. That fact shall never change. All I ask is for you to trust me."

88

"If you had such a strength of affection for me when we were young, then why did you put a frog in my reticule, or steal my doll?"

His brow drew down as he huffed. "You stood by your mother with that ridiculous reticule and toyed with the ribbons when I attempted to talk to you. As for Matilda, I wanted you to go riding with me or walk the trails around Pemberley. Instead, you had tea parties with her. You did not even see fit to invite me."

Could he be serious? Jealous of a reticule and a doll? The notion was preposterous! She bit her lip and held back her laughter, but it twitched, and the breath she was holding burst forth when she could no longer restrain it.

She clapped her hand over her mouth. "Forgive me."

A corner of his lips lifted. "No, I fully understand the ridiculousness of it all. We were young, I was headstrong, and I wanted to be friends. At least, that is what I believed at the time.

"You were fourteen when I last saw you. Along with my own father, I attended your father's funeral, and when Darcy returned to the house after the service, we accompanied him. My father joined your brother in the master's study where they spoke of business—primarily how to prevent Lady Catherine from assuming control of you, while I followed the most haunting, melancholy music to a pianoforte in the music room."

While he told the story, her smile faded and her eyes blurred. "I remember that day well. You startled me after I played the final chord."

"I had not intended to do so. I was merely listening at the door."

She laced her fingers together in front of her. "You apologised and insisted I continue."

"I would have preferred to talk," he confessed, "but I also enjoyed hearing you play. I thought you would prefer the latter, and since it brought me comfort as well, I made the request."

"Losing myself in music has relieved many a worry. I improved greatly while mourning my father . . . and at other times in my life."

"I hope you will share your worries with me one day."

Her chest was heavy as though a weight was settled upon it. "I do not know if I should. You would be better off finding another who is more capable of returning your affections."

"I do not want another."

She turned away. The sadness in his eyes was heart-wrenching. "I doubt I shall ever be capable of offering you more than friendship."

He stepped closer. How she wanted to step away, but she would not yield. She had been a coward thus far, and Nathaniel would never cause her harm, of that she was certain.

"I have agreed to your arrangement, yet I am not a patient being when it comes to you. I have waited a long time. I cannot help but dream that you will one day make me the happiest of men." A finger trailed from her temple to her chin in a caress so soft, it was as though a feather stroked her flesh.

As he turned her head towards him, she could not tear her eyes away from his. Her heart pounded in a heavy cadence against her sternum, and fear was not the cause. Instead, the sensation was a novel one, and unknown. The impulse to flee was overwhelming, yet she was rooted to the spot.

"Nathaniel . . ." Her voice trembled. Why could she not better control her emotions?

"You have the most beautiful eyes—clear, crystal blue eyes that catch the light in the most becoming fashion."

Her hand caught his as he meant to return it to his side. She held it in both of hers with a firm grip. "I am in earnest when I say it is unlikely we can be more than friends. I have no wish to hurt you."

"Are you cold?"

She started. "Pardon?"

"You are shivering. I can feel it in your hands. Is your heart beating as rapidly as mine?" He placed her hand to his chest. "I have caught you blush at my words or looks, and I have heard your voice waver. I have every reason to hope, as long as your mind does not lead your heart astray."

"There are matters you do not know."

His gloved hand rubbed over hers where it rested against his waistcoat, yet the sensation was as though no barrier lay between them, as though flesh touched flesh. "Then tell me." His voice was soft and beckoning, like the gentlest chords of a pianoforte.

Her vision hazed. "I cannot. I do not know how." A wet droplet fell upon her cheek. He brushed it away with his thumb.

"I still need to gain your trust, then?"

"You would change your opinion of me if you knew." She withdrew her hand and folded her arms tightly over her chest.

"Georgiana Darcy, look at me."

He lifted her chin with his finger so their eyes met. "Regardless of what your secret is, I will not abandon you. I just wish you had enough faith in me to share what bothers you."

The door swung open, and they backed apart with haste.

"Nathaniel George Henry Howard!"

Georgiana dug her teeth into her lip as Lady Lindsey grabbed her son's arm and dragged him back from her.

"Did you know Darcy is searching the house for Georgiana? What if he found the two of you in here alone?"

He lifted an eyebrow. "We would be forced to marry?"

His mother slapped the back of his head. "Not likely. I believe he might just set the former Colonel Fitzwilliam the task of offering you a choice between pistols or sabres."

"I did nothing untoward," he defended in a high-pitched voice. "We needed to speak without being overheard. I thought to talk in the garden, but the weather was too poor."

"That it is. Ladies wear several layers, but not as heavy as men's clothing. She would freeze, and then where would you be?"

Georgiana placed a hand to Lady Lindsey's wrist. "I should return. I do not want my brother to worry needlessly."

She glanced at Georgiana's gown. "You should return Nathaniel's topcoat. I admit to enjoying my husband's from time to time, though not in company."

She pulled the coat from her shoulders and returned it to its rightful owner. "Thank you."

While he put his appearance to rights, his mother looped her arm through Georgiana's. "We shall make our entrance together and Nathaniel may follow." She gave a disapproving glare in her son's direction. "If you can find an alternate route to ours, it would aid in our deception."

"Mother, would you allow us one more moment?"

She gaped at him with a slightly dropped jaw. "No, I will not."

Georgiana pressed her lips together. His pouting expression was reminiscent of when he was a boy and did not have his way, but before he could object, Lady Lindsey put a hand to Georgiana's back and pressed her towards the door. When they entered the corridor, the voices from the celebration increased in volume.

"If the two of you require more time to speak, the next time you ride out would be the simplest and best method of achieving some modicum of privacy. I could invite you to tea and sit across the drawing room, yet I am certain my son would not appreciate my presence."

She regarded Georgiana with a tilted head and inquisitive expression. "If I thought you might accept his suit, I would not hesitate. Nathaniel is usually even-tempered, though you must understand his eagerness when you are involved. He has waited for some time."

Georgiana stopped and clutched her hands together. "I wish I could give him some assurance. I enjoy his company, which is an improvement from when we were children, but I . . ."

Lady Lindsey placed her palms upon Georgiana's cheeks. "You need to decide whether what frightens you should stand in the way of your happiness.

Even if your future is not with my son, do not hide from all life holds for you." Her words were similar to those said by Lizzy on numerous occasions, yet carried more significance. Her sister was as accomplished a lady as Lady Lindsey, but the lady before her had been friends with her mother. She could almost hear her mother's melodious voice as Lady Lindsey spoke.

"If only matters were so simple."

She took Georgiana's arms and took her hands. "They can be. You should never cower to fear."

"I get so tired of summoning my courage. At times, I lack the strength."

"A Darcy? Lack strength? My dear, I have never known more strength of character in one family. Your mother, your father, your brother, and I am certain his wife all possesses the trait in abundance. I know you do as well." Lady Lindsey examined her for a moment. "Should you ever wish to confide in me, I will never fail to make myself available. You need not send word either, simply arrive on our doorstep."

Georgiana could not help but give a small smile. "You would not be pleased if I called during dinner."

"If you required me, then I would not be vexed at all. Do not doubt my sincerity. I promised your mother, and I will not fail her." Lady Lindsey tugged her towards the bright, golden glow of the hall. "I wish we had more time, but we should return."

Lady Lindsey remained with her until they located her brother interrogating Nathaniel, who appeared to have just returned from the garden. Once he saw her with Lady Lindsey, his questions ceased.

The remainder of the wedding breakfast was spent with family, though Nathaniel and the Lindseys joined the Darcy and Fitzwilliam party. When the bride and groom departed for their short honeymoon trip, Lizzy declared herself fatigued and Fitzwilliam ensured the carriage was brought around post haste.

During the rest of their time at the Raeburns', she and Nathaniel were never alone, which left little time for private conversation. She had agreed to ride when the weather next permitted, but could she prevent further discourse on subjects discomposing and disconcerting? A heavy weight, like a rock sitting in her stomach, said she would be unsuccessful.

Chapter 11

January 14th 1817

While Nathaniel's inquisition has been delayed by two days of rain and one day of church, I am restless at being too long indoors. Lydia and I played cards, practiced our music, embroidered until our fingers bled, and read until we can do so no longer. As a result, we have staged a rebellion against the diversions of an accomplished lady!

After services, we returned and pestered Fitzwilliam until he taught us chess. I am also pleased to announce that I have learnt to fence. Fitzwilliam was horrified when Lydia and I made the suggestion, yet I am convinced Lydia's whingeing could persuade even a deaf man to capitulate!

Though I cannot see it through the clouds covering the sky, the sun rose this morning. The ground has dried a vast deal with the sun yesterday, and thus far, I have espied no rain. Despite my reticence about meeting Nathaniel again, I am dressed in my habit with my riding gloves on the escritoire beside me, itching to leave this house for the trees and views of the Serpentine. The note he sent to Fitzwilliam late in the evening indicated he would come as before. Though I dread our conversation, I will welcome the outdoors with open arms.

Despite the weather, Mr. Hanson called on Lydia twice, so I have had time to spend in solitary pursuits. I confess much of this I have spent contemplating the words of Nathaniel and his mother. I cannot deny I am envious of Lydia's happiness, but do I want to marry Nathaniel? And, if the answer is yes, how do I find the courage to take the chance before me?

She stared at the entry as she placed her pen in its holder. Little progress had been made since Richard's wedding breakfast. The days of respite had done well to restore her equanimity. However, as she had been told on occasions too numerous to count, she could not hide from her problems—or would-be suitors in this instance.

William's babyish giggle startled her from her musings, but when she rose and opened the door to her bedchamber, he was not there. She glanced up and down the corridor. The little imp must have hidden.

With a quiet step, she tiptoed down the passage until a little figure jumped before her. "Boo!"

Without pause, she scooped her nephew into her arms and jumped back as the pedestal within the niche where he was hiding swayed, the bust atop it rocking precariously.

"Oh!" Mrs. Wynn jumped from the open door opposite them and hugged the sculpture to prevent it from falling to floor below. When the column steadied, she rested the heavy burden back upon its stand. "William Darcy, you will be the death of me!"

She pressed her hand to her heart. "I thought I was clever and locked the door, but he still escaped." A glance revealed the key in the lock. "I put the key on the bookcase. Good Lord! Do you think he climbed to fetch it?"

"I believe it likely." Georgiana kissed her wiggling bundle and passed him back to his nursemaid. "He is too quick for all of us."

"Well, the key shall be in my apron from now on. 'Tis a miracle he has not been hurt during one of his escapes. I say a prayer of thanks for his safe return after each scare. I would never forgive myself if he came to harm." She hugged William a little tighter. "Come, why do we not play with your blocks."

"Yes, blocks!" exclaimed William as Mrs. Wynn set him down and shooed him back into the nursery.

Once the nanny closed William's route of escape, Georgiana giggled to herself as she proceeded down to the hall. When she passed her brother's study, she peeked inside.

"William is up to his usual mischief this morning. We might want to ask Mrs. Rowley to have the bust across from the nursery moved until he is old enough to have his own chambers."

Fitzwilliam's eyes widened. "Dare I ask what he was doing?"

"Hiding, but he nearly tipped the pedestal. He climbed the bookcase in the nursery to retrieve the key and effect his escape."

"Elizabeth will be beside herself when she learns. I have wondered if perhaps Mrs. Wynn requires a maid to assist her. If there are two, then he would never be alone."

She stepped forward and placed her hands upon the back of a chair. "He could still escape during the night. Will you hire maids to remain awake and watch him while he slumbers?"

A long exhale caused the papers on his desk to make a slight shift. "I know. Perhaps not being blessed with another child so soon was a blessing in itself. We have more time for William to outgrow his impetuousness before a sibling comes along."

He shifted a document to the side and handed her a neatly folded letter. "Mrs. Annesley has written. The rain delayed her departure, but she should arrive in London on Friday."

The note did not contain much more than news of the delay. As she folded the missive back into its original shape, the sound of the knocker reverberated through the house.

"Sele has arrived, it seems."

She lifted her eyebrows. "Why do you believe it to be Sele?"

He glanced at the clock upon the mantel. "Mr. Hanson calls later, and we expect Sele for your ride. Did you have an enjoyable conversation with him at the wedding breakfast?"

"Others occupied much of the discourse, we only spoke for a short while."

Fitzwilliam leaned back in his seat. "I believe the two of you had a rather lengthy talk when you departed into the back garden."

Her hands dropped from where she was picking at a fingernail. "How did you know?"

"I saw Sele pull you through the door." He held up a hand with a firm expression. "Before you become angry, I would have you listen. I know he would never harm you, and I thought perhaps you might come to some resolution—whether it be to remain friends or to allow his suit. I do intend to speak with him after your ride since I will not have him endangering your reputation in the future. You were fortunate no one took note of your escape or your return on Lady Lindsey's arm."

A knock sounded upon the door.

"Enter!"

"Sir, Lord Sele awaits Miss Darcy in the drawing room."

Her brother picked up his pen, and with a grin, pulled his ledger back before him. "Sele might come searching for you if you keep him waiting for too long."

She gave a frustrated growl. "It would serve him well to wait. Perhaps he would learn some patience."

"I do not mean to irritate, Georgiana. I have let you be since the ball because I know I can trust Sele, and I have faith in your judgement. I simply do not want you taking further chances which might incite gossip." He glanced to the empty doorway and back. "He has waited long enough. Do you not think so?"

With a huff, she strode from the room, retrieved her gloves from the table in the hall, and pulled them on as she entered the drawing room.

Nathaniel jumped up from the settee. "I began to think your brother might not have informed you of my message, but I see my concern has been for naught."

"Yes, he was kind enough to inform me of your note." They stood staring at one another for a moment. How awkward! She glanced to the window in an attempt to see their mounts. "If the horses and chaperon are present, then shall we depart?"

He started. "Yes, of course."

Again, Nathaniel helped her to mount, and the girl accompanying them fell a horse-length behind as they began their ride to Hyde Park.

"We were unable to finish our last conversation."

"You are certainly persistent, but I am afraid my response is much the same as it was. I can give you no assurances." She could not turn to meet his eye, though she was certain he was watching her.

"I do not require assurances as much as a fair opportunity."

A small bark of amusement escaped before she could stop it. "Why do I feel akin to a business transaction?"

"You know you are nothing of the sort."

They entered the gates of the park and steered their mounts in the direction of Rotten Row. Her thumbs rubbed a rough patch of leather on the reins. Could she take the chance?

"Allow me to court you?"

Her incredulous laugh startled a bird in the tree above, prompting it to take flight. "I have not even accepted your calls as a suitor. What if we find we do not suit? The ton would be speaking of it for months."

"Then allow me to call."

She closed her eyes as her stomach lurched. Lord, but she despised being a coward! "Very well, you may call."

"Truly?" His voice was amazed. She lifted her eyes to his face where he wore a faint smile, but his eyes were bright and glowed. Was he holding his breath?

Her heart quickened, and she gripped the reins tighter so she would not place her hand to her chest. "Yes, you may call."

"If we were not on these horses, I would be compelled to shock all of London by sweeping you up and twirling you in my arms."

She bit her lip to keep from smiling. The ridiculous grin upon his countenance spoke of his joy. He was almost giddy, but his boyish enthusiasm was endearing. He did, indeed, harbour feelings for her.

"Far from a proper response, Lord Sele. I daresay you would have scandalised all who would have borne witness to such an unseemly display."

"Then I should purchase a roomful of flowers. I cannot have you forget how happy your agreement has made me. I know! I shall have to find a shade of blue to match your eyes."

"No! Any colour but blue! I implore you."

Her outburst only served to make him laugh. "You do not care for blue?"

"I do not dislike it, but my aunt has always purchased fabrics of that colour to complement my eyes. Before arriving in London, most of my gowns were the shade of the sky. I refused my aunt's offer of more fabric when we visited the draper's a few days after our arrival. She was quite put out with the pale tea green and sprigged muslin I chose in its stead." She scrunched her nose. "You do not want to discuss fashion. I am certain."

"I prefer other topics, though I do not abhor the thought."

"Oh! Did Fitzwilliam inform you that the Theatre Royale at Drury Lane is playing Sheridan's *School for Scandal* Friday next? Richard and Julia will have returned from their wedding trip by then."

"Your cousin and his wife did not plan a long journey."

"No, they travelled to an estate owned by Lizzy's uncle in Cambridgeshire. The property is normally let, but is empty at the moment, so Mr. Gardiner offered its use as a wedding gift. When they return, Mr. Raeburn purchased a home in Mayfair for them."

Nathaniel's odd chuckle interrupted her.

"May I ask what is so amusing?"

He shifted upon the saddle. "Your cousin is a proud man, in the best sense of course. I cannot think he appreciated Mr. Raeburn's support."

He was correct. Richard had always been insistent he would create his own future. Julia's fortune would help, but the credit for the estate would be to him.

"I had not considered the matter as such, but your assessment is likely true. I am unaware if the home is a part of the settlement or her fortune."

They approached the beginning of Rotten Row, but before Georgiana could cue her horse, Nathaniel spurred his to a canter.

Without thought, she followed suit. She would love a good gallop, but too many people were riding along the popular route today. Besides being unfashionable, it would not do to collide with another horse and rider.

When they had ridden the full length of the Row, they doubled back until they were once again where they began, their horses puffing clouds in the cold morning air from the exertion.

When she pulled her mount back, she looked over to Nathaniel with a smile and a warmth spread from her chest and kept the chill from penetrating through her entire body. What a glorious time! The sky had cleared of the dreary clouds, and she was riding unfettered through the park.

As she pulled her horse towards the grass, a couple walking along the Serpentine caught her eye. The man could be any of quality, but it was the woman who made her squint to ascertain her identity. The bonnet was the same as that day on Bond Street, but what would *she* be doing on this side of London?

"Miss Darcy?" Nathaniel's horse stopped beside her while he regarded her with a lifted brow.

"Forgive me. I thought I saw an old acquaintance." She looked back to the water's edge, but the couple must have moved into the copse of trees since they were no longer there. She shrugged. "I must have been mistaken."

She cued her horse and Nathaniel followed, trotting their horses in the grass. When their mounts were no longer breathing as heavily, they then repeated their original route. The wind whipped against her face and chilled her nose, but the sensation was wonderful. Even the foul air of London was heavenly after so long indoors!

After exhausting their mounts, they walked them back through the park, winding along the Serpentine for a portion of the way. Georgiana glanced about for a familiar hat, but none was to be found.

Upon their return to Darcy House, they no sooner stepped across the threshold than Mrs. Rowley was upon them. "How you can ride for so long in such cold weather! You must be frozen! I have hot water prepared for you to warm and refresh yourselves, and Mr. Darcy's valet is awaiting Lord Sele to see him to rights as well."

Nathaniel halted in his steps. "I appreciate your offer, but I can return home to wash and change."

Mrs. Rowley gave a tut. "I have known you since you were a wee lad, so I hope you will forgive my mothering, but you will remain and warm yourself before you leave. Luncheon is prepared and you must have some tea or brandy to ward off the cold."

His shoulders shook while Georgiana covered her mouth with her hand. At least he found amusement in Mrs. Rowley's ministrations rather than taking offence.

"Clarke will brush out your clothes—though, by the looks of the two of you, the park was not terribly muddy—and see to your needs. If you will follow me, my lord."

They trailed Mrs. Rowley up the stairs and down the corridor. With a parting glance, Georgiana entered her suite where Lucy awaited her. Once Lucy had her washed up, changed into her green muslin, and her hair tamed from the damage the wind wrought upon the style, she returned down to the hall.

"Lord Sele is in the master's study," explained Jobbins with a small bow.

"Thank you."

She paused before she knocked upon the door. The two of them were laughing, which was a good sign. While he did deserve censure for his actions, hopefully, her brother did not take Nathaniel too much to task for whisking her away from the wedding breakfast.

With a deep breath, she lifted her hand and rapped upon the door.

"Enter!" When she stepped inside, Nathaniel and her brother rose. "I am pleased to see you have returned. Mrs. Rowley was beside herself due to the length of your ride. She continued to mutter of you catching your death and being drenched in filth."

"The park was not as sodden as one might think." She shifted and brushed her hand down the front of her gown. Nathaniel appeared to scan the garment.

Fitzwilliam glanced between the two of them. "Well, Lydia has desired Cook serve luncheon for the last hour. If we do not make haste, she might have the entire meal devoured before we can take our seats." He looked again. "Shall we?"

Nathaniel's lip curved upwards on one side. "Of course. I appreciate the invitation to remain."

"What of the servant and the horses? Brother, they will need to be taken into the stable."

"Do not fret on their account," responded Nathaniel. "As you know, we live nearby, so I had the servant return the horses home. Clarke was good enough to send a footman to convey the message. By now, she has surely brushed Viola and returned her to her stall."

She placed her hand upon Nathaniel's sleeve and they followed Fitzwilliam. "Oh, I am glad. I would not want her to be waiting all this time."

He pulled her closer to him. "No, I would not want her to remain in the weather either. Besides, the horses required tending." He dipped his head down. "Is this the tea green gown you preferred over the blue?"

Did he not understand how leaning close in that manner discomposed her? His breath could elicit such strange responses: tingling, shivers, and shudders. They were not necessarily unpleasant, but they were disconcerting.

She cleared her throat. "Yes, I thought the shade pleasant, and Lydia—Miss Bennet—assured me the colour suited."

"It certainly does. I find it very becoming. Your eyes appear to have a slight greenish tinge to them where they normally do not."

A painting she always favoured hung upon the wall, and she diverted her eyes to examine it as they passed.

"Have I made you uncomfortable?"

Her face warmed. "I do not know how to respond to such compliments."

When her brother entered the dining room, Nathaniel paused, affording them a little privacy. "I require no response. I have a suspicion that you do not know how lovely you are. I may never alter your perception of yourself, but I want you to know, without a doubt, my feelings on the matter."

Lydia poked her head through the doorway. "Are you to keep us waiting all day?"

Nathaniel reddened. Once they had entered and Georgiana was seated, he took the chair beside her and leaned closer. "Do you think she was eavesdropping?"

Lydia seated herself across the table near Lizzy, wearing a grin from ear to ear. "I believe it likely."

Despite their proximity, Georgiana turned and her eyes met Nathaniel's for one long moment. They broke out in laughter.

A pleasant discussion of Sheridan's plays and the upcoming trip to the Theatre Royale dominated the luncheon conversation. Once they had all partaken of their fill, Lizzy and Fitzwilliam excused themselves to play with William before his nap while Lydia accompanied Nathaniel and Georgiana to the drawing room.

Lydia's ploy to force them into the sole company of the other was not as blatant as the now deceased Mrs. Bennet's would have been, but she made a show of picking a book from the small shelf, sitting in a chair near the fire, and reading.

Nathaniel gestured to the chessboard. "Do you play?"

"I learnt a few days ago due to the foul weather. I fear I am no proficient."

He took her hand and led her to the table, seeing her seated across from him. "The best way to become accomplished is practice."

His thumbs trailed across her knuckles as he released her. Her acceptance of his calls rendered his behaviour more forward than before. How would he change if she agreed to a courtship? Not that she would at this time—but someday . . . maybe?

"Georgiana?" His voice was low and vibrated through every pore of her body. "You have the first move."

She clenched her hands together in her lap as their eyes met across the small table. Her breath caught in her throat.

"Georgiana?"

She raised her hand. Do not tremble! She lifted a pawn, moved it forward two spaces, and set it down.

He rubbed his hands together with a huge grin while he contemplated the board before him. The cut of his topcoat accented his broad shoulders and clung to his chest. As her eyes traced up the lapels to his cravat, a slight cough distracted her from her study.

His eyebrows were raised when her eyes darted back to his face. Oh no! He had caught her inspection of his person. As if his manner was not forward enough, he might take that as permission to be more so.

What had she done?

Chapter 12

January 22ⁿᵈ 1817

Mr. Hanson has declared his intentions. He had been granted permission to call, but last night after dinner, he requested Lydia's agreement to a courtship.

Georgiana looked up from her journal to where a snoring Lydia lay sprawled upon her bed and stifled a giggle. Mr. Hanson would have a rude awakening on his wedding night!

I thought Lydia would never fall asleep last night with the excitement. She chattered away until the wee hours of the morning, and I believe I now know as much of Mr. Hanson as Lydia does! She is happy, and I cannot begrudge her felicity. She penned a note for Mr. Hanson to deliver to Mr. Bennet when he calls at Longbourn today. I suppose I shall have to keep Lydia occupied while she frets over her father's reaction to the news. I cannot fault Lydia for her worry as I believe I would feel the same if I were in a similar situation. Mr. Bennet's sense of humour alone is cause for concern.

Nathaniel has surprised me with his manner since I agreed to accept his calls. He is not overly formal, and in the privacy of Darcy House, we refer to one another by our Christian names. If we had not known one another as children, I am certain Fitzwilliam would take issue with the familiarity as he does not allow Lydia and Mr. Hanson the same liberty. Not that Lydia minds. She has taken to calling him "My Mr. Hanson" when the gentleman is not in attendance.

We attended a dinner last night at Lord and Lady Lindsey's. I have not been in company with Lady Lindsey since Richard's wedding breakfast, so her enthusiastic hug was not unexpected. Nathaniel had mentioned he confided my agreement (or should I say capitulation) to his calls to his mother. She is overjoyed. I suppose it is a relief. What if I agreed to a gentleman whose mother despised me? What a nightmare that would be!

We have had word from the Bingleys. They are delayed in leaving Rosings this year due to Miss Bingley (Why am I not surprised?). I am not certain of the problem, and Fitzwilliam has not seen fit to elaborate on the subject. I anticipated seeing the children, but as they shall arrive in February, I shall not have a lengthy wait for their society.

A groan came from the bed. "What I would not give for a cup of tea?"

Georgiana rose and prepared a cup that she delivered to the lady herself. Despite the late night talking, Georgiana had risen with the dawn while Lydia remained abed, snoring.

Lydia looked at her morning gown and frowned. "You are already dressed. When did you awaken?"

"Not long after eight. I would have liked to remain abed, but found I was too awake. You are the one who has slept until nearly eleven. I suppose you continued talking after I fell asleep?"

Lydia leaned against the headboard and gratefully accepted the fortification. "Until I noticed you were no longer listening, I did. What was the last you remember?"

"Oh no!" laughed Georgiana. "I have heard enough of Mr. Hanson's virtues to last me a fortnight, at least."

"Then you should speak of Lord Sele. You have given him permission to call, have you not?"

"I am certain Lizzy or Fitzwilliam have shared that knowledge with you."

Lydia frowned. "They have told me nothing." She blew into the steaming cup before taking a sip. "I do know Lord Sele has called almost daily since your last ride in the park. I thought you must have provided some encouragement else he would not be seated beside you on the settee day after day."

"Lydia Bennet! You exaggerate!" Georgiana picked up a pillow and poised it, ready to swing.

"I have tea!" she exclaimed, holding the cup and saucer aloft. "You would not want poor Lucy to have to clean the mess."

Having tea-stained sheets was not an appealing notion, so she hugged the pillow and sat upon the bed. "I gave my permission, though I have doubts every day."

"He loves you, Georgiana. I have seen the looks he bestows when you are not aware. The man is besotted and painfully so."

Her heart quickened but her insides stirred at the same time. Her heart was surrendering itself to him one tiny piece at a time. What would happen when he possessed it all? What had to occur was obvious. She would need to tell him of Wickham, and she would lose his respect and his love with one heart-wrenching confession.

"Georgiana?"

She shook herself from her thoughts. "Forgive me."

Lydia perked up and pulled herself taller. "I know! Do you think Mrs. Annesley would be averse to an outing?"

Since her return, Mrs. Annesley had resumed her duties, with a few small exceptions. She had never been required to serve as a chaperon, so those responsibilities were now a part of her position when they had not in the past.

"I do not see why she would. What do you have in mind?"

Lydia wore a slight smile as though she hid a secret. "I thought after we make calls with Lizzy this morning, we could go to Hatchard's and perhaps purchase some new music. After our trip to the theatre, you could play the pianoforte while I sing."

"I do not know." She stared at her hands as her fingers fidgeted. "Nathaniel will be there, and I have yet to play before him. I believe I would prefer to do so when we are not in the presence of a group."

"Then you have until Friday." Lydia giggled and set down her cup. "You have nothing to fear. You play beautifully."

She narrowed her eyes at Lydia. "Cease your matchmaking!"

"Well, you need to give him some encouragement. One moment you laugh and appear to enjoy his company and the next you become testy or seem uncomfortable."

"I am not like you, Lydia. I cannot flirt or flutter my eyelashes at a man. I simply do not possess the talent. I would appear an imbecile should I make the attempt."

"He cares too much to ridicule you. He enjoys teasing you, but from what I can see, it is done with fondness. Despite your dislike of him when he was a child, he is a good man."

"I know he is, and I am trying. Whether I can care for him as he deserves is a question I must answer for myself. I cannot hurry intimacy without deciding in his favour."

Lydia huffed and put her hands on her hips. "Oh, very well. I must admit you do care for him very well indeed else you would not be so cautious with his heart."

"We have known one another since we were young. I would not wish to injure his feelings."

"Unless you are honest with him, you will wound him."

"Must we discuss this again? I do know your thoughts on the matter."

With a kick to dislodge the bed sheets, Lydia scooted to the side. "Very well, but I believe you should just tell him you will marry him. Would be ever so much fun to shock him, would it not?" She put on her dressing gown and made for the door, but Georgiana called her name before she could exit.

"Perhaps I will do so when you ask for Mr. Hanson's hand."

Lydia opened the door and turned before pausing. "Do not tempt me," she dared, cackling as she let the door swing shut behind her.

Georgiana stared into the fire. What was she going to do? The situation with Nathaniel was not what she planned, but why did the thought of never seeing him again also bring her so much pain?

Her vision blurred and she blinked several times fast and hard. She needed her pianoforte! With a sure stride, she did not stop until she reached the music room. After searching through her music sheets, a piece she longed to play called out to her.

All sense of what surrounded her disappeared once her fingers began to stroke the keys. The music filled her surroundings and the melody flowed from her fingers through her being, calming the trembling within her chest.

When she released the final chord, she remained where she was, her fingertips resting ever so gently against the keys. An odd noise came from behind and she pivoted around with haste.

"Forgive me," whispered Nathaniel. He took a tentative step forward and paused. "I had no wish to disturb you."

She stared, taking in his tousled hair and broad shoulders. His eyes, which were more often than not full of mischief, were serious and tentative.

"You have indeed improved since I last heard you play," he added. "You have nothing to fear performing before an audience. No one who has heard you could find anything wanting in your performance, I assure you."

"Thank you." The words were hoarse and rough. What was wrong with her voice? Why was it so difficult to speak all of a sudden?

"Forgive me for startling you. I heard you playing when Jobbins admitted me. I begged him to leave you undisturbed so I could listen." He scratched the back of his neck in an awkward fashion. "I feel as though I have broken a piece of crystal or expensive china at a party." Their eyes met for a moment before they both began to laugh.

"I have never considered you clumsy."

He looked to the floor and shook his head. "No, I am not."

She slid to one side of the bench. "You once promised to play if I exhibited first. You have now heard me."

Even from across the room, the pink in his complexion was obvious. "If you wish it."

"I do. I do wish it."

After a slight hesitation, he moved to the music, selected several sheets, and held them before her. "Which would you like to hear?"

Each of the works were strikingly different, but none of them were simple. All had been difficult for her to master when she had learnt them. He was quite accomplished at the art if he could choose them at random to play at her whim. She pinched the corner of the piece she particularly favoured and tugged.

He relinquished it to her and set aside the remaining sheets before taking the vacant seat beside her. "Shall I give you a nudge when I require the page turned?"

She should have known! Before she could retort, his shoulder brushed hers and the woodsy and masculine scent of his cologne flooded her senses.

"Georgiana?"

"Hmmm?" His deep chuckle vibrated through her.

"Shall I begin?"

A rustling caused them both to turn to where Mrs. Annesley entered and sat in a chair near the fire. She pulled her embroidery from her basket and set to work.

When Georgiana turned back to him, he watched her expectantly, so she nodded. "Yes."

He set the tips of his long fingers upon the keys, paused a moment, and even on the first note, his fingers caressed the instrument as though the pianoforte was precious. The tune was light and delicate, and his touch was never forceful.

Before she could turn her attention to the sheet, his knee bumped hers and she started.

"Turn the page," he whispered.

"Oh!"

Once she had done as he asked, her gaze returned to him. His eyes never moved from the notes upon the page, though his shoulders swayed and shifted with the melody. He was talented!

His knee tapped hers again, though more of his leg brushed hers with each turn of the page. When he released the last note, her hands were clasped in her lap and her face was aflame.

She opened and closed her mouth a few times before a sound emerged. "That was lovely."

"I am glad it pleased you."

Her eyes met his and were trapped—she could not look away. "It did, very much."

A feather-light touch upon her wrist sent a shiver up her arm. She glanced down to where his finger was stroking from the base of her thumb to her wrist. She had thought her hand felt bare before! How naïve she had been. Without the impediment of gloves, the tingling sensation was multiplied tenfold.

"Nathaniel—"

"Oh! Were you playing a duet?"

Nathaniel jerked his hand back to the keyboard as she closed her eyes. When had Lydia entered?

"No, I promised Miss Darcy I would exhibit for her." He stood and gave a short bow. "I hope you are well this morning, Miss Bennet."

"Very well, thank you." Lydia looked back and forth between them. "Lizzy would like to know if you intend to make calls with us. Lady Fitzwilliam invited us to tea, but Lizzy said it was not necessary for you to come. It will only be a small party."

Georgiana peeked at Nathaniel, who lifted his eyebrows in silent question. If she decided to depart with Lizzy, he would surely understand, though he would, no doubt, be disappointed.

She bit her bottom lip and stared at the keys. "I believe I shall remain behind as long as Lizzy is certain she does not require my company."

When she found the courage to lift her head, Lydia was beaming. "We planned that trip to Hatchard's after luncheon, but if the two of you become bored, I would not mind if Lord Sele attended you in my stead."

Her chin gave a jolt back. What was Lydia doing?

Nathaniel stood and linked his arms behind his back. "If Miss Darcy still desires an outing to the bookseller's, I would be pleased to escort her."

"I would not wish to disrupt any plans you might have." Georgiana searched his expression. Did he wish to go or was he merely being polite? "We do not have to go today. We were merely attempting to pass the time."

"I had no engagements this morning other than my call here. Hatchard's is one of my favourite shops in London. Accompanying you would be no hardship, I assure you."

Lizzy entered with a pleased glint in her eye. "Are you to visit Hatchard's? Mrs. Annesley should enjoy such an outing. I know she was anticipating a particular volume of poetry."

"You do not object?" she asked. Lizzy usually insisted Georgiana accompany her on calls. Why did it feel as though the entire household was pushing her into Nathaniel's arms?

"Of course not. You have spent a prodigious amount of time with your aunt these past few weeks. She will not begrudge you a day with your pianoforte or a trip to the bookseller's. You have done much to satisfy our whims as of late. Do as you wish for today."

With a nod, she clasped her hands in her lap. She had no wish to pay calls. Tea at her aunt's would not be a difficulty, but she would much prefer to avoid those Lizzy was to visit. Her gaze met Nathaniel's. Her reticence and dogged determination to evade his advances had hurt and disappointed him in the past. The notion of disappointing him again caused a sharp pain in her heart.

"I would prefer to remain. I would not mind a journey to Piccadilly Street to see if anything new has arrived. Perhaps I could call on Lady Lindsey?"

Nathaniel smiled. "My mother would take great pleasure in your company.

She has no fixed plans this afternoon. If you call at Howard Place, be warned she will not rest until you stay for tea."

After slipping on her gloves, Lizzy strode forward and placed a kiss upon her cheek. "Have a delightful time." Lydia followed Lizzy out with one last glance and a giggle.

"Shall we spend some time at the pianoforte or would you care to go now?" He leaned in her direction to await her answer, his proximity making it difficult to hold his gaze.

"Do you have a preference?"

"I am at your disposal. Your wish is my command."

She chuckled as he tilted his head. "I beg your pardon, but had that been your method from the moment we became reacquainted, you would not be pursuing me now."

With a laugh, he shook his head. "If I have sufficient time to win your heart, and you tell me there is no hope, I shall accede to your wishes. Until then, all but my absence is yours to dictate."

He was impossible! "Let us go then."

Mrs. Annesley placed her needlework back in her basket and trailed them into the hall. Once a carriage was ordered, Georgiana and Mrs. Annesley fetched their coats, bonnets, and gloves.

Nathaniel was not as talkative as was his wont with her companion joining them, but once they arrived at Hatchard's and began to browse, Mrs. Annesley moved further down the shelves while Nathaniel remained by Georgiana's side.

"Did you have a particular book in mind?"

She glanced around, taking in the long rows of shelves. Where to begin? "No, I just thought to . . ." A title she recognised beckoned to her, which she withdrew and opened.

"Your brother would approve of such reading material?"

Did he really ask such a question? "Fitzwilliam does not restrict me from any of the contents of our library. I admit that I have only been told of Lady Caroline Lamb's novel.[1] I have heard it is quite scandalous."

"Do not forget that her authorship is a secret," he teased in a whisper.

"Oh, yes! So secret I heard of it in Derbyshire." She replaced the book and strolled further down to the poetry.

"Lady Caroline's exploits do not interest you?"

"No, I would also prefer to sketch the characters within myself. I have heard she painted some of society with a rather unforgiving brush."

"That she did."

She pulled another volume and opened the cover while he leaned against the shelf behind him. "I thought you enjoyed the bookseller."

With a wide grin, he crossed his arms over his chest in a cocky fashion. "I do, but I find I enjoy watching you more."

She could not hold his eye, so she glanced at the first page of the poem inside.

"Do I make you uneasy?"

She gave a lift of her shoulders. "I am not certain." Her insides fluttered. What a lie she had just told! He discomposed her thoroughly, but he knew it. A confession of the truth would only render him more forward than he was now.

"I suppose that is better than a definitive yes."

After snapping the book closed, she walked around to another row of books and began to look over the titles as she took slow steps. His form could be discerned from the corner of her eye as he followed.

Before she reached the end of the shelf, Nathaniel grasped her elbow, startling her, but bringing her attention to a couple standing where she was about to step. Her hand flew to her chest as she gasped. "Forgive me."

When she had a chance to see the features of the woman before her, she swallowed hard and fisted her hands. Her eyes rested upon the lady—no, no lady—*that* woman's bonnet. It *was* her she had seen on occasion since her arrival in London. Words bubbled in her throat and fought for release, but she gulped them down.

"Miss Darcy, it has been such a long time." The woman gestured to the man beside her. "Allow me to introduce—"

Who she was to meet was never heard as Georgiana hastened past the woman, placed the book on the counter, and hurried from the store. She paid no heed to the direction she took, but began to walk as swiftly as her feet would carry her from that wretched, horrid excuse for a human being. As people strode towards her, she twisted and pressed herself between them to hurry her way.

Her eyes stung, and she heaved great gulps of air as she attempted to calm herself. She took in her surroundings. Where was she? When she slowed, a hand to her elbow pulled her to stop. She whipped around, her reticule at the ready, brandished as a weapon, but her arm dropped when she saw Nathaniel's worried face.

"Georgiana." His voice was not loud, on the contrary, his tone was frantic but soft. "Tell me what is wrong."

She put her hand to her forehead and dropped her arms.

"I gather you know her."

She bobbed her head as she fought not to yell and cause a scene. Unlike what she expected of herself, this time, she had not run in cowardice, but to prevent herself from causing a scandal. It would not be wise to have that confrontation in such a public setting.

Mrs. Annesley hurried towards them and stepped around Nathaniel, placing a palm to each of her cheeks. "I saw her. I cannot believe she had the audacity to speak to you. Of all the nerve."

Georgiana searched Mrs. Annesley's face, her heart beating like a frantic rabbit. "How do you know her?"

"She came to Darcy House, while your brother was in Hertfordshire, to collect the belongings she left behind. I was there to fetch your mother's shawl. If you will remember, you requested it of me not long after you moved to Clarell House."

After a quick nod, she placed her hand to her chest. "I want to go home." The words were choked and forced.

Nathaniel, whose eyes were worried, flinched at her tone. "If you would allow me to escort you. Despite the presence of your companion, I feel it is my responsibility to do so. I would also prefer to remain by your side until I know you are well."

"Your assistance would be most welcome, my lord." Mrs. Annesley glanced up and down Piccadilly Street. "Perhaps we should find the carriage and return at once to Darcy House. I fear this will prevent Miss Darcy from calling upon your mother today."

She should be the one saying those words, but her teeth were grinding against each other with such ferocity her jaw was beginning to ache. If she opened her mouth, all would pour forth. She could not do so on a crowded street.

His shoulders dropped, and he presented his arm. "I understand. I believe our carriage is that one." He pointed to the horses, which were only a few shops away.

She allowed him to lead her to the equipage and hand her inside. Once he aided Mrs. Annesley, he took his place and rapped the top to signal the driver.

They passed Hatchard's one last time, but Georgiana would not lay eyes upon the storefront. Instead, she studied the buildings across the street in great detail as they passed. She had no desire to set eyes upon *her* again.

Why was she on this side of town? Who was the gentleman? Of course, if she had only remained a moment longer and not lost her temper, she would know that information. Stupid, stupid girl! She became so upset and angry, she fled.

Her mind whirred with more and more questions, and the continual spinning did not cease until they reached Darcy House. She accepted Nathaniel's hand to help her alight before he escorted them inside the hall.

As their coats and hats were taken, Fitzwilliam stepped from the corridor with a creased forehead and a frown. "Elizabeth said you were to call on Lady Lindsey. I didn't expect your return for several hours. What has happened?"

"*She* was at Hatchard's."

The lines upon his forehead deepened. "Who was at Hatchard's?"

Georgiana's fingernails dug into the tender flesh of her palms as she steeled herself. "Mrs. Younge."

---

¹*Lady Caroline Lamb published Glenarvon in 1816. It was a gothic novel in which she fictionalised her affair with Lord Byron and made unflattering caricatures of several prominent members of society. Her authorship was a well-known secret.*

Chapter 13

A disbelieving sound erupted from Fitzwilliam. "You must be joking. She is nigh on destitute. What would bring her to this side of town?"

Georgiana shook her head in a frantic gesture as a large hand enveloped one of hers at her side and held firm. "I have no idea. She approached when I was not attending, and I nearly ran headlong into her and her companion. She greeted me and made to introduce me to the gentleman, but I was furious and overcome. Rather than expose myself and my anger, I fled."

Fitzwilliam looked between each of them with his jaw slightly agape. "I am shocked, nay appalled. I had not thought her so brazen. Forgive me, but I should like to hear the tale from the beginning." He made to shake Nathaniel's hand. "Sele, I appreciate your seeing my sister safely home. I would be happy to send a note this evening assuring you of my sister's well-being if you wish it."

Wait? Was Nathaniel departing? They could discuss the incident without speaking of the past, could they not?

"Must Nathaniel leave?" Her eyes flickered to her brother's surprised visage. "Mrs. Annesley was not nearby when I stumbled upon Mrs. Younge, but Nathaniel was at my side. He might remember what I do not."

Her brother's eyebrows lifted in silent question, but she took Nathaniel's elbow. "Mrs. Younge was a servant who misled us and betrayed us. One day you will know all, but for now, I beg your indulgence on the matter."

Nathaniel covered her hand with his own. "Of course."

Fitzwilliam extended his arm to invite them to the parlour. "Then perhaps we should sit."

Once they were settled, Nathaniel fetched her a glass of wine, which she sipped as he sat beside her. Meanwhile, Georgiana told the story in as much detail as she could remember. Nathaniel and Mrs. Annesley helped by making observations and additions as required.

During the entirety of her recollection, Nathaniel's hand never left hers. Fitzwilliam either ignored or failed to notice the breach of propriety, but more remarkable was the comfort the simple gesture provided. Despite her gloves, her hands had been frigid when they returned, yet the one he held no longer felt the cold. That hand had also lost its tremor since he had taken it into his possession.

Fitzwilliam was frowning, his expression furrowed in concentration by the time their recitation was completed. No doubt, he wondered at Mrs. Younge's motives as well. What would she have to gain by approaching them? Was she up to some nefarious scheme or was it no more than simple happenstance?

"No one heard the name of the gentleman she accompanied?"

"No, sir. Mrs. Younge gave an air of affront when Lord Sele chased after Miss Darcy," explained Mrs. Annesley, "but she did not complete her introduction nor call the man by name even after Miss Darcy departed. I did not remain long, however, as I hurried after Lord Sele and Miss Darcy."

Her brother gave a guttural exhale. "Richard and I shall have to speak of this, and soon. Fortunately, he and Julia have returned from Cambridgeshire. Perhaps I can manage to lure him over for some brandy and conversation prior to our trip to the theatre."

He extended his hand to Nathaniel. "I owe you a debt of gratitude for ensuring Georgiana came to no harm and returning her in such a swift manner. I do apologise if the afternoon with your mother was spoiled."

Georgiana's stomach settled like a rock. Mrs. Annesley and now Fitzwilliam both assumed this incident would prevent her from calling on Lady Lindsey, but why should it? She was merely a bit harried and did not come to harm. Besides, her fit of pique had passed.

"Could I not still call?" She peered from person to person within the room. "Why should I allow that wretched woman to ruin my plans?"

"Are you certain?" Nathaniel's hand tightened upon hers. His eyes were hopeful as they held hers without wavering.

Was she certain? Would she regret her fortitude once she was no longer within the safe confines of her own home? She would not know unless she made the attempt.

"Yes, I wish to go."

"Sir," addressed Mrs. Annesley to Fitzwilliam. "Unlike Miss Darcy, I could use some quiet after the tumult this morning. Perhaps Lucy could accompany Miss Darcy to Howard Place."

Her brother looked to Nathaniel. "I have no objections, though the grooms are sure to object. I am certain they have already brushed down the horses."

Nathaniel leaned in order to peer through the window. "The weather is as fine as one can expect for a winter's day. The house is not far. We could always walk."

"Two footmen will see you there," instructed Fitzwilliam after glancing outside himself. "If your mother would extend the same courtesy when Georgiana returns. I am likely being too wary, but I hope you will indulge me."

"I foresee no problems with your request. Mother would always wish to ensure Miss Darcy's welfare."

"I do not doubt she would, but I admit to being overprotective of those in my family."

Nathaniel's expression remained easy. He did not tense or give any hint that he took offence. "I cannot blame you. I would do the same in your position."

Georgiana glanced between them. "If I could but refresh myself for a moment, I will be ready to leave upon my return." The gentlemen rose until she departed with Mrs. Annesley at her side.

"You cannot be as comfortable as you seem," Mrs. Annesley observed while they ascended the stairs. "She gave you a great shock. No one would think less of you if you rested rather than insisting upon your schedule prior to this morning's outing."

She placed a palm upon her long-time companion's forearm. Mrs. Annesley was such a mother hen. While she had encouraged Georgiana to be stronger, she always offered to coddle her. She was such a contradiction! "I will no longer allow the actions from so long ago to dictate my life. I cannot. Today's meeting was sure to be a coincidence, and I will not cower to a woman who wished me ill."

Mrs. Annesley placed her free hand atop Georgiana's. "I know you have Mrs. Darcy and Miss Bennet, but should you wish to speak of it later, you know I shall attend you."

"I do, and I appreciate the offer." Without thought, Georgiana embraced the older woman, who returned the gesture. "You helped me through the worst time of my life. I can never repay you for your kindness and understanding."

A sniff came from Mrs. Annesley as her companion withdrew and began to rummage through her reticule. "It has been my honour, Miss Darcy." She dabbed eyes and nose with a folded handkerchief. "If you do not hurry, your young man will wonder what has become of you."

"He is not my young man!" she cried.

Mrs. Annesley giggled and pressed the fine cloth to her chest. "Oh, I remember those looks from when my husband courted me. Lord Sele loves you, and while you are more circumspect, you crave his attention. Those feelings are still very present in my mind—as if they happened yesterday."

Georgiana opened her mouth, but Mrs. Annesley put up a hand.

"I have seen your manner in his presence. You are attempting to guard your heart, but failing in a spectacular fashion." She sighed and took Georgiana's hands. "I shall be glad to see you find happiness. You and your brother both deserve a lifetime of joy after the sadness you have overcome." She gave her head a shake as though it required clearing. "Enough! Lord Sele is awaiting you."

"Mrs. Annesley—"

Her companion wagged a finger in her direction. "Do not keep that young man waiting, though I daresay he would sit in the drawing room all day if he thought he might gain your society." She pressed the handkerchief to her cheeks once more and bustled in the direction of her bedchamber.

Once Georgiana entered her dressing room, Lucy helped her tuck a few pins and attend to the necessary adjustments to her gown, then she and her maid returned to the hall. A moment later a footman joined them, and they departed for Howard Place. The walk was truly not a journey by any means. The mere stroll to the end of the square and one street over was simple enough.

Nathaniel hugged her arm close to his side as he escorted her with Lucy following just behind. Fitzwilliam's two footmen trailed after her maid.

"I am glad you decided not to cancel the remainder of our day on account of this morning."

"Lizzy always says her courage rises with every attempt to intimidate her. I suppose I understand her meaning more today than usual."

"You are unaccustomed to such feats of bravery, then?" His eyes twinkled and his impish grin made her laugh.

"I suppose it depends upon the situation. With family or at Pemberley where I am familiar with all and sundry, I would say yes, but in a crowded London ballroom or street, I have never before felt such stirrings."

Where did this odd sensation of confidence come from? Her courage had been lacking since her arrival in London, but had suddenly emerged with the presence of Mrs. Younge.

They turned the corner and crossed the street, pausing only briefly at the door. The butler allowed them entry, and once their coats and gloves were left with a housemaid, they were led through a hall bedecked with marbled columns to a comfortable, yet richly furnished drawing room where Lady Lindsey sat with two ladies unknown to her.

When Lady Lindsey noticed her arrival, she sprang from her seat. "Miss Darcy! I am so pleased you could call."

Nathaniel steered her forward until they were standing directly before his mother. "I have done better than you presume, Mother. Miss Darcy is to spend the afternoon with us. I even ensured she will stay for tea. All you must do is provide two footmen to accompany her and her maid on their walk back to Darcy House when she is ready to depart."

Lady Lindsey clasped Georgiana's hands within her own. "Of course I can grant such a simple request. I would never send her unaccompanied as you well know." She gave a sly look from the corner of her eye in the direction of her son. "You will ensure her safe return as well."

With a grin, he dipped his chin. "I had no other thought in mind."

"Is this Lady Fitzwilliam's niece?" asked the lady seated closest to them while she stood. "I should be pleased to make her acquaintance, as would my sister."

"Lady Jersey, Lady Bessborough, this young lady is indeed Miss Georgiana Darcy, and you have met my son, Lord Sele." The ladies all curtseyed a greeting.

"Word has spread through town of your début this Season." Lady Jersey looked Georgiana up and down as Lady Lindsey gripped her hand. "Few ladies wait as you have for their first season, which makes you a bit of a novelty. I know several who have questioned why you were shuttered away for so long."

Georgiana held herself as straight as she could at their direct manner. She would not cower. "Not shuttered away at all, my lady. I have simply been content at Pemberley and had no desire for my circumstances to change. While many young ladies look for a gentleman to marry in order to gain status or money, I have no need for such affectations. If I wed, I will do so for love—nothing but a stout and healthy love will induce me to wed."

Lady Bessborough regarded her with her head tilted and a raised eyebrow. "A singular attitude, indeed."

"I agree, Sister," responded Lady Jersey before turning her attention back to Georgiana. "I admire your convictions. I expect we shall see you at Almack's before the season has concluded."

Lady Jersey fetched her reticule and kissed Lady Lindsey's cheek. "I have enjoyed our visit, but we have intruded for too long. I hope you enjoy your afternoon, ladies." Lady Bessborough joined her sister before them, they all made their curtseys, and the callers exited into the hall where the butler awaited them.

When the door closed behind Lady Bessborough, Lady Lindsey laughed and placed her hands upon Georgiana's shoulders. "Well done! Lady Jersey enjoys provoking a reaction from people, though your response was certainly not what she expected. She will admire that you did not bow to society's conventions and expressed your own opinions instead."

"I hope my words were not too shocking."

Lady Lindsey led her to the settee where they both sat and faced one another. "Lady Jersey will respect you for stating your convictions with the confidence you displayed. Due to connections or fortune, she and the patronesses of Almack's have sent vouchers to some ladies, but I know Lady Jersey presses for invitations to those who impress her."

When she peered towards Nathaniel to ascertain his view of the matter, he stood before them with a frown. What had soured his milk? He had been positively chatty on the walk to Howard Place, but now, he appeared more a dejected puppy.

His mother giggled and wrapped an arm around Georgiana's shoulders. "Nathaniel, be a dear and tell Cook we will have one more for tea."

His jaw dropped a bit and Georgiana pursed her lips in order not to laugh.

"Oh, do not be so dramatic," his mother chided good-naturedly. "You have, no doubt, been in Georgiana's company all morning, as well as a number of other times over the past se'nnight. You can stand to be separated for a few moments." A sly smile graced her face. "Perhaps we should have a talk between girls. Find your father and join him for a time. I daresay he could use the company."

"What could you possibly have to say that I could not hear?" Nathaniel's voice was higher than was its wont and a mite petulant.

"I am certain I could think of some information or discussion that would require privacy," she said firmly. Without further argument, his hands dropped to his sides as he stalked from the room. "He is a kind young man, but he needs to be denied his own way from time to time. I knew you would be different than most young ladies who curry his favour, but I am pleased to see you do not allow him to lead you."

Georgiana, who suddenly had the urge to wiggle in her seat, began to pick imaginary pieces of fluff from her gown. "He does press for me to agree to his wishes."

"Yet you do not. You have not been in each other's company in years, and even then, propriety dictated your interactions because you were not yet out. The two of you needed to become reacquainted—to grow accustomed to the adults you have become." She gazed towards the fire. "When you both were still very young, your parents, my husband, and I considered arranging a match between you. We thought you would do well together, and Nathaniel doted upon you so."

"Why did you not?"

Lady Lindsey's attention darted back to her. "Because we agreed we never wanted you obligated towards the other. We could not imagine marriage without affection, and did not want to condemn you to such a fate."

She shifted in her place and began to chew at the inside of her cheek. A strange sensation gnawed at her and twisted her stomach. Would an agreement between the Darcy family and the Lindsey earldom have prevented Wickham's machinations? He might not have pursued her if he had no hopes of obtaining her dowry. How a part of her heart wished the contract had been signed. So much misery could have been prevented!

"Georgiana?"

Without warning, a sob tore from her throat and she covered her mouth with her hands. What had come over her? Why had she allowed such a desire to enter her head? Now, look what she had unleashed!

"Oh, dearest!" Lady Lindsey's arms enfolded her as Georgiana wept in her embrace. "What did I say? I had no intention of making you cry."

"If only you had arranged matters, Ramsgate would have never happened." She took in a great pull of air between each statement as her hands shook. "My life would be so different, and I would not be plagued with these dreadful memories."

Warm palms cradled Georgiana's cheeks, brushing the damp trailing down her face. Oh, God! What had she done? She blinked to clear her vision, but no expression of shock or disgust was to be found. Instead, the eyes of her mother's greatest friend were bright and glistened with unshed tears.

"What terrible misfortune could have occurred to give rise to such desires? You are far too young for these regrets."

"Oh, no! I should have never mentioned it." Georgiana withdrew with haste and began to tug frantically at her reticule. How could she have been so indiscreet? She had assumed happening upon Mrs. Younge had no lasting effect, but perhaps she was mistaken.

"Georgiana?" Lady Lindsey removed Georgiana's bag and loosened the top before handing it back.

Once Georgiana retrieved her handkerchief, she began to dab with shaky hands at her cheeks. "Are you friends with Lady Jersey or merely acquaintances?"

The older woman grasped Georgiana's wrists and held them in a firm grip between them. "Georgiana Darcy, you will not change the subject. You are distressed, and I will not ignore what just occurred."

"Why ever not?" Her voice was petulant, even to her own ears.

Lady Lindsey's gaze held Georgiana's and never wavered. "When did you spend time in Ramsgate?"

She folded the embroidered piece of muslin and pressed it smooth across her leg. "My brother formed an establishment for me there in summer of the year eleven."

"You were young."

"I was not yet sixteen," mumbled Georgiana. Lady Lindsey had relaxed her grip and now ran her thumbs back and forth across the top of her hands. "I was accompanied by my companion, Mrs. Younge."

The lady's forehead creased. "When did your brother hire Mrs. Annesley?"

"August of that same year."

After a moment of staring at Georgiana, Lady Lindsey leaned against the back of the sofa. "Have you ever fancied yourself in love?"

Georgiana started. "To what purpose is your question?"

Lady Lindsey sighed. "Companions of young ladies who are a certain age are seldom dismissed unless they have been remiss in their duties and allowed something untoward to occur. Either the charge has fancied herself in love and behaved in an inappropriate fashion or a young man has used the poor girl very ill indeed."

With a wince, she began to fiddle with her reticule once more.

"Should you ever require a willing ear, you can speak to me in confidence. I would never divulge a word to anyone—even Nathaniel."

Georgiana shook her head and stared at her busy fingers. She had never given a thought to love with George Wickham! Why the very notion turned her stomach! How repugnant!

Her head was stilled by warm palms, which took her by the shoulders. Lady Lindsey's eyes insisted upon her attention.

"Georgiana, who was the gentleman?"

"George Wickham was no gentleman," she spat.

Chapter 14

Lady Lindsey's hands dropped and her jaw went slack. Without a word, she rose, walked to the door with measured steps, peeked into the hall, and said a few words to whoever was nearby. When she returned, she eased back onto the settee in an odd manner—as though in a stupor.

"No, he certainly is not." The lady's hands rested upon her own stomach and she swallowed. "I learnt too much of Wickham's proclivities upon your father's death to doubt what must have occurred. Your brother requested my husband's counsel in regards to a living your father wished for that young man. I hoped your brother would distance the both of you from his evil."

"He did. You must know he did. Wickham conspired with Mrs. Younge." As much as she tried to take measure of Lady Lindsey's reactions, she could not keep her eyes from darting to the door every minute or so. Would Nathaniel return while they spoke? Would his mother insist Georgiana tell him all?

"I requested no one disturb us." The faint voice of Lady Lindsey drew her gaze from the entry.

"You did?"

"I made the assumption you might have had a slight flirtation with a young man a few years ago and been hurt by his departure for school or a grand tour. I thought to reassure you." Lady Lindsey turned to face her with tears welling upon her bottom lashes. "I never dreamt . . . Forgive me for pressing you so. I, of course, will never refuse should you need to unburden yourself, yet I never would have forced such a confession."

"Nathaniel and I happened upon Mrs. Younge this morning at Hatchard's. Foolishly, I convinced myself the incident gave me no more than a fleeting pique of temper, but perhaps, the experience made me more emotional than I would be otherwise. I also have not spoken of Ramsgate in so long. I have had no wish to relive that time, yet I know well how holding in my emotions wreaks havoc upon my equanimity. I have nightmares when I fret or when I restrain myself more than I should."

"You mask your feelings as your brother does and your father did before you," observed Lady Lindsey. "Your mother helped a great deal with your father's reserve as Mrs. Darcy does with your brother's. Personalities like theirs are never free unless in the presence of those with which they are comfortable."

Lady Lindsey wrapped a comforting arm around Georgiana's shoulders and gave an uncharacteristic growl. "Your mother never saw the harm in indulging that boy, though I thought it might breed resentment in the servants. After all, your father could not be so generous with all of the children on the estate. I was appalled to hear what Wickham had become."

"He is dead," added Georgiana. "He can no longer harm anyone."

"I should not feel relieved at another human being's death, yet I cannot feel anything but."

Georgiana laid her head upon the older lady's shoulder. "I believe we all had some measure of relief and gratitude that he could no longer cause the pain he once did."

"This is why you have insisted you would never marry?"

"I could never imagine what I must . . . How I could . . ." How did one explain without embarrassment?

"Oh dearest, I know of a few women who lived through similar experiences. Most were wed to a suitor who required their fortune, but one was betrothed when another man forced himself upon her. Her husband, thank the Lord, is the best of men and they wed regardless of the incident. She once confided that while the marriage bed can bring back unwanted recollections and render her uneasy at times, that the experience is so different with her husband. He is also an exceedingly gentle man, which helps her be more comfortable with him."

"Fitzwilliam believes Nathaniel is my best chance at happiness."

Lady Lindsey squeezed her hand. "I cannot disagree with your brother, though you must tell him."

"I have always intended to speak with Nathaniel should we become closer to an understanding. I have been unable thus far because I fear his reaction."

"My son has loved you most of his life," stated Lady Lindsey matter-of-factly. "He will be angry with Wickham, and your pain and suffering will break his heart. Yet, his affection for you will not die or be diminished. I am certain of that."

How could she not trust his mother's words? Georgiana stood and stepped before the fire, watching the coals glow with their heat. "He is so different than the boy I remember, but in some ways the same. I know not what to make of him."

"You must trust him."

She turned to face Lady Lindsey, the warmth of the fire not warding off the chill that permeated the room since Wickham's name was mentioned. "I would trust him with my life."

"You need to have faith in his constancy."

"I am making an attempt. I am still becoming accustomed to the Nathaniel I know at present as opposed to the boy from all those years ago."

The lady's throaty laugh drew her attention. "He has matured and seeks your notice by means other than being a nuisance. You must remember he was a spoiled only son. We had despaired of having a babe of our own when I discovered I was with child. My confinement was difficult and I never conceived again. Nathaniel is our pride and joy."

"You and Lizzy have much in common. She did not have a difficult confinement—at least not from what I understand—but little William was not conceived immediately after their wedding and kept them in suspense for a year. He is now two, and Lizzy has yet to fall with child again."

Lady Lindsey nodded in understanding. "I pray she does manage at least one more. We fretted Nathaniel's first few years. I still thank God for my son's life. So many children do not survive to become adults."

Why was Lady Lindsey still advocating her son? How could she desire her family to be polluted by her ruin?

Nathaniel's mother watched her, studied her. "What troubles you?"

"You adore your son."

"Yes, of course."

What an inane statement! "What I meant was you love your son, so why would you still wish him to marry me?"

"Because he adores you, and I know you will make him happy."

She gaped at Lady Lindsey. How could she honestly see the situation in such simple terms? "But I am ruined." A gasp escaped when the lady gave her a quick but hard jolt.

"I do not ever want to hear those words from you again. Do you understand?"

Georgiana could do nothing but bob her head up and down.

"Ladies of our station seldom come into marriage as maidens, despite their protestations, and a large number by their own choice and inclination. You had no such decision since the ability was taken from you in a cruel and demeaning fashion. I think no less of you."

"What if I cannot bear a child?" whispered Georgiana. When she claimed she had no interest in marriage, the ability to carry a baby had never been a concern, but now, her mind whispered the worry whenever she had a quiet moment.

"Then Frederick's imbecile of a cousin inherits the title—or his son if the addle pate is no longer living. Some matters are beyond our control. God gives no one assurances or guarantees of their fortunes or misfortunes. A child is a blessing, but so is felicity in marriage. Do not lose the opportunity for love.

My son will not love you less for failing to provide an heir."

Georgiana's eyes widened. "You are not concerned about why I asked?"

"I can only imagine one reason you would have that concern," clarified Lady Lindsey. "Many women lose a child and go on to carry and deliver many more."

She could only continue to stare.

"Did you believe I would throw you from my home? Forbid my son from you?" The lady's voice was incredulous. "I loved your mother, and I have cared for you since you were born. I would never cast you out. I may not have been as present in your life as I would have preferred these last few years, but I intend to rectify that mistake now."

She took Georgiana in her arms and held her close. Warm, wet droplets coursed down her cheeks and collected upon Lady Lindsey's shoulder. After a shuddering breath, she relaxed into the lady's embrace, allowing her to soothe the ache that had blossomed anew when she laid eyes upon Bridget Younge in Hatchard's.

A raised voice broke the quiet that had overtaken the room, and Lady Lindsey gave a noisy exhale. "I am amazed he managed this long." The voice became louder and an insistent knocking reverberated around the room.

"We no longer require privacy, Joseph," she called when the rapping paused. "Allow my son inside."

Nathaniel burst through the doors and looked about the room while his mother drew back from Georgiana, though she kept an arm around her. His shoulders dropped when he saw her and then narrowed his eyes at his mother. "What have you done? I leave the two of you for no more than a half-hour and you have reduced her to tears?"

"Request a small bowl of cool water and towelling from the footman, and we will talk. I wish to know more about this morning."

After Nathaniel poked his head into the hall, he hastened to Georgiana's side and took her hand. His mother raised her eyebrows at his familiarity and Georgiana's face became heated, but he did not relent.

"Fitzwilliam intends on discussing the incident with Richard," she informed Lady Lindsey. "I am certain they will ensure she is not following me, though she has not noticed me when I have seen her prior to today."

"You have seen her more than once since your return to London?" Lady Lindsey's tone was one of concern. "You are certain she was not aware of your presence?"

Georgiana looked to Nathaniel. "Do you remember when we met at the hat shop on Bond Street?"

His brow creased as he sat forward. "I am sure Mother and I both recall that day, though I do not remember Mrs. Younge."

"No, she was not inside the shop. Lydia and I departed a few moments after you. When I looked up and down the street for Lizzy, I noticed Mrs. Younge's favourite hat, which has not changed in these last five years. She was on the pavement across the road, and on the arm of a man—I assume the same man from today.

"Then, I saw her when we rode Rotten Row. She and a man were strolling along the Serpentine. I remember I took my eyes from her for a moment, and when I searched for her again, she was gone."

"She is always in company with this man?" Lady Lindsey's eyebrows drew down in the middle. "Unless she married, she could have taken a protector. If he is wealthy, it would explain why you continue happening upon her on this side of town."

Would Mrs. Younge do such a thing? Fitzwilliam had, on several occasions, commented of her relationship with Wickham. He supposed they were lovers, but she had her boarding house. Would she require a relationship of that nature?

"But Mrs. Younge had a boarding house. I do not know its location, but she would not have required such a position unless she wished it."

Nathaniel glanced between her and his mother. "Is this discussion necessary? I do not believe Georgiana needs to hear the sordid details of the habits of some men."

Georgiana pulled her hand from his. "Really! Despite my propensity for tears today, I am not some frail flower who cannot cope with what is published in the gossip columns. My brother ceased shielding me from that sort of knowledge years ago. I may be sheltered to a degree, but not naïve." A giggle came from across the room and they both turned to Lady Lindsey.

"Bravo, my dear!"

"Mother!"

His appalled expression made withholding her laughter quite difficult, but she held her breath for a moment, until the urge subsided. "Why do you prefer I not hear of such happenings?" she asked, schooling her features to appear truly curious. "Do you intend to indulge in such dissolute practices or do you now?"

His head whipped to face her and if possible, his mouth opened a bit wider. "Georgiana!"

"Really, Nathaniel," scolded his mother. Lady Lindsey's shoulders shook as she stifled a laugh, but that was the straw that broke the camel's back. Chuckles erupted from Georgiana, and Lady Lindsey followed suit.

Nathaniel glared angrily at them both. "I am uncertain as to the source of your humour, but I assure you this has not been amusing in the least."

A maid entered and set a bowl and towelling upon the table, curtseyed, and departed with haste. Nathaniel dampened a cloth and pressed it into Georgiana's hand. She folded it and placed it upon one eye.

A corner of his lips twitched as he watched. "You are aware both of your eyes are red?"

"But I cannot see you if I cover both."

His teeth appeared as he smiled that impish grin that made her insides flip. "You enjoy looking at me then."

"Do not feed his vanity, dearest," whispered his mother.

Georgiana could not help but smile at a remembrance from when her brother and Lizzy first met. "You are tolerable, I suppose."

Lady Lindsey burst into gales of laughter. "Well done!"

He shook his head and attempted to maintain an insulted expression, failing dreadfully. "We should return to Darcy House."

She removed the damp cloth. "You must be joking. We just arrived, and I am to remain for tea."

"In your brother's home, I do not have you and my mother conspiring to insult me."

"Are the ladies treating you unfairly, Son?" When they all started and looked in the direction of the voice, Lord Lindsey stood in the door. "Do not take umbrage at their good humour. A lady's mood can vary like the weather—happy and pleased with the world in one moment, and temperamental and stormy the next."

Georgiana placed her palm to her mouth, then hastily removed it as it contained the damp towelling, while Nathaniel laughed under his breath.

"Are you not concerned of the displeasure that could arise from such a statement, my dear?" A spark lit Lady Lindsey's eyes as she gazed adoringly at her husband.

"Perhaps you should allow me to finish." He stepped forward, his cane rapping along the floor at the end of the rug. "While the moods of our English roses vary, both have their advantages: a happy wife is always a joy, and I find my wife's agitations a pleasure to calm."

He came to a stop before Georgiana and gave a slight bow. "Miss Darcy, welcome to Howard Place."

"Thank you, sir."

"Is that all, then?" asked Lady Lindsey. "Am I to be placated by your enjoyment of my capricious behaviour?"

Her hand was brought to his lips. "Passionate, but not capricious by any means. Am I to be forgiven?"

With a roll of her eyes, Lady Lindsey withdrew her hand. "I shall consider it."

Despite their words, the arch manner of both of them displayed their true feelings upon the matter. They teased much like Fitzwilliam and Lizzy did, though her brother and sister did so without such suggestive words; at least they did not in her presence.

"Perhaps I should return Georgiana to her own home if you persist in this blatant lack of decorum."

Lord Lindsey chuckled at his son. "You should be accustomed to our banter by now, and Miss Darcy is family. Her parents often teased one another—particularly her mother. Besides, you are one to lecture us on decorum when you hold the young lady's hand in yours."

She withdrew as though singed. How could she have forgotten? Nathaniel was indulging in that liberty more today than was his wont. Before the morning's upheaval, he might grasp her hand and lead her to the chess table or the settee. He never held it for any length of time, until now.

"We have been invited to join your family for one of Mr. Sheridan's plays. Have you read the work, Miss Darcy?"

Her head lifted to Lord Lindsey from where she had stared at her lap. "Oh, I have read *The School for Scandal* and enjoyed it very much."

"As much as Radcliffe? My wife adores Radcliffe, and would, no doubt, be the first in the theatre if a play was crafted from her work."

"I cannot deny a preference for *The Romance of the Forest* or *The Mysteries of Udolpho*."

"Your mother was a great admirer of the lady's work," said Lady Lindsey with a fond smile. "I am not surprised you enjoy her as well."

Nathaniel was quiet all of a sudden. He was attending the conversation, but had ceased to speak after his father called attention to their holding hands. "Are you looking forward to the play?" asked Georgiana.

"I am," he admitted, "though more for the company than the performance."

She shifted in her place. The statement did not expressly state her society, but he certainly did not mean Fitzwilliam or Richard. Her mouth opened and closed a few times in an attempt to make a retort, but how to respond?

Fortunately, two maids bearing tea and refreshments entered, saving her from the need to speak. By the time the service was set out and they departed, Lady Lindsey enquired of Georgiana's preferred diversions while in London, which, as conversation does, led to other discussions until the time came for Nathaniel to return her to Darcy House.

"My mother enjoyed having your company. I thank you for visiting with my family."

"I have wished to become reacquainted with your parents." She tilted her face so the breeze would graze her face just so. "I feel closer to my mother than

I have in years. I know it must sound strange, but your mother's stories of my parents have done much to contribute to that feeling. I am ashamed to say I have forgotten so many little details."

"You were quite young when your mother passed. She would understand and not wish you to feel guilty over what you cannot control. As long as you remember how much she loved you, I know she would be satisfied."

When she turned, he continued to look forward as they walked. "How do you know?"

His eyes met hers and held them without wavering. "Because it is what I would wish you to remember most about me."

Chapter 15

The shouts of drivers and the sound of an armada of wheels rattling along the uneven cobbled road heralded their arrival to the Theatre Royale, just as it had when Georgiana first visited years before. This time, however, rather than her brother sitting across from her, Nathaniel and his father watched through the window at the crowd of conveyances while Lady Lindsey had the place at her side.

"It seems we are not the only occupants of London who thought a night at the theatre a pleasant diversion," observed Nathaniel as they pulled closer to the front entrance and came to a stop. "Will you be well?" His gaze was soft and earnest when he looked at her.

"I will manage. We have a large enough party. I should never be without companionship."

Lady Lindsey wore a sly smile as she patted Georgiana's hand. "Unless you chase him away, I am certain Nathaniel will not stray from your side for the entirety of the evening, my dear. You have no reason to fret."

Nathaniel's complexion adopted a pinker tinge, but instead of being affronted, he lifted one corner of his lips. "Do not give her the idea that she can keep me from her society."

"Heaven forbid." His father chuckled as he lifted his eyebrows and gave a meaningful look to his wife. Before any further comment could be made, the thud of the step brought her attention to the door, which was opened directly.

Nathaniel alighted first, followed by his father, before his hand reached inside to help her step down. She lifted her cloak and gown as much as possible to prevent it from being soiled by the filth and the remnants of the horses that preceded them when her foot came in contact with the street.

He pointed forward, but slightly to the right as she placed her hand upon his arm. "I believe this way is our best route."

With a nod, she followed his lead as he wove around the widest path to the pavement before the theatre where she allowed her skirts to fall.

Lord and Lady Lindsey stepped to join them but a moment later. "Do you see your brother's carriage?" All four scanned the sea of horses and different conveyances that clogged the road, but the Darcy carriage was not to be found.

She dropped from her tiptoes, which had done nothing to help her locate their party. "No, I do not."

"'Tis too cold tonight to remain out of doors," commented Lord Lindsey, who glanced about them. "We should await them inside."

The gentlemen led the ladies into the much warmer entrance hall of the theatre, which was bustling with people and activity. Who knew so many were already in London before the start of the season? Or was it the choice of play that attracted the crowd?

"There you are!" At the sound of her brother's voice, Georgiana looked around her. Fitzwilliam squeezed between two men, who both glanced disdainfully back at him, to reach them. "We must have arrived just before you. Forgive me, but we could not keep the ladies in the weather to wait. Richard had just departed with the remainder of our party to the box when I spotted you from across the room."

Lord Lindsey clapped Fitzwilliam on the arm. "Do not trouble yourself. We brought the ladies inside for the same reason, particularly since it looks like snow."

Her brother helped her remove her cloak. "I would not be surprised to find the weather has turned by the time we depart for the house." After a glare at a red-faced man who was obviously already in his cups and stumbling past, he motioned towards the stairs. "We should make our way to the box. I have never seen the theatre this crowded before the beginning of the Season."

"Sheridan is particularly popular," offered Lady Lindsey. "I have oft times found his plays more attended than some."

When they entered the box, Jane stood just inside. "Georgiana, I am pleased to see you again." They had just kissed one another on the cheeks when Lizzy rushed forward and grasped her hands.

"I told Fitzwilliam you could not be far behind. He fretted so when the carriage behind us did not have the Lindsey crest."

Fitzwilliam came to stand by his wife's side. "Men do not fret, my dear. We show appropriate concern."

The clear laughter of Lizzy carried around their box while Richard, Sir James, and Mr. Hanson, who had Lydia on his arm, gave a spirited, "Hear, hear!"

"You forget, dear husband," Lizzy teased, "Georgiana and I frequently witness your 'appropriate concern' for the members of our family. You and Richard expressed a great deal of the emotion before we departed this evening."

Georgiana put a hand to Lizzy's shoulder. "Their concern does them credit, though the two of them exhibit more feeling than an 'appropriate concern' warrants. I would characterise it more a prolonged affront. I believe they express more worry than us ladies."

"A gentleman's lot in life is to care for his estate and his family." Nathaniel's chest puffed and his voice was haughty. "The responsibility is not one to be taken lightly. Men who are dedicated to those duties cannot leave them behind like they would a story in a book."

The ladies all watched Nathaniel as he finished his speech while the men murmured their agreement. Georgiana glanced to Lizzy, Jane, and Lady Lindsey before the four of them began to giggle.

Lady Lindsey motioned to the rest of the men. "You are as bad as they are." She looped her arm through Georgiana's and led her towards the edge of the box. "If you will excuse us for a moment."

While the remainder of their party continued their conversation, Lady Lindsey leaned closer when they stood before the balustrade. "I have made calls and listened to a prodigious amount of gossip since your trip to the bookseller's."

Her head whipped around to face the countess. Why mention that now?

"Your former companion's name has been bandied about a great deal," she whispered. "A gentleman by the name of Mr. Browne, who has recently come into his inheritance, has installed her in a home on Berkeley Square."

Her eyes hurt they widened so. "Berkeley Square is—"

"Is just around the corner from Grosvenor Square, which is why you have seen her in the park and at the bookseller's. Talk has it the gentleman has purchased her an extensive new wardrobe over the past fortnight, and would explain her presence on Bond Street."

Lady Lindsey scanned the boxes across the theatre. "I do not imagine your meetings to be by design. While your brother is unlikely to be friends with Mr. Browne, due to that gentleman's habits, Mr. Browne would have no desire to offend the Darcy family, and by extension the Fitzwilliams and the Howards. He is extremely knowledgeable of connections. He married for wealth and is ever searching for ways to improve his standing."

"I never thought my sightings were more than happenstance. It is possible Fitzwilliam and Richard believe otherwise, particularly after an experience Fitzwilliam had while betrothed to Lizzy."

"Then, they will be none too pleased this evening," she commented with a tilt of her head towards the back, opposite side of the theatre.

Georgiana shifted and looked as a man, who did indeed appear to be the same from Hatchard's, stood in a box with a woman on his arm. If she did not already know his partner, she would not have recognised Bridget Younge. Her gown was a far cry from the worn muslin from their previous encounter, rather she glowed in a daring scarlet silk that complemented her pale complexion and ebony hair.

"I would not have known her at a glance."

A head poked between them, and they jumped at Nathaniel's sudden appearance. "What do you discuss so secretly? I would not think either of you prone to idle gossip."

"While Fitzwilliam waited to meet with investigators and has yet to receive any information, your mother has used her time and connections to great success." His forehead crinkled, and he frowned as she gestured towards Mrs. Younge in much the same manner as his mother.

He narrowed his eyes and stared hard for a few moments before his head gave a jerk. "That is Mrs. Younge!"

Georgiana clapped her hand over his mouth. "Shhh! We do not want to announce her presence to our entire party."

"If your brother does not notice her during the course of the evening," explained Lady Lindsey while she peered at Fitzwilliam, "I shall inform him after dinner. He should not be paying an investigator for what I have discovered in the drawing rooms of Mayfair." A low chuckle came from Nathaniel though he attempted to press his lips together to stifle the sound.

Georgiana crossed her arms over her chest. "What amuses you?"

"The idea of my mother employed as an informant for the Bow Street Runners. She, no doubt, believes herself an expert since she discovered what your brother's investigators have not." A high gasp and a slap to his arm from his mother made him step back.

"I have said no such thing! I made two days of calls before I heard the first rumour. I then called upon the acquaintances I knew who kept company with that man's wife. They are a fickle set with no loyalty to one another, but maintain acquaintances based on status. His wife boasted of her husband's more prosperous situation, and those ladies now take great pleasure in what they perceive as his wife's humiliation."

Nathaniel's expression tightened, disgust evident upon his features. "The practice is all too common, yet I find it abhorrent."

"Their disdain or the husband's infidelity?" His eyes met hers, but before he could answer, the curtains began to open, and those in their party moved to the seats. Georgiana settled between Nathaniel and Lady Lindsey. As the play began, his shoulder pressed against hers.

"Both." His breath was warm and sent a shiver through her.

"Pardon?" she whispered.

"His infidelity and her so-called friends' disdain are both abhorrent."

She turned from the stage and held his gaze. His expression was open and earnest. No doubt existed that he meant precisely what he said. Someone cleared their throat behind them, and with a sigh, Nathaniel shifted away. The tone of the cough sounded like Richard, but without looking, it was difficult to be certain.

The play began on the stage, which demanded her attention, yet a part of her could not dismiss the presence of Nathaniel beside her. Every movement or laugh from him was more noticeable than those of the rest of their group.

Upon the arrival of the interval, Nathaniel leaned in her direction. "I shall not be long." He jumped from his seat and shifted around Richard and Sir James, disappearing through the door.

"Are you enjoying the performance?" asked Julia from behind her.

Georgiana pivoted and set her arm along the back of the chair. "It is very diverting. Have you enjoyed the play thus far?" Some of their party remained in their seats while they spoke and some milled around the box, stretching their legs while they chatted.

"I have. I am glad your brother chose a comedy over a tragedy for our outing this evening. At the moment, I have no wish to lower my spirits by watching the characters all perish by the end."

Lizzy grinned as she sat beside Julia. "But do you not enjoy crying from time to time? I find there is little that compares to crying over beloved characters upon their demise, and a great satisfaction for the evil doers when they meet their fate." How like Lizzy! She felt matters keenly and appreciated every emotion while Georgiana attempted to shutter away feelings that caused upset.

"I do enjoy a melancholy tale when I am in a particular mood," explained Julia, "though I have not been of that bent for some time."

"Perhaps you are too happy since your betrothal and have no desire to lose your good humour so soon after your marriage?" All eyes turned to Lady Lindsey, who had turned to join their conversation. "I was much the same from the moment Frederick requested to court me until almost a year into our marriage. I do not mean to imply your happiness fades, but it changes when you become more comfortable with one another."

Julia shifted forward and bit her lip. "Has Lord Sele requested to court you yet? I know Lydia was adamant he admired you before Richard and I wed, and he is very attentive to you this evening. I could have swatted Richard for clearing his throat when he did. Neither of you were behaving improperly."

Her cheeks began to burn and she opened and closed her mouth twice, unsuccessfully attempting to speak before Lady Lindsey lay her palm over her hand. "It does no harm for my son to have to work for what he wants—especially in this instance. Georgiana is right to delay until she is at ease accepting his offer, and though Nathaniel is impatient, I am certain he will wait until he knows she will respond in his favour."

Lady Lindsey gave a motherly smile and rested against the back of her chair. "I understand you have a rather precocious young man at home,

Mrs. Darcy."

A laugh bubbled from Lizzy's lips. "William is never idle unless he is asleep, and even then, I am surprised he does not wiggle about while he slumbers. At Fitzwilliam's insistence, I hired a maid to assist Mrs. Wynn. She is often overwhelmed by our son's active nature."

"He eludes her whenever possible," elaborated Georgiana. "He has climbed bookcases to retrieve keys, crept from his room to hide, and escaped when Mrs. Wynn thought he slept. He is more than a handful for the poor woman, and she had five children of her own."

Lady Lindsey clasped her hands before her. "He sounds delightful. I hope you do not think me impertinent by saying that I hope to make his acquaintance soon. I enjoy the man he has become, but I miss cuddling Nathaniel in my lap and telling him stories. I did much the same with Fitzwilliam when he was a little boy. I had to wait for my son for several years, and when we visited Pemberley, I took your husband on walks and read to him while Anne tended to her household duties. I believe the nursemaids were sad to see us depart at the end of the month. They had quite an easy time of it while we remained."

The soft glint in Lizzy's eye and the hint of a smile were the same as when Aunt Charlotte told stories of Fitzwilliam's youth. "I am certain William would adore your visit. He naps most afternoons, so during calling hours or earlier would be best. We can remove the knocker from the door for the day so we will not be disturbed."

"I thought you might care for a glass of wine."

Georgiana startled and turned abruptly in her seat to face Nathaniel where he stood almost behind her. "How kind of you." She took the glass and sipped the deep red liquid, which was a bit sweet.

"Father and I were surprised at its quality. I am oft times disappointed, but Father thought it suitable for my mother." As he resumed his seat, she glanced to find Lady Lindsey now standing near her husband as they spoke to Fitzwilliam and Lizzy. She held a glass of wine in her hand as well.

"I thought perhaps we could ride again this week if the weather permits. With the number of people in attendance this evening, riders might be sparse on Rotten Row on the morrow." Nathaniel regarded her with raised eyebrows.

"If we are very late this evening, then I may not wish to ride tomorrow."

"I have no care whether it is the fashionable hour or not. We could take the horses out later than is our wont or we might stay inside and play chess. I do not have a preference as long as I am with you."

A sip of wine, or maybe a gulp, was taken to help settle her. Was Julia watching from behind? She must if Richard was keeping such a close eye on them.

The opening of the curtain saved her from responding, but the remainder of the play was not without its distractions: Nathaniel's low chuckle rumbled near her ear, he leaned in to whisper some observation or another while his breath tickled her neck, and he set his hand disturbingly close to her own, his little finger brushing hers periodically and nearly prompting her to spill her wine on the first occasion.

They did not remain for the later entertainments but departed upon the conclusion of Sheridan's play. The later crowds were known for their rowdy behaviour as the food and drink of the evening had more and more of an influence on those in attendance. Better to depart now than sit in a sea of carriages containing drunken revellers later.

Upon their arrival to Darcy House, they were not long in the drawing room before dinner was announced. Nathaniel escorted Georgiana to the dining room, then took his usual place beside her.

With a tap of his leg against hers, he leaned his head in her direction but dipped it towards Lydia and Mr. Hanson. "How long before you expect an announcement from that quarter?"

His close proximity caused her to stiffen. "They have only been reacquainted but a month. I do not expect Lydia to be so impulsive for such a big decision."

"Yet they were acquainted in the past. Would that not forward their attachment?"

Georgiana examined his expression as he turned and their eyes locked. "Both are greatly altered from the last time they were in company together. Besides, they knew very little of one another then."

"Then they are vastly different than us."

"How do you mean?"

"Well, our families have been close for all of our lives. I know you well."

She straightened and narrowed her eyes at his confident grin. "You do, do you?"

"Your doll's name was Matilda. Your favourite colour as a child was pink, but has changed since to green, if I am not mistaken—you favour your new gown of that shade and you complemented the materials in my mother's green drawing room. You prefer wine to sherry, though you will drink the latter if offered, and you tap your finger to your lips when you are uncertain of your next move in chess."

Did she indeed tap her finger to her lips? Who knew she was so predictable?

"I am certain you could claim to know as much of me as I do of you."

The first course was placed before her, and she took a deep breath to keep from forgetting herself in Nathaniel's gaze. "I do not think—"

"Do not be coy, Georgiana. Not with me." His voice was soft so as not to be overheard. Why did that particular tone unnerve her? She could quiver as badly as one of Cook's jellies if she gave into the notion.

"What do you remember of when we were children?"

She set down her fork and gripped her hands in her lap. "You had a pony called Badger, though I do not know what inspired the name."

"He was named when my father gave him to me. I was young and never enquired as to why."

"Your current horse is named Puck, so I assume you enjoy A Midsummer Night's Dream."

"When I first read the play," he explained, his attention remaining upon her despite his plate being placed before him. "I took great pleasure in the silliness of it all. Puck was my favourite character."

"Do you prefer a different character now?"

He laughed and looked off for a moment, considering her question. "I confess to having not read it in some time, but I believe, were I to read the play again, I would still like Puck best."

Georgiana stared at her food and took a bite or two lest her plate be removed at the end of the course and she had not touched it. What did she remember of Nathaniel other than frustration being her constant companion while in his company?

"I am afraid I do not recall you ever showing a preference for a particular colour." While she spoke, the conversation at the table quieted, and her voice carried further than she had anticipated. She swallowed the food in her mouth with more noise than was ladylike.

"My son has always liked blue," responded Lady Lindsey with a sly grin. "I do remember he expressed a disappointment that you did not favour the shade. It would go beautifully with your eyes." Lydia began to cough, but it was evident to all assembled that the fit was to cover her giggles while Georgiana's cheeks and ears burned.

"I do not dislike blue. I have a number of gowns in a particular shade and wished for a change. I am afraid, since they were delivered, I have worn my newer purchases more than the gowns I brought from Pemberley."

Lady Lindsey glanced at her son with a mischievous eye. "Every lady prefers to wear what is new to what has been in their wardrobe. One cannot fault you for that."

"I do not find fault with Miss Darcy, Mother. Though I am not familiar with ladies' fashion, I find the colours Miss Darcy chose each complement her in their own way."

Richard chuckled and lifted his wine as if toasting Nathaniel. "As diplomatic a response as I have ever heard." A few people laughed behind their hands before they began to return to their previous discussions.

Georgiana filled her fork, but did not lift it to her lips. "Books, what think you of books?"

"I enjoy them a great deal."

"Do not play games," she huffed. "You know what I intended."

His shoulders shook with his suppressed chuckle. "I do, but the question was rather broad. Did you mean books of poetry? Novels? Histories? Perhaps treatises on the latest farming techniques?"

"Very well! You have made your point. Do you like poetry?"

His eyes held hers. "More so now than when I was younger. I have found solace in the works of several poets these last few years."

"Does one touch your heart more than most?"

Nathaniel's head shook as he sat forward and began to pay more attention to his food. "No, no, no," he answered in an amused tone. "One day, perhaps I shall share such personal details, but for now, I think them best kept to myself."

"Hardly a fair response when you were the one who insisted upon our knowing one another better."

He lifted one brow, finished chewing his bite, and swallowed. "Have you read Malthus' views on the Corn Laws?"

Infuriating man!

January 24ᵗʰ 1817

Why insist upon a topic only to change one's mind when matters become too close to the heart? They must have been too close to the heart, else why would he not share? He was the one who challenged me, claimed I knew more of him than I did. I merely asked a question, a question of poetry no less, and he refused to oblige me! I shall never understand that man!

The remainder of the evening was enjoyable. The play was performed well, and the crowd better behaved than I have seen in the past—only a small amount of fruit was thrown at the stage. I admit it is a relief to know why Mrs. Younge is frequenting this side of town rather than remaining in the neighbourhood near her boarding house. My temper must remain in check if I stumble upon her once again, which is likely to happen with her living so close. Fitzwilliam was too occupied to take note of her this evening, so Lady Lindsey pulled him to the side, before she departed, to inform him of Mrs. Younge's new situation. I am certain he will wish to discuss matters in the morning.

Nathaniel was a gentleman and ensured my comfort throughout the evening until dinner. When the men joined the ladies after the meal, I remained by Julia and Lizzy, who eyed me suspiciously, but did not insist I go to his side.

What could be so personal he could not share? He expects me to trust him, but do I not deserve the same courtesy?

Enough! No more of Nathaniel for this evening! When I put down my pen, I shall lose myself in The Mysteries of Udolpho *once again, and forget Nathaniel Howard. Why do I not believe myself—even when I commit it to paper?*

Chapter 16

When she released the last chord, Georgiana carefully lifted her fingers from the keys, placed her hands in her lap, and stared at the music sheet in front of her. Oft times, she found solace in the pianoforte, but not today. She was too unsettled. Her mind was not occupied so much with thoughts as it was a feeling or attitude she could not identify.

She slumped and rose from the seat, determined to rid herself of this feeling, but how did one rid themselves of what they could not name? As she departed the music room, voices could be heard from the drawing room, so she peered inside. Lydia and Mr. Hanson sat on the settee, though not close together while they spoke. Mr. Hanson faced away from Georgiana, but Lydia's animated countenance as she described what sounded like a story from when she was a little girl was visible to her.

She had no need or want to disturb their conversation, so she made her way to Fitzwilliam's study. He sat in a familiar position, his pen poised over a piece of paper, and his forehead creased in concentration.

"What is giving you such difficulties?"

His head shot up with a start before he relaxed back in his well-worn chair, his hand resting upon the desk. "Nothing of note. Elizabeth received a letter from Mrs. Reynolds, requesting her advice on an issue with one of the servants, and I was attempting to respond."

"It is unlike Lizzy to avoid addressing those sorts of problems herself."

"She was unwell this morning, and I hoped to save her the trouble." He looked to the empty paper before him with a frown. "Instead, I should just have a maid deliver it to my wife as I fear she will be upset if I give Mrs. Reynolds the wrong instruction."

Georgiana turned her head and eyed him with a sidelong glance. "You speak as though Lizzy is ill-tempered, which she is not."

"No, but she is adamant that she manage the household without my help. Even after these past five years, she worries of maintaining the servants' respect."

"She earned their respect and their loyalty within the first few months. None will think less of her if she allows you to make one decision in her stead and should you make the choice incorrectly, well, you enjoy your wife's ire, do you not?"

Fitzwilliam's lips curved at each end. "You are too aware of some matters, but yes, I, at times, provoke my wife because I enjoy the spark in her eyes when she becomes angry. Infuriating her in this way, however, is different. I doubt she would be so easily soothed."

She grinned and held out her hand. "Give me the letter from Mrs. Reynolds. I shall give it to Lizzy, so you no longer need worry about upsetting your wife."

"Be careful, Little Sister. I might seek retribution for your teases when you least expect it. Sele may have had business today, but I would wager he will be at our door soon enough. Just remember, I know all your embarrassing stories."

"As I know yours, Fitzwilliam."

He laughed as he placed the correspondence in her palm. "But you, Mrs. Reynolds, and Richard have all enlightened Elizabeth of my childhood misadventures. I doubt any remain she has yet to hear."

She strolled to the door but just as she walked through, leaned back. "What of Miss Jameson? Have you told Elizabeth of her?" His eyes bulged, but she darted away from the study and towards the kitchen before he could catch her.

Cook glanced up as Georgiana entered, abandoning her kneading and wiping her hands upon her flour-covered apron. "Is there somethin' ya be needin', Miss Darcy?"

"My brother said Mrs. Darcy was not feeling well this morning and I hoped to bring her some tea."

"Her maid requested some tea and biscuits not five minutes past. I was about to add tha water to tha pot when ya entered. Yer not gonna be wantin' Mrs. Darcy's tea, so I'll add another pot." She took a steaming kettle from the stove and filled the teapot from Lizzy's favoured setting and an additional one, adding a few other items before she appeared satisfied. "Let me get a maid to carry it."

She poked her head in an adjoining room and soon returned with one of the upstairs maids in tow, handing her the tray. "Now, be careful and don't spill it before it's delivered to the mistress." She looked to Georgiana. "Millie's new, just started yesterday, so she might get turned around."

"I can help her find her way. Thank you."

With a curt nod of her head, Cook pounded the dough in front of her and set back to work while Georgiana led the maid up the stairs to the family wing, through a passageway that led out of the servants' corridor, and to the outer door of Lizzy's chambers. She knocked and her sister's voice bade them enter.

"Georgiana!" she exclaimed. "I had not expected you." She rose from a chair by the fire still clad in her dressing gown.

"Fitzwilliam mentioned you were unwell. I went to the kitchens to arrange tea, but it seems your abigail made the request before I could manage it."

She gestured to the nearby sofa. "I see Cook has added a setting for you. I do hope you will join me."

"I confess I had hoped we could talk, but if you are feeling too poorly I have no wish to disturb you." The dark circles under Lizzy's eyes stood out against her fair skin and she appeared a tinge green.

"I am not certain I will be an entertaining companion, but would welcome the company and the distraction." The girl placed the tray on the table in front of Lizzy. "I hope you do not object to preparing your own tea?"

"Not at all." Georgiana sat and set to work, not paying particular attention to Lizzy's and why it was different until a scent she had not smelled in some time wafted across to her. "Lizzy, is that ginger?"

Her sister poured her first cup, which was pale and made the odour more pronounced. "A bit of tea with ginger, yes." Lizzy moved the milk before Georgiana. "You are welcome to every last drop of that this morning. I cannot even stomach the idea of it at the moment." She added honey to her cup and relaxed into her seat, nibbling on a biscuit.

Georgiana picked up a biscuit and brought it to her nose, narrowing her eyes at Lizzy. "Cook's ginger biscuits and ginger in your tea—the last time you required these remedies was when you suspected you might be carrying William."

A soft smile appeared upon Lizzy's face as she placed her free hand upon her waist. "I have reason to hope I might be with child, but I can do no more than speculate at this time."

"So speculate!" She leaned forward and held the arms of her chair.

"I have felt unwell most mornings and certain foods," she glanced at the milk with a frown, "are not appetising and do not agree with me. My breasts are sore, and if I lay on my stomach, I feel as though I have a knot right here." She pointed to a place below her waist.

Georgiana clasped her hands together and squealed. "If you were not holding that tea, I would be hugging you!"

"Allow my stomach to settle, and you may embrace me as much as you wish."

"How is Fitzwilliam coping?" asked Georgiana with a giggle. He had been beside himself with worry when Lizzy was ill during the first months with William. Thus far, he had not been coddling her as he had before. "I believe I now understand more of this." She held up the letter. "I found your husband attempting to pen a response."

A small line formed between Lizzy's eyebrows. "This is to me from Mrs. Reynolds."

"Fitzwilliam wanted to help but was afraid of giving Mrs. Reynolds instructions you would find objectionable."

"He can be such a dear man, but he is well aware that I prefer to oversee the household matters myself." She scraped her teeth across her lip for a moment before giving Georgiana a sheepish grin. "I am afraid I became a mite capricious in my moods when I carried William. I became upset over the silliest things and cried for no good reason."

"Why do I remember none of this?"

"Because I never became moody while in your company. For some reason I cannot explain, I reserved all the anger and tears for Fitzwilliam. The poor man will walk on eggshells until this child is born just as he did with William."

"I have never witnessed you and Fitzwilliam having more than a tiff. You cannot have been too intemperate."

Lizzy laughed and shook her head. "I swore after the Netherfield Ball that I would be more reasonable, and as long as I am not with child, I do give your brother the opportunity to discuss any differences of opinion we might have."

"I never understood how you believed Fitzwilliam could conspire against your sister. If Mr. Bingley had been at liberty to court your sister, my brother would not have had an objection."

After Lizzy blew on her tea, took a sip, and swallowed, she watched Georgiana. "Do you really not understand?"

"No, Fitzwilliam is the best of men. You had to know that if you accepted his offer of courtship."

Lizzy broke off a bite of ginger biscuit. "Our misunderstanding at the Netherfield Ball had nothing to do with your brother's character, but fears I had yet to acknowledge."

"I could never imagine you afraid of anything," confided Georgiana. "You always appear so confident—so fearless."

"You met my mother. She never failed to tell me how much prettier Jane was than me or how Lydia was so much more agreeable. When I misunderstood Fitzwilliam's conversation with Mr. Bingley, I believed it confirmed my own worst fears—that your brother did not care for me as I did him. He was from a higher sphere, and I had no fortune or connections to tempt him. I loved him, but I did not believe he could love me."

"But he did," exclaimed Georgiana. "He was distraught when he returned to London."

"Which I learnt at your aunt and uncle's ball." She set her cup upon the saucer and rested it in her lap. "I was terrified that evening. As scared as I was of my own feelings, I knew I needed to face your brother and apologise, but I dreaded the encounter. I feared he would not forgive me."

"I cannot imagine—"

"Because you and I met after I decided to put aside what scared me so and take a chance on Fitzwilliam. I did not want to be hurt, but realised I would be heartbroken if your brother did not forgive me. I had to face my fears or lose the man I loved."

Georgiana stared into the dregs of her tea. She pretended all was well when Nathaniel told her he could not call today. He had no grand plans but to attend a meeting at the solicitors on business, yet she was put out. He had called daily since their trip to the Theatre Royale a fortnight ago. Was today's discontent because she missed his presence?

Was she in some ways the same as Lizzy? She had never believed she deserved Nathaniel or any man after Ramsgate, but if Nathaniel returned to Ireland, would she be heartbroken? The pain in her chest and the burning of her eyes at the idea of his departure answered her question more than the shivers and flutters he unknowingly caused.

"Georgiana?"

She started and disturbed the china in her hand, causing the cup to rattle precariously upon the saucer. "Forgive me. I cannot explain why, but I have been out of sorts today."

"Perhaps you are merely accustomed to Lord Sele's society and feel his loss since he has not called. He is here every day, either to ride Rotten Row or to play the pianoforte." A mischievous glint appeared in her eye. "I do wish Fitzwilliam would have learnt how to play. I never realised how attractive the accomplishment is in a man."

They both burst into giggles, but after a moment or two, Lizzy, without warning, stood and rushed for her dressing room. Now that Georgiana understood the nature of her sister's illness, she followed and dampened a towel in cool water, placing it on the back of Lizzy's neck as she knelt before the chamber pot.

Three deep breaths and exhales could be heard as Lizzy rocked back and forth upon her knees. "Forgive me." She swallowed and pulled the cloth to wipe her face. "I do not remember it being this bad with William, but I may have just forgotten."

"You have done nothing to require forgiveness." She dropped to her knees by Lizzy's side. "Has it passed or do you need more time?"

"It has passed."

Georgiana stood and assisted Lizzy to do the same. When they were once again ensconced in their chairs before the fire and sipping tea, Lizzy eyed Georgiana as though searching for something. "Do you wish to speak of Lord Sele?"

"Not particularly, no." Her finger studied the pattern upon the fabric beneath it. "I told Lady Lindsey of Ramsgate—not intentionally, of course."

Lizzy's eyebrows rose upon her forehead. "When was this?"

"The day Nathaniel and I happened upon Mrs. Younge in Hatchard's. Are you angry with me?"

"No," she replied, her tone puzzled. "Why would I be angry? You are an adult and though I am but acquainted with her, I doubt Lady Lindsey would break a confidence. Besides, it is your secret to keep or share, not mine."

"I did not intend to divulge as much as I did. She knew enough of Wickham's character to guess what occurred."

"I hope her acceptance brought you peace of mind."

She crossed her arms over her chest. "I confess it did."

Lizzy watched her while she chewed and swallowed a bite of her biscuit. "You are still worried about telling Lord Sele." The statement was not a question. She had become quite adept at reading Georgiana over the past few years.

"Of course, I am. How could I not be?"

"Because that man loves you, Georgiana. Not by halves, but with his entire being, and his affection is evident to all who care to notice. He will be pained, more for what you endured than what you have become. He will wish to kill Wickham, as did your brother and Richard, but he will not abandon you. I am certain of it."

Georgiana sat without speaking while Lizzy continued to nibble on her biscuits and sip her tea, giving her the chance to think. Lizzy was quite perceptive and thoughtful on those matters, which was one of the reasons she was so well suited to Fitzwilliam.

The clock chimed and Georgiana started. "Forgive me."

"You know well there is nothing to forgive." She placed her cup and saucer upon the tray. "I am feeling a little better, so I had best dress. Your brother promised William a ramble in Hyde Park, and I do hope to join them."

"Of course, you do. You love a walk in the outdoors as much as William, and I daresay the cool air, even London air, might do you some good."

Once Lizzy departed into her dressing room, Georgiana walked the family corridor without purpose. She could play her pianoforte—no, she had already made that attempt and it failed to tempt her, even now. She could read in the library—no, if music could not hold her attention, then neither would a novel. She blew out a noisy breath as she descended the stairs.

Jobbins passed, moving towards the door, and she paused. Had someone knocked? If so, she had not heard it. Not that it mattered. No one was to call for her, at least not today.

She began to head in the direction of the music room, but a low voice speaking to Jobbins gave her pause. Her body straightened, and she pivoted as Nathaniel handed off his great coat. Something within her chest jumped at the sight of him.

Before he took note of her presence, she watched as he kindly interacted with and thanked their aged butler. He was a handsome man, with his broad shoulders, dark eyes, and thick hair; however, it was the sincerity of his actions and expressions that rendered him even more attractive, if that was possible. Their eyes locked when he turned and her insides fluttered as though her stomach were made of a jelly.

Not a word was said as he strode forward, took her hand, and led her to the music room. The door had been left ajar, but the room was empty. She shivered, and he moved them closer to the fire, his eyes returning to hers as swiftly as they had left.

One of his hands continued to hold fast to hers, while the fingers of the other traced from her temple to her cheek. "Georgiana?"

She trembled from head to toe as she opened her mouth to speak, yet not a sound emerged. Her teeth wore at her lip and she covered his hand upon her cheek with her own.

He touched his forehead to hers, his shaky breathing more noticeable because of their intimate position. She had done all she could to resist him these past weeks. She had no desire to fight him or her heart any further.

His thumb grazed along her cheek as he leaned closer and brushed his lips against hers. Her eyes fluttered closed and a moment later he drew back. "Breathe."

"Pardon?"

"You were holding your breath," he whispered with a chuckle. "While some men might enjoy a lady swooning when they kiss them, I would prefer you did not." Her face warmed and she shifted to withdraw from his embrace, but he wrapped an arm about her waist, keeping her close. "Tell me, am I to request a courtship or make you the offer of my hand?"

She had difficulty holding his gaze and instead, looked lower to study his cravat. What did she want? Was she prepared to accept his proposal of marriage? His bent first finger to her chin brought her eyes back to his.

"Georgiana Darcy, will you allow me to court you?"

"Has that not been your primary occupation these past weeks?" she asked, her voice a little breathless.

"Yes, but you required time to consider the question I asked a moment ago. While I wish to call you my wife, a courtship brings me one step closer to what I desire most. I cannot be anything but overjoyed at your acceptance." His eyes searched hers. "Will you allow it—allow me to go to your brother?"

With only a brief moment of hesitation, she nodded, and a wide grin appeared upon his countenance as he took her into his arms. She should pull away, but she had no desire to.

Before she could react, he pressed another soft kiss to her lips, then her forehead. "I need to speak to your brother," he whispered.

When he shifted away, she grasped his sleeve. "There is something I must tell you."

He regarded her expression, his eyes tracing her face and the set of her shoulders. "I will not like what you have to say." It was a statement, definitely not a question.

"No, but I should not keep this from you any longer."

He stepped closer, cradled her face in his palms, and again brushed his lips between her eyebrows. "I understand. But might it still wait? I want to remember how happy you have made me. I promise to listen at the first available opportunity."

How could she deny him when it would indeed pain him? No, she had to tell him now before he went to her brother. "I fear what I need to say will cause you great upset, yet I feel I must not delay."

His forehead furrowed. "Yes, of course."

"Georgiana!" When Nathaniel and she jumped away from one another, they found Lydia and Mr. Hanson standing just inside the door. "I thought I heard voices! But why are you in here all alone?"

Chapter 17

February 6th 1817

I am being courted by Nathaniel Howard, Viscount Sele. The notion is still odd. I had hoped penning it thus would make my present circumstances more real, yet it has not. A part of me feels this a dream, and I fear I will awaken when the time comes to speak to Nathaniel of Ramsgate.

I was prepared to tell him before he sought out my brother, but Lydia's interruption prevented any further discourse. While in company with Mr. Hanson, I could not very well request more time alone with Nathaniel, and although I do not believe Mr. Hanson would gossip, it would be most improper to make such a disclosure with him present. Mrs. Annesley's entrance after Lydia only caused my resolution to crumble.

Fitzwilliam was pleased when Nathaniel approached him requesting a courtship and wasted no time in giving his permission. Lizzy's smile when she hugged me held a question I needed no translation to understand, and Lydia whispered that I should not retire before we talk this evening. At the moment, how I wish to avoid that discussion!

Georgiana flipped to a fresh page and picked up her pen.

February 9th 1817

A loud sound caused her to jump as the door to her dressing room opened and slammed shut.

"Georgiana Darcy, you have avoided me for the past three days and you will do so no longer!" Lydia came to a stop not far from the writing desk with her arms folded over her chest.

"I have not avoided your company. We live in the same house and see one another every day. I could not have hidden from you if I tried."

"You knew I wished to speak after you accepted Lord Sele's courtship, yet you have retired early each evening, not answered my knocks, and locked your door. I allowed you time before I forced myself into your presence, but you will answer my questions.

"I began exploring the servants' hallways two days ago. I found your dressing room this morning and thought there was no time like the present. How could you keep such matters to yourself?" Lydia exclaimed, stomping her foot.

She winced at the loud thud. "I do not force confessions from you. Can you not allow me to confide in you in my own time?"

Lydia watched her for a moment, her hands upon her hips. "No." She grabbed Georgiana's arm and hauled her from the chair. "Come, we will sit upon the sofa, and you will tell me what has made you finally agree to Lord Sele's courtship."

"Perhaps I felt the outcome inevitable and resisting became tiresome."

Lydia's eyes narrowed as she pressed Georgiana to sit and then studied her countenance. "When Mr. Hanson and I entered, you were in Lord Sele's arms. I do not believe for one moment he would force his attentions upon you, just as I know you would not accept them if you were decided against him."

"What is it you wish to know?"

"All that occurred before we entered." Lydia's tone was emphatic, as though Georgiana should be aware without asking.

"I am not as open as you are, Lydia. I cannot divulge intimate matters with such ease."

Lydia dropped with a huff beside her. "Well, he had to have some reason to broach the subject! What did you do?"

"I am not certain. Nathaniel arrived as I was wandering the house after speaking with Lizzy. I was restless all morning, but unable to reason why."

"Music did not soothe you?"

"No," she replied, shaking her head.

"Instead you had Lord Sele soothe you." Lydia burst into a fit of giggles.

"Lydia! I will not have this conversation with you if you insist upon being vulgar." She made to rise, but Lydia grabbed her wrist and pulled her back.

"Forgive me. I could not resist." Lydia drew her knees up and hugged them in front of her. "You must have given him some indication you would accept his offer?"

"If I did, it was unconsciously done. He looked at me and whisked me to the music room where we spoke."

"You are infuriating. How am I to enjoy this if you cannot tell me more?"

"What do you want me to say?" cried Georgiana. "I was relieved upon his arrival. The disquiet I had felt until that moment disappeared."

"You missed him." Lydia's finger pointed at Georgiana's chest in an annoying fashion. "Finally! *You* missed him!"

"Possibly."

"You did, but you do not want to admit it." With a suspicious eye, Lydia leaned away. "So, he recognised your feelings had grown, he rushed you to the music room. Did he kiss you?"

Her cheeks were warm, but her ears were burning as Lydia clapped her hands together and laughed. "Ha! I knew it!"

"Lydia—"

"I do not mean to embarrass you. You must know how pleased I am. I have hoped you would see his worth and how handsome he is." The last was added on almost as an afterthought, though it was obvious it was not. Lydia was incorrigible.

"I still must speak with him on matters of which he should be made aware. I intended to before he went to Fitzwilliam, but had not the chance."

"Do you mean your dreams?"

Georgiana stared at her hands in her lap as her fingers fiddled with one another. "Yes, but more what caused them."

"You mean who, do you not?"

Her head jolted, and she looked hard at Lydia. "Why do you ask?"

"When you have had your nightmares, you have spoken in your sleep," confessed Lydia, taking her hand. "I am fairly certain of what transpired. I have been for a while now, but you never wished to speak of it after that one time, so I did not press you."

She adjusted the way she was seated and attempted to clear her throat. "What do you think you know?"

"That George Wickham forced himself upon you."

Georgiana closed her eyes. Lydia was indeed aware, and since they had not slept in the same room for a while, had known for some time.

Lydia squeezed Georgiana's hand to get her attention. "I have heard rumours of such happening, so it was not difficult after witnessing several of your dreams. I needed only to piece together the bits to discover the truth. I require no details and I do not expect you to tell me of what occurred unless you wish to speak of it. What I would like to know is why you are going to tell Lord Sele? What if he changes his mind and ends your courtship?"

"Lydia!" she exclaimed. "I will not lie to him. He deserves to know the truth."

"You are not lying. You are merely omitting what he has no need to know."

Shaking her head, Georgiana held out her hands in front of her. "Enough! I cannot conceal something of this sort. Do not attempt to persuade me further. Besides, he knows I wish to speak to him, but we have not had the opportunity. While Mrs. Annesley is aware, I would prefer privacy for a personal disclosure."

"Well, I cannot argue with you, but if he does indeed flee, I shall be a willing ear."

With Lydia's lack of understanding, she could not imagine seeking her for comfort. "I hope to tell him soon. If all else fails and we cannot find a private moment, I can request it of Fitzwilliam. He will understand. With the dinner at Audley House and the arrival of Mr. Bingley and Anne, we have been too much in company."

Lydia rolled her eyes. "I still cannot fathom how they were delayed so by Miss Bingley."

"You mean Mrs. Davis," clarified Georgiana.

She sucked air between her teeth with a grimace. "Can you imagine the tantrum she threw at the altar?"

"How much did Lizzy tell you?"

Lydia leaned closer. "That Miss Bingley found herself in the family way, and Mr. Bingley was forced to marry her off as swiftly as possible."

After she laughed ruefully, Georgiana settled against the back of the sofa. "Miss Bingley always was avaricious, and I suppose she hoped allowing an earl his way would promote her in some fashion. When Mr. Bingley confronted her, she apparently had grand assumptions of what she expected from the earl, but from what Fitzwilliam has said, the earl already had a mistress in town and had no intention of replacing her. In fact, when he suspected Miss Bingley was with child, he severed all ties with her."

"And she became wed to a farmer," finished Lydia, shaking her head. "I hope her husband was pleased with her fortune, since she will not be pleased with her new situation."

"No, Mr. Bingley told Fitzwilliam that he had to stand at Miss Bingley's side so she would recite her vows. She attempted to refuse, but Mr. Bingley threatened to send her to some remote estate in Scotland. I do not know who he would have employed for her companion as no one would take the position any longer. Miss Bingley ran them all off."

Lydia swallowed with a grimace. "Could you imagine being that woman's companion, though? I knew her a little, and I doubt I could manage for more than a day."

"No, I would never wish such a position on anyone." A rapping at the outer door prompted them to turn. "Enter!"

One of the younger maids bustled inside. "I beg your pardon, but Mrs. Darcy wanted me to inform you that Mr. and Mrs. Bingley are in the drawing room with their children."

"Thank you," replied Georgiana as she and Lydia rose and made their way down the stairs where they began to hear the chatter and din that accompanies a group of children. When they entered, Lydia joined William and the Bingleys' boys, Lewis and Peter, upon the floor playing a sort of ninepins with their fathers while Anne held a babbling baby Catherine on her lap as she spoke with Lizzy.

Georgiana kissed Anne's cheek and held out her arms for the baby. "May I?"

"Of course." A wiggling Catherine was passed into Georgiana's arms as Anne relaxed back into her chair. "After the struggle I have had to keep her from the boys' game, I welcome the respite. Thank you."

"You have no need to thank me for something I am happy to do." Catherine regarded Georgiana with a wary eye for but a second before she giggled. "What do you find humorous, little one?" Her little cousin wiggled her legs in an attempt to slither down Georgiana's body, but she held her firm. "Where are you going?"

They walked to the window and Georgiana pointed at various things in the garden as Catherine watched. Why did all babies like the outdoors? When William was little she could entertain him for a quarter hour, at least, by merely standing before a window. Now, the task was not so simple. He desired more than the birds or the clouds to occupy him.

"Lord Sele," Jobbins announced in the partially open door. He pushed it further open, and Nathaniel entered. Once Lizzy introduced him, he made his way to her side.

"I did not realize you would have guests this morning. Your butler never said a word when I arrived."

Georgiana bounced Catherine and smiled while the baby babbled happily. "We are courting. If we wed, the Bingleys will be family—as will my aunt Lady Catherine. Besides, your parents were considered family by mine, which makes us as good as related."

He laughed and lifted his eyebrows. "Though not too closely, thank goodness."

After hoisting the baby up so they were face to face, she pointed to Nathaniel. "What do you think, Catherine? Should you like to call him cousin?"

Catherine let out a string of babbles, pressed her chubby hands to each of Georgiana's cheeks, and planted a very wet, open-mouthed kiss to Georgiana's lips. The deep rumble of Nathaniel's chuckles came from beside her as Georgiana allowed Catherine to finish her messy gesture of affection and clap.

She took the handkerchief Nathaniel held before her and wiped her face. "She was not kissing a few months ago when the Bingleys visited Pemberley."

"Your shocked expression was beyond words," grinned Nathaniel. He glanced about the room, then with a light finger, shifted a curl from her face. "You are a doting aunt. How will you enjoy being a mother?"

Something inside her gave a jolt. She had never allowed herself to consider the possibility of children of her own. Having sworn off marriage, it was simpler to convince herself she would never have more than her nieces and nephews to spoil. Now, imagining a sweet face with Nathaniel's dark eyes and hair was not so difficult.

"I suppose I will be quite happy."

"You suppose?" He held out his hand and allowed Catherine to hit his palm. "It is obvious you adore William, and you appear content with this little one in your arms."

"How can I not be? Babies are innocent and helpless and easy to love."

His expression shifted as his face tilted and he appraised her with more care. "You never intended to marry, so you never considered the experience of having a child."

"If I carried any hope of such an eventuality, I would be disappointed."

"We never did speak of what you wished to tell me."

She pressed a kiss to Catherine's wispy hair. "No, I wish for a moment to ourselves for such a talk. If we cannot happen upon one, then we can speak to Fitzwilliam. If he understands why, he might indulge us."

"With your guests, today would not suit," he observed, as William cheered at his ball knocking over the last of the pins.

"No, but we will find a way. I am uncomfortable leaving this unsaid for too long."

February 12ᵗʰ 1817

Why is it when I require a moment without guests, we are inundated with them? Not a day goes by that someone does not visit—Lord and Lady Audley, the Bingleys, Aunt and Uncle Fitzwilliam, Richard and Julia, Nathaniel's parents, not to mention callers! We cannot escape them to have a quiet moment. I spoke to Fitzwilliam. Though he understands the necessity of the conversation, he will not allow it with so many family and friends about. I do agree with him, but on most days, the drawing room is full or we are paying calls.

I know I should not be so unfair. None of our family are aware that I need to speak to Nathaniel. As far as they are concerned, I am talking to him when he calls, which is nearly every day when he becomes a part of the rabble. I must admit I have missed the Bingleys and the Audleys, especially the children. They grow and change with a swiftness I cannot fathom. They are already all taller than when they visited Pemberley several months ago.

We had a large family party at services yesterday, and Nathaniel attended with us. Lady Lindsey enjoyed the gimlet eyes and hateful stares directed our way as a result. Miss Thorpe and Lady Harriet, who we met in the hat shop not long after our arrival, were present, and after whispering and gawking at us through nigh on the entire service, they approached as we neared the door to speak to Lady Lindsey. I shall never forget the roll of her eyes when those two girls looked to one

one another for a moment. I suppose they never forgave Nathaniel for his defence of me and now have reason to despise me for catching his notice. Not that I care. He would not have spared them a glance even if I were not the object of his affections.

The object of his affections? I still find the notion of this to be strange in every way. I, who swore I would never marry and would teach my nieces to embroider cushions and play the pianoforte, am being courted by a gentleman, and not just any gentleman, but Nathaniel. I now wake every morning and anticipate the moment he enters this house. I take comfort in his steady presence when he is at my side. When did I become so dependent upon his presence? It seems one moment I was fighting to resist him and the next his willing subject. I exaggerate, but I can think of no other words to describe this alteration in myself.

Lord and Lady Lindsey are to plan our next outing to the theatre. Lizzy, Lydia, and I will stop at the draper's on the morrow before our appointment at the modiste for new gowns. As much as I have avoided blue since our arrival in town, I shall seek a fabric in that colour, though perhaps a different shade to that preferred by my aunt. Lord! But I am hopeless!

Chapter 18

"Lizzy?" Georgiana looked around the breakfast parlour and then down the corridor. "I had not expected you down so early—and without Fitzwilliam."

"I am as at a loss as you are." She sipped her tea and dabbed her mouth with her napkin. "I awoke, feeling better than I have in the last se'nnight to find Fitzwilliam missing. Jobbins has told me he departed early this morning, but cannot tell me where or why. I went to the nursery, helped William dress, played with him, and sat at the table while he ate his meal. Now, Mrs. Wynn is reading him a story, and I am eating my own breakfast, on St. Valentine's Day, alone." She bit her bottom lip with worried eyes. "Could he have forgotten?"

"I find it unlikely. He has never failed to consider you—spoil you, really—on this day. I would not fret about it. I am confident he will return soon."

"He has always planned a special meal in the morning, but with my queasy stomach most days, I suppose he could not lest I become sick."

Georgiana took a plate and helped herself from the sideboard before sitting across from Lizzy. "That would be certain to spoil the day."

One side of Lizzy's lips curved upwards and her eyebrow rose with it. "Enough of my woes, will Lord Sele be calling?"

She took to cutting her bacon as though it were the most important task of the day. "He indicated he would."

"Have you a gift planned?"

"I have," she confessed, "but I am not sure if he will like it."

Lizzy picked up her toast, but before she took a bite, a wicked gleam lit her eye. "Oh, I wager you could purchase him the most unattractive item you could find, and he would adore it merely because it came from you."

Her sister's response was not surprising. How Lizzy had always loved to tease! Georgiana schooled her features as best she could. "I shall have to test your theory some time, but I will require your aid in locating a suitably ugly purchase."

The only response to her impertinence was a tinkling laugh before they continued to eat, discussing their shopping from the day prior until Jobbins entered almost a half-hour later. "I beg your pardon, Mrs. Darcy, Miss Darcy, but Lord Sele has arrived. He is in the blue drawing room."

"Thank you," she replied as she made to rise. As both had been finished for a while, Lizzy followed and joined them as Nathaniel kissed the back of Georgiana's hand. "Good morning." He looked to Lizzy. "Good morning, Mrs. Darcy. I hope you are well." Nathaniel was aware Lizzy had been indisposed on several occasions over the last few weeks, though he was not yet aware of the reason why.

"I am quite well, thank you."

"Where is my lovely wife?" came Fitzwilliam's booming voice from the hall. Lizzy began to laugh as the strident tones of his boots on the tile of the entry carried into the drawing room. "Do not trouble yourself, Jobbins. I can hear her laughter." Not a second passed before he appeared in the doorway, a bundle of red roses in one hand and several parcels in the other. "There is my beautiful bride."

"I have not been a bride in years, you silly man!" she exclaimed. He swept forward and pressed a loud kiss to her lips.

"Regardless of how much time passes, you will always be my bride." He peered over to where Georgiana stood with Nathaniel. "You must forgive me, Sele, but I have no desire to be proper today."

Georgiana laughed and crossed her arms over her chest. "Fitzwilliam, you have never been entirely proper. You often hold Lizzy's hand and kiss her cheek before me and other members of the family. I am amazed you have not yet forgotten yourself in public."

A wide grin adorned Nathaniel's face while he watched the scene before him. "Have no fear. I am accustomed to such inappropriate displays from my parents. You will not shock me."

Fitzwilliam handed Lizzy the roses and the first parcel. "For you, my dear."

She untied the string and pulled the paper open to reveal a wooden box, which could only contain jewellery. "I have no need for more jewels. I hope you did not spend too much." With shaky fingers, she opened the lid to reveal a stunning ruby and diamond necklace. "Fitzwilliam!" she gasped.

"Before you scold me for what you believe to be a great expense, allow me to explain." She nodded as she gaped. "When I showed you the Darcy jewels, you commented that two of the necklaces were rather heavy and not to your tastes. Do you remember?"

A small line formed between Lizzy's eyebrows. "Yes, of course." Her eyes widened. "Are you saying this was made from those pieces?"

"From both sets would be more correct. Between the earrings, the bracelets, and both necklaces, the jeweller made this. I thought it more suited to you and your tastes."

"It is exquisite."

Her brother beamed and passed the second and smaller parcel to her.

"Then, you should open this as well."

Lizzy placed the necklace on a nearby table as she took the next gift. "Was the choker not enough?" He smiled at her teasing while she opened the second box, which contained ear-drops and a bracelet to match. "Apparently not," she mumbled, touching her finger to one small rosebud of a single ruby with diamonds that alternated between larger rubies surrounded by another ring of diamonds. The ear-drops were thankfully the rosebuds, so not so large as to weigh down the ears. Lizzy refused to wear the larger, more ornate ear-drops from the Darcy collection.

Fitzwilliam leaned forward and down to catch his wife's eye. "You will wear them when we next attend the theatre or a ball, will you not?"

"Of course." Lizzy placed her hand to Fitzwilliam's cheek. "I would not dream of wearing another." Lizzy started, as though remembering others were in the room. "Georgiana, have you seen them?"

Georgiana stepped forward to get a better look. "My brother has excellent taste."

"That he does." Lizzy closed the box and gathered her gifts. "My present for you is in my rooms, and I should not leave these here." With a look between Georgiana and Nathaniel, she paused. "If you will excuse us, we will call for Mrs. Annesley to chaperon."

"I need to fetch something from my chambers. If you do not object?" she asked Nathaniel.

After a quick shake of his head, Georgiana hastened to her rooms and pulled two small packages from her dressing table. It was not much, but what would he like more? Gifts on St. Valentine's Day were not supposed to be grand, on the contrary, they were typically nothing of consequence—tokens, really.

When she returned, Mrs. Annesley sat reading a book, by the fire, but Nathaniel stood near the sofa, holding a small box.

"What is this?" she asked, pointing to what was in his hand.

"Perhaps you should open it and discover for yourself?"

His cocky smile prompted a sidelong glance. "I am not certain I should."

He grabbed her hand and pulled her to sit beside him. Once the parcel was held in her palm, he gazed at her expectantly. It was not the right size or shape for jewels. Thankfully, he had not followed Fitzwilliam's lead. She lifted it. It was not heavy, but when it tilted, a faint knock could be heard from inside. What could it be?

Georgiana lifted the lid on the little wooden box and stared at the metal instrument inside. He gave her a key? "I do not understand."

"When I was a boy, my parents took me to Italy for a short time. In Padua, it is a tradition to give St. Valentine's keys as an invitation to unlock the giver's heart."

She looked from the white metal key to Nathaniel. "So you are inviting me to unlock your heart?" His words of affection were always well spoken, but this gesture was beyond what she expected. Wait a minute! "Nathaniel? When, did you purchase this?"

"I bought your key in Padua when I was fourteen," he replied with steadily reddening cheeks.

The metal was cold when she fingered the teeth that did not resemble those on the keys within English houses. He bought it when he was fourteen? How did she have no concept of his devotion until recently? When she glanced in his direction, his shoulders were tense and not at all the relaxed posture he usually bore.

"Forgive me." She closed her fingers around the keepsake and held it tight. "I thought you might have a trinket of some sort, but this . . ." She swallowed and gripped the key tighter. "This is unlike anything I imagined. You have said you loved me for as long as you can remember, but I never took those statements to be serious until now."

He relaxed and took her hand. "If you had asked me at the time, I doubt I would have called it love. I desired your attention, and I was determined we would marry one day. My father bought a key for my mother, so I bought a key for you. My feelings grew more and more with time, but you were still too young when I graduated Oxford, so I went to Ireland to manage our property there, only returning for Christmas each year until I knew if you were to have your first season."

His fingers entwined with hers as his soft voice made her insides quiver. "The more time we spend together only confirms my feelings, and I become more determined to have you as my wife."

Georgiana placed the key in its box and smiled. "Thank you, I shall treasure it."

He laughed and nudged her with his shoulder. "You do not think that is my only gift, do you?"

"The key is more than sufficient, Nathaniel. I am not certain it would be appropriate for you to give me more."

After reaching around, he returned with a much larger box and placed it in her lap. "Then, consider this as my returning what rightfully belongs to you."

"I do not understand," she muttered in a bewildered tone. "What could you have of mine?"

When the fabric protecting the mysterious item was shifted away, she gasped and pressed her hands to her chest. "I cannot believe you kept her!" She lifted the battered doll while Nathaniel removed the package from her lap. "It is

Matilda," she explained, holding her old friend so Mrs. Annesley could see.

Her companion nodded with a knowing smile before returning to her book. Georgiana gaped in amazement at her beloved long lost toy. "I never dreamt I would see her again." Before she gave it much consideration, she threw her arms, which still held Matilda, around Nathaniel's neck. "Thank you for Matilda and my key."

His hands barely touched her back when Mrs. Annesley cleared her throat and they withdrew. Georgiana's arms were rather empty without him. Did he feel the same? His feelings were of a longer duration than hers. Could he feel her absence more than she did his?

"This is the last. I promise." He held a small bouquet of pink Camellias, which she took as she smiled.

"You long for me?"

His ears pinked, and he gave a devastating grin. "I was not sure if you would be familiar with the language of flowers. I should have known you would."

"Give me one moment." She hopped from the sofa and stopped the first maid she found, requesting the flowers be put in water and placed upon her dressing table. Upon her return, Nathaniel watched her with a furrowed brow. "I wanted them brought to my chambers. If Lydia or Lizzy see those, I shall never hear the end of their teasing."

"Perhaps Mr. Hanson will purchase a bouquet equally embarrassing for Miss Bennet?"

"I find it unlikely Lydia would be flustered. When I first made her acquaintance, she was not as she is now; she was brash and headstrong. Her father even called her and her sisters, Kitty and Mary, three of the silliest girls in England. I have yet to witness Lydia become mortified. She blushes at times when speaking with Mr. Hanson, but it is not the same."

"No, it is not."

She stroked the fine, sprigged muslin of Matilda's handmade gown, sewn with her mother's own fingers. He saved her all this time! His hand covered her free one where it rested upon the sofa.

"I remember when my mother made her gown," she confessed. "I had one with the same fabric, and she had requested the spare materials to sew one for my doll."

"I apologise for taking her. I was young and should never have done it."

When she looked, his eyebrows were shifted down a fraction and his mien was serious. He was truly contrite. The behaviour of neither, if strictly examined, was irreproachable. They had been children, and headstrong ones at that. "I should have been more polite. You incited my ire like none of my acquaintance. I became intolerant as a result. I hope I have learnt to correct my temper by now."

"I have never been the most patient of beings, and I remember being quite persistent. I am sure I deserved more than my share of your fury."

"You are still persistent," she chuckled, "but I am not in a mind to fault you for it."

He did not rise, but gave a mock bow. "Why thank you."

She took her small packages from where she had set them beside her. "I am afraid it is not as thoughtful as yours, but I do hope you will like it."

He pulled the string and opened the lid. When the miniature was free of the fabric, he did not say a word. He just stared.

"If you do not like it—"

"No, I . . ." He cleared his throat and blinked. "I was merely taken aback by the expression in your eyes. You were not as content with your life as you are now."

"The likeness was taken in the year after Fitzwilliam and Lizzy's marriage. I had a troubled time in August of the year prior, which haunted me for a time—still does once in a while."

"Is this what you wish to discuss?"

Georgiana nodded and glanced to Mrs. Annesley. "She knows, but to tell you in her presence would be awkward at best."

"When the time is right, you will tell me. I know you will. You will also see that no matter the secret, I will remain by your side."

Her vision clouded, and she blinked several times. "Do you not like the miniature, then?"

"Forgive me," he begged. "I had not expected such a treasure and found myself drawn to examine each detail. I should have thanked you sooner."

"To be honest, the portraitist who was commissioned to paint this insisted I required more than one. Fitzwilliam and Lizzy wanted a miniature for a cabinet at Pemberley, but the artist was adamant I would need one for a fortunate suitor, as he put it, when I came out. Lizzy indulged him rather than argue." She held out her hand. "Do you have your pocket watch?"

His forehead crinkled as he pulled it from his pocket and placed it in her palm. He then watched as she opened the cover, and fit the small, thin piece of porcelain into the lid, the confusion upon his face clearing. "I must learn the name of this artist, so I might have him paint a new one in the future."

"I must see if it fits first. He did indicate that some watches would not accommodate it, and yours might be one."

With a frown, he took both the portrait and his watch. "Then, we shall have to make a trip to Bond Street to find a watch that does." He picked up the cloth used to protect the fragile portrait, and spread it across his leg. "Georgiana, is this a handkerchief?"

"Yes, I embroidered two, one for each gift. They are no more than your initials. I could not imagine you desiring flowers."

He pulled the string from the second of the handkerchiefs and startled when a ribbon and her embroidery scissors were revealed.

"I also thought you might wish for a lock of my hair," she almost whispered. "I figured you would desire to choose the token yourself, rather than me doing so."

His lips parted to display his full smile. "I would indeed." He slid closer, his fingers separating the curls at the nape of her neck. When one was cradled in his hand, he leaned forward to meet her eye. "May I?"

"Of course," she replied. A series of light tugs indicated he was binding it with the ribbon before the snip of her scissors reached her ears.

He wrapped his token with her miniature, and hid them away in his coat pocket. When his hand grasped hers once more, the corners of his lips were slightly turned upwards giving him the appearance of contentment. "Thank you. I shall treasure these more since you bestowed them upon me freely rather than me requesting them of you."

"I would not have denied you."

"No, but you considered what would be significant to me without extravagance. I cannot tell you what that means to me."

"Then I am pleased." The words were whispered, but he heard them. His eyes held hers and she could not look away. Was he coming closer? Mrs. Annesley coughed and Nathaniel straightened and ran his fingers through his hair.

She needed to tell him of Ramsgate, and soon!

February 14th 1817

I admit to being uncertain of what this day would hold. I can never predict Nathaniel's words or his actions, and today was no different. He said the miniature, the lock of hair, and the handkerchiefs were significant to him, yet his gifts were more heartfelt.

Before this journey to London, I could not have mentioned a cordial conversation between us because I remembered our arguments and disagreements more: though today, we spoke of when he and Lord Lindsey came to Pemberley after the death of my father.

Nathaniel was not his usual self, but more respectful and subdued during that visit. We did not see much of one another, but I now recall several discussions we had on books and horses. Most of these were during dinner or in the drawing room with Fitzwilliam, but were instances I had long forgotten. Why did I choose to remember nothing but his insufferable behaviour? I suppose it was because that visit was but once, and he was a pest for the remainder of our acquaintance.

I am troubled by the delay in telling him of Ramsgate. He promises constancy despite knowing I have information of importance to reveal, but am I incorrect in believing we require privacy for such an emotional confession? I can only hope I am correct in hoping for a quiet moment, and that he shall understand.

Chapter 19

Lucy placed the last of the pearl hairpins and stepped back, her hands held out before her. "I think I have managed it, miss."

Georgiana picked up the *Belle Assemblée* on her dressing table while her maid looked over her shoulder, comparing her hair to one of the tamer styles illustrated. "It is close, but I do not give a whit about the differences. I prefer what you have done."

A grin spread across Lucy's face. "Thank you, miss. 'Tis such a pretty gown, and I believe this hair suits you more than the hat on the pattern."

She turned her head to the side and traced her reflection. The vivid, deep blue ribbon twined around her head and the tiny pearl hairpins placed here and there through the curls were definitely an improvement over the feathered monstrosity on the fashion plate! When she stood and shifted to the long mirror, Lucy followed, tugging and straightening the skirt and the tucked, short sleeves.

The gown was not a style she would normally choose, but she thought it more mature than the patterns she usually favoured. "Lucy, do you think he will like it?"

"He would be a fool if he did not," her maid stated definitively, "and I have never thought of Lord Sele as a fool."

She bit her lip as she appraised her new purchase. The gown she had Madame prepare for this evening was a rich, dark blue, the colour of lapis, with a striking white adornment that fit similarly to stays, but over the bodice. The piece fastened in the back, and appeared to stretch and button in the front, leaving parts of the blue underdress exposed. Tiny pearls trimmed the bodice and her sleeves, purloined from her mother's old gowns. Lizzy had been kind enough to save them when she sorted through the trunks hidden away in the attics. The gowns were in such disrepair they were not salvageable, but tiny pearls and various other adornments were saved in order to be used again.

She started at a knock upon the door. "Yes?"

In the mirror, she saw Lizzy enter and smile. "Your brother will not appreciate that gown. You appear very much a grown lady. While he may have granted this courtship with apparent ease, I hope you know he will be loath to part with you when the time comes."

"I am in no great hurry to wed," she confessed. "I am content with

Nathaniel's courtship." A light giggle from Lizzy prompted her to turn and see Lucy's grin. "Do you believe me to say other than what I feel?"

"I beg your pardon, miss, but I should have departed upon Mrs. Darcy's arrival." She dropped a curtsey and made a swift exit.

"Lucy and I have known one another long enough for her to speak her mind. Why would she not simply tell me?"

"Because though you may be happy with the progression of your courtship now," explained Lizzy. "Once you discover you are prepared to marry, your mood shall alter in but a moment."

Georgiana shook her head while she gathered her reticule and gloves. "I require more time than other ladies."

"Once decided, the heart is impatient. You might be surprised at how swiftly your desires change."

Lizzy was rarely mistaken, yet Georgiana could not imagine wanting to rush before the altar. So much was still unsettled. She could not be certain of herself or Nathaniel at the moment, despite his fervent assurances to the contrary.

"Have you forgotten your cape?" asked Georgiana in an attempt to change the subject. "Lucy claims the weather is cold and damp this evening."

"You know Phoebe will bring it down as Lucy will do yours." Lizzy looped her arm through hers. "We should make our way to the drawing room. I daresay Lord Sele will arrive before long, and we do not want to keep him waiting."

"You are incorrigible."

"No, I am delighted you have found a man worthy of you, and that you have chosen to embrace a future with him." Georgiana opened her mouth to speak, but Lizzy held up a hand. "I know your future is hardly set in stone, yet you must admit it is as good as settled."

"I suppose," she conceded. "I have thought more of the eventuality as of late."

"I should think it strange if you had not." Lizzy tilted her head and studied her. "You appear much more comfortable in his presence and with his expectations than you were." They proceeded down the stairs, and upon entering the drawing room, Fitzwilliam stood as did Nathaniel, who gave the sudden appearance of a fish out of water.

Fitzwilliam stepped forward and kissed his wife's hand. "You are lovely, Elizabeth." When Nathaniel did not behave similarly, Fitzwilliam glanced back, rolled his eyes, and looked at Georgiana. "If what she wears elicits that reaction, I do not like it. Go change."

A giggle bubbled from Lizzy as Georgiana hit her brother in the arm with her fan. "Hush! I shall not change. I adore this gown and Nathaniel's expression was precisely my object when I selected the pattern."

"You wished to make him a dreadful bore, then."

"Fitzwilliam!" exclaimed Lizzy and Georgiana simultaneously.

Nathaniel shook himself from his insensibility. "If my opinion matters, I think you look splendid."

"The style is too mature." None in the room could deny the petulant tone in her brother's voice. He was looking to find fault, now. "And 'tis not appropriate for the theatre."

She scoffed. "According to the modiste, the pattern is an 'opera gown,' so perfectly suitable."

Richard and Julia were shown in by Jobbins. When all had greeted one another, Richard made a detailed study of her new blue silk. "Darcy, do you not find this too mature for one of her age?" He made motions around his chest area. "Too much protrudes."

All three ladies gasped and Julia elbowed him in the ribs. "Lizzy and I both approved her choice when she made the order, so are you implying we allowed her to make an inappropriate selection?"

"You could not have known how it would appear once on—"

"We viewed the gown at her last fitting," interjected Lizzy, peering back and forth between the two men. "Madame Guiard just received that pattern a few days before our initial appointment and set it aside with Georgiana in mind, not making it available to her other customers until after tonight. Even she was confident Georgiana would be well-received in such a gown."

Lydia entered with a smile. "Are we not to depart soon? I do not want Mr. Hanson to be forced to wait for our arrival."

The sound of horses and the Darcy coach came from the front of the house. "That should be our carriage," announced Georgiana, taking Nathaniel's arm. "We may as well proceed to the theatre. I shall go as I am."

With a squeeze to Nathaniel's bicep, he led her to the front where Lucy helped her don her cape, and then, out to the equipage where he handed her inside. He took the seat across from her and grinned. "Well done. I would wager your sister and Mrs. Fitzwilliam are now attempting to smooth your brother's and your cousin's ruffled feathers."

"Fitzwilliam does not often treat me like a child, but I cannot abide when he does. He forgets at times that I am twenty and no longer an impressionable fifteen."

"You are much like a daughter to him. I believe were your father here, he would behave in much the same fashion."

She lifted one shoulder. "Perhaps, but I would not tolerate such treatment from him either."

Nathaniel grinned. "No, I do not suppose you would." After a quick glance at the front door of the house, Nathaniel leaned forward and took her hand.

"What are you about?"

The corners of his lips curved further. "I should think it obvious. I am taking liberties I could not when your brother was present."

His fingertips traced up her arm to the small bit of uncovered skin between her long gloves and her sleeves. When flesh met flesh, she shivered while her eyes held his. "Fitzwilliam and Richard could come at any moment. Someone might see you." After another peek outside, he shifted beside her.

His feather-light touch to her neck was a shock, and though she tried, not a word would come from her lips. His thumb grazed her jawline as he bent down, his warm breath fanning against her cheek, creating gooseflesh in its wake, and her eyes fluttered closed. When his lips pressed ever so softly against hers, she held her breath.

Suddenly he was gone, and with a sizeable exhale, she looked around her. Voices floated into the carriage while he settled back in his place across from her and the laughter and speaking grew louder just before the remainder of their party began to enter.

Lizzy's pesky eyebrow sat high upon her forehead as she took her seat beside Georgiana, whose face warmed while she took a sudden interest in her hands upon her lap. This was ridiculous!

She turned to Fitzwilliam. She would not look at Nathaniel. "You have yet to tell me what play we are to see. I do not know why it has been such a well-guarded secret, but you have no further reason to withhold the information."

"The selection of the play was Sele's," revealed her brother with a grin, as they began to move. "He wished it to be a surprise, which is why you were not told."

Her eyes found Nathaniel's and her cheeks and ears burned. Why did he seem so unaffected? The only hint of his bold manoeuver was a wide grin, his dimples on full display.

"Would you care to know?" His inordinately pleased expression never faltered, but remained fixed in the most annoying fashion.

"If you would be so kind as to tell me." Fitzwilliam's shaking shoulders were difficult to miss in the corner of her eye. "Brother, you take too much delight in his attempts to vex me."

"Yet you allow him to have his success," he laughed.

"You should practice more of the vaunted Darcy reserve," said Lizzy in a teasing tone, "then he might believe he has no effect on you at all. He might even believe you merely look to find fault." Though Lizzy leaned in as she would when sharing a confidence, her voice was not hushed, and discernible to the entirety of their party.

Her brother struck his walking stick upon the floor. "Hardly charitable!"

"Be careful, Darce. You begin to resemble Lady Catherine with that manoeuver." Richard's crooked smile overspread his face. "You are well aware you are a right prat in company. I am still amazed you found a lady to tolerate your boorish behaviour."

Nathaniel's gaze heated her cheek while she watched her family's antics. His presence could not be forgotten as easily as one might misplace a pair of gloves or a reticule. He filled the room as he did her head, and her surroundings were too warm as it was. Fitzwilliam's coach easily fit six people, but with Lydia, their party numbered seven, leaving the ladies packed together uncomfortably to accommodate them all.

Lydia appeared when she bent forward to speak around Julia. "Well? Why are you not asking him again?"

"Thank you. I had not thought to do so before now." Georgiana spoke through her teeth as she glared at Lydia. Georgiana would not embarrass her so before Mr. Hanson, so why did Lydia insist on embarrassing her before Nathaniel?

"*Much Ado About Nothing*," he said softly.

"Pardon?" Her head turned swiftly to face him as Lizzy asked Julia a question, distracting the remainder of their party. How she adored her sister at that moment!

"We are to see *Much Ado About Nothing*. You said your preference is for Shakespeare's comedies, and I believe this play is a favourite of yours."

"It is. I appreciate your thoughtfulness."

"'Tis not thoughtfulness. I have my reasons." He surely wanted to earn her favour, though he had already done so. Gestures such as this were hardly necessary. As the equipage moved through the streets of London, she listened to the talk around her until the theatre appeared through the windows.

When the door opened, Nathaniel handed her down from the carriage, wrapped her arm about his, and led her inside behind Fitzwilliam and Lizzy. "You are too quiet. What has your mind so occupied?"

She watched the crowd around her because she could not hold his eye without blushing or behaving like a silly young girl. "You do too much."

"In what manner?"

"You bring me flowers oft times when you call, you arrange for us to see one of my favourite plays. You need not go to such lengths to prove yourself to me." The muscles of his arm tensed under her hand, and she looked away so as not to see the disappointment that was sure to be evident on his countenance.

When they reached the entrance to their box, Fitzwilliam and Lizzy entered and Nathaniel halted, turning to face her. Richard stopped beside them with Julia on one arm and Lydia on his other side. "Sele?"

"I only require a moment. We will follow." Nathaniel's tone was not angry or frustrated but disheartened, and left a dreadful hole in her heart. She should have kept her thoughts to herself. Lizzy would certainly have told her as much, yet no more than his company was required. He had to see that, did he not?

Richard glanced in her direction, so she gave a nod. When they disappeared into the box, Nathaniel ran his hand through his hair and exhaled heavily.

"I do not bring you flowers or do what I have tonight for gratitude or to prove myself to you. I confess my reasons are purely selfish."

"Nathaniel—" she attempted to interject, but he only continued.

"Your eyes light up—especially when I bring you lilies from the hothouse—you smile so peacefully when I play the pianoforte, and your surprised expression when you learnt of the play tonight are my true motivations. I need nothing more than to bring you happiness to make me content. So, Georgiana Darcy, I intend to spoil you for the rest of our lives whether you object or not. Do you understand?"

"I only meant that I do not require gifts and trinkets to enjoy your company. I do not require such gestures because I care for you as it is."

He cocked his head a little to the side. "You do not wish to care for me more?"

"That's not what I mean, you silly man, as you are well aware!" She attempted to swat his arm, but he grasped her hand in his and brought it to his lips, making her legs tremble. "I require no more than your society."

"Be that as it may, become accustomed to my extravagance."

"I would hardly call you extravagant."

"No, probably not," he conceded, "yet you behave as though I am."

"I do not."

He reluctantly released her hand. "Do too."

"Are we arguing like children?"

A dimpled grin appeared upon his face. "I do believe we are behaving as when we were children. You never agreed with me then either."

She laughed and turned to peer at him over her shoulder while she stepped towards the box. "No, you were insufferable."

One large step brought him toe to toe with her. "No more insufferable than you," he responded while their eyes held each other's without wavering. "I wished to hear you laugh tonight. 'Tis why I chose this play."

"You have heard me laugh," she whispered. He was so close—too close. Her heart stuttered against her ribs and her breathing quickened.

"I have, but not often. You are more apt to smile. I know it is not fashionable, but I hoped I might hear at least a few giggles. You laughed more before your mother's death. I have missed it for some time."

"I hardly sound the same as I did then."

"No, but that never mattered. I merely enjoy the sound of your happiness." Voices passed close behind her, making Nathaniel start and draw back to a more proper distance. "We should join the others."

As she placed her hand in the crook of his elbow, the sound of footsteps drew closer and she glanced in that direction, only to flinch. Nathaniel followed her line of sight and became rigid.

"Miss Darcy," greeted Mrs. Younge when she stepped in front of Georgiana. "It has really been too long."

Neither she nor Nathaniel spoke. Instead, he stepped to the side and tugged Georgiana with him, effectively cutting Mrs. Younge. A few loud whispers reached her ears from those milling about while he led her into the box, but she took in a breath that filled her chest in an attempt to blow out the nerves. That woman would never rile her again!

"I hope she has not ruined our evening?" Nathaniel's whispered words were so close, his breath tickled her ear and sent a wave of gooseflesh down her arm and chest.

"I will not allow that woman to spoil my evening or my life. She is not in a position to hurt me as she did before and will never be so again. I will not permit it." She squeezed his arm. "I need to finally tell you. I do not believe the time will ever be ideal, but perhaps the next time we ride we might find a moment?"

"Of course," he responded, his warm eyes reassuring, "I should welcome the opportunity to finally know it all." His free hand came to cover hers. "Do not fret. I swear to you, my heart will remain yours, no matter the revelation. I could no more turn my back on you than I could remove my own soul. 'Tis impossible."

He led her to the front of the box. Once she was seated, he took the chair beside her, adjusting his topcoat before he settled. "I have anticipated this evening."

"I hope the performance does not disappoint."

"The performance does not matter. I am certain the company will prove infinitely superior."

She bit her lip and glanced to Fitzwilliam and Lizzy, who spoke with Richard and Julia behind them. Mr. Hanson and Lydia stood to the side of their box, conversing quietly.

"Your brother explained he and your cousin would leave us to our own conversation tonight. They shall not depart but shall not interfere. I hope you do not object. I confess I take great pleasure in the prospect of uninterrupted time with you."

Her mouth opened to respond but movement on the stage caused those in attendance to take their seats, though they still spoke, causing a low murmur around the theatre. The remainder of their party took their own seats with Mr. Hanson and Lydia sitting in the same row as the play began.

Those around her appeared to become engrossed in the actors upon the stage, but Nathaniel's presence at her side was palpable, though no part of him touched her. As she smiled at Beatrice's description of Benedick, a light caress on her thumb pulled her attention from the play and her heart quickened. She looked to find Nathaniel's little finger reaching over to touch her as surreptitiously as possible.

She turned her hand over and opened her fingers, inviting him to join their hands. Richard would surely notice, but what did it matter? Nathaniel's solid presence steadied her, his cheer lifted her spirits, and his touch . . . well, his touch made her believe she could be a woman in the truest sense of the word. At one time, something she never would have thought possible.

His palm pressed flat against hers, and his fingers slipped between hers, interlacing. She stared at their joining rather than the play—it was infinitely more interesting. Her heart still beat against her ribs in a furious cadence, and her body was sensitive to the slightest shift of his; yet an odd sense of peace overtook her.

She had fought and denied he could become a vital part of her existence, but he inched his way into her soul despite her well-intentioned motives for keeping him at bay. Lord help her, but she *loved* him! She hoped to tell him of Wickham before he possessed so much of her, but the fates had conspired against them.

Her vision blurred and a warm, wet droplet fell to her cheek. Nathaniel peeked behind them before raising his knuckle to brush away the lone teardrop. His eyebrows drew down in the centre as his eyes held hers. "Are you well?" he mouthed.

She put on as much of a smile as she could manage and gave a barely perceptible nod. His expression remained the same. She had not convinced him, but she could not do so without speaking and allowing those around them to hear such personal revelations. He should be the first to hear those words. He deserved to be the first she told.

When they next rode, they would have the groom hold the horses while they walked nearby. They would not manage enough privacy another way. Regardless of his reaction, she would tell him everything.

Chapter 20

February 28th 1817

Nathaniel promised we would ride today, but while he can control many things, English weather is certainly not one of them. The rain is not terrible so he may still call, though we shall not be able to speak openly within the house. The knocker is upon the door, which means callers wanted or unwanted will descend upon us today. Again, we shall have a house full of family, friends, and acquaintances preventing me from confiding in him.

I suppose we shall have to be content with our lot, but I have no desire to be content. I no longer want to avoid the long-delayed conversation threatening to burst from me at any moment. I love him and I cannot continue to keep such a secret. Nathaniel deserves to know before he commits himself to me for a lifetime. He will know. Soon!

She set her pen in its stand and sanded the page. The entry was short, but she could not sit idly and do nothing but write. She needed to move about or find some method to occupy herself. If she were at Pemberley, she would hurry to her favourite walk and run as fast as she could to quell the unease and agitation possessing her. No, it was not ladylike or proper by any means, but it did help when she was as unsettled as she was.

When she passed the nursery, she smiled at the sound of Lizzy singing with little William, his childish mispronunciations making Lizzy giggle from time to time. For a moment, she stood still simply listening. He was such a dear child and despite his energetic nature, very caring. He adored hugs and cuddles, particularly when someone read to him. If she could sit without bouncing, she would have joined them, but the likelihood was low with her present state of mind. She listened to one more line, and then, moved to the stairs.

Jobbins stepped from the dining room when she entered the hall. "Ah, Miss Darcy, I was about to seek you out. A messenger brought this letter for you a short time ago." He picked up a note from the salver and held it in his outstretched hand. "You have not received correspondence from Lady Grace since your arrival. I thought it might be of some importance."

She stared at the penmanship. The handwriting did resemble Lady Grace's, but they had not been friends since school. Grace simply never contacted her, and Georgiana never desired to know why. The rumours since their arrival in town were surely more than enough reason for the respectable daughter of a peer to cease their acquaintance. She had likely long forgotten Georgiana.

Walking to the music room, she rubbed her finger across the smooth wax seal. It had no imprinted crest or design—another oddity. She sat in the chair near the window and stared at the neatly folded paper. The hair on her arms stood on end. Grace had cared little about contacting Georgiana for the past five years. Why make an effort now?

She held the letter closer to her face, studying the writing. Her fingers stroked the paper. It was not as fine as what the daughter of an earl would use.

Before she could change her mind, she broke the seal, biting her lip as she unfolded the missive with trembling hands. Inside, she found a familiar handwriting. One she thought—no, she hoped she would never see again. She clenched her free hand into a fist, wrinkling the skirt of her morning gown. She should have known!

February 27th 1817

My Dear Miss Darcy,

For one who has been the cause of my current situation, you have some nerve refusing to speak to me. Oh, I am certain you believe me to be the author of all your misfortune. Everything that has befallen you since Ramsgate, no doubt, lies upon my shoulders, but though you may not acknowledge it, I have suffered for your stubbornness.

I possessed little before being in your brother's employ. When my husband died, he left me a pittance; a run-down boarding house and his father's watch. Your marriage was to provide me the funds to repair my home and live comfortably for a very long time. Wickham would have made for an agreeable husband if you had allowed him the opportunity. Of course, nothing of the sort ever occurred and I became destitute.

While you have pranced about London this Season, going to Gunter's, visiting the modiste on Bond Street, and being courted by a handsome viscount, I languished in my boarding house that has long-since fallen into further disrepair. My debts had become such that I would soon be taken to debtor's prison and I would lose my property. I can no longer remember when I sold the watch. It did not bring much, but I ate for a week—I do know that.

Now, I live in a house not far from your brother's, while this drooling sop has his way with me night after night. I have no choice but to pretend to enjoy myself, but in my mind, I remember how you are the cause of my misfortunes. You would not have suffered as Wickham's wife. After all, you were his means of improving his situation, but you had to refuse. You put me here, and to add insult to injury, I am faced with your presence wherever I go. Well, I have decided that now you will provide me with the means to escape.

I want nothing more than the ten thousand pounds I would have received when you wed Wickham, and you will pay it. You will provide me those funds or I will spread the tale of your ruin from one end of London to the other. I may no longer be a respectable lady, but my situation will be of no matter. Too many wish to know why you absented yourself from town for so long, and the reason behind your sudden return. I am certain they will accept my story—even if it is true.

You have a week to acquire the funds. I have no care for how you do so, but I will expect you to meet me in Hyde Park Friday next with the money. I will wait by the Serpentine near Rotten Row. You know of the place I speak. You saw me walking with Mr. Browne in the very spot several months ago.

I know you must tell your brother to acquire the funds, but I have left information with several acquaintances who will bring this knowledge to the gossip columns should I find myself in the gaol. So, you must see that the only way to save your reputation is to provide me the money. I doubt Lord Sele will want you if the truth of your past is made public. You would return to Pemberley alone and in disgrace, if you are lucky. I doubt even your brother's wife would wish to keep your company once news of your attempted elopement and ruination were made known.

B.Y.

Georgiana swallowed the burning bile that had risen into her throat. She was going to be sick. Without hesitation, she jumped from the chair and rushed back to her chambers, nearly pushing Lydia into the wall when she passed her.

"Georgiana?" she called after her.

She did not pause but burst through the door to her bedchamber, barely making it to the chamber pot in the dressing room before losing the contents of her stomach. When she finally stopped retching, she gasped in a breath as she let out a sob. Before another could escape, she pressed her lips together as tight as she could.

A cloth appeared beside her face. "Here. Take this."

The cool, damp cloth soothed the lingering nausea when she pressed it to her cheeks, which she did until the next wave passed. When she was fairly certain she would not again cast up her accounts, she leaned back against the nearest wall and wiped her mouth.

Lydia followed and handed her another cloth, taking the warm one and rinsing it in the basin. "I rang for Lucy. We should open a window and move to your bedchamber until she can sort out this mess."

She helped Georgiana stand, cracked the nearest window, and followed her to the sofa in her bedchamber. Once they were seated, Lydia held the cursed letter in front of Georgiana. "You left this on the floor near the chamber pot."

Georgiana took the horrid article as though it might bite, which was a ridiculous notion, but why did she only use her thumb and first finger? She did not look at it. She could not look at it. If she did, she would be kneeling over the chamber pot for what remained of the day.

"Did you read it?"

"No," admitted Lydia. "'Tis your letter, and you did not give me permission." Lydia's head tilted while she watched Georgiana. "Is that," she pointed to the missive, "the reason you were sick?"

Georgiana nodded.

"What could you have received to provoke such a reaction?"

When she did not answer, Lydia placed her hand on Georgiana's wrist. "Perhaps we should start with a simpler question. Who wrote the letter?"

"Mrs. Younge," burst Georgiana with a sob.

Lydia's eyes widened and her hand tightened where it gripped her arm. "You mean the horrid woman who you have happened upon all over town since our arrival? The one who was your companion for a time?"

"The very one." Her voice was flat—emotionless. She could not breathe. Her chest was so restricted, it was as though her stays were laced impossibly tight. She pressed her hand to her eyes and began to pant.

"May I read it?"

Georgiana choked back another sob while she dipped her chin enough to give Lydia her consent. She lay her head upon the back of the sofa in the hopes it would cease its infernal spinning. She exhaled in bursts of air and grasped the front of her gown in an attempt to pull the restrictive clothing away.

"Stop or you will tear it."

When she leaned forward, Lydia released the fastenings and helped pull her sleeves from her shoulders. Georgiana sat forward and shifted so the gown was pulled away. Her shaking fingers managed to loosen the ties on the stays Lydia then pulled over her head.

She still could not breathe. Why did it feel as though she was still all trussed up? A glass was pressed into her hand while she hiccoughed.

"Drink this," ordered Lydia as the glass tilted upwards. Before she could ask what it contained, the pungent smell of brandy filled her nostrils just before the sharp liquid singed her tongue. Lydia did not drown her, but dispensed a sizeable swallow.

"Lucy, if you would ask Mr. and Mrs. Darcy to join us here. Oh! Before you go, fetch Miss Darcy's dressing gown."

While Lydia spoke, Georgiana shifted the brandy around her mouth. She did not like the strong liquor but it was definitely preferable to the taste that lingered from earlier.

Lydia brushed back Georgiana's fringe and pressed a cool palm to her forehead. "Are you better?"

Another sob broke from her control, but she sucked it back before her upset overtook her. She took the glass from Lydia and downed in several large gulps what remained. Perhaps that would numb the pain inside, even if it only did so for a short time.

When she handed Lydia the empty glass, she looked inside and shrugged. "I suppose that is one way to calm yourself. I had not intended for you to drink the entirety."

Only a minute passed before Lucy returned with the dressing gown and helped Georgiana put it on. When she curtseyed and departed once again, Lydia dropped beside her and stared at the note. "When did you see Mrs. Younge last?"

"Nathaniel and I gave her the cut direct last night at the theatre."

"Do you think—"

"She was angry. I am certain of that. She has probably been planning this for some time, but I do believe in her anger she sent the letter earlier than she might have otherwise."

"What a cruel, vindictive piece of baggage."

Georgiana's lip curved on one side as she peered at Lydia. "Baggage? I can think of better words to describe Bridget Younge, can you not?"

"Bunter¹?" Lydia spoke low as if someone would hear and be offended.

"Better," urged Georgiana.

"Buttock and file?"

She leaned her head on Lydia's shoulder. "Where did you hear that one?"

"The innkeeper in Meryton called a beggar woman that once. I asked Papa what it meant."

"What does it mean?" She hiccoughed.

"It is a whore and a pickpocket."

Georgiana lifted her head and looked at Lydia, who was beginning to appear a bit bleary. "We could just call her bitch."

Lydia gasped and began to giggle harder than before. "Georgiana! If your brother heard you!"

"He would agree."

"Probably, but he would surely die hearing such words from your lips."

"You certainly have not lost your flair for the dramatic, Lydia," said Lizzy as she entered with Fitzwilliam behind her. "Lucy said Georgiana is ill?" She stepped around Lydia's legs and placed her hands upon Georgiana's cheeks. "You are not feverish."

Lydia scoffed. "A malady is not at fault, unless you consider Mrs. Younge an infectious disease of some variety."

"Mrs. Younge?" Fitzwilliam glared at the mere mention of her name and Lydia passed him the note. He glanced at the direction before turning the paper to read the contents. Lizzy remained at Georgiana's side and rubbed her back.

Georgiana felt around in her hair, searching for the pins. Her head was beginning to throb and she simply wanted to crawl into her bed and forget the outside world existed for as long as possible. She found one and began to tug, but it would not give.

Lizzy's hands stopped her. "Here, let me."

Fitzwilliam dropped the note against his leg and swore. "When did you receive this?" His voice was furious and unrelenting.

"Jobbins claimed it was delivered this morning, but I do not know how." She swayed in her spot and steadied herself with a hand to the seat cushion.

"Have you been drinking?" he asked, his voice shocked.

Lydia stood and clasped her hands in front of her. "She was sick when I followed her to the dressing room. When she became overwrought, I gave her brandy. I did not know she would finish the contents of the glass." Lydia bit her lip and leaned slightly away from Fitzwilliam.

He scratched the back of his head with an exhale that sounded as though the weight of the world on his shoulders forced the air from his lungs. "I am not angry at you, Lydia. I can imagine my sister's state of mind when she first read this."

Lizzy took the pins, disappeared into the dressing room, and reappeared a moment later with Georgiana's brush. Georgiana closed her eyes as the bristles worked their way through her long waves and massaged her scalp.

"Georgiana," called Fitzwilliam, "I need to know what you wish to do."

She blinked blearily. "Pardon?"

He took the seat Lydia vacated and clasped her hand in his. "Do you wish me to pay her? Do you want me to notify the constable? Do you want me to set Richard on her?"

She could not help but give a half-hearted smile at the last. "As much as I would enjoy that, you cannot. She would ruin me. If she ruins me, it would affect you. It would affect Lydia. The scandal might even touch your children. Too many people would suffer."

Lizzy's hands covered Georgiana's where they rested in her lap. "Then, will you dole out ten thousand pounds whenever she finds herself in a poor situation?"

"Elizabeth!" Fitzwilliam's voice held a tone of warning, but his wife did no more than give him a frown before she turned back to Georgiana.

"Your brother would never object or complain but if he pays what she asks, she will reappear whenever her prospects again become dire. This could never end. If she squanders the money as Wickham did the bequest from your father, she might insist on thirty to forty thousand before the end of her life."

Georgiana pressed the heel of her hand to her forehead while Lydia whispered, "Lord, such a sum to give away."

"I would do so without hesitation to ensure my sister's happiness, Elizabeth. You should be well aware of that."

Lizzy gaped at him. "I do not doubt your devotion to your sister, but where does it end? I do not wish her unhappy or shunned, yet we must think of the future. What of this child I now carry? You have noble intentions for any younger sons we might have, but will you give away our younger son's future? Or a daughter's dowry?"

"No! I do not want you to argue!" Georgiana stood and put her hands on her brother's shoulders. "You have protected me since our father died."

"Not well enough."

"As well as you were able. You could not have known Wickham's scheme, and I will never allow you any share of the blame. I do want all of this to disappear, but Lizzy is correct. Once we hand her those funds, she will return for more. I will not see you sacrifice yours or your family's future to that woman."

"I would not hesitate to do so. You must know."

"I understand that you would give all you have. I am at a loss as to how to proceed from here, but arguing will not bring about a solution."

"What do you want?" asked Lizzy from behind.

She dropped her arms to her side. "I know I cannot avoid this for long, but all I want is to climb into my bed and forget the world around me exists. Mrs. Younge has provided us a week. We need not rush to a decision today. Perhaps, if we delay until tomorrow, a better idea than what we have concocted in anger, fear, and haste will present itself."

Fitzwilliam pressed a kiss to her forehead. "I shall send for Richard. He will want to be of aid."

She nodded. "Of course."

Lizzy wrapped her in a warm embrace while she pressed her lips together. Only a moment more and she would be free to release the tears she struggled to contain.

When Lizzy and Fitzwilliam departed, Lydia lifted an eyebrow. The expression was not used as often by Lydia as it was Lizzy, but the small change rendered them so very similar. "I hope you do not expect me to leave because I have no intention of returning to the drawing room for idle conversation. I will see to it you are well."

"What of Mr. Hanson?"

"He shall have to understand."

Before Georgiana could object, Lydia pushed her to the bed where she tucked her snugly into the covers and sat beside her. She did not speak, which was unusual for Lydia, but she must have understood Georgiana was just not equal to the effort.

The brandy helped her eyelids become heavy, despite the constant turning of her mind. Her eyes fluttered as the sound of a door latch opening reached her ears.

"Miss Bennet?" The whispered voice was Lucy's. "Lord Sele is here. He wishes to call upon Miss Darcy." Who spoke at the door did not matter, yet what she said did have great consequence. She needed to talk to him, but would he understand? Would he agree and abide by the decision she made for herself? Could he reconcile himself to what occurred in Ramsgate?

She dissolved to the luxury of tears and never heard Lydia's response.

She needed to speak to him, but then again, perhaps he would be better off without her.

---

[1] *Bunter - A low dirty prostitute, half whore and half beggar.*

Chapter 21

Georgiana tossed, turned, flipped the coverlet down and huffed. Lydia had long since fallen asleep and snored incessantly beside her while rain pelted against the window. Nothing could be seen through the darkness outside and the water dripping in heavy rivulets down the slick surface of the glass. How long had she slept?

Her legs twitched with the need to move, to pace—to be anywhere but in this infernal bed twisting the sheets about her calves! Careful not to wake Lydia, she stood and paced beside the bed, her mind spinning with the contents of the letter and what followed. How dare Bridget Younge behave as though she were the injured one! Had she not done enough at Ramsgate to ruin Georgiana's life? She needed to return to make matters worse? Why did that revolting woman rear her ugly head now? Revealing everything to Nathaniel would be difficult enough without this looming over her.

If she did not pay Mrs. Younge, the evil woman would divulge the entire affair with her own sordid twisting of the events. The note did not indicate what Mrs. Younge would say, but that woman's version of events would never match hers.

She jammed her arms through the sleeves of her dressing gown, cracked open the door to her chambers, and peeked through the slit. No one should be about at this hour. Lizzy would have retired after seeing William put safely to bed in his cot, and surely, Fitzwilliam followed them directly. He never lingered long unless he had a great deal of work to be completed. A loud snore, resembling the sound of a pig, came from behind her. Of course, Lydia slept like the dead.

She glanced back at the clock upon the mantelpiece—half-eleven. No servants would be about at this hour, would they?

With no one in the corridor, she slipped out and quietly closed the door behind her. The turn at the top of the stairs was dark, but she did not require light to lead her way. She tiptoed down to the drawing room where embers still glowed in the grate, giving off a slight warmth to the room. There was no need to add more coal. She would not remain for long.

The glow in the cut crystal of the decanters caught her eye and gave her pause. The dark amber liquid within also reflected the fire, but in a strange, distorted fashion. Brandy helped her find sleep earlier, perhaps it could be of aid to her now? The thoughts going around and around in her head had slowed just long enough for Morpheus to take her away—that was all she required to see her until morning.

She approached the table and gingerly lifted the stopper. Just as brandy always did, the vile smell stung her nostrils a bit, but Mrs. Younge's words and face loomed before her as though she was in the very room with her. She had to forget, even if for a short time.

She tipped the glass back, took a generous swig, and relished the lingering burn as it travelled to her stomach and warmed her from within. She brought the brandy to her lips once more.

"Georgiana?"

Nathaniel! She jumped and brought a hand to her chin to wipe the small amount of alcohol poised to dribble down her neck.

Her eyes closed in horror. What would he think of her? She turned to face him as he approached. His eyes traced down her form, no doubt, taking in her improper attire, before they settled upon the brandy in her hand.

"I have yet to see you drink brandy."

She drew herself as straight as she could. "I woke and could not go back to sleep." She peered at the glass. Would he notice the slight shake of the contents? "I did not know you were here."

"Your brother said you were not well. I was worried, so I waited all day for word of you. This evening, your brother invited me to remain for the night. He thought being closer to you might put my mind at ease.

"He retired a short time ago, so I went to the library to select a book." He held up a hand, which contained some unknown volume. "I was about to retire when I thought I heard noises from this room."

He set the book upon a table, stepped closer, and removed the glass from her hand, placing it upon the tray. "I once asked for your trust."

She shook her head.

"No, Georgiana. When we began this courtship, you were so unpredictable—one moment you confided childhood memories or treasured pieces of your heart, and the next, you withdrew into yourself and hid. You have since promised to confide in me. I beg of you to do so now."

Tears stung at her eyes and her vision became hazy. "I know, but you cannot understand how difficult it is." She choked on a sob and covered her face with her palms.

A hand slid along the back of her neck and pulled her close until she was engulfed in warmth. Her fingers clenched the lapels of his topcoat as she struggled to regain her composure. If only she could remain thus forever, safe and protected within the haven of his arms. If only he could protect her from Mrs. Younge, yet he could not. He would be made part of the scandal if he remained.

"Georgiana Darcy, I love you. I cannot remember a time when I did not love you. Nothing you tell me will change how I feel."

"This could." Her voice came out as a strangled whisper. Why was she so infernally weak?

His hands cupped her cheeks and drew her face back until his eyes held hers captive. "No! Nothing could change my feelings for you."

She wrenched herself from his grasp. "Do not make assurances when you have no concept of what I hide. What I have struggled to keep hidden these last five years. I swore I would never marry, so I need not reveal any of it, yet I never counted on you."

He stepped forward with his arm stretched towards her, but she held up her hand, palm out, and shifted back.

"You were patient and charming."

"Not so patient," he said with a slight curve to his lips.

"Very well." She wiped the damp from her cheek with the backs of her hands. "You managed to wheedle your way into my heart. I could not prevent myself from falling in love with you, though I tried with all I had in me. The effort, in the end, was useless. I was in the middle before I knew I had begun."

She crossed her arms over her chest. "Now, the one person who could destroy me has made her threats, and if I do not comply, she will ruin me—she will ruin us."

"Who?"

She tightened the grip around herself.

"Who?"

"Mrs. Younge!"

His eyes searched hers. "I know she once held the position of your companion, but what does this woman hold over you? Just tell me and we need never fear her."

"She will not see it end there."

He rushed forward and with tender fingers brushed her damp fringe from her cheeks. "Tell me once and for all, and then, we will discuss a solution— together. You need not shoulder this burden on your own."

"Why not?" she whispered. "It happened to me alone."

"What happened?" His voice was just as soft.

She withdrew, picked up the glass of brandy, and took a swallow. "In the summer of eighteen-eleven, Fitzwilliam and Richard removed me from school, and an establishment was formed for me in Ramsgate.

"I had a companion, Mrs. Younge, who accompanied me to the seaside." She smiled weakly. "I was so excited to be on my own and to enjoy the fresh sea air. Those first days were wonderful. I collected seashells and took long rambles along the shore. Then, a few weeks after my arrival, George Wickham appeared as we walked along the sea wall."

"George Wickham?" Nathaniel's tone was hard yet disbelieving. "George Wickham, the son of your father's steward?"

She nodded. "The very one."

He removed the glass from her hand, finished the last gulp, stepped over to the tray, and filled it to the top once again.

"Nathaniel?"

A shaky breath left him as his shiny eyes set upon her face. "I know his . . ." He placed his hand over his mouth. "He often . . ." His hand, holding the glass, trembled. "Did he?"

"He continued to happen upon us on our walks. Mrs. Younge allowed it and began to persuade me to consider him a suitor." His Adam's apple bobbed as he gulped and closed his eyes.

"I summoned Fitzwilliam. I wrote him directly. In the meantime, my maid and I made plans to flee Ramsgate because we feared Fitzwilliam would be unable to arrive before Wickham proposed or insisted we elope. The night before we intended to take the post coach, Wickham came to the house and Mrs. Younge allowed him a private audience."

Nathaniel gasped and slammed down the glass upon the closest side table. "The bastard had the temerity to propose marriage! He would be interested in naught but your fortune."

"Which he was, indeed. I declined, but he refused to accept my answer." A hiccough came as she attempted to stifle another sob. "He thought ruining me would force my hand."

His eyes closed. Was he so horrified he would never wish to look upon her again? How would she bear his rejection if that was indeed what he did?

"Good God."

She clenched her arms more tightly around herself. She would require every bit of fortitude she possessed to keep her composure if he cried off now. "I have no desire to recount every detail. I will only say the ordeal was painful and terrifying, and when it was over, I informed him his actions made him the last man in the world I could be prevailed upon to marry. He slapped me and said I would come to my senses. He would see to it.

"I managed to make it to my chambers. I know not how I had the strength to say what I did to him much less climb the stairs, but I did. Lucy was horrified upon her return. She still feels to blame, though I have assured her no one but

Wickham is at fault."

Warm, wet tears flowed freely down her cheeks. "I tried to fight him, but he was just too strong."

Nathaniel looked up with a line between his eyebrows, strode forward, and pulled her to his chest. "You feared I would blame you, but he was taller and stronger. I have no doubt of that. You were also not the first woman he ever . . ." He gulped. "You were not the first woman he forced himself upon."

The remnants of Nathaniel's cologne soothed her as she wrapped her arms about his waist. "My brother told me as much."

"Your decision to never marry was based on Wickham's actions, was it not? Why you are at times, reluctant in my presence?"

"I dreaded this conversation. A simpler solution, in my mind, was to avoid the intimacy, which would lead to another proposal of marriage, but you would not relent. You were determined."

His fingers combed her hair back from her face and he pressed a kiss to her temple. "I knew you held a secret, but I never dreamt . . ." His voice was hoarse and his shoulders shook. "I am sorry. I am so sorry I could not protect you."

She withdrew far enough to look in his eyes. "No one is at fault but Wickham. Fitzwilliam took a great portion of the blame upon his shoulders, but my aunt and uncle, as well as Lizzy, have helped. He could not have prevented Wickham's actions and neither could you."

His thumb traced down her cheek. "You feared my reaction."

"I confess I did."

He touched his forehead to hers. "You need never fear me. I may not care for what you say, but I will love you regardless of what you tell me."

After swallowing her nerves, she pressed her palm to his chest, raised onto her tiptoes, and brushed his lips with hers. He did not attempt to deepen the kiss but allowed her to express her affection in its simplest form.

She buried her face into his chest. "You deserve to know the entire story."

He ran his hand down her arm, leaving a trail of sensation in the wake of his fingers, and grasped her hand. He tugged her to the sofa where he sat and pulled her into his lap. The intimacy of their position made her face and neck heated. Hopefully, no one would catch them thus!

His arms wrapped around her, keeping her protected and secure. "I dread what you will say, though I would not have you keep secrets from me. We must put the past behind us if we are to ever have a future."

She reached to grab the forgotten glass of brandy, took a drink, and passed it to him. A curve of his lips was his response as he gulped a measure of the fortifying liquid and rested the glass upon her thigh.

His head tilted as he opened his mouth twice as though trying to speak and failing before finally managing, "How long before Darcy arrived?"

"He was in Ramsgate by early the next morning. He travelled through the night, you see." She rested her arm around his shoulders and leaned against him. His embrace was of such comfort and conveyed his continued affection, which put her more at ease. "Upon his arrival, Lucy informed him of what occurred. After threatening Mrs. Younge with Richard's ire, he immediately had her packed and on the first post coach to London. Lucy packed my trunks, and we returned to London that very day."

"The journey must have been taxing."

"I cannot remember a carriage ride being more so. I remained within the carriage while horses were changed at the larger coaching inns. In the smallest of villages, my brother ensured we had a private room. I kept my head down to hide the bruise upon my face from Wickham's hand."

His hand, resting upon her waist, tightened.

"My aunt, upon hearing of Wickham's evil, took me into her home. Fitzwilliam had accepted Charles Bingley's invitation to stay at Netherfield in Hertfordshire a month prior. He did not want to leave me, yet he was obliged to go. I remained with Aunt Charlotte and waited."

"To see if you were with child?" His voice was flat and his sorrow-filled eyes sparkled in the dim glow of the embers.

"Yes."

"Were you?" he asked as though he was barely containing his anger.

"We believe so."

He took another generous gulp of brandy and bared his teeth as he swallowed. "You believe so?"

"If I was, the babe never quickened. My aunt believes I miscarried. I was ill for some time after. That was when the nightmares returned."

The wet trails where tears streamed down his face shown in the sparse light of the room. He was such a dear man. Beneath the sense of humour and the handsome face was a sensitive soul. How could she ever have doubted him?

"Do you still have the dreams?"

"Only when I am afraid or nervous. I had them after I decided to return to London a few months ago. I feared the rumours from remaining at Pemberley and not coming out when I was seventeen. They have waned since I decided to ignore those of no consequence to me." She swallowed and steeled herself. "I do still worry that I will be unable to give you a child."

He cleared his throat. "As long as I have you, I shall be content. I would adore a child with your eyes and gentle smile, but that is not as necessary to me as you are." He hugged her a little closer. "I returned from Ireland for the beginning of every season. Did you know?"

"I did." Her tears began to flow anew. He had been waiting for her.

"I would remain until I discovered whether you would come out. When you remained at Pemberley, I would journey back to Ireland. This year, however, I vowed to come to Derbyshire if you did not come out."

She could not help but smile. "I remembered a boy who pestered me when I was but a girl. I would have still been stubborn." She traced the line of his nose with her finger. "I dreamt of you on the carriage ride to London."

His head gave a slight jerk back, his brows rose on his forehead, and a slight grin graced his lips. "You did?"

"You are incorrigible."

"You said you dreamt of me. You know not how that makes me feel."

"I was eight and you were twelve. You and your parents brought Fitzwilliam to Pemberley before my mother's death. When you professed you would marry me, I woke with a start."

His hand took hers and laced their fingers. "I have hoped to marry you for as long as I can remember, but you have yet to tell me you are ready."

She watched their hands and her heart dropped. The conversation of the letter was required but not wanted. "What of Mrs. Younge?"

His grip became tighter. "I assume she has made some demand of you?"

"I received a letter this morning. She wants what she would have received from Wickham had we eloped."

His breath shifted the silk of her dressing gown when he exhaled and set his forehead against her shoulder. "How much?"

"Ten thousand pounds."

"She is mad!" He was incredulous.

"I believe desperate would be more accurate. If she has Wickham's habits, she likely owes a great deal of money. She mentioned debtor's prison and the possibility of losing her boarding house."

His hands slid up her neck to hold her face. "Marry me," he begged. "Marry me, and I will ensure Mrs. Younge never breathes a word."

Chapter 22

Georgiana placed her hands over Nathaniel's where they rested on her cheeks and pulled them to her lap, keeping them firmly in her grasp. "Nathaniel, I do not desire marriage to keep Mrs. Younge at bay. If we wed, I want the reasons to be our feelings for one another and our wish for a life together. The threat she poses should be why you wait rather than rush to make me the offer of your hand."

He closed his eyes and placed his forehead against hers. "I worded that dreadfully." He straightened and his gaze held hers, steady and sure. "I love you. I have always loved you. I have returned every season in the hopes of courting you, and you finally returned this winter. I had to persuade you to accept my courtship, but you would not be my Georgiana if you fell at my feet and accepted easily—not that I would have minded if you had." One side of his lip twitched upwards as he caressed her knuckles with his thumbs. "My reason for begging your agreement now is that I am impatient to begin our life together, though I cannot deny that I am impatient to protect you as my own as well. You are my heart, a part so vital to me that I cannot simply leave you behind."

While he spoke, her vision became hazy and a warm droplet landed upon her cheek, gradually making a damp trail to her chin. Nathaniel brushed the tear away with his thumb.

"You do not play fair," she whispered with a sniff.

"Good. I require every advantage I can gain." His fingers threaded into the top of her loose braid and drew her towards him. He looked to her lips and lifted his eyebrows, asking permission as he came closer and closer. His warm breath fanned against her cheek, sending little sparks of sensation down her neck and further as her eyelids fluttered closed. His lips were soft when they cupped hers and moved slowly, but before she was ready, he paused, remaining unbearably close. "Marry me, Georgiana. Marry me because you love me as I love you."

When she opened her eyes, his dark brown ones were before her, searching hers and imploring her. Surely, he was so close he could see into her soul? He could not be in doubt as to her feelings, her eyes must have betrayed the love threatening to burst from within. She might not have said the words, but her reluctance to tarnish his family's honour had to speak to the affection she held for him. When she opened her mouth in an attempt to speak, no sound emerged.

His palm rested against her cheek. "I love you, Georgiana Darcy."

"I love you, too," she managed in a raspy voice.

An enormous grin overspread his face. "Does that mean yes?" She nodded and a short laugh burst from her. "I am afraid I must hear that precious word, my love."

She rolled her eyes. "Yes." She kissed his nose, the words now coming with ease. "Yes." She kissed his forehead. "Yes," she whispered just before he lunged to claim her lips. At first, he remained still and inhaled deeply—his lips merely pressed to hers. Then, they parted a hairsbreadth and began to move, brushing and gently teasing. She hesitated for a moment before she attempted to mimic his movements, which made his fingers tighten in her hair and against her scalp. A groan rumbled from his throat that vibrated through her and urged her closer. Her mind was a muddle. He wreaked havoc with her ability to think, but she could not complain. Her greatest fear had been for naught. Nathaniel still loved her.

Meanwhile, his thumb traced an invisible line up and down the sensitive shell of her ear, creating a frisson that did not disappear but only became more intense as he repeated it over and over again. She jumped when his warm tongue darted out and tasted her, but he did not comment or criticise. He merely continued those tender, feather-light touches that made reason impossible and her breath come in pants. She could not speak. She could not move. She could do no more than feel. Her entire body was sensitised in a way she could not have put into words even if she tried. He was easy with her, as if he tamed a skittish foal, murmuring, "I love you. Let me show you." He kissed one corner of her mouth and then, the other. When she melted in his arms, he did not hesitate and began to kiss her like before.

This time, however, when his mouth covered hers and his tongue slipped inside, she welcomed him instead of drawing back. Her hand found its way to the side of his face, threading her fingers under his collar, while she turned in his embrace and pressed herself to him. She needed to be closer, to feel his warmth and his strength, but he still wore the layers required of him by propriety, which were in the way.

A groan escaped as he tore his lips from hers and trailed kisses along her jaw and down her neck. When he gazed back up at her face, his fingers shifted a curl from her forehead.

"I must look affright," she confessed. "I slept most of the day before you found me here."

"You are beautiful," he stated matter-of-factly yet with an unmistakable reverence. His fingers traced from her chin down the arm of her dressing gown and back to her shoulder. His heated gaze rested on her face once again before she began to tug at his cravat. "What are you about?"

She shrugged while she worked, but he did not object and helped her remove the impossibly tied piece of lawn. The collar of his shirt fell open, and she indulged in stroking the smooth skin from his Adam's apple around his neck where his curls tapered against the soft flesh.

His eyes closed, and she took advantage and bestowed a kiss under his ear, much as he had earlier. His swift intake of breath betrayed his pleasure in her first timid attempt, so she forged ahead and traced her fingertips along his ear to the lobe where she kissed him again. The last brush of her lips was against the small hollow at the base of his neck, except she tried her tongue this time, which made him hiss and moan her name. Her heart quickened at the sound.

Before she could experiment further, he drew her head back and claimed her lips more confidently this time. He wrapped an arm around her waist, and pulled her so close her breasts crushed against his chest. Her dressing gown bunched tight where he clenched the fabric at the small of her back and her leg became cold when one panel fell away, leaving it exposed to the cooling air in the room.

His hand upon her back became impatient and travelled down her hip and thigh, halting when he reached bare skin. He relinquished her lips and spread light pecks across her eyes, her cheeks, and ended with one last to her lips.

"The last thing I desire is to stop what we are doing, but if we continue, we will have no choice but to wed in the morning. If I survive your cousin's wrath, that is. I also do not wish to rush you."

She closed her eyes in an attempt to regain control. She did not want to stop. Nathaniel's touches and kisses started as pleasant, but with each moment they continued, her body craved more than what she expected to ever want—more than what should certainly happen in her brother's drawing room!

Her heart raced, her body thrummed and trembled, and her breathing was ragged. She buried her head into his neck and breathed in the remnants of his cologne while he stroked her back until her body calmed.

She shifted more onto his shoulder so she could see his face. "I hate to mention her at this moment, but what do we do about Mrs. Younge?" The woman was a menace, but how did they prevent her scheme without the secret of Wickham and Ramsgate becoming fodder for the gossip columns?

After a tender peck to her forehead, he wrapped an arm around her shoulders. "I do not know, but am I wrong to believe you have told my mother?"

"I had not intended to reveal so much before I told you."

"Shh, I am not angry you confided in her. Your talk did cause her upset, but I do know she was pleased she could give you comfort. I merely asked because I believe she could be of great aid. My mother does not gossip, but she listens and remembers all she is told. Her knowledge could be of infinite use."

"She did discover the identity of Mrs. Younge's protector."

He combed his fingers through the part of her hair not in the loose braid. "She did and before your brother's investigators. I think we would do well to seek her opinion. I shall send her a note in the morning, requesting her presence when we speak to Darcy."

"What if we cannot prevent Mrs. Younge from revealing what she knows?"

His warm palms cradled her cheeks and lifted her face so their eyes met. "Then we wed and ignore the whispers. We could return to Ireland if you wish. No one would be aware of the gossip and while the estate is not large, it is a beautiful country. I have never seen grass so verdant and lush."

She gave a small smile. "I would not object to seeing it, but I do not want to leave Fitzwilliam and Lizzy to brave the repercussions on their own."

"When a lady is ruined, she is typically redeemed by marriage. I do not believe they would suffer. The event also did not occur last week or last month. Since this happened years ago and no threat of a by-blow exists to entice the talk to linger, I believe the scandal would die quickly."

"Are you certain this is your desire?" she asked. Her heart constricted at the possibility of his changing his mind, yet she had to ask.

"I am not so alterable or so easily frightened away. I have no intention of departing now."

"Good, I do not want you to go." She nuzzled back into his neck while his arms tightened around her.

"Unless you banish me, my place is with you. You belong just as you are, in my arms."

They remained quiet, savouring the close contact they rarely had and were unlikely to have again until they wed. The clock chimed the quarter hour then, chimed again before he stirred. "I do not want you to leave but I shall fall asleep if we remain thus, and you should return to your bed."

"I shall never sleep," she laughed softly while she lifted from his shoulder.

"Are you still so awake?"

"No, I am sleepy, but Lydia sat with me when I was so upset after receiving the letter. I am afraid she retired to my bedchamber so I was not alone, and remains sleeping in my bed."

His brows furrowed as he watched her with heavy eyes. "You are not accustomed to sharing a bed? It is understandable. You never have been required to do so."

"No, she snores *dreadfully*."

He smiled while his eyelids drooped and opened again. "She cannot be so bad," he murmured.

Georgiana giggled. "She has slept in my bedchamber on several occasions after we fell asleep, talking. The next morning, I can still hear her in my dressing room—with the door closed. Besides, I would prefer to remain a while longer."

His chest shook with his own laughter. "I do not want to leave you either." His earnest gaze drew her closer. "We must not sleep so late we are discovered."

She stroked his cheek until his eyes finally closed and, after one last sigh, his breathing became steady and even. He was such a dear man. Who would have known the annoying pest of a boy would be this considerate and devoted as an adult?

His features relaxed as he fell further into Morpheus' spell and his arms tightened around her, keeping a firm hold as though she might disappear if he loosened his embrace. While he slept, she watched his eyelashes flutter and his expression change as he dreamt, fascinated by every nuance. He was so handsome.

When her eyelids became weighted and it was a struggle to keep them open, she leaned against him, resting her head on his shoulder. She would only remain there for a moment, for one last embrace, and then, return to her bedchamber. He was so warm and so comfortable. She would only close her eyes for a few seconds . . .

"What is the meaning of this?" Fitzwilliam's stern voice rang in her ears as the mattress beneath her jumped. The pillow expanded, lifting her head, and she blinked. Wait . . . the pillow moved? Oh, no, no, no! She had fallen asleep in Nathaniel's arms! She had intended to return to her bed, but his embrace comforted her and lulled her to sleep.

"Georgiana Eloise Darcy, rise at once!"

She placed an arm to the cushion beside Nathaniel and pushed herself from his chest, her face and neck burning in mortification when she found her leg thrown over his hips. With care, she removed herself as they both rose to a seated position. He brushed his fingers through his hair and stretched. How did they end up lying on the sofa?

"Fitzwilliam," she said in a raspy voice. "'Tis not what you think." A sound almost like a high-pitched hiccough made her look up. Lizzy stood to her brother's side, with a hand over her mouth, her shoulders shaking.

"Since Sele remains clothed with the exception of his cravat, I do not believe the worst, if that is your concern. That still does not excuse your spending the night together. You know how damaging rumour and gossip can be, Georgiana." Fitzwilliam's countenance did not hold the fury she might have expected, but instead, his features were hard but twitched periodically like . . . like he was attempting not to laugh? "I assume you confided the letter and the complete history behind Mrs. Younge."

Georgiana rubbed her eyes and nodded, stifling a yawn. "Yes, I could not sleep with Lydia's snoring. Nathaniel found me pouring myself a brandy, and we were able to discuss all of it."

"And?" he asked, looking back and forth between them.

Nathaniel cleared his throat. "Darcy, I would like to request the honour of marrying your sister."

"I suppose that answers one question, though not the question I intended."

Georgiana glanced at Nathaniel, who gave her a slight smile. "Nathaniel feels we should not give her the money. He would prefer to see if we can gag Mrs. Younge by some other means."

"As it happens, I agree with him," her brother admitted, as his shoulders relaxed. "I know I said differently when I first learnt of her threats, but Elizabeth and I discussed this at length yesterday. I agree that if we give her one shilling, she will become a leech we cannot remove without injury." He turned to Nathaniel. "Do you have any ideas on how to prevent her from speaking?"

"I believe we should send for my mother. As you know, she discovered the identity of Mr. Browne. She could be helpful now as well. She mentioned Mr. and Mrs. Browne are both exceedingly concerned about their place in the ton and their connections. A well-placed threat with either of them could get us far, but we need to consider every possible outcome before we proceed."

Her brother nodded but levelled Nathaniel with a hard glare. "I agree, but what happens if Mrs. Younge makes her information public? What are your intentions then?"

"I will not abandon your sister if that is what you are asking. I have waited and hoped for her acceptance of my hand for too long, I will not allow the revelation of another person's evil to change my mind. You and I both know what Wickham was and why the fault of Ramsgate should be blamed on no one but him and Mrs. Younge, since she was as complicit as him. I would personally take great pleasure in seeing her locked in the gaol."

"As would I," agreed Lizzy. "Do you truly believe your mother can help?"

"My mother is well-connected and knowledgeable when it comes to the families of the ton and their connections. Ladies sometimes find her haughty, but it is merely because she listens rather than speaks—particularly when in company with a large group of ladies."

"I have one more question."

Georgiana looked to Nathaniel and then, to her brother. What else could he possibly want to know? Had they not discussed all they could at the moment?

Fitzwilliam smiled and chuckled. "Did Sele propose last night or seek my permission this morning due to your inappropriate sleeping arrangement?"

She could not help but grin so widely that her cheeks ached. "He asked last night, then we talked until he fell asleep. I meant to remove to my chambers, but I must have dozed before I could do so. The last I remember, we were in a seated position. I do not know how we came to be lying down."

"Well, you are fortunate Jobbins discovered you," said Lizzy. "He locked the servants' passage and closed the door to the hall, refusing the maids entry until your brother could be notified."

Nathaniel gave a lop-sided grin and a one-shouldered shrug. "I would not have objected to a rushed wedding."

Fitzwilliam sat in the chair across from them. "But Georgiana could use the time to adjust to her new situation, and she still has her début in a fortnight."

"We could announce the betrothal at the ball," suggested Lizzy. "The début was a formality anyhow."

Georgiana waved her hand between them. "Not that I do not enjoy when you discuss me as though I am not in the room, but first, we need to take care of Mrs. Younge."

Her betrothed's intense stare sent a tremor through her. "First, you need to dress while I write my mother a note, requesting her presence and a change of clothes."

"Then why are the two of you just sitting there?" Lizzy's favourite eyebrow arched. "Georgiana, perhaps you should let me go ahead of you. We do not want the servants to make assumptions based on your lack of dress."

Georgiana rose and followed Lizzy to the door. Just as her sister let her know the hall was clear, she ducked out as Nathaniel's voice carried through the door, "Let them assume."

"Six weeks, Sele," growled Fitzwilliam in response. "My sister deserves a betrothal and planned wedding rather than an impromptu affair. You must wait at least six weeks."

The last thing she heard as she crept up the stairs was Lizzy's bubbling laughter.

Chapter 23

March 3rd 1817

After a weekend spent discussing the letter with Lady Lindsey, my Aunt Charlotte, my brother, and Lizzy, we have concocted a plan. Whether this will work remains to be seen, but my aunt and Lady Lindsey are certain we shall prevent any damage to my reputation by proceeding in such a way. I can only hope they are correct.

I have been assured by Lady Lindsey that any gossip or scandal that erupts from this will be survived by the Lindsey earldom, yet I still worry. Nathaniel, the dear man, promises me daily he would prefer me with all the ton pointing and staring than another. What have I done to deserve such devotion? I cannot say. I never thought myself worthy of love in the past. Now, I must accept that Nathaniel deems me worthy of his love. Perhaps one day, I shall believe the notion myself.

Today, we begin our plan to rid ourselves of Bridget Younge. We do not know how this will end, but we all pray for a swift resolution in our favour. Mrs. Younge will hopefully have her comeuppance once and for all.

The paper of her journal fluttered in the exhale she blew across the pages. The knots in her stomach appeared when she awoke first thing that morning and persisted for the last few hours. She had not eaten breakfast, afraid she would cast her accounts on the floor when they made the call in . . . she peered at the clock. Oh Lord, in a half-hour!

With a slight tremor to her hand, she placed the pen back in its holder and dried her damp palms on a nearby handkerchief. She never had problems with such dreadful nerves, but today, they were certainly persistent. This was the third cloth in four hours! At this rate, she would need to stuff her reticule full of them to survive the day.

"You need not speak a word, you know." Lydia stood in the open door, leaning against the frame. "Your family will protect you and handle her. You merely need to sit tall and demonstrate that you will not cower in fear."

Georgiana stood, fetched her reticule, and an extra handkerchief before she approached the door. "Whether I need speak or not, I must still remain composed and my behaviour must be, for all intents and purposes, perfect. I am allowed to find the prospect daunting, Lydia." She searched her dressing table until she found her new blue gloves to match the gown Nathaniel favoured. Nathaniel noticed the gloves in a shop during their courtship, but for some reason, waited until they were betrothed to present them to her. They were now her favourite. "Is Mr Hanson to call?" she asked, changing the subject.

"He is. Mrs. Annesley will chaperon." Lydia smiled widely like she did whenever Mr. Hanson's name was mentioned, but her happiness soon faded from her face. "I did ask Lizzy if I could join you this morning, but she felt my presence was not necessary."

"Why would you wish to be a party to this? Despite it being a social call, there is nothing friendly about it. Besides, you counselled me to keep matters to myself."

"And it appears I was mistaken. I know it must sound silly, but you are my dearest friend and my sister, and I wish to be there to support you. Even if I did no more than hold your hand, I would be satisfied."

Georgiana hugged Lydia and kissed her cheek. "You are my dearest friend and my sister, too. I appreciate your willingness to help, but I want you to have your visit with Mr. Hanson. I am still waiting for you to propose to him."

Lydia laughed. "If only propriety would allow it! I cannot even confess my feelings unless he has done so first. 'Tis all so frustrating! His family is invited to your ball, and I am terribly worried they will not like me."

"They can do naught but adore you, Lydia. Stop fretting."

"Well, is it not the pot calling the kettle black," commented Lydia, as they turned and headed for the stairs.

"Perhaps, but you do not need to acquire my nerves."

Lydia only laughed harder. "You remind me of my mother. Do we need to purchase salts for you?"

"No, once we have today sorted, I shall feel inordinately better."

When they entered the drawing room, all a party to the scheme were present and waiting. Nathaniel stood, stepped over, and lifted her hand to kiss her knuckles. "How are you this morning, my dear?"

"She suffers from an acute case of the nerves, my lord," interrupted Lydia with a mischievous countenance. Georgiana glared in her direction, but Nathaniel merely gave a gentle squeeze to her hand.

"I am hopeful we can end Mrs. Younge's plan in as swift a manner as possible, but do remember, that you have no reason to fret. We shall not abandon you should the worst happen." His thumbs rubbed over the backs of her wrists. "You are wearing my gift, I see. If you need my comfort, think of them as me holding your hands, giving you strength." Thank goodness he whispered the last! If Richard or her brother had heard him, they would tease them both mercilessly.

But how she wished they could disappear for even a few minutes so she could lose herself in his embrace. She craved his strength. Strength visible when one looked at him and tangible when in his arms.

He pressed her hand between his palms before bringing it to his arm and leading her further into the room where Lord and Lady Lindsey, Lord and Lady Fitzwilliam, Richard, her brother, and Lizzy all awaited her within. Lady Lindsey had been adamant about including her husband, and though Georgiana was reluctant to reveal the events of Ramsgate to another person, Lady Lindsey's persuasive entreaties that her husband would aid their endeavour peeled away her reservations until she relented.

"Are you well this morning?" asked Aunt Charlotte. "I know you are quite ill-at-ease with today's confrontation, but I do hope you are prepared."

She took in a measured breath in an attempt to stifle the urge to pace from one end of the room to the other. "I am as prepared as I can be. I could never be completely at ease with what we are to do."

Her brother brought her a measure of brandy. "Just enough to calm you."

She shook her head and swallowed. "I cannot. My stomach would not tolerate it."

The glass was taken from his hand by Richard, who emptied it and set it firmly upon the nearest table. When they gaped at him, he shrugged. "Would have been a shame to waste it. Now, let us get this done. I should like to return to my wife before long."

Two carriages awaited them outside Darcy House. The Fitzwilliam coach with the crest on the door in front of the similarly adorned Lindsey coach. Nothing in regards to pressing their connections or advantages was ignored.

Nathaniel escorted Georgiana to the first coach and handed her in with the ladies before he joined the men in the other that would take them in a different direction.

"Where are the men meeting Mr. Browne?" asked Aunt Charlotte as the carriage began to move.

Lizzy adjusted the edge of her glove. "Richard and Fitzwilliam thought meeting him at White's would be preferable to ambushing him in his home. They feared too many of us there for the same purpose might not achieve the desired results."

Rubbing her gloved hand down her skirt, Georgiana shifted in her seat. "What of anyone who could eavesdrop?"

"They have reserved a private room. Your brother would never be so indiscreet."

"Relax, Georgiana," soothed Lady Lindsey. "I can understand you must be exceedingly anxious, but you are by no means unprotected. Your brother is of consequence and you have two earldoms behind you. Regardless of what happens, we will ensure this woman's threats do you no harm." She took Georgiana's hand and held it tight until the equipage came to a halt in front of a sizeable home on Berkeley Street.

The butler admitted them without delay and ushered them to a well-appointed drawing room. Unfortunately, the lady they sought had previous callers, so they made their curtsies, were seated, and joined in the current conversation. When the two other ladies took their leave five minutes later, the door closed behind them, and Aunt Charlotte wasted no time.

"Mrs. Browne, I hope you will forgive us for being presumptuous. We must speak with you on a matter of the utmost importance to not only to our family, but also to the reputation of yours. We are in a quandary, you see, and must do whatever is within our means to remedy this threat against us all."

Mrs. Browne's beady eyes examined each of them before coming to rest again on Aunt Charlotte. "I do not understand, Lady Fitzwilliam."

"No, we did not expect you would," said Lizzy. "You see, your husband has taken company with a woman who was for a short time a companion to my dear sister, Miss Darcy." Lizzy gestured to Georgiana, who stiffened. "Not long after she took the position, my husband learnt how unqualified and inappropriate Mrs. Younge was to be of such influence in a young lady's upbringing. When he discovered her decided lack of character, he dismissed Mrs. Younge without reference, which she still resents to this day."

Mrs. Browne shook her head. "I still do not see why this affects me." Her voice exuded impatience and irritation, but Aunt Charlotte ignored her tone.

"We shall arrive at the point soon," explained Aunt Charlotte. "If you will afford us a little more time." With narrowed eyes, Mrs. Browne dipped her chin before her aunt continued, "This Mrs. Younge conspired with a man, who wished to elope with my niece for her fortune, and in return, Mrs. Younge would receive ten thousand pounds."

Georgiana pulled herself as tall as she could. "My brother learnt of the plot and removed me from the care of Mrs. Younge before their plan could succeed and I could come to harm. After, I heard naught of Mrs. Younge for five years, but I have not been so fortunate as of late. The woman has been determined to speak to me, and I recently learnt why. Several days ago, I received a letter disguised to be from an acquaintance, but instead was an ultimatum from Mrs. Younge. Unless we pay her the ten thousand pounds she lost when her scheme failed, she intends to slander my name by claiming I was ruined by the man with whom she conspired."

"Miss Darcy," interjected Mrs. Browne before Georgiana could say another word. "While I sympathise with your plight, I do not understand what you would have me do. The woman to which you refer is hardly a friend or confidante. As a woman, I have no recourse on the behaviour of my husband."

Lady Lindsey, who had stood and weaved her way through the furniture while she listened, stopped before the fire and stared down Mrs. Browne. "Do you not? You could not be so blind, could you?"

Mrs. Browne's eyes began to dart to each of the ladies in the room. "I am afraid I have no idea what you could mean?"

"Why, your husband's connection to this woman," laughed Lady Lindsey. "Miss Darcy has the support of her brother Mr. Fitzwilliam Darcy, but she also has my son, Viscount Sele's, support, as well as the resources of the Lindsey and Fitzwilliam earldoms behind her. I am certain Lady Fitzwilliam will not object to my saying that we are more than willing to use every resource at our disposal to ruin Mrs. Younge and those who protect her." The threat was succinct, it was direct, and by the sudden pale complexion of Mrs. Browne, quite effective. "Might I enquire of your connections?"

The woman gulped.

They knew well that the Brownes possessed a modest income in comparison to most of the quality and no illustrious relations or friends. They closely resembled, in nature, the former Caroline Bingley—too interested in status and money and not as high as they behaved. If the Lindseys and the Fitzwilliams wished to bring about their downfall, the task would be ridiculously simple.

"You could have her arrested," responded Mrs. Browne. Her voice wavered, but she schooled her features, composing herself quickly.

Lizzy feigned an interest in her reticule while she fingered its ribbons. "Mrs. Younge claims to have made arrangements for the release of her information should that happen, so we felt another course might bear more fruit than such a direct manoeuver. Mrs. Browne, I am unaware of your relationship with your husband, but I find most wives have some influence over their husbands. We simply expect you to exert yours."

A loud, incredulous bark came from the lady. "You wish to be blunt and disregard proper discourse, then very well, we shall do just that." She stood and drew herself up to her tallest height. "Before my husband came into his inheritance, I might have had some sway over him, but now, he is rarely home. He spends most of his time at his club or with his mistress, and to be frank, while I held an affection for my husband when I married him, my feelings changed when faced with the reality of him. Since then, I have come to accept and welcome his absence. Should you wish to control this woman he is so infatuated with, then I urge you to speak with him."

"Oh, there is truly no need for such a measure," said Lady Lindsey with a smile. "Our husbands, if we are fortunate, are persuading him to our cause at this very moment. When we depart your home, we shall call upon my dear friend Lady Jersey. Are you acquainted with her?"

"Only by reputation," she nearly croaked.

Lady Lindsey cast a fond glance at Georgiana. "She was quite impressed with Miss Darcy from the moment she first met her."

"We wish to speak with anyone who could be of aid, you see," Aunt Charlotte continued. "I can assure you that we will leave nothing to chance. My niece is innocent of any wrongdoing and we will ensure her reputation by what means we have at our disposal. Mrs. Younge's reputation, however, is quite simple to tarnish, but ruining her alone will not prevent her from spewing her lies. Instead. we require you and your husband's interference, so perhaps we must examine your character. What of you, Mrs. Browne? What do you have to hide?"

Mrs. Browne's eyes widened just a little. "You know nothing of me." She pointed towards the door. "I want all of you to leave—now!"

"Does Mr. Browne know of Mr. Lewis?" Aunt Charlotte's eyebrows lifted as she asked. Lady Lindsey had ferreted out the information, though no one knew how, but they had sworn to use it only as a last resort—only if Mrs. Browne remained implacable. Well, she was not exactly the model of agreeability!

The lady of the house cleared her throat. "I do not know a Mr. Lewis. I believe I asked you to leave."

Lady Lindsey returned to her chair and sat. "Come now. You wear different gowns and veiled hats when you visit the small home that was once his mother's, but it is certainly you. You are not so dissimilar from many women whose husbands take up with another, but would your husband object? You have borne his heir, but some husbands would prefer their wives not take a lover. Mr. Browne is exceedingly conscious of status as well. Would he object to Mr. Lewis? He is a tradesman, is he not?"

The lady sank into her chair. If she was pale before, she was positively ashen now. She opened her mouth once, twice, but nothing emerged. Her hands grasped and twisted at the flesh of each other. The woman was at sixes and sevens.

Before she could manage to utter a word, the door opened and the butler announced another caller. Mrs. Browne lifted her shoulders and schooled her expression, composing herself. Then, she greeted the newcomer, and sat stiffly as though waiting for one of them to do the opposite of what Napoleon once suggested and air her dirty linen in public.[1]

"I believe we have stayed longer than we ought," announced Georgiana before anyone else could speak. "Thank you for your gracious welcome, Mrs. Browne." She stood and curtseyed to the lady and the new guest, with her relations following suit.

Mrs. Browne stood and curtseyed. "I shall be most attentive to the matter we discussed in the future, Lady Lindsey." She nodded at Lady Lindsey. "Lady Fitzwilliam." She nodded at Aunt Charlotte. "Mrs. Darcy, Miss Darcy, I hope you will call again soon." Her voice was welcoming, but the words were contradictory to her clenched hands and tense jaw.

They remained quiet until all of them boarded the carriage and the door was closed behind them. When they began to move, Georgiana looked at her aunt and Lady Lindsey. "What do you think?"

Aunt Charlotte shrugged and sighed. "Unfortunately, we shall not know much more until the men return from White's."

"I thought we agreed not to bring Mrs. Browne's lover into matters," said Lizzy faintly. Lady Lindsey and Aunt Charlotte's eyes met.

Lady Lindsey took Georgiana's hand. "Mrs. Browne is known for bragging and taking great pride in her husband and her position, but she is also known to be quite ruthless. Charlotte and I agreed we must use every weapon in our arsenal. Mrs. Browne must know we are aware of her behaviour or she will not lift a pinkie finger to help us."

Georgiana peeled off her gloves and dried her hands with her handkerchief. "We never requested she keep our confidence."

A laugh came from Lady Lindsey. "She will not breathe a word, my dear. If she told anyone, she would have to discuss her husband's mistress as well as her own lover. No, she will keep her mouth closed. I would wager on it."

They did not lie to Mrs. Browne as the ladies did call on Lady Jersey. They did not discuss the particulars of the letter or her blackmail of Georgiana, but Lady Lindsey insisted on the call while they constructed the plan in the hopes of controlling any damage should Mrs. Younge make her knowledge public fodder.

After Lady Jersey rang for tea, the conversation flowed until another caller complained of her issues with several maids, and Aunt Charlotte pounced on the opportunity. "There is nothing more ghastly than problems with servants. I have always been quite envious of my nephew and Mrs. Darcy. They have always had the good fortune to hire the best servants and rarely have problems." She put a finger to her chin and looked up a little as though thinking. "I believe the last I remember was that terrible companion he hired for my niece before your marriage." She turned to address Lizzy at the last. "Did he ever mention her?"

Lizzy rolled her eyes. "Mrs. Younge was her name, and yes, he and my my sister have spoken of her. Of course, she remained in his employ only a few short months before he let her go."

"Mrs. Younge?" asked Lady Jersey with wide eyes. "If she is the same Mrs. Younge referred to in the latest gossip, I must admit I have heard her name mentioned in the most dissolute of ways."

Lizzy sipped her tea and swallowed. "Unfortunately, she is one and the same, my lady, though she was not a woman of ill-repute when my husband hired her. She presented herself as the widow of a colonel in the Regulars who had become a companion due to necessity. Her references appeared to be exemplary, but my husband soon discovered those were nothing more than a fabrication."

"'Tis so difficult to find good help," commiserated the lady who was once bemoaning her own problems.

Aunt Charlotte nodded and turned back to Lizzy. "He also discovered she conspired with a man in order to swindle Miss Darcy's fortune, did she not?"

"We were fortunate my husband discovered her scheme before she could make good on her plans. My sister could have been lost to us forever."

"I am simply fortunate my brother happened upon the proof of her lies." Georgiana fiercely gripped the saucer in her hand. She could not shake! "I only wish Mrs. Younge would stay far away from me, but she has attempted to speak to me as of late as though we are friends. Can you imagine?"

Lady Jersey gasped and placed a hand to her chest. "Of all the nerve! Once a lady's status changes as hers has, she cannot expect to maintain the same acquaintances. No respectable lady would admit her."

"She seemed quite put out when Lord Sele and I cut her at the theatre," said Georgiana with her best dramatic sigh. Living with Lydia certainly taught her a few skills she had not previously possessed. "I do hope she makes no further attempts. We were hardly friends when she served as my companion, and I definitely have no desire to be friends now."

Lady Lindsey, who sat on the sofa to her left, patted her knee. "Well, of course you do not, my dear."

Miss Darcy," began Lady Jersey with a side-long glance, "I understand you have entered a courtship with Lord Sele. I must offer you my congratulations."

Georgiana genuinely smiled at the lady's comment. "I am pleased Lord Sele found me worthy of courting. He is a true gentleman."

"He is indeed," agreed her Aunt Charlotte.

Their rumour planted, Georgiana sipped her tea, her stomach finally beginning to settle. "Lady Jersey, your gown is beautiful—I particularly adore the colour."

"Oh! Why, thank you. It was just delivered from Madame Guiard yesterday, and I found myself anxious to wear it."

The remaining ladies all gave their compliments while Lady Jersey preened. When the topic shifted again, Lizzy winked subtly in Georgiana's direction while sipping her own tea. Their work for today was completed, but what of the men? Could they have found success? It was doubtful. Such a swift resolution was unlikely, but she could hope!

Chapter 24

March 5th 1817

Two days! It has been two long days and we have heard nothing of Mrs. Browne, Mrs. Younge, or Mr. Browne. I do know I am being unrealistic—that a solution could not be forged so swiftly, but with each day that passes, I become more worried.

As disheartening as the lack of resolution from the men and Mr. Browne was when we returned from calling on Lady Jersey, the men at least reported Mr. Browne appeared horrified by the notion of making an enemy of three peers. He had not apologised or promised to make amends, but instead, became argumentative and angry, which puzzles me exceedingly. I suppose it is impossible to predict how someone will react, yet I hoped he would be more willing to help resolve the matter.

Our attempt at starting gossip has proven successful, however, and we have had proof of our good fortune with that endeavour. One of our callers yesterday declared Mrs. Younge "pure evil" and that it was "no wonder I delayed my coming out." Our little rumour seems to have spread like pollen in the breeze in the short time since we first mentioned it. Apparently, Mrs. Younge's scheme for my dowry has become the accepted explanation among the entirety of the ton for my long absence from London. I am still amazed at its effectiveness as we never even told the entirety of the story, but Mrs. Younge has been vilified and I have become the innocent victim. How like the truth a lie has become!

One lady, who called yesterday upon learning of Mrs. Younge, confided how a man whose family had lost their fortune at the card tables attempted to force her into marriage some years ago—his desire nothing more than an attempt to gain her substantial fortune. Their scheme failed when her family learnt of their plan and whisked her away from London to their Lancashire estate, yet the experience still left an indelible mark upon her. I am surprised she shared her experience. I still cannot believe the gossip has done as it ought.

She started at the sound of the knocker and paused, her pen hovering over the fine sheet of paper. Loud voices and a general commotion filtered through the open door, so she set her pen in its holder, rose, and stepped into the hall where something hit her in the legs with an "oomph."

"Gee! Up!" With a smile, she lifted the little imp into her arms. He kissed her cheek and wrapped his arms around her neck, squeezing tight. "I want go park!" he cried when he pulled back. "Come with me?"

"You are to go to the park with your Mama and Papa after your nap. I would be pleased to go then, but you must sleep for Mrs. Wynn first."

His eyebrows drew together, making him look more like a serious and put out Fitzwilliam. "No nap."

She pressed her forehead to his. "You must take a nap, or no Aunt Georgiana."

His shoulders dropped before he held up his fingers a hairsbreadth apart. "Little nap?"

Pursing her lips to keep herself from laughing at the gesture Lizzy often used with him, she glanced to Mrs. Wynn, whose shoulders shook. "If you take even a little nap, I shall accompany you to the park."

He wiggled his little legs to get down, grabbed Mrs. Wynn's hand, and led her into the nursery. His nap was not for another hour, but with her help, he climbed upon his cot, closed his eyes, and feigned sleep. The child was entirely too clever for his own good! Any child of Lizzy's and Fitzwilliam's would be intelligent, but who knew they could create one so mischievous! That part had to come from Lizzy.

While his eyes were shut, Georgiana placed a finger to her lips, grinned at Mrs. Wynn, then crept in the direction of the commotion downstairs. When she reached the hall, all appeared to be quiet until Jobbins exited her brother's study, and the voices became loud again before the door closed and muffled the din.

"Jobbins, who has called?"

His eyes widened when he noticed her, peered back from where he came, and back to her. "Mr Browne called for the master, miss."

She placed her hands on her hips and narrowed her eyes. "That is too much noise for just my brother and Mr. Browne."

"Colonel—I beg your pardon, Mr. Fitzwilliam and Lord Sele arrived an hour ago and have been speaking in the master's study. They remained when I showed Mr. Browne in a moment ago."

She took two steps towards the door, but Jobbins put out his hand. "Forgive me, miss, but Mr. Darcy requested they not be disturbed."

Her eyes travelled from Jobbins' hand to his face. "You have done as you were instructed. I shall be certain my brother is made aware." The aged butler's eyebrows rose when she stepped around him and hastened to step inside and close the door before he could stop her. All heads in the room turned to her. Her brother, Richard, and Nathaniel all frowned.

"I told Jobbins we were not to be disturbed." The tone of her brother's voice was low and unfriendly, though certainly not meant to frighten her.

"He informed me of your request," said Georgiana, "but as this pertains to me, I wished to know what has happened to cause the yelling I heard when Mr. Browne arrived."

The man himself stepped around Richard, so he stood closer than she liked, but Nathaniel edged his way beside her in a protective gesture. "Do you wish to know why I am angry? You and the other ladies in your family called on my wife, did you not? Did you think I would allow that threat to go unanswered?"

"The threat was no more than we delivered to you ourselves," drawled Richard, who rolled his eyes. "What I find baffling is your waiting until today to address the ladies' call. Why is that, Mr. Browne?"

"Because I only learnt of it this morning," boomed Mr. Browne. "My wife sent footmen and messengers all over to find me once the last caller departed that day, but I was attending . . ." He glanced at her, cleared his throat, and turned back to Richard, "important business. I did not receive my wife's message until I returned from my club early this morning."

She startled a bit—not at the tone but at the content of his words. He had not received his wife's messages for two days? He had not laid eyes upon his family for the same time?

"Important business, you say." Nathaniel laughed and shook his head. "I would say Mrs. Younge persuaded you of her innocence and slandered Miss Darcy's good name, did she not? Then, I would wager she convinced you further for the remainder of the time. She kept you so occupied, you would not consider the truth of the matter much less the comfort or peace of mind of your family. Particularly when you had her comforts to avail yourself of."

While Nathaniel spoke, Mr. Browne's face turned several shades of red, deepening more and more through the speech. He opened his mouth.

Richard dropped into his chair as though watching a play. "By the beetroot complexion of the gentleman, I congratulate you on your winning hand, Sele. The woman must be quite a piece to make the man a blunderbuss[2] as well as blind."

"How dare you! And before a lady no less!" Mr. Browne clenched his hands into fists at his sides and a vein pulsed on his forehead. "Though I should not be surprised with the threats levelled by your women towards my wife and my children. They have done nothing to you, yet you treat them with such callous disregard."

"We merely warned her of the repercussions to her reputation and that of her family should you continue your relationship with Mrs. Younge," explained Georgiana, speaking as evenly as possible lest her voice shake. "Your ignorance of the woman's actions and her nature will be their ruin, not us."

"You spoke of my family to Lady Jersey and her callers!" he screamed. "My wife has heard of the call you made after you departed my home. Do you deny it?!"

Georgiana held her hands up with her palms out. "That we mentioned your family, I deny completely. We made no reference to your wife or your children. As for the call, we told your wife ourselves that we intended to speak with Lady Jersey. Since we will not pay what Mrs. Younge demands, we hoped to prevent any damage from her falsehoods."

"You lie!" he cried and stepped closer. Nathaniel wedged himself between them, but Georgiana moved to the side of her betrothed. Despite the quivering of her limbs, she could no longer shield herself behind the men of her family or Nathaniel.

"We spoke of what occurred with Mrs. Younge. Her connection to you is well-known among the gossips in London. We never mentioned your name nor your wife's. If Mrs. Younge was linked to you by the rumour mill, 'tis no one's fault but your own. We had naught to do with it."

Her brother opened a drawer, rose, and walked around until face to face with the man. "Sir, you will believe what you will, but you will not abuse my sister in her home. Should you continue, I shall have you removed from this house, and I shall not aid your family should Mrs. Younge harm mine."

Mr. Browne's jaw stiffened, but he stepped back, his eyes round and his arm outstretched with his finger pointed. "What do you hold in your hand?" Mr. Browne jumped when her brother pulled a letter from his side, holding it before the man.

"I thought you might benefit from reading this," said her brother in a tired voice.

His eyes rested upon the item. "What is it?"

Georgiana steeled herself. The note in his hand was well known to her and she fought the urge to cringe. She could not allow any hint of weakness. She could not!

Richard growled, stood, took the paper from her brother, and held it closer to Mr. Browne. "'Tis correspondence found in Mrs. Younge's rooms after she packed her belongings and departed his home."

The man snatched it from Richard's grasp. "It should have been returned to her possession immediately. What it contains is no one's concern but her own."

Richard stood toe to toe with Mr. Browne, who did not retreat in the slightest. "Perhaps you should read the passage where your lady suggests Mr. Wickham force himself upon Miss Darcy should she not accept his hand in marriage—that she might accept him rather than face ruin."

Nathaniel's hand wrapped around hers before she could clench the fabric of her skirts, but he shifted closer so their joined hands were hidden in behind the folds.

"I know Bridget Younge more intimately than you. She would never do such a thing."

"Do not presume you know the woman as well as you believe," sneered Richard. "She has no love for you and will not hesitate to swindle you should she happen upon the opportunity."

"My maid found the correspondence, sir." When he looked at her, Georgiana held his eye and did not shrink. "She knew the reason for Mrs. Younge's departure, recognised the name of the recipient, and brought it directly to my brother. The article is genuine. I assure you."

While she spoke, Richard removed the letter from Mr. Browne's grasp, unfolded it, and held it before the man. Mr. Browne shifted his eyes to the side in an attempt to avoid the slender writing on the pages, but as quickly as they darted away, they returned and he leaned closer. After a moment of studying the missive, he took it carefully, moved to the window, and tilted the document in different directions. "This is truly her handwriting."

"Indeed," her brother agreed a bit sarcastically.

They watched while his eyes roved over the words once and then again, his shoulders dropping and his body nearly sagging by the time he was done. "I would like to see the proof of her threats against you."

Her brother looked at her and she nodded while Nathaniel's grip tightened on her hand. "Are you certain?" he whispered.

"No, but I am hoping my instinct serves me well."

Another letter was removed from the drawer and handed to Mr. Browne, who unfolded it with careful fingers and treated it in much the same manner as the first, only his reaction differed drastically. Instead of the dejected countenance like the first, his spine stiffened and, when he lifted his head, a crunch sounded from his jaw as he clenched it. "This man did offer you marriage—to elope?"

"Mrs. Younge attempted to persuade me in his direction, but I had no love for the man. I refused him."

Something about the expression upon his face disconcerted her. He opened his mouth three times as though he would ask a question, but a sound never came. Was he going to ask if Wickham attempted what Mrs. Younge suggested? The question would be improper to say the least, which might have explained his hesitance.

Nathaniel cleared his throat. "Sir, you have your proof. Now, I ask if you will aid our endeavour to keep the woman from spreading her falsehoods or will you remain wilfully blind to her evil? I have chosen to support Miss Darcy as has the Lindsey earldom, and we will do all in our power to ensure she remains unharmed."

"As will the Fitzwilliams," added Richard.

"I believe my allegiance is obvious." Her brother glared at the man. "What part will you take?"

"She made a fool of me," he seethed. "She has pretended to care, pretended to be what she is not. I—"

"Mrs. Younge is clever, as well as a practiced deceiver." Richard poured himself a brandy and took a sizeable gulp. "Darce and I did not even consider checking her references until after Miss Darcy was in her care. The fault of this calamity lies with us."

Georgiana took the glass of brandy from Richard's hand and set it aside. "'Tis too early for that, and it shall not help one jot. Besides, Julia will throttle you if you drink more than you ought before noon."

She laughed at Richard's fiercest glare. "Such a hateful look might have frightened me when I was a child, but has no effect on me now."

Mr. Browne watched them before he turned his attention back to the letter. He tensed and released his free hand several times and shifted on his feet. Then, he held the papers out to her brother. "I appreciate your candour and willingness to share this. I need to . . ." He cleared his throat. "I must depart. I beg your pardon."

Before Richard or Fitzwilliam could show him to the door, Mr. Browne hastened himself out, giving a passing nod to Lizzy who stood in the door of the drawing room. Jobbins did not even have the opportunity to open the door before he exited. With Mr. Browne gone, they followed Lizzy back into the drawing room and Richard closed the door behind them.

"Well?" asked Lizzy, her eyes darting expectantly to each one of them.

"It appears Mrs. Younge convincingly persuaded him to believe her innocence in all of it." Richard's tone was biting as he swaggered near the fire and dropped into the closest chair. "That woman must have some sort of magic power to render a man stupid by bedding him."

"Must you speak so with ladies present," chided Nathaniel.

"Do I offend you, Sele?" he chuckled. "Lizzy has borne a child, so I doubt what goes on is a mystery to her, though you never know with my uptight cousin here. As for Georgiana, I see no reason to shield her from reality since Darce and I ceased to do so years ago. You are aware of why, so I shall not explain further."

Georgiana bit her lip and peered at Nathaniel out of the corner of her eye. How would he handle such a statement from her heedless and blunt-spoken cousin?

He did not balk or flinch, but instead turned to her brother. "My mother desired a visit with Georgiana. Would you mind if we walked to my parents' and remained long enough for perhaps some tea?"

She nodded at her brother's raised eyebrows, so he nodded. "Of course, but please have Lucy and at least a footman accompany you."

"I doubt Mrs. Younge will attempt an abduction or some sort of violence on the street," she scoffed. "She merely desires money."

Richard pointed at her. "Do not dismiss her so easily. Do not forget it was her idea for Wickham—"

"I do not require reminding," she said, tensing and exasperated. "The situation, however, is quite different this time."

Mumbling came from Richard, but she could not understand what he said while he turned towards the fire, so she ignored him. With a kiss to Lizzy's and her brother's cheek, she took Nathaniel's arm and headed for the hall, but Lizzy's voice caused them to pause.

"Do not forget the Audleys, the Bingleys, and Lady Catherine will join us for dinner."

She smiled. "I shall remember. Besides, I promised William to join you in the park. Do not fret. We shall return before long."

Once Lucy and a footman joined them, the walk was but a quick stroll. The butler showed them inside where they were placed in a drawing room and informed Lady Lindsey would join them shortly.

"My mother must have had a long morning with the housekeeper. The knocker is not even up yet."

"If she is too busy, I can call another day," offered Georgiana. "I do not mind."

A handsome grin spread across his face. "I am in no hurry for her to join us." He glanced at the cracked door. Unless someone stood at a particular angle or poked their head inside, the two of them were more or less concealed.

He stepped towards her while she stepped back. "What are you about?"

"If we stand behind the door, we cannot be seen."

His low tone sent a ripple of something down her spine, and she bumped a small table, making a vase teeter precariously on its surface. Before it could plummet to the floor, she darted to grab it and settle it. When she removed her hands, Nathaniel's arms wrapped around her waist from behind, pulling her flush to him.

"I have not had a moment alone with you since I asked you to marry me."

"Since we spent the night together and Fitzwilliam does not allow us to remain unchaperoned." Her breathless voice always sounded like someone else's when he flustered her. She turned in his embrace—such solace after the confrontation with Mr. Browne. "He will not be pleased if we flaunt propriety again."

His lips seared the skin where her neck met her shoulder. "We shall not flaunt it much. I promise." His whispered breath left a trail of gooseflesh in its wake. If she had not been in his arms, she would have swayed on the spot.

He trailed small kisses up to her ear and down her jaw until he claimed her lips. A small almost squeak escaped, but she closed her eyes and gripped the shoulders of his jacket to hold herself up. Thoughts blurred until all she could do was feel—feel the coarse wool of his jacket against the bits of skin uncovered by her gown, feel the softness of his lips as they caressed hers, and feel her heart thrum against her ribs in a flutter instead of an even rhythm.

One of his hands slid around to the small of her back and pressed her closer while the other followed the curve of her waist up to her ribs, finally resting almost under her arm where the heel of his hand and his wrist touched the side of her breast. She inhaled sharply and stood on her tiptoes. She had to get closer, to burrow as close as she could until they were joined from head to toe.

His deep, throaty groan only made their surroundings disappear further. Her fingers wove through his soft hair, clenching when his lips suckled under her ear. Her eyes rolled back in her head and she whimpered at the need pulsing through her.

Then, from somewhere in the distance a throat cleared.

---

[1]*Napoleon was quoted in 1815, amending a French Proverb "Il faut laver son linge sale en famille" ("we should wash our dirty linen in private").*
[2]*A stupid, blundering fellow*

Chapter 25

March 10th 1817

We cannot explain it, but Mrs. Younge seems to have vanished from London. After their initial meeting with Mr. Browne, Fitzwilliam and Richard hired men to search for her, but she has even eluded them. Initially, she remained at the house provided by Mr. Browne until just before the weekend when she departed in a hackney. Alas, the hack was lost in a sea of carriages when it travelled down several busy streets and the investigators, who lacked enough men to follow every possibility, became confused which carriage contained her and followed the wrong one. Richard mumbled for days about inept reconnaissance and how he could have fared better, but without knowing where she went, he could not even make an attempt to watch her.

In the event she made an appearance along the Serpentine, my brother was present at the time and place she specified to claim her ten thousand pounds, but she never appeared. Grooms and footmen took shifts watching that particular spot in Hyde Park all weekend, yet not one caught a glimpse of her. We assume she must have known he would not pay.

Despite what occurred, naught of what she threatened has appeared in the gossip columns as of yet. I am braced for the worst, but a small part of my heart hopes she has been thwarted in some manner. Without direct knowledge of her whereabouts and her intentions, all I have is hope.

Georgiana sighed and set her pen on its stand. The longer they went without word of Mrs Younge, the more her stomach churned. Today it was a writhing mess. How could she fall into a sense of security when there was none to be had?

Perhaps happy thoughts to dispel her fears would be of aid. Carefully, Georgiana shifted back several pages and bit her lip.

March 5th 1817

I have just returned from the Lindseys' and I am positively mortified! Lord Lindsey caught Nathaniel and I kissing in the drawing room. I confess matters progressed a little further than mere kissing since Nathaniel had a hand on my side as he did, and though his touch was tentative, I am still overwhelmed by the strength of the sensation that seeped through my gown and filtered through my body.

And Lord Lindsey saw us thus! It is in every way horrifying! I know we should not have been behaving so in the drawing room with the door cracked even the slightest bit, but once Nathaniel pressed his lips to mine, I forgot our surroundings completely. His touches only added fuel to that fire. I never understood those who declared themselves helpless to resist a man's or a woman's charms, yet I am powerless to Nathaniel's.

I do appreciate that Lord Lindsey did not scold as he should, but simply ordered his son to set a date with my brother before the end of that day, insisting he not accept a wedding further than six weeks from the date of our betrothal. I suppose to reduce our chances of flaunting propriety again before we are wed?

My flesh burned so intensely in embarrassment that if Nathaniel had touched my cheek, I am sure I would have scalded him. How I wish I could have buried my face into Nathaniel's chest and hidden! I would have closed my eyes, breathed in his scent, and never withdrawn. Well, perhaps once we were alone, I would have. It would be impossible to kiss Nathaniel otherwise.

Despite what occurred, I still remained for tea with Lady Lindsey, but I could not look Lord Lindsey in the eye for the remainder of the day, no matter how hard I tried. Nathaniel was amused by my mortification and laughed quietly while I stared everywhere but his father. Impertinent man!

I am grateful Lord Lindsey has not breathed a word of our behaviour to my brother or his wife. He informed Nathaniel that if the date was settled that evening, he would not tell, and I do believe he has upheld his end of the bargain. Lady Lindsey would not hesitate to give her opinion on our behaviour if she was aware, and she did not say a word of it this afternoon.

Of course, after my call and tea with his mother, Nathaniel returned with me to Darcy House and immediately petitioned my brother to set the date for the wedding. Fitzwilliam attempted to delay a week or so, but Nathaniel pressed based on my brother's words from the morning we were betrothed. Fortunately, Fitzwilliam asked no questions and eventually capitulated without further explanation, though if my brother knew of our lapse of propriety that day, he would likely have us wed within the week. As it is, I think he is loath to part with me.

Now, Richard has taken to persuading me to change the date of the wedding so I might still stay with him and Julia this summer. Though I am certain he means to tease more than to truly cause me guilt, I do believe he is hurt I became betrothed so swiftly. He knows he could not find a more worthy man for me, yet I suppose I am little like a daughter to him and my brother, which makes them more sentimental. They have their wives, so they can allow me a husband, *can they not?*

She stood, walked to the window, and watched a horse and then a carriage pass before the house. Just before she could turn, however, the familiar stride and shoulder set of her betrothed caught her eye at the end of the square. With a smile, her eyes followed him as he approached and she pressed a hand to the glass. He might not be able to see if the angle of the sun created a glare on the pane, but she would know.

A wide grin split his face and he winked in her direction, making something in her chest flutter, replacing the earlier uneasy sensation. He was so handsome. He stood tall and sure, his confident walk suited him, and his humour and outgoing attitude complemented her quiet nature. She would never find anyone better—at least not for her.

Before he could approach the front of the house, she hurried from her room and down the stairs so she awaited him in the hall when Jobbins opened the door. His eyes lit when he saw her standing there, and he rushed forward, lifted her in his arms, and twirled her around, his hat falling to the ground.

"Nathaniel!" she cried, laughing. "My brother will have a fit should he find us thus." Her feet hit the floor as Jobbins quickly passed behind her, picked up the hat, and took Nathaniel's coat before disappearing into the servants' passage. "What has you so happy?"

"Come!" He grabbed her hand and pulled her to Fitzwilliam's study door, which opened when they drew near.

Fitzwilliam's expression was not shocked, but resigned. "What are you doing to my sister before the servants, Sele?"

"Celebrating," he responded, pleased and almost exultant. "I have news. Nothing definitive, but enough to give me hope."

Her brother's eyebrows lifted and he gestured them inside, swiftly closing the door behind him. "About Mrs. Younge?"

Nathaniel nodded and squeezed her hand before it could tremble. "My parents attended a dinner party last night. I do not recall the host, some peer or another, but that is not important." Her brother waved his hand, urging Sele to get to the point. "Mr. Browne was the subject of much of the gossip when the ladies separated after the meal. It seems the man informed several of his friends at White's that he intended to end his agreement with Mrs. Younge."

She gasped. "When did this occur?"

"The very same day he arrived here full of ire, and we enlightened him of the woman's character." Nathaniel was so pleased, she was surprised he did not bounce in place. "Apparently, he indicated to the men present that her skills as a courtesan were lacking and he would ensure his next mistress suited his needs better." He lifted her hand to kiss the back. "Forgive me for saying as much in front of you."

"I do not want you to keep things from me—even should they be considered improper for a lady's ears by most of society. I shall not suddenly become dissolute by hearing of such matters, nor will my ears suddenly set themselves aflame. Besides, we shall wed in four weeks, and Lizzy has told me that many matrons are far too candid in regards to marital advice with a newly wed lady. I am certain I shall not be exempt from their salacious advice."

With a groan, her brother returned to his chair. "I should not have allowed her to be alone at those first few dinner parties. Thank goodness when Anne and Bingley returned to London after their wedding. Anne and Elizabeth, together, managed to successfully change the subject when it was broached, so we attended most functions together since neither Elizabeth nor Anne wanted their ridiculous counsel." He gave Nathaniel a stern look. "Be certain Georgiana has a lady she knows at every party you attend for a year or so after you wed."

He nodded and laughed. "I will be certain to do so, though I hope Georgiana would know better than to listen to a word they say."

"I do," she said with a smile, "but I understand they can be quite shocking in their advice—even Lizzy was taken aback by their candid speak. She could barely keep from giggling while Fitzwilliam discussed the most mundane subjects with the husbands."

"She nearly spit wine on the Duke of Cheltenham after his wife decided to enlighten Elizabeth on how she avoided her husband's nightly visits." Fitzwilliam shook his head. "We have strayed from the point. Has the gossip said where Mrs. Younge is at the moment?"

Nathaniel's shoulders dropped just a little. "No, no one has mentioned where she might be at all. It is as though she disappeared from London without a trace."

"She could not have just vanished." Georgiana led Nathaniel to the chairs before Fitzwilliam's desk and they both sat. "She departed Mayfair in a hackney, which is strange since your investigators discovered Mr. Browne had a carriage and horses at her disposal. I have wondered if she was fleeing from him."

"It is possible," agreed Nathaniel. "If she became aware that he knew of her deception and was angry, she might run. We do not know enough about either of them to know their actions for certain. With his gossip, he ensured she will find no other protector among the quality. 'Tis my hope she has fled for good."

Her brother sighed and stared at the papers on his desk. "Yet she never fails to turn up like a bad penny. I still want Georgiana protected. I know you would never allow her to come to harm, Sele, but I insist you take footmen with you if you leave the house. I believe you planned a walk in Hyde Park?"

Georgiana leaned towards the desk. "Fitzwilliam—"

"I would never argue when it comes to her safety," explained Nathaniel. "I already planned to have a couple of footmen with us along with a chaperon—"

"I am still in the room." Georgiana looked between the two of them. "I do not believe she is a concern. She wants money, not revenge. Surely no more than a maid is necessary?"

"If Mr. Browne has frightened her into hiding, then she might be desperate." Fitzwilliam pulled a piece of paper before him and began to write. "No, I believe Sele's plan is prudent. I am pleased to find him considering your safety before his wishes for a stolen moment."

"We would hardly find a 'stolen moment,' as you put it, with a maid accompanying us." Her reply had a slight sting to it, but she despised when her brother became overprotective. Now, he urged Nathaniel in the same endeavour. She decided long ago she had no wish to be cossetted as it did naught to help her feelings of insecurity. Instead, she faced those fears, banishing them swifter than she believed she would otherwise.

"I trust Lucy to prevent your reputation from coming to harm, but she is quite devoted to you. I would not put it past her to act as a lookout so the two of you can misbehave." He looked between the two of them accusingly.

"What do you believe us to have done?" she asked. Please do not let him know of the Lindseys' drawing room!

"Only what occurred the night of your betrothal, which was bad enough. I recall how I searched for every opportunity to have Elizabeth to myself before we were wed, so I know the temptation." His complexion reddened a little and he cleared his throat.

Georgiana burst into gales of laughter. "Yes, I recall Aunt Charlotte's complaints. Your chaperons were dreadful and turned their backs on you and Lizzy, and the two of you took full advantage—despite their being nearby."

Nathaniel covered his mouth to restrain his amusement while Fitzwilliam coughed and shifted in his seat. "We were not so bad, Georgiana."

"Oh yes, you were. I remember quite well. Besides, we are unlikely to steal away in Hyde Park during the fashionable hour. I would prefer to forgo the torture altogether, but Lady Lindsey and Aunt Charlotte insist we must make at least two appearances in the next week."

A warm hand covered hers. "My mother and your aunt only want to ensure the announcement of our betrothal at your début does not seem precipitate."

"The ball is a formality," she groused. "I never desired the event and we would not be hosting a ball were it not for Lydia's presumption."

Nathaniel stared at her with his eyebrows drawn down in the middle. "I do not understand."

"No formal début existed before the day we met in the hat shop. Lydia created the entire affair in an attempt to encourage you towards me."

"Not that I required any encouragement," he smiled.

"Lydia knew," explained Fitzwilliam. "She was certain your interest lay in Georgiana and hoped to throw the two of you together."

"I must thank her then." Nathaniel's dimples deepened with his grin. "If she has helped you along even a little, then I owe her a great debt." They started at a knock on the door.

"Enter!" called her brother.

As they stood, Lydia, who wore her best day gown, and Mr. Hanson entered, the former with an enormous smile upon her face. "Lizzy said you and Lord Sele were to walk in Hyde Park this afternoon?" When Georgiana dipped her chin in answer, Lydia glanced at Mr. Hanson before continuing. "Would you mind terribly if we joined you? I have not yet walked during the fashionable hour and it sounds ever so interesting."

She glanced at Nathaniel who shrugged a shoulder. "I do not object."

Lydia clasped her hands and stared at Georgiana expectantly. "Georgiana?"

"I do not object either, and I am certain Lucy will be relieved she is not required to go along with us. She has never been fond of walking, and I am sure she would prefer to attend to her duties here."

The youngest Bennet sister bounced on her toes. "I would think we should be departing soon?"

At Nathaniel's nod, Georgiana poked her head through the doorway, finding a footman close by. "Would you have Miss Bennet's and my maid bring our pelisses, hats, and gloves to the hall?"

"Of course, miss," he said with a swift bow.

Once they were clad in their best coats and hats, they strolled the short distance to Hyde Park where Georgiana and Nathaniel walked just ahead of Lydia and Mr. Hanson. A footman was positioned on each side of their group, keeping a watchful eye on those who passed and those who approached.

"Miss Darcy!" When she turned, Lady Jersey approached with her sister Lady Bessborough. "I am pleased to have happened upon you. I trust your family is well?"

"Yes, my lady, they are very well."

"And yours, Lord Sele?"

He nodded in acknowledgement. "My mother and father are enjoying a quiet afternoon at home. They do not have such an opportunity often this time of year."

"I sympathise with their predicament." She peered around Georgiana to

Lydia and Mr. Hanson who remained close behind and speaking softly. "Would you introduce me to your friends?" They both stepped forward at Lady Jersey's request.

"Lady Jersey, Lady Bessborough, may I present Mrs. Darcy's youngest sister, Miss Lydia Bennet, and Mr. David Hanson."

Once they all bowed and curtseyed, Lady Bessborough dipped her chin towards Lydia. "We heard Miss Bennet was in town, though we have not had the pleasure of making her acquaintance until now. I do hope you are enjoying your stay?" As Lady Bessborough spoke, she eyed Lydia's gown and pelisse, likely attempting to place a value on the fabric and dating the style.

Lydia offered a controlled curve of her lips. "Thank you, my lady, I have enjoyed London immensely. I am thankful my sister and brother extended the invitation for the season."

"I believe Mr. Hanson has requested a courtship?" asked Lady Jersey as she acknowledged the gentleman.

"Yes, my lady. I am honoured he chose me for such a request." Anyone who knew Lydia well could see her restraining herself until she nearly shook, she was so pent up with emotion. The poor dear was desperate to make a good impression and not to shame Mr. Hanson. She would make herself ill if she continued thus.

"I was acquainted with your father," Lady Jersey informed Mr. Hanson. "He was an honourable man. You must have felt his death keenly."

He nodded. "I assure you I do, thank you."

"Now," she returned to Lydia, "you must tell me where you found the satin for your pelisse. I have searched for months for just that shade of rose."

Lydia's severe grip on her reticule and Mr. Hanson's arm relaxed and a grin spread upon her face. Fashion was something she could discuss easily and without fear of saying the wrong thing. "My sister purchased the fabric as a birthday present not long after our arrival in town. I do not know the name of the establishment, but if you like, she can send you a note with the direction of the shop."

Lady Jersey's eyes crinkled at the edges as she smiled. "I shall look forward to her message then." After a glance at her sister with raised eyebrows, she turned back to the group. "It has been lovely making your acquaintance. We shall need to return to our carriage soon, so we should start walking towards the gates. I anticipate speaking to the lot of you at Almack's."

As soon as they curtseyed and departed, Lydia's eyes bulged. "Did she say she would see the lot of us at Almack's?" Her voice was breathless and a mite controlled, as though she would burst when someone affirmed her question.

"You did very well," complimented Mr. Hanson, proudly standing tall.

"May I request the first?"

Lydia playfully slapped his arm. "I have yet to receive my invitation, you silly man, and I shall not accept any dance requests until I have."

Mr. Hanson pretended to be pained as he replied, "I believe that is the closest you will get to an actual voucher this early in the Season."

When they continued on, Nathaniel bent closer. "I believe you have just been guaranteed your own Almack's voucher. If I request your first now, will you make me wait or will you relieve my suffering and consent now?" A shiver ran down Georgiana's spine and his warm breath tickled her ear.

She gave a sidelong glance and bit her lip. "I might be persuaded."

Both dimples appeared, and a warm, deep chuckle made a few passers-by stare. "Then, I shall certainly enjoy applying my best persuasive skills to garnering your acceptance."

"I have no doubt," she laughed.

Chapter 26

When Georgiana made her entrance, candlelight glittered in the decorative cuts of the fine crystal and luminous silks and satins glistened against the dark windows of the ballroom. Her body trembled at the sea of eyes staring exclusively at her on her brother's arm, but she stood tall and refused to cower. After all, she was a Darcy, and proud of her heritage and her brother. She would not disappoint her family.

Nathaniel stood in the centre of the room, which would soon be the midst of the dancing when the music began—though that was part of their plan. Her brother led her through the crowd, who parted when they approached, until he stood between her and Nathaniel, with a hand raised.

"I would like to thank all who came to wish my sister well this evening and to join us on this joyous occasion. I have considered Georgiana out for quite some time, so I am pleased to make it all official." The Fitzwilliams, the Bennets—who travelled to London for the ball—the Bingleys, the Lindseys, and the Audleys all smiled.

Her family comprised the innermost ring surrounding her, their presence supporting her intangibly. The friendly faces before her soothed her more than the strangers who lurked behind them.

"Tonight, however, is not merely her début. I am certain many of you are aware of the courtship between my sister and Viscount Sele, but not that a fortnight ago, he proposed marriage." Murmurs broke out among the crowd, so her brother paused until they subsided. "Tonight, we not only mark my sister's first season, but I am also proud to announce her betrothal to Lord Sele." A footman with a champagne laden tray appeared beside him, and Fitzwilliam took a glass and raised it. "So, I ask you to raise your glasses to my sister, Georgiana Darcy, the future Viscountess Sele."

A sea of glasses raised above the throng and just as swiftly disappeared.

"While I am certain my sister would dance the first with me and not complain in the slightest, I have no doubt she would prefer to dance with Lord Sele in my stead. Sir?" Fitzwilliam shifted back and cleared the path to her for Nathaniel, who beamed brilliantly as he stepped beside her and she placed her hand upon his arm.

Lady Lindsey stood directly before them, dabbing her eyes with her fine handkerchief, while Lord Lindsey tugged her to their place in the line. When Georgiana looked around them, they were again surrounded by family, with Lizzy and her brother to her left and Richard and Julia to her right. She was fortunate to have such relations who knew she would be ill at ease and would attempt to alleviate some of her distress.

She and Nathaniel both honoured their partner as she curtseyed and he bowed. When he took her hand, he squeezed it gently. "Are you well?"

"I am nervous."

"I know," he said softly. "I could feel you shaking when your hand rested upon my arm. No matter what happens, I shall not be far, so do not fret." He added, "I did notice one or two annoyed men leaving after the announcement of our betrothal, which gratified me."

"You do not wish me to dance with other men?"

"I have no issues with those who are your relations, but you are forbidden from dancing with the others." The twinkle in his eye belied his demand.

"Then, I would be unable to dance with you." With a glance through her lashes, she took Richard's hand as he led her through the next part of the pattern.

"Must you flirt with him in my presence," Richard groaned dramatically.

When she stepped back to Nathaniel, he rolled his eyes. "Is he complaining again? He should really see his reflection when he looks upon his wife. If only we could have him view that pathetic countenance in the mirror." Once they had taken their turn, she took her brother's hands for the next.

"I know I told you before we entered, but I am prodigiously proud of you. I had not anticipated giving you away. I would have been content to have you remain with us forever."

"Yet that is not the way of the world, is it?" she asked as she released him and placed her palm upon the back of Nathaniel's hand. "Are we to dance only the first tonight?" They had discussed the first while planning her entrance, but Nathaniel had not yet secured a second dance.

"Of course not." His brows drew down and he frowned. "I did not expect the first until your brother mentioned it. I did, however, count on the supper dance and the last set of the evening."

"Three? Would that not be too much?" His heated stare thrilled her. How she wished she could draw out her fan, but if she did, he would know how he affected her. He needed little encouragement or more confidence than he already possessed.

"When you leave with me at the end of the night, I shall relinquish the final. Until then, I claim three."

Oh my! They split and she walked around the group, using the moment to catch her breath. He did love to discompose her. When she reached her place in the line, she faced him and did her best to hold his steady gaze and pretend she was unaffected until one corner of his lips began to curl. "What is it?"

He shook his head as they joined hands and turned.

"What amuses you?" she asked.

He passed her to Richard, who leaned closer. "Do not enquire?"

"Pardon?"

"He enjoys knowing he has flustered you. Do not rise to his bait. You are a Darcy, you must know how it is done. You have witnessed your brother doing it often enough." When she stood before Nathaniel again, she did her best to hold his gaze before they shifted down the form.

What if she feigned amusement? She lifted one side of her lips in what she prayed was a seductive expression—or flirtatious at the very least. A crease formed between his eyebrows. "Georgiana?"

She said naught but continued with their dance while he watched her intently. When they were required to take a turn, he would whisper, "What are you about, my love?" but she did not respond. She pretended she had a secret and could do naught but giggle when he enquired of her mood.

When her set with Nathaniel ended, her brother claimed her before Nathaniel could pester her about her alteration. She must seem rather silly for her attitude to have shifted as swiftly as it did, but Richard's advice did turn the tables on the ever-confident Lord Sele.

Fitzwilliam handed her off to Richard for the third in what was to be the last of her male family members for the time being. They were dear to give her a reprieve from the curiosity of those in the room, but she needed to face them at some point. Her uncle, Mr. Bingley, Mr. Bennet, Lord Lindsey, and Sir James all remained nearby in the event she required an excuse.

Of course, Nathaniel was never far. From his place near the column on the edge of the dancing, his dark eyes had followed her every move since the first set ended. Even when her back was turned, she could feel their caress, giving her a certain thrill she had never experienced before.

If she had as she wished, she would have danced with merely her relations for the entirety of the night, but such a circumstance was not possible—and it would be rude, as it was her ball. When her set with her cousin ended, her aunt introduced her to some lord or another, who looked her up and down more than once as one would a prize mare at an auction while he made insipid conversation. She stiffened to prevent a shudder from wracking her body.

She peered towards Nathaniel. Had he noticed the direction of her partner's looks? He would not take kindly to such actions from any man. Two ladies cleared the path before him, revealing his reddened visage, but when his gaze met hers, it softened.

She bit her lip and made another attempt at flirting. She likely appeared as ridiculous as she felt, but his posture relaxed and he grinned at her silliness. Much better!

"Miss Darcy, why have I not danced with you before? You have avoided the best social events the season has had to offer thus far."

Oh, good Lord! She suppressed an eye roll. "I have attended the balls my brother and family sanction as well as made several trips to the theatre, including Lord and Lady Fitzwilliam's ball during the holiday season." She raised herself up in the best impression she could of her aunt when insulted. "Are you insinuating the Fitzwilliams' ball is somehow wanting?"

His eyes shifted back and forth and his forehead creased as though he were working out a particularly difficult riddle. She continued on through the set, pretending he was not her partner.

When the dance concluded, Nathaniel stood at her side. "May I escort you for some punch, Miss Darcy?"

"Thank you, my lord. How did you know I would be parched?" She gave a barely perceptible dip of a curtsey to Lord . . . She should have listened when her aunt made the introduction! "Pray excuse me, my lord." The gentleman pursed his lips and appeared displeased, but she had no desire to spend another second in the intolerable man's company.

"Why do we not hide away so I do not have to share you?" he whispered as they approached the refreshment table. He handed her a glass of punch as she laughed.

"You know we cannot."

Before he could respond, her aunt approached and introduced her to another gentleman and soon she stood back in the line for the next set. This one was not a talker and did not leer, thank goodness. He moved with grace through the dance, thanked her politely when the music concluded, and escorted her back to Nathaniel's side. A perfect dance for one with a gentleman not her betrothed or close family.

As the evening progressed, she never lacked for partners, and though some were preferable to others, Nathaniel disapproved of them all, behaving more akin to her personal guard than her betrothed. She continued to flash saucy little looks in his direction to which he would usually smile.

His manner during the supper dance was much different than the first. He remained quiet, but his eyes held hers for every moment they were partnered. His provocative expression could melt ice and did nothing for her equanimity.

When he made to lead her to the supper rooms, the crush moved little once they reached the doors. Before she could comment, an energetic tug relocated her into the servants' corridor and through to the library.

"Nathaniel!" she exclaimed. "Why do you persist on stealing me away? You know we cannot be caught thus!"

He pulled her into his embrace and bestowed a tender kiss upon her lips. "By the time we get into the supper rooms, all the food will have been eaten, so I thought a moment alone would do much to restore my humour before the latter half of the ball."

She wrapped her arms about his neck. "My brother will not be amused."

"I will tell him the fault is yours."

She pulled her hands back to his arms and stepped back slightly. "I beg your pardon?"

He shifted her flush to him and pressed his cheek to hers. "You kept giving me such seductive glances that I had no choice but to whisk you away."

"I had no idea how I appeared. I felt ridiculous."

His warm laugh rumbled against her chest and melted her insides. "I do not understand what began the coy little looks, but when I decided not to worry about why you were behaving so, I rather enjoyed it."

The sensation of his breath against the sensitive skin of her ear sent a shiver through her. His strong arms brought her comfort and stability, and his complete acceptance brought a sense of belonging she had never experienced before. For the first time since Ramsgate, no feelings of shame clouded every encounter. She had a freedom she had craved but had not known how to attain.

"I love you," she whispered, threading her fingers through the curls at his nape.

His face was visible only long enough to see his huge grin before he claimed her lips. He inhaled as they touched, but the kiss remained tender and heartfelt. His hands tightened in the folds of her gown, and he gradually tensed as their lips met again and again until he wrenched himself away.

"Perhaps we should speak of the weather, or your brother would do as well." He stepped to the fireplace, scratching the back of his head.

As though Fitzwilliam had heard Nathaniel, her brother's voice carried into the room from the closed door to the study. "What is the meaning of this, sir?"

She and Nathaniel looked at the door and then one another. "What do you think that is about?" he enquired.

"I could not tell you," she replied. "I am surprised he is not at dinner, and wondering why we are missing. I do know he would be furious if we were not only caught alone together, but also eavesdropping."

After the initial outburst, the voices were slightly raised but muffled. Nathaniel approached and took her hand, removing her glove and placing a feather-light kiss to her palm. He traced his fingers across the flesh while she held her breath.

"I agree. We should return, though I have no desire to share you again."

Nathaniel handed her the glove, playing with the curls at her nape while she replaced it. "You are tickling me," she whispered.

When she was set to rights, he pulled her into his arms. "Georgiana?"

"Yes?" She smoothed his unruly locks, but his worried countenance gave her pause. "Whatever is the matter?"

"I want you to know that if you are ever uncomfortable with a kiss or my touches, you can ask me to cease my attentions. I do not want you to feel you must—"

She placed her fingers to his lips. "Though I do worry I shall forget where I am and who I am with at some time in our lives, I have not done so yet. I do promise to tell you should I become overwhelmed. Now, what brought this on?"

His lips brushed her fingers and with one last kiss to her lips, he relaxed in her arms. "While I have enjoyed our encounters, recently I have a sudden fear you would suffer my attentions rather than confess you are frightened or ill at ease."

A sarcastic giggle escaped her. "Suffer your attentions, indeed. I never imagined I could crave a man's touch as I do yours."

With a sigh, he took her hands in his. "As much as I would prefer to remain and discuss this further, we should return before we are missed."

Hand-in-hand, they tiptoed into the passage, but as they approached the study door, voices inside became louder. The door opened and Georgiana froze when her curious gaze landed upon none other than a bloody and battered Bridget Younge sitting in a chair before her brother's desk.

Richard halted in mid-stride lest he walk into them, and her brother closed his eyes, likely in horror, and groaned. "Why are you not at the ball?"

Almost the same fearful tremor welled up in her chest as when she was a little girl and her parents caught her doing wrong. She impulsively lurched back, but Nathaniel's hand shifted to her lower back and urged her forward. "Supper was a crush. We decided to forgo the meal."

Richard's jaw clenched and released. "Everyone moved to the supper rooms nearly a half-hour ago. Where have you been in its stead?"

"The library," responded Nathaniel as though the library was the most obvious answer. "Now, Fitzwilliam, do not go off at half-cock. You are beginning to appear much like a beetroot. Besides, I believe we have more important matters to attend." He dipped his head in the direction of Mrs. Younge.

Her brother stepped closer. "People will wonder where you are, Georgiana."

"I am with you, of course." She slipped around Richard, pulling Nathaniel along behind her, but came to another abrupt halt when Mr. Browne came into her line of sight. He stood against the wall, his stare shooting daggers at his mistress.

The man paused the assault of his eyes to bow. "Miss Darcy. I hope you are well."

She greeted the man, but gaped at her former companion, who would not meet her eyes and stared with one eye at the portrait on the opposite wall, the other was black and blue and swollen shut. "Who did this to her?"

"Mr. Browne brought Mrs. Younge by this evening to deliver these," her brother explained, holding out a handful of letters.

She gingerly took them in her shaky hands and perused the directions. One was to each of the papers, two belonged to the most notorious gossips in London, and one was written to, of all people, Lady Jersey.

Richard closed the door and cleared his throat. "Mr. Browne intends on having Mrs. Younge travel to one of the colonies."

A small part of her suddenly lightened. Her departure from England would solve their dilemma. If she remained, she would always be a threat, yet this did not answer her initial question.

"But who did this to her?" She studied her brother and Richard before she noticed Mr. Browne's hateful glare had not wavered in the slightest. A knot rose in her throat. "Sir, did you do this?"

"Her actions threatened myself and my children," he seethed. "I implored her to relinquish those letters, but she adamantly refused. So, I confess, I beat her until she gave over the information."

Georgiana looked about the room. Her brother's expression tightened. He did not approve, but he would not interfere, while Richard's jaw pulsed as he again clenched and unclenched his teeth. Nathaniel's gaze remained on her as he squeezed her hand.

"I apologise for disturbing your evening." Mr. Browne took a menacing stance before Mrs. Younge's chair, but addressed her brother. "Now that you have what you require, we shall depart. You have my word, Mr. Darcy, she will be on a ship within the next fortnight. Come, they have a ball they must return to."

Mrs. Younge did not look at him, but continued to stare at the portrait. He repeated his order but she still did not move, so with a hand to her arm, he hoisted her from the chair and yanked her behind him as they turned towards the door.

While Mrs. Younge resisted the man's attempts to wrestle her from the house, Georgiana's eyes met those of her former companion's and her stomach lurched at the glimmer of something in their depths, something she had never believed Bridget Younge was capable of experiencing—fear.

Did it matter what happened to the woman when she left Darcy House? After all, Mrs. Younge had not cared what happened to her in Ramsgate. Mr. Browne's hand settled upon the latch, and Mrs. Younge flinched.

"Wait!"

Chapter 27

Mrs. Younge could not leave with that man! Regardless of the wrongs Mrs. Younge had done to her, she had no wish to see the woman tortured or even killed, and something in her heart screamed and yelled and ranted that would be the end result.

"Wait!"

"What is wrong?" asked Nathaniel, drawing closer than he should. The gesture spoke of protection rather than intimacy.

Georgiana turned to her brother. "Fitzwilliam, I would be more at ease if we saw Mrs. Younge aboard a ship ourselves. I need to witness her departure from England to know she will never bother me again. 'Tis my peace of mind that requires it. I beg of you."

Her cousin threw his hands up and let them fall to his sides. "She will be gone regardless. Why do I believe there is more to this than you are saying?"

"Believe my motives to be what you wish, but I speak the truth. I want us to ensure she is gone from England forever."

Her brother shook his head. "I do not think it prudent. She would see you come to harm if it suited her intentions, and I daresay she would do the same to Elizabeth or William. Forgive me, but I cannot risk any of you."

Mr. Browne had paused by the door at her objection, but at her brother's decision, he moved to depart once more.

Georgiana rushed forward and barred him from leaving. "Wait!" She looked between each of the men who had such influence in her life. "There has to be somewhere."

Nathaniel took her hand and pulled her away from the door. "Are you certain this is your wish?"

"Yes, I want to ensure Mrs. Younge boards that boat and remains until it sets sail."

His lips did not curve at the ends or even frown, but instead, remained in a thin line while he searched her eyes. It was so difficult to know what he was thinking with that expression! After a moment or two, he looked at her brother. "I know where she could stay until you arrange transport," Nathaniel offered. "I have a small home not far from here. I have never used it since I have been so rarely in London these past few years, but a small staff exists for its upkeep. If you can provide a footman or two to guard Mrs. Younge, she could remain there for now. There are plenty of empty servants' rooms in the attics."

"This is bloody insane!" bellowed Richard. "After all she has done, you cannot seriously be considering this, Sele!"

"She would be isolated and guarded. No one would know she is there with the exception of the servants who care for her and us, and those in my employ are loyal, having served in that household or my parents' household for years."

Her brother ran his hands through his hair and growled. "We are in the midst of a ball. How would we accomplish her removal from this house and relocation to yours without being noticed?"

"He could do it," said Georgiana with a sudden lightness that comes from a revelation. "We are not to dance again until the last, and everyone is at supper. While you make the arrangements, Nathaniel could return with me to the ball, then when the dancing begins again, he could sneak away to escort Mrs. Younge and the footmen to this house. He can join the festivities again once he has returned."

"What of Mr. Browne?" Richard looked from one to the other while he crossed his arms over his chest. "He has an interest in this, yet no one has thought to ask if he takes issue with your interference."

The man in question laughed derisively. "You have just as much if not more incentive to see her banished from this country than I. If you wish for the trouble of ridding us of her, then I shall not object."

"Why help her?" Richard's arm stretched towards Mrs. Younge. He was obviously not done objecting. "You will not receive one word of gratitude from her. She will board that boat and continue to hold you in contempt for how she believes you have wronged her. Why show her mercy? Even the most dissolute beggar on the streets would be more worthy of your efforts."

"Richard?" Georgiana pled. While she did long to see Mrs. Younge depart England for good, she did not necessarily need to witness it. She merely refused to see any woman come to such harm—her conscience would not allow it. "Since we are so different, I doubt I could explain my motivations so you would accept them, but this is something I must do."

Her brother nodded and sat back down at his desk as Nathaniel approached him. "If you will provide me with paper, I can pen a note to the housekeeper so she can prepare a room. I would make a swifter return should everything be ready when we arrive." While Nathaniel quickly penned a note, Richard was too angry to stand still, so he volunteered to locate a footman to deliver it.

Georgiana wrapped her fingers around Nathaniel's arm. "We should make our way to the ballroom. We have surely been missed by now."

Just then, Richard returned and interrupted them. "You cannot just reappear on Sele's arm without tongues wagging. I shall escort you. Sele, you wait for five minutes and then follow."

Sele did not frown or appear put off by Richard's brusque manner—he certainly recognised the prudence of the scheme. After the door to the study closed behind them, Richard let out a long, almost weary sounding breath. "You are too kind to her."

"You do not understand," said Georgiana softly.

"I understand more than you know. I saw your horror when you noticed the bruises and marks upon her face. She has had worse done to you and does not deserve your sympathy. I feel little sympathy for her."

"We do not know for certain what happened to me was worse, do we?"

"Georgiana—"

"No, we cannot know what Mr. Browne did to her in his anger. We set him upon her and I feel responsible for her current state. I wanted her gone, but I did not desire her injured in the endeavour. She looks dreadful and he is still so angry. I could not allow her to leave with him. What if he killed her?"

"Then she would never bother you again." His lips pressed into a rigid line, his jaw clenched, and his shoulders remained unyielding. He meant the words; his experiences with the army made him more callous than her. What he witnessed on the continent could only have hardened him.

"I cannot live with her death on my conscience. I beg you to understand. I do not fault you for your opinion, yet I pray for your understanding of mine. I cannot turn my back and pretend all is well."

He uttered an odd growling moan as they stepped through the doors into the glittering surroundings of the ballroom. "You have never failed to be generous, even as a child. I can never find fault with such a trait, yet I do not wish to see you hurt. I also would not mind seeing her pay."

She watched his profile for a moment, his strong jaw working as it always did when he was upset. "I understand life aboard a ship is perilous," she said softly. "She will be alone and unprotected. As a woman, it will be necessary for her to find a protector if she survives the journey or she will have a more difficult time of it. I am not asking for more than to see her depart safely. Nathaniel and my brother will see to it she can cause no one harm until then."

"I hope you are correct, because I do not trust her."

She glanced around the room that was just beginning to fill again after supper. "Neither do I, but it is only for a short time."

A moment later, Nathaniel walked through the doors leading to the supper room and strode in a direct line to stand before her. "Miss Darcy, would you care for some punch?"

She fluttered her eyelashes. "Why thank you, Lord Sele. I would care for a glass very much."

Richard groaned and Nathaniel gave a wicked grin. She rarely behaved in a coy fashion, but he did seem to enjoy it when she did, which was why she took every opportunity since that discovery to surprise him if she could.

"Can you not wait until I have crossed the room for that," groused Richard. "I shall be forever scarred."

"You exaggerate, Fitzwilliam." He pointed towards the supper room. "I believe I saw your wife speaking to Lord Dunleavey near the pianoforte. You might wish to rescue her before he uses that quizzing glass he favours to peer down her gown." While Richard stalked off muttering curses, Nathaniel offered her his arm and whispered, "We should make a circuit of the rooms before I must depart."

Once she had wrapped her hand around his elbow, he led her through the ballroom to the supper rooms. They moved more quickly through the card room since he knew she did not care for the smoke from some of the men's cigars. Lastly, Nathaniel escorted her to the punch table and then, to his mother, who was speaking to Lady Jersey. Nathaniel pressed one last precious kiss to her knuckles, and her gaze followed him until he disappeared into the crowd.

"I must congratulate you on your betrothal," said Lady Jersey with a sympathetic tone. "Several ladies have set their caps at him these past few years, but Lord Sele never showed any interest in a lady until your arrival in London this winter. He is so attentive. You are to be envied."

"Thank you, my lady. I am honoured by his proposal. I hope to be everything he needs."

"You already are," replied Lady Lindsey with a direct look.

Georgiana squared her shoulders. "I must express my gratitude for the invitations to Almack's delivered this week, Lady Jersey. Miss Bennet is beside herself with excitement at the prospect."

Lady Jersey laughed. "Yes, she thanked me earlier. She is a spirited little thing, but does well to temper it as she does."

"That she does." Lady Lindsey peered behind her where Lydia spoke with Mr. Hanson's parents. "She rarely loses her good cheer. I daresay she has been an excellent friend to Miss Darcy."

"She has indeed." Georgiana's head tilted while she studied her friend, who appeared happy at a glance, but whose neck and shoulders were rigid, as though she had a tree limb pressing against her spine. The poor dear! She would be sore if she held herself thus for the entire evening.

"Is aught amiss?" asked Lady Lindsey.

With a start, Georgiana shook her head. "Oh, no. Lydia looks nervous, is all."

"She will be well." A hint of reassurance laced Lady Jersey's voice. "I believe all ladies are quite at their wits' end making the acquaintance of their suitor's families—particularly if they have never met before. I remember being unable to eat for several days when I was in a similar position."

A giggle erupted from Lady Lindsey. "I shook so I thought I would spill my tea." She patted Georgiana's arm. "You were fortunate we were previously acquainted."

"I beg your pardon?"

The ladies lips pressed closed to suppress their unladylike giggles as they turned to the tall, spindly gentleman who stood at Georgiana's side. "May I be of aid?" asked Lady Jersey.

"Miss Darcy promised me the next and they are lining up as we speak."

Georgiana looked to the line beginning to form. "Forgive me. I had not realised the music would begin so soon." After curtseying to Lady Jersey, she followed the young man to the floor. When that set finished, her next partner, this one broad and balding, awaited her near Lady Lindsey. She wilted a little at the prospect of another two dances. She enjoyed dancing, but since Nathaniel's departure, the night had begun to drag as though it would never end.

Five partners later—or was it six? She steeled herself for the company of some man she had only made the acquaintance of that evening who would speak endlessly of himself, his property, or the latest gossip for the time they were partnered. The last spoke with unceasing praise of the meal, which was appropriate since he still had part of it in his teeth.

"Why, you do not appear to be enjoying your own ball." She inhaled sharply and started, finding Nathaniel standing before her with a smug grin. He leaned towards her just a little to continue in a quiet voice, "My housekeeper had all prepared when we arrived." Despite the nature of the information he conveyed, his low, rich tone soothed her nerves after missing his presence for the last hour.

"I am so glad you have returned." The words rushed out before she gave them much thought, yet his pleased grin and steady gaze prevented her from being mortified at speaking so freely. A tiny part of her still had a difficult time being so open with him. They shared feelings and kisses, but confessions from the heart were still rarely spontaneous. The reserve she embraced for years was a challenge to overcome.

He brushed a kiss to her hand and squeezed before allowing it to slide in a gradual motion from his, caressing her fingers as they released. "I am as well." He reached into a pocket and removed a small velvet pouch. "I retrieved this while I was there. I meant to do so before now but preferred to spend my time with you."

Before she could enquire of what was inside, he spilled the contents into his palm, revealing a single ring. The gem faced away from her, but when he lifted it and held it to slide upon her finger, she stared into the barrel-shaped sky blue stone set on a carved floral band.

"'Tis your betrothal gift. May I?" As though he had problems keeping his hands from her, he pressed his palm to hers, slipping the ring into place. "I hope you like it."

She bit her lip and blinked rapidly in an attempt to ward off tears. "I do. I like it very much."

"I do not know why, but I kept it in my study there. I do not go to that house often, but I always liked the idea of keeping it in our future home."

"I thought we would live with your parents. I suppose I did not think it to be forever, but I did not know you had a house."

"'Tis on Curzon Street. As I said earlier, Gray's Corner is not large—particularly when you consider the other homes on that street, but comes with my title. If we have a son, it will become his when I assume my father's role." He traced his fingertip over the aquamarine. "I am certain my parents would welcome us, but I want for us to do as we wish without regard to others. I want to begin my life with you, not you and my parents." He shrugged. "The house has been empty for some time. I could never bring myself to lease it, though my father thought it prudent. I am afraid it is also in sore need of redecoration."

She could not help but smile. "I have helped Elizabeth often enough. I believe I shall manage."

"I am parched," complained Lydia as she approached, fanning herself. "Mr. Hanson is fetching me a glass of punch. I hope you do not mind if I remain with you until he returns." Her eyes wandered to their joined hands, and she tilted her head. "I should have known the stone would be blue." She giggled and peered around several people towards the refreshment table. "I see Mr. Hanson is returning. I shall leave you to your discussion." She wore an exasperating grin when she swayed into the crowd.

Nathaniel laughed and kissed the ring upon Georgiana's hand. "Her behaviour is strikingly different with you than in company."

"Yes, at one time, she was rather unguarded in her manner and still feels the brunt of her past behaviour when she is in Hertfordshire. She behaves in a stricter fashion in public than in private for fear of causing talk again."

Her next dance partner appeared at Nathaniel's shoulder. "Miss Darcy, I believe the next is mine."

Her betrothed pivoted on his heel and glared, which prompted Georgiana to giggle. "You resemble my brother with that expression. Have you been taking lessons?"

"I shall be waiting here when the set is complete."

As the man led her away, she looked over her shoulder and held Nathaniel's gaze. She did not mind his protective nature as long as he knew her heart belonged to no one but him. She watched for him along the periphery as she made her way through the pattern, and he remained in the same spot, solid and dependable, until she was escorted back to his side.

"You have returned," he observed, stating the obvious.

"I am particularly attached to you, you know." She peered up at him through her lashes. "I shall always return to you."

Chapter 28

March 31ˢᵗ 1817

My wedding clothes are prepared, my wedding gown is completed, and today, the last obstacle to my future sails from England's shores, never to return. I forgave Mrs. Younge long ago for her actions in Ramsgate—more for my own happiness than any debt or request on her part. I had stored a well of hatred deep inside for her and George Wickham and found by releasing my pent-up anger, I released myself. Now, I simply wish to see her gone for my own peace of mind and security.

My brother located a passage to Halifax, and while the wait was a little longer for Mrs. Younge's departure, I thought it preferable to the other choices. I have heard the winters are difficult, but I could never send her to a penal colony, though Richard still argues for her exile to Van Diemen's Land.

I returned to Gray's Corner yesterday with my brother and Nathaniel to view the redecoration Nathaniel and I arranged just after my début. Why he did not bring this to my attention when we were first betrothed still vexes me, but the work is proceeding at a swift pace. Nathaniel surely has paid more than he ought for the wall coverings to be hung before our wedding, though he insists it is no bother, but I dislike the waste. There will be one advantage to the excess spent: I adore the fabrics I chose for my chambers and I am eager to finally see the end result. Nathaniel, however, is being mysterious and did not allow me to view our suite yet. He has a plan afoot. I would bet my life on it.

I must finally confess that the name Gray's Corner for a house is quite odd, but though I have only been there a handful of times, I now find the appellation suits since it seems but a small corner of Curzon Street compared to the grandiose homes surrounding it. I believe it also suits us. We do not require twenty bedchambers or five drawing rooms. When Nathaniel inherits his father's title— hopefully far into the future—the home he will inherit as Lord Lindsey is quite grand. We have no need for such extravagance now.

"The coach is in front of the house. Do you still intend to accompany them?" Her head jerked up. The voice was Lizzy's as she peered inside the slightly opened door. "Your brother will understand if you have changed your mind."

"No, I have not changed my mind. I merely wished to pen my thoughts before I lost them."

Lizzy stepped inside, revealing William perched upon her hip. "Gee!" He wiggled to the floor and ran with his arms outstretched to her. She scooped him up and held his precious little body close. The realisation that she would no longer see him every day dawned in the last week, but when her heart hurt at the thought, she took a deep breath and sought him out to give him a cuddle.

Mrs. Wynn was forever bathing him due to the messes he favoured, and the faint lingering scent of soap in his soft little locks soothed her. Just a few days ago, they returned from Hyde Park with William covered head to toe in muddy water. Despite Mrs. Wynn's hesitation on bringing him out when the pavements and ground were so damp, he sorely required the exercise after a week of wet and dismal weather. Only, instead of just exercise, he found great entertainment in jumping from puddle to puddle, much to his nursemaid's dismay.

She kissed his forehead and smiled. "I must go, but I shall return and we can play with your blocks or cup and ball. Would you like that?" He bobbed his little head up and down, bouncing in her arms while she and Lizzy laughed at his boundless enthusiasm.

"Your brother departed with the earlier carriage, several footmen, and Richard to escort Mrs. Younge. Lord Sele awaits you in the music room. I do not believe Mrs. Annesley prepared for a trip to the docks, so she will remain behind to chaperon Lydia and Mr. Hanson. Lucy will accompany you."

Georgiana grabbed her gloves and reticule and tossed them inside her bonnet, carrying that in one hand while she continued to hold William in the other. When they passed the nursery, Lizzy hugged Georgiana and took William. "I hope you find the peace you seek."

With a kiss to Lizzy's cheek, she took her free hand. "Thanks to my brother and you, I have peace. Now, I have Nathaniel, who has filled my heart and made me whole again, and today is to relieve my conscience. Regardless of Richard's objections, she will have a small amount of money so she is not destitute, and we shall never need worry of her again."

Lizzy squeezed her hand as she gave a slight smile . "I am proud of you. I know Richard has made matters difficult, but he only means to shelter you while he still can. He will protect all of us whether we desire it or not. He is a good man."

"He is, but I do wish he remembered at times that I am no longer a child."

Lizzy giggled. "I am certain he is reminded more and more as your wedding draws near, but we must not stand here all day. Lord Sele awaits you."

After a last kiss to William's pudgy cheek, Georgiana made her way to the music room to find Nathaniel bent over the keys of her pianoforte, picking out a melody with one hand. Taking advantage of the absence of a chaperon, she set down her bonnet, tiptoed behind him, and slipped her arms down his shoulders and around his neck.

He groaned and leaned back into her stomach, looking up into her eyes. "You must promise to do that when we are married so I can pull you into my lap and kiss you senseless." Something about the thought sent a thrill through her, but one small detail marred his plan.

She leaned down and pressed her lips to his. "Yet you have no pianoforte at Gray's Corner."

A lazy smile curved his lips. "Then, I had best run out and purchase one as quickly as I can."

She laughed and swatted him in a playful manner on the chest. "You are incorrigible."

He put his hands on her cheeks and pulled her back down to his inviting lips. "I love you and I love making you laugh. It is the sweetest sound in the world."

He brushed one more lingering kiss to her lips before he stood, took her hand, and pulled her closer. "I wish we could remain here and play the pianoforte and talk all day with no worries to address."

She opened her mouth to speak, but he wrapped his arms around her before a sound could escape. "Do not apologise. I understand and admire your decision. You have every reason to detest and place her in the worst possible situation, yet you show mercy. You are a better person than I, Georgiana Darcy."

"You would not wish a human being to suffer," she said softly, fingering the folds of his cravat.

"No, I would not, but Mrs. Younge hurt you. In my eyes, that is unforgivable."

Their eyes held and in that moment, she understood his dilemma. He had not argued or contested her decision, but allowed her to do as she wished so she was content. He was the best man of her acquaintance.

A throat clearing caused them to separate and they turned to find Lucy standing near the door with Georgiana's pelisse in her hand. "I beg your pardon, miss, but we should be going if we are to arrive on time."

"Thank you, Lucy."

Jobbins helped Nathaniel with his coat and hat while Lucy aided Georgiana with hers. When they were prepared for their trip, they boarded the carriage and proceeded in the direction of the docks. With Lucy present, she and Nathaniel did not speak. Their conversations never failed to touch on the personal and private, which they had no desire to share with a chaperon present, but Lucy did not watch them like a hawk. Instead, her attention was focussed on the goings on outside of the window, affording them a little privacy, though not enough for their liking.

With Nathaniel sitting across from her, there was little they could do without being observed, but Nathaniel grinned while he tapped her foot with his. Georgiana widened her eyes at him and pointed to Lucy, but he only grinned more, showing those dimples that did not help her with her rebuke. He then lifted his eyebrows and stretched his leg across the floor so his booted ankle rested against hers. He was quite bold, but how was that a surprise? He never failed to shock her in some manner.

Just before the equipage came to a halt, he withdrew his foot and straightened before Lucy turned and witnessed his improper behaviour. The step knocked against the door when it was set, and he stepped out first, handing them both down once he had looked around.

The shrill cry of gulls echoed overhead and the odour of the seawater, reminiscent of Ramsgate, flooded her senses. The scent mingled with that of putrid, decaying fish, prompting her to swallow before she gagged. As Nathaniel escorted her to a nearby warehouse, she pulled a scented handkerchief from her reticule and held it to her nose while Lucy did the same. When they approached the smaller building, her brother and Richard exited with Mrs. Younge.

"You are late," groused Richard. She was certain his ill mood was due to leaving his wife to help with Mrs. Younge.

She removed the cloth from her face. "Not very. We have not missed it, have we?"

"No," responded her brother. "The ship is out in the harbour and departs in an hour. The captain needed to speak with his employer, so she will take the ship's tender with him when he returns. He should not be much longer."

Her brother was indeed correct and a tall man emerged from the same door about five minutes after her brother and Richard. He bowed to them. "If you are ready?"

They followed him to a nearby boat where four men loaded the last of some crates on board. The men climbed inside, and the captain held out his hand to Mrs. Younge to help her aboard, but instead of taking his hand, she turned at the last minute and stepped towards Georgiana.

Nathaniel wrapped an arm around her and pulled her close while Richard jumped between them and growled, "Like hell."

"I shall not harm her. I only want to speak to her for a moment." Mrs. Younge's voice sounded tired, even though she had done naught since arriving at Gray's Corner. She had been isolated in a servant's room for the entirety of her stay. Georgiana had not even seen her when she visited to arrange for its decoration.

Richard leaned into her face and sneered, "What could you possibly have to say that my cousin would wish to hear?"

"An apology." Mrs. Younge released a heavy breath as though a weight rested upon her chest.

Georgiana pressed against Richard's arm and shifted to his side. "I shall hear her, Richard. Too many people are about for her to do any real harm. I do not believe she wants to go to gaol." With a huff, he stalked over to her brother and ranted in his ear, while Nathaniel assumed a familiar protective posture at her shoulder.

"Thank you," said Mrs. Younge, her eyes darting to Richard, then Nathaniel, and back. "I realise I owe you a huge debt, Miss Darcy. I do not know your impulse for preventing my departure that night with Mr. Browne, but I know you saved my life. He was furious and would have beat me further had I gone with him, and I would not have blamed any of your family for allowing it. I had a lot of time to think while I was locked away in that room, and I realised I became so desperate to find security, I became what I do not recognise. I was not always this way. My husband died and left me with little but that run-down boarding house and no money, and I began to do what I needed to survive.

"When I met George Wickham, he convinced me I deserved better, and I listened to his manipulations and his lies. I know I hurt you, Miss Darcy—not only by what I did in Ramsgate, but by the letter as well and I would like to apologise. I do not deserve your forgiveness, so I do not expect it of you, but I wanted to have my say."

She turned, but Georgiana grabbed her arm. "I forgave you long ago."

"Do not feel you must say it. I thought to clear my conscience before I start anew. Your brother settled the matter of my boarding house with my creditors and a little money was left when all was said and done. I shall not be completely destitute. I hope to remember who I was before Wickham."

Georgiana wrapped her hand around Nathaniel's arm, drawing strength from his solid presence. "I discovered long ago that anger is a difficult beast to tame. It can eat you alive from the inside and leave you hollow or you can set it free and remain whole. Forgiving you was a selfish act, you see. I had to release the anger before it consumed me. I did forgive you, though."

Mrs. Younge nodded with a tight smile. "I appreciate you saying as much." She glanced back at the boat before she curtseyed. "Farewell, Miss Darcy." She allowed the captain to hand her into the boat and did not look at them again as it was pushed back from the shore.

The wind blew the ribbons from Georgiana's bonnet in her face while she watched the small boat make its way to the ship moored in the harbour. When all its occupants were aboard and the tender hoisted and secured, the anchor lifted, and a portion of the sails unfurled. The process was a lengthy one, yet no one suggested returning to Mayfair or even spoke until the ship began to slowly float away.

"Are you well?" whispered Nathaniel into her ear.

"I am, but I am ready to go home." She leaned her head against his arm, receiving a glare from Richard.

"I shall take you to Darcy House, and in another week, I promise to take you home."

She lifted her face to capture his earnest gaze. "Do you promise?"

His finger trailed down her cheek. "I do—with my whole heart."

"Good, now, we should be going. I have a promise to William to uphold."

"Should I be jealous?"

She could not help but smile. "I do not believe so unless you want to play blocks or cup and ball with us."

His warm laugh vibrated down her spine and curled her toes in her boots. "I believe I would enjoy that. We could take him to Hyde Park if your sister does not object."

He began to lead the way back to the carriage, keeping her tight to his side while ignoring Richard's incessant evil eye. Richard could relax. No one they need worry over was about, and she would be married in a week's time. Richard certainly would not be accompanying them to Gray's Corner after she wed Nathaniel. He could return to his own home with Julia and leave them to themselves.

After he helped her inside the equipage, he took the seat across from Lucy while her maid assumed the same posture as before. How tiresome this was becoming! She did not want to maintain a proper distance or have a constant chaperon anymore.

They began to move and Georgiana looked to Lucy and then to Nathaniel and tugged at the tie, allowing the drapery to fall over the window. At the change of the light, Lucy turned. "Miss?"

"Close the other and change seats with Lord Sele," she requested. Lucy's eyes grew the size of horse chestnuts, and Georgiana reached across to tug the tie beside her. "Oh, for heaven's sake, you are present. We shall not do anything untoward. Is it too much to ask to sit beside him and be able to talk privately?"

"No, miss, but I am supposed to sit with you."

"And I swear I shall not tell my brother. Besides, in a se'nnight, you are in my employ."

Lucy started and paused for a moment before leaning forward and allowing Nathaniel to aid her way across so she did not fall with the movement of the carriage. He then shifted beside Georgiana, his thigh flush with hers while Lucy held the fabric over the window out a little and concentrated on her view.

When Georgiana leaned into his side, Nathaniel wrapped an arm around her shoulders. "Your cousin will have his back up if he discovers us thus."

"We shall change seats again before we arrive. Lucy will be certain to let us know when we are near, and she will not say a word for fear of reproach from my brother. Are you properly scandalised at my willingness to throw propriety to naught?"

She closed her eyes and savoured his laugh. "No, not at all. I take great delight in your impetuous expressions of affection. In many ways, you are like your brother, planned and controlled most of the time. His open manner with his wife never fails to amaze me, but since the night we spent talking, you are less restrained in my presence. I treasure the expression of trust you have shown by more freely sharing your heart."

After removing her glove, she stroked the line of his jaw. "I shall never forget your tenderness," she whispered.

He untied her bonnet, removed it, and pressed his lips to her forehead. "The great danger of being thus is not that I am scandalised, but that we shall scandalise Lucy. I do not think I can help but touch you when you sit so close."

"We shall need to learn some restraint before appearing in public together." She sighed as his hand covered hers on his chest. "We cannot attend a ball and behave as we are."

"Why not?" He dipped his head a little closer to her ear. "I would prefer to remain home in your sole company, but this would definitely make a ball more tolerable."

She drew back. "You enjoy balls and the theatre and all forms of revelry. Why do you speak as such?"

He trailed a finger along the line of her neck. "Because I do not have you at home. When I do, alone with you at Gray's Corner will be the ideal way to spend an evening."

At that proclamation, she could do nothing but smile and bestow a swift kiss to his lips whether Lucy gasped in shock or not.

Chapter 29

April 5ᵗʰ 1817

Here I sit, in my wedding gown, writing in this journal as I have done to ease my thoughts for these past few years. This time, however, Lizzy would have an apoplexy if she were in the room, afraid I might spill ink on the white silk, yet I had an overwhelming urge to pen my thoughts for my last hour as Georgiana Darcy.

My aunt, Lizzy, Lady Lindsey, and Julia have all told me the stories of their weddings and the nervous flutterings they had before taking their vows, but I find I have no such affliction. I slept without disturbance all night long and did not wake until later than is my wont. Even then, it was only due to the whispers of Lydia and Lizzy, who stood beside my bed and debated on the best method of rousing me.

Lizzy, however, has hastened from room to room and exhibited enough nerves for the both of us. I know she wants nothing more than the day to be perfect and for her careful planning not to be for naught, which is endearing but I have had to remind myself of it. Otherwise, I must admit she would greatly test my fortitude before the clergyman even arrives. How would I make it through the wedding breakfast?

I wonder if Nathaniel is nervous this morning? Are the men plying him with spirits as Mr. Gardiner did my brother when William was born? The situation is vastly different, yet the men of my family are quite predictable—brandy cures all nature of ills. It is a wonder none of them are drunkards. One might wonder of Richard if they did not know better, but Julia would throttle him. I do like her! At least if Nathaniel is in his cups, we wed in my brother's home and not in a church.

Nevertheless, the special license is purchased, and we wait for naught but the parson so I can become Lady Sele.

"Georgiana! You will spill ink on your gown!" gasped Lizzy, who stood in the doorway of the dressing room.

"I only wished to pen a few thoughts before the wedding. I have been careful."

Lizzy bustled to the basin of water, grasped the cloth, and presented it to Georgiana. "Wipe your fingers before you touch your gown. You do not want to accidentally mar the fabric. It would be impossible to clean."

She had been careful and had a mere drop or two on her fingers, but instead of arguing, Georgiana took a breath and bit her cheek while she accepted the rag. As she scrubbed away the offending black, a knock rang through the room. "Enter!" she called.

Her brother entered and paused just inside while he closed the door behind him. "When did you grow into such a lady?" A sad smile graced his lips while he approached, removing the cloth from her hand and returning it to Lizzy. "It seems one day you picked our mother flowers and kicked Sele in the shin, and now you are to marry him. What will we do without you?"

Georgiana giggled. "You will have more privacy with Lizzy. I doubt you will miss me much."

His jaw tightened and his brows drew down. "On the contrary, you are my sister, and since our father's death, I have felt something akin to a fatherly affection for you as well. I became accustomed to the thought of you remaining with us forever, so I fear I will be very poor at letting you go."

She blinked repeatedly in an effort not to cry, but her vision clouded and she sniffled as she threw her arms around her brother's neck. "You have Lizzy and William and a baby coming who should occupy your time more than a much younger sister. I shall miss you, too, though." When she stepped back, a teary-eyed Lizzy held a handkerchief before her. While she dabbed her eyes, her brother cleared his throat and stared at the floor until he regained his composure.

"Nathaniel and I shall never be far. Gray's Corner is a short walk and we shall visit Pemberley when you deign to have us—I do not want to miss the birth of my new niece or nephew. I will be married and shall not cause such a scandal this time."

A garbled giggle burst from Lizzy. "Such a ridiculous thing to create gossip over. I expect the quickening any day, but you would be more than welcome to attend my lying-in. I hope you know you will always be welcome."

"I do. We may never live in our own home except in London between you and Lord and Lady Lindsey."

"So, you do not plan on returning to Ireland?" her brother asked.

"Nathaniel might be required to inspect the mines on the property next year, but he assures me we can remain in England if it is my wish."

They all jumped when the door opened and Lydia strode inside. "Why does everyone look as though they have been crying? She is not leaving forever." Lydia hugged Georgiana and kissed her cheek. "You look very well indeed. I cannot wait to see Lord Sele's expression when you enter the room." She held a box out to Fitzwilliam. "You forgot this in the library."

He closed his eyes and laughed softly. "That is the reason I came up."

"What is it?" asked Georgiana.

Her brother offered the box. "A wedding gift from your betrothed. He asked that you might wear it today."

She glanced between each of her loved ones and gingerly lifted the lid. The light reflected and played off the barrel-shaped sky blue stones in the choker, bracelet, and ear bobs within and she inhaled sharply as she held up her ring. "I had no idea it was part of a set."

Lydia appeared spellbound. "I can almost hear Mama's raptures. 'Oh, the pin money! The jewels! How grand you will be!' "

An undignified and uncharacteristic sound came from Lizzy's nose. "She would have said much more if she were here."

"Too true," Lydia agreed, lifting the necklace from the bed of velvet it rested upon. "What do you think, Georgiana?"

Georgiana reached back and unclasped the simpler amethyst necklace she wore and handed it to Lizzy while Lydia helped her with the gift from Nathaniel. When the box was empty, she turned to the mirror and fingered the stones at the base of her neck. When they visited the drapers for the fabric for this gown, Georgiana had considered a pearl coloured silk, but had ultimately decided upon the stark white. She was now glad she had since the ivory would not have looked as well with the sky-blue stones.

Her brother's face appeared over her shoulder. "The parson arrived before I came upstairs, so all is in order when you are ready. I shall await you in the hall." She gave him and Lizzy both one last hug and kiss on the cheek before they left her alone with Lydia.

Her best friend took her hands. "I am so pleased for you. I hope you know."

Georgiana smiled. "If I could but see you so happy."

"I daresay you will soon," giggled Lydia, sauntering towards the door.

"Lydia!" With a lunge forward, Georgiana grabbed Lydia's arm and pulled her back. "Whatever does that mean?"

"I asked Lizzy and Fitzwilliam to wait until after your wedding to announce it."

"He finally asked?" Georgiana covered her mouth with her hands and restrained herself from bobbing up and down.

"Heavens, no! For a man who was bold enough to approach me as he did at your aunt and uncle's ball, he kept becoming tongue tied. I assumed he lacked the courage, so I did as you suggested. I proposed for him."

"What did he say?" she squealed.

"He laughed at my keen perception and declared he should be the one to ask, so he dropped to one knee and proposed."

Lydia's radiant smile lit her entire countenance, which glowed with her happiness. How had Georgiana not seen it before?

"So, you see, we shall be two of the happiest couples in the world."

She wrapped her arms around Lydia's shoulders. "So, we shall. I am delighted for you."

Pulling back from the hug, Lydia shook her head. "Enough of this or we shall all have red eyes and red noses for your wedding." She examined Georgiana from head to toe. "I cannot think of anything we have missed. Have you?"

"I do not need much, Lydia. I would do as an indebted widow and marry him barefoot and in my shift if it was required."[1]

"Thank goodness it is not! Could you imagine your brother's reaction?" Once their giggles were spent, Lydia took her hand and squeezed. "Let us get you married."

When the two arrived in the hall hand-in-hand, Fitzwilliam awaited her, a proud smile upon his countenance. "You look beautiful," he said as Georgiana took his arm. Lydia slipped into the drawing room and Georgiana suddenly began to shake. "Are you well?"

"I am marrying him, Fitzwilliam."

He leaned as though he were whispering in her ear. "If you want to wait or have changed your mind—"

She could not help but laugh at his hopeful tone. "Thank you, but I have no doubts. I believe it is simply the magnitude of it all."

His bearing slumped just a little. "I had to be certain."

Jobbins bowed as she neared the drawing room door, then opened it so they could enter. Her eyes latched onto Nathaniel's handsome face and everything else disappeared, including her trembling, with the pure and true love radiating from his gaze. Her attention never wavered and neither did his. He said, "I will," but she did not think about why until an elbow to both sides of her ribs made her jump.

She glared at Lydia and then, her brother who still stood between her and Nathaniel, while he dipped his head at the clergyman. The parson pursed his lips and huffed. "Wilt thou have this man to thy wedded husband, to live together after God's ordinance in the holy state of Matrimony? Wilt thou obey him, and serve him, love, honour, and keep him in sickness and in health; and, forsaking all others, keep thee only unto him, so long as ye both shall live?"

"Oh! I will," she answered quickly. Nathaniel grinned widely while Lydia, Lizzy, and a few other female giggles came from around her as her brother "gave" her to Nathaniel.

Rather than be caught unawares again, she spared a little attention for the clergyman—enough to know when to say her vows and respond if necessary.

When he began the speech which would end in him proclaiming them man and wife, she glanced down to their joined hands and back to his face, her eyes stinging at the tears now obscuring her vision. Their families cheered when they were declared man and wife and crowded around them to offer their felicitations.

Lady Lindsey hugged Georgiana first. "I wish you such joy, and I know your mother and father would wish for the same were they here. They would be so proud of you, my dearest girl." She kissed Nathaniel's cheek and whispered a few words in his ear before clasping her hands together at her chest and watching them proudly.

Aunt Charlotte used her handkerchief to dab Georgiana's tears as well as her own while Uncle Henry laughed and patted his wife's back. Richard hugged her tightly. "I am pleased for you, Moppet."

She closed her eyes and groaned. "You have not called me that in ages. Why now?"

"You know I had to save it for a special occasion," he chuckled. "I believe today suits."

Her aunt swatted her son with her fan. "I believe Lizzy planned a grand wedding breakfast, though I do wish you had allowed us to invite more than family."

"Aunt, between the Bingleys, the Fitzwilliams, the Audleys, and the Darcys, we have quite a large party. We need no more than our family around us today. Besides, you already have a crush planned in a fortnight."

"And do not think you can send your regrets at the last moment." Her aunt wagged her finger in Georgiana's face. "You are just like your brother, you know."

"What a disturbing thought," mumbled Nathaniel in her ear. She pressed her lips together in order not to laugh and reached around where she could not be seen and pinched him. He could not say such things and expect her to remain composed!

She hugged Jane and Sir James before her new husband tugged her closer. "That was most uncharitable, my love."

"Then do not speak so when we are in public."

"Allow me through! I must have my say!" Her fingers clutched Nathaniel's arm as Lady Catherine waved her walking stick to clear a path. When she finally stood before them, she rapped her walking stick on the floor. "I am quite put out that you did not consult me on this important of a matter, yet despite the lack of my guidance, you have done well for yourself, Niece."

Her aunt might have knocked her down with a feather, she was so taken aback. Had her aunt just complimented her? "Thank you."

"Now, where is that butler of yours? I require some sherry."

"Mother, no!" scolded Anne, whose face changed promptly to a smile as she hugged Georgiana. "I wish you great joy. If you will forgive me, I shall see Mother seated by the fire."

As they walked away, Nathaniel leaned his head over. "How much sherry do you think she has drunk thus far today?"

It was all she could do to refrain from burying her head in Nathaniel's arm and dissolving into giggles. His warm palm rested in the small of her back as he whispered, "I am pleased you wore the jewels." The sensation of his breath on her neck sent a trail of gooseflesh down her spine as it did whenever he spoke near her ear.

"They are exquisite. Thank you."

Lady Lindsey returned and kissed her son's cheek and then Georgiana's while Lord Lindsey laughed silently at his wife. "I feel fortunate to be gaining you for a daughter, Georgiana."

"As I am fortunate to be gaining you for a mother."

The lady dabbed at her eyes with her handkerchief. "I see he finally gave you the rest of the set. The colour of the stones complement your eyes. They are lovely."

"Are they a Howard piece or were they yours before your marriage?" asked Georgiana, who assumed they were a family heirloom.

Lady Lindsey frowned. "Did Nathaniel not tell you the story of them?"

She glanced between them, noticing the sudden red hue of her husband's cheeks. "No, my brother delivered them just before the ceremony."

Nathaniel suddenly cleared his throat. "If you will excuse us for a moment." Before Georgiana could object, he led her out of the drawing room and into the music room. The door barely closed behind her when he pulled her into his embrace and laid claim to her lips, brushing the top and then the bottom before drawing back an inch. "I have wanted to do that since you entered on your brother's arm."

"We shall be missed," she managed before he kissed her again, this time teasing her lips open to deepen the kiss. His fingers dug into her hips and her heart began to beat so swiftly. What if she swooned?

"We are married. What can they do?" His devilish grin made her tummy flutter.

"You make an excellent point." His lips caressed her collarbone while she struggled to remain standing. He could render her a quivering mass with no more than a brush of his lips, but this was more. If he continued, she might just collapse at his feet in a heap.

"Tell me about my ring and the necklace," she said, breathless.

He groaned into her neck. "My mother enjoys a laugh at my expense far too much."

"I do not understand." She combed her fingers through the dark curls near his neckline.

"Do you remember your key?" While he spoke, he stood straight, but his hands still roamed over her back and her hips.

"Of course." Her head jolted back a little. "Did you buy my betrothal and wedding gift when you were fourteen?"

"No," he responded with a shake of his head. "I was sixteen." The last he mumbled against her hair at her temple. "My father brought me to Thomas Gray's establishment on Sackville Street to be of aid in purchasing an anniversary gift for my mother, only I saw this." He touched the stones at her throat, but his finger skimmed her neckline, making her shiver. "Mr. Gray designed and made the piece ten years before, but had purchased it back from a widow requiring funds to discharge her debts. I saw the necklace before my father and entreated Mr. Gray to reserve the set for me until I could return with the money. Meanwhile, Father found the bracelet and was put out that I claimed it before him. Poor Mr. Gray was terrified he had angered an earl, but when I told my father why I wished to buy the set, my father paid for it with the gift we found for my mother. I returned his money that evening."

"How did you acquire enough to pay for such a set?"

"Aquamarines were not terribly fashionable at the time. Mr. Gray only bought the pieces because he paid a good price for them and because he claimed to have a fondness for the floral engraving on the ring. My father was also teaching me how to run the estate in Ireland at the time. The funds were mine to do as I chose, but I never used any of them until then." He bestowed a kiss to her hairline.

"What reason did you give for desiring them?" she asked.

With reddened cheeks, he pulled back and traced his fingers down her cheek. "I told him they matched your eyes, and I intended them to be your wedding gift."

She smiled and tilted her head. "That was a little risky, do you not think? What if you had wed another lady and her eyes were hazel? She might not have appreciated them at all."

"Such impertinence! You were meant to marry me."

"I could not deny you, but I must say that I yielded upon great persuasion, and partly to save your life, for I was told you were in a consumption."[2] She burst into giggles as he tickled her ribs, stepping back in an attempt to flee his agile fingers until she backed against the wall.

"Peace," he growled, "I will stop your mouth."[2]

Before she could duck under his arm, he covered her mouth with his own, ceasing any and all rational thought. His tongue grazed hers and his fingers sought further intimacy than in the past, stroking the swell of her breast not covered by her gown. When his lips joined his hand, she sank against the wall and closed her eyes in a feeble attempt to concentrate on something besides what he was doing to her.

"We must return before we are searched out."

"I wish to go home," he whinged, his forehead resting against her chest and his curls tickling her chin.

With her palms on his temples, she lifted his head. "I do not want to be caught thus—especially if you continue your acquaintance with my bosom."

His wicked grin made her heart stutter. "I hope to have particular attachments to those."

She rolled her eyes and slapped his arm. "I knew better than to wed you. You may call me impertinent, but you are insufferable."

At odds with his last words, he pressed a sweet kiss to her lips. "First and foremost, I have a particular attachment to you. The rest is a close second. It is your heart that mine attached itself to when we were but children and it is your heart that will be bound to mine forever. I cherish that more than anything."

At the not so unexpected knock upon the door, he stepped back and took a deep breath. "This seemed a good idea when it came to mind, but I believe it only made matters worse."

"Georgiana?" came Julia's voice through the door. "I know you are a married lady now, but it has been all I can do to keep Richard from interrupting. I am afraid Darcy is not faring any better."

"Perhaps one day they will cease to think of me as a child."

He entwined his fingers with hers. "I do not think of you as a child."

She laughed and leaned her head against his arm. "And what a relief that is!"

He kissed the crown of her head. "How much longer must we remain?"

"Until it is over."

He gave an affected sigh. "I was afraid you would say that."

---

[1] *In the 18th century, it was a practice for widowed women who had debts, or whose husbands had debts to remarry naked, though usually she was barefoot and wearing a shift. The idea was that she brought nothing to the marriage, so the husband-to-be was not liable for the debts.*

[2] *Shakespeare, Much Ado About Nothing*

Chapter 30

Georgiana gritted her teeth at the strength of Lizzy's grip. When William was born, Mrs. Gardiner held her hand, but Lizzy's aunt could not make the journey for this child, so Georgiana had offered. How had Lizzy's aunt never complained?

"Forgive me," panted Lizzy when she relaxed. "I know it probably hurt. You need not continue if it is too much."

She stretched out the fingers on her hand and winced. "I do not mind if you truly require the aid."

"You were speaking of Lydia."

"Oh!" With Elizabeth breaking all of the bones in her hand, she had completely forgotten the story she was telling Lizzy about Lydia. "Mr. Hanson became frightened when he realised she had been losing the contents of her stomach every morning and insisted on taking her to the seaside."

Lizzy giggled tiredly. "What did Lydia want?"

"Lydia insisted she was well, but adamantly refused to tell him her suspicions. His birthday is near the time she would quicken, so she hoped he would not discover before then. But she decided a trip to the seaside sounded ideal and agreed readily."

Lizzy shifted and rubbed a hand over her swollen belly. "The letter you received yesterday? Was it the first since their journey?"

"Yes," she responded with a grin. "Of course, Lydia would not listen when I attempted to warn her of the dangers of a rocking carriage during the early months. She spent half the trip by the side of the road, sick, and at the first inn, her husband refused to travel further until a physician examined her."

"Please say Lydia told him."

"Yes, she relented, though she called Mr. Hanson frustrating and impossible."

"Oh, Lydia," sighed Lizzy while she closed her eyes and breathed.

"Another pain? So soon?"

"No, my back hurts."

She helped Lizzy to her side and kneaded her thumbs into her lower back. "Is that better?"

Lizzy groaned. "Much, thank you."

"What was the letter you received this morning?" Georgiana continued digging her fingers into Lizzy's impossibly tense muscles. The poor dear had already been labouring for hours and was exhausted. Any relief she could give would certainly be more than welcome.

"It was from my father, but I have not had the opportunity to read it."

"Would you care for me to read it to you? I understand if you are afraid the contents are too personal and wish to wait."

"I would appreciate it if you would, and no, it is unlikely to contain anything I would not share with you anyhow. I confess I have been quite curious since I received it. Sarah is so close to her confinement, I hoped it might have news of her." She pointed to the small writing table near the window. "I put it there when I returned after breakfast."

Georgiana stretched her fingers as she walked over. The letter sat atop a few empty pages, and she picked it up and broke the seal. "Nathaniel found Mr. Bennet entertaining at Lydia's wedding. He found much to appreciate in your father's wit."

"His sense of humour has altered little since I left Longbourn. He still enjoys the folly of others and took great pleasure in studying those acquaintances of 'quality.' " Every part of Lizzy went rigid and she held her breath as another pain gripped her.

She dropped beside her sister and clutched her hand. "Breathe. I cannot think it good to hold it in as you are. Just think, when this is over, you will have another baby to love and cuddle."

"Can we not pass this by and get straight to the cuddling?" she said breathlessly.

"That one was worse than the last, was it not?"

"Yes," she nodded. "Where is the blasted midwife? Mrs. Reynolds sent for her hours ago."

Georgiana pressed her lips together while she wiped Lizzy's sweat-dampened forehead. The words usually reserved for Richard and her brother were now escaping her sister's lips. Where was the midwife indeed? She had no desire to deliver the baby. She might have been present at William's birth, but to be the person to . . . no, a midwife would be preferable.

"I am certain Mrs. Withers will arrive soon."

"She had best do so or Fitzwilliam might need to get over his aversion to seeing me in pain and bring this baby into the world." Lizzy's finger lifted and pointed at Georgiana's chest. "And, your husband better not be putting him in his cups!"

"Nathaniel would not as he would not want Fitzwilliam to do the same to him." She unfolded the letter. "Do you still desire to hear your father's message?"

"Yes, of course," she replied moodily.

"My dear Lizzy,

"When Lydia was born and the midwife told your mother and I we would have no further children, I felt it was a good thing since we could not afford any more girls as it was. Your mother, who realised she would never bear an heir, turned silly and I, at a loss as to what to do, hid in my book room.

"Sarah, as you know, pulled me from my self-imposed exile and became my world, and I cannot express how terrified I became when she informed me she was with child. I am sure your husband has similar feelings of helplessness and uncertainty as I did. But, for the first time, I never worried whether the child was a boy or a girl. Well, God certainly has a sense of humour!"

Lizzy frowned and struggled to draw herself up to sit. "What does that mean?"

Georgiana opened her mouth to answer, but Lizzy leaned forward. "Well, what does it say?" She bit back a laugh and trailed her finger down until she found where she left off.

"My beautiful wife began having pains while I slept, yet kept me in the dark until I rose for the day and she could no longer hide her discomfort. The midwife was summoned and I remained at her side and held her hand until the wretched woman refused to do her job until I departed.

"Kitty's and Mary's husbands awaited me in my study and good men that they are, tried to distract me from what was happening above, but to no avail. It was quiet, too quiet. Your mother's wails began from her first pain until she delivered, yet if Sarah made a noise, I never heard it.

"Seven hours later and after an entire decanter of brandy, Mrs. Hill entered to tell me I was needed in my wife's bedchamber. I climbed the stairs, my heart full of dread that some misfortune took my Sarah from me, but when I opened the door of her chamber, she cradled a baby in her arms looking lovelier than I remembered. She laughed when she told me I had a daughter, because what else could we do but laugh?"

Lizzy sighed. "Poor Papa. It seems his lot in life is to be plagued by daughters. I so hoped for a brother. It would be nice to see Mr. Collins usurped, would it not?"

"He would travel to Longbourn in a fury if your father suddenly had an heir. The petty little man would not take losing his inheritance well. I am willing to wager he would expect your father to owe him some recompense."

Her sister's eyes lit. "Sarah is still of child bearing years. They could have another child. What would you care to wager?" Lizzy doubled over in pain, and Georgiana sat there with her mouth gaping.

"You truly wish to wager on whether you have a brother?"

"Yes," she gritted out.

While Lizzy panted and groaned at the pain gripping her stomach, Georgiana looked back down at the note.

The laughter did not last long, however. Before I knew what was happening, Sarah cried out in pain, Mrs. Hill took the baby, and the midwife began barking orders. I suppose she found herself too occupied to eject me from the room once more, so I remained and held Sarah's hand, terrified I was about to lose her.

Her agony lasted another hour before the midwife placed a squalling baby boy directly from Sarah's womb to her chest. Then, I fainted.

Georgiana gave a shrill inhale and covered her mouth with her hand before laughing madly.

"Georgiana?" Lizzy tore the letter from her fingers, her eyes roving back and forth over the paper until she must have reached the same place Georgiana had. Her hand containing the creased paper dropped to the bed and Lizzy gave a sobbing laugh. "Twins? I have a brother! Fitzwilliam!"

Dear Lord, how could Lizzy yell at such a volume? She covered her ears in case she called again. Thank the Lord, he had sent word he would be working in his bedchamber, else she might have yelled louder.

"Fitzwilliam!"

Her brother tore into the room a moment later like the hounds of hell were on his heels. "Elizabeth? Whatever is the matter?"

She held the letter aloft with tears running down her cheeks. "I have a brother."

"And a sister," added Georgiana.

"Twins," clarified Lizzy, "My sister was born first and then, my brother surprised them all."

Fitzwilliam looked over the letter and a low chuckle rumbled from him. "He fainted! Hah! And he thanks me for the excellent bottle of French brandy I gave him when Lydia wed. It seems he celebrated late into the night."

That one eyebrow of Lizzy's arched to her hairline. "Do not make sport of him for fainting, dearest. Unlike you, he actually remained and made it through the birth. Since you have yet to even attempt such a feat, you should not find humour at his expense."

He scratched the back of his head awkwardly. "Yes, well." After a glance about the room, his face contorted into a menacing glare. "Have you no one but Georgiana to attend you? Mrs. Reynolds sent for the midwife hours ago."

"I am uncertain what has occurred. I began labouring and all and sundry vanished."

"That is unfair, Lizzy. Phoebe has come and gone several times and continues to ensure we have need of nothing, the scullery maid has replenished the fire, and a maid brought tea and broth not even an hour ago."

Lizzy grabbed her stomach and cried out, and Fitzwilliam turned as white as snow, prompting Georgiana to jump up and steer him to the side of the bed.

"Sit and put your head between your knees. Neither of us can move you if you swoon."

After a few long and heavy breaths, her brother turned and grabbed Lizzy's hands. "I am sorry. I am so sorry."

"Why are you apologising?" she panted. She arched her back and whimpered. "On second thought, you should be. You took great enjoyment in doing this to me."

Georgiana bit her lip to keep from giggling at her sister's words and her brother's bewildered look in her direction. "She does not mean it," she whispered. "Comfort her. You should know how it is done."

He turned and brushed the hair from his wife's eyes while she grasped his arm and growled. Georgiana had to give him credit. He did not complain. The only hint of any pain on his part came from him staring at the hand mercilessly gripping his arm with wide eyes. When the pain subsided, he let out the breath he had been holding. "I love you."

"You should," she muttered, winded. "Where is the midwife? This baby will not wait much longer."

Hurriedly, Georgiana pulled the bell, but Lizzy's lower back pulled away from the pillows behind her and she cried out again before anyone could respond. "I need to push."

Georgiana rushed to her sister's side while Fitzwilliam stood paralysed, watching his wife writhe in pain. "Oh, for heaven's sake! Fitzwilliam! Do not just stand there! You must help us!" He started from his stupor, his eyes moving from Lizzy's head to her feet and back.

"What do I do?"

"Fitzwilliam! You have helped horses and sheep give birth. Is it really so dissimilar?"

"I do not appreciate being compared to a sheep! Or a horse!" Their heads both jerked around to Lizzy whose hands fisted the sheet below her, her knuckles white with the strain. Her head dropped back, a low moan hummed from her lips, and her knees drew up under the bedclothes. Before Georgiana could scold her brother further for his inaction, he whipped the covers from his wife and sat at her feet.

"I see the head," he yelled. "Elizabeth, you should see the hair! He has a full head."

Lizzy slumped back into the pillows as Mrs. Reynolds bustled in and gaped at her master. "Sir, I have sent for the midwife, but I have not had so much as a message from her."

"Why has no one been assisting my wife and sister?" he asked angrily as Lizzy moaned once again and gripped Georgiana's hand as though she were trying to fold it in half.

"I have checked on Mrs. Darcy since her pains began this morning. I sent for the midwife, as I just said. Your wife took so much longer with Master William. I never thought she could be this close this soon."

While Mrs. Reynolds spoke, Fitzwilliam watched his wife's progress with a creased forehead and wary eyes. "Do you know how to deliver a child?"

"No, sir!" She backed from the bed so fast she nearly tripped on the rug. "Forgive me, but I have only been present at two births, that of your son and that of Lady Sele."

Lizzy collapsed against the pillows and heaved in gulps of air. "I am so tired."

Georgiana wiped her sister's face with a damp cloth. "I know you are, but you are so close. You want to hold your child, do you not?"

"Elizabeth, the head is out, sweetheart. I am holding our baby's head in my hand. You just need to push the rest of him out." Georgiana watched her terrified and reticent brother, who had all of a sudden transformed into the commanding presence she had not seen since Ramsgate. Thank God! Mrs. Reynolds handed him a towel and whispered something in his ear.

Then, Lizzy tensed once more and crushed Georgiana's hand with hers as she bore down with all her might. Fitzwilliam's countenance was the picture of concentration while he urged her to continue and praised her. After a minute or two, Fitzwilliam's laugh filled the room as he lifted an exceedingly angry and squalling baby and placed it on Elizabeth's chest. "We have a daughter!" he laughed.

"Oh!" she cried, wrapping her arms around the naked little body. Mrs. Reynolds brought a few more towels so Georgiana could help Elizabeth cover and clean her.

Mrs. Reynolds held out a ribbon. "Sir, you must cut the cord and tie it off."

Her brother took the ribbon and levelled a good-humoured glare at their long-time housekeeper. "For someone who claims to be unable to deliver a baby, you have a great deal of knowledge on the subject."

"Really, this is common sense, sir."

Lizzy giggled and winced but helped turn the infant over so her husband could do as he was instructed. When all was done, Georgiana took her new niece to a table set up near the fire to finish cleaning her.

She was so beautiful! And that hair! It was not like the spattering of fine hair William had when he was born, but was thick like Lizzy's. She had yet to open her eyes, but she had the longest eyelashes and the sweetest little rosebud mouth. Georgiana took an additional moment to kiss her little feet and caress her tiny fingers. Once she was swaddled snugly, she returned the child to her mother. "Does she have a name?"

"Rebecca," said her brother as he took the place beside Lizzy and wrapped his arms around her. "Rebecca Anne Georgiana Darcy."

A wet drop landed upon Georgiana's cheek as she covered her mouth with both hands. She lowered her fingers just enough to say, "Truly?"

"We would be pleased if you would be her godmother." Lizzy's voice was faint. Poor dear was exhausted!

"Of course. I am honoured." After kissing each of them and giving Rebecca an extra on the nose, she clasped her hands. "You should sleep while you can, and I need to tell my husband of his new niece."

"Lord Sele has been wonderful at keeping young William occupied," added Mrs. Reynolds. "He took him for a long walk around the pond and to see the horses. Mrs. Wynn said the dear fell asleep for his nap the moment his head touched the pillow."

Lizzy smiled. "He will make an excellent father."

"I believe so," beamed Georgiana.

Fitzwilliam and Lizzy turned their attention to the baby, so she slipped from the room and hurried from the family wing, down the stairs, and to the hall. She had not asked Mrs. Reynolds where he was. How silly of her!

She stood there a moment longer, looking at the different doors, when the faint sound of a pianoforte sounded from the direction of the music room. "Nathaniel!" she whispered. He sat bent over the keys when she entered, so she tiptoed behind him and twined her arms around his neck.

"I did not think to see you again until after the birth." His voice was low and rumbling.

"We have a niece."

He swivelled around with his mouth agape. "But the midwife has not yet arrived."

She giggled as he pulled her into his lap. "Babies do not come according to any schedule or the presence of a midwife."

"I know that, Georgiana, but are you saying you delivered her?"

"No, my brother did."

He lifted his eyebrows. "Truly?"

"Yes, she called him in to tell him of her father's news—his wife gave birth to twins, one boy and one girl—and when he realised the midwife had not yet arrived, he remained. I do not believe he would have done so if he had the choice. Her father was present for his son's birth—though inadvertently—and fainted." At Nathaniel's chuckle, she leaned away from him. "Do you think you could perform better?"

His warm palm pressed against the swell of her stomach and his thumb caressed her in a soothing back and forth motion. "I have no objections."

"You cannot deliver this baby!"

"You are the one who issued the challenge," he said with a cocky grin.

"Because I did not believe you would rise to it."

He pulled her closer to his chest and rested his chin on her shoulder just like she adored. "We shall remain until the churching and christening, and then we return home to Thornhill. No more travelling. I want you rested before your confinement. I do not want to take any chances with you or the child."

"When was the last time you visited Thornhill?"

"When your mother was ill. When we did not stay here at Pemberley, we often resided there when we were in this part of the country. Father managed most of the business while I was in Ireland. No doubt it is also in need of decoration. I thought that would keep you happily engaged until the birth."

"Your mother said she will attend me, and Julia has offered to come as well."

"Thornhill is but thirty miles. Could Lizzy make the trip?"

"I do not expect it with such a new baby." She hoped Lizzy could make the trip, but her new mother would be as much of a comfort as Lizzy. She would make do.

Their baby kicked where his hand rested and a beaming grin suffused his face. He bent over and kissed where the little hand or foot pressed, then kissed her softly.

"I never knew," she whispered against his lips.

"What?" he responded, stroking the swell of her stomach.

"That I could be so happy." Her vision clouded with tears. "You have been so patient with me and I love you so much." He had indeed been the most patient of men. While she had been willing to give herself to him on their wedding night, he wanted to wait, though all evidence suggested it pained him to do so. Instead, they kissed and touched until she was more comfortable with the intimacy—and the lack of clothing. She did become uncomfortable from time to time, but he never pressed. He held and cuddled instead, which only made her love him more.

"How could I be anything but when you are my whole heart? Lord help me if this child is a little girl with her mother's eyes and gentle smile."

"She would wrap you around her littlest finger the moment she entered the world." His chest vibrated with his soft laughter.

"You will always be my first love." He spoke with his lips barely touching her temple, the warmth of his breath making the flesh prickle. "I shall always be particularly attached to you."

"I shall hold you to that." Holding his hands, she shifted them so she could stand and tugged for him to follow.

"Where are we going?" he asked.

"I am in need of a nap and I thought you would enjoy tucking me in."

"I would indeed." Though his voice was tempered, his eyes betrayed his thoughts. The look was quite familiar and made something besides the baby flutter in her tummy.

Georgiana and Nathaniel remained at Pemberley until Rebecca's christening, when they were named her godparents. Three months later, Thornhill's walls were the ones filled with the angry squalling of a child as Arabella Elizabeth Grace Howard entered the world.

Despite the challenge issued at Pemberley, her husband did not deliver his new daughter, though he refused to leave his wife during the birth—much to the consternation of the midwife and the amusement of his mother.

When Arabella's eyes first opened, she had the blue-grey eyes common in most infants, but Nathaniel insisted they would be crystal blue like her mother's. For a time, it appeared as though he might be correct until they began to change a month before her first birthday, turning a dark brown like his.

Still, she wrapped him around her tiniest finger with her gentle smile and little cupid's bow pout, and he swore she would never have a particular attachment to any gentleman—at least until she was five and forty, that is.

The End

Acknowledgements

The story of Georgiana and Nathaniel almost stayed locked inside my head. I have friends who were raped, and I'd been told their stories but I really worried about doing it justice and making Nathaniel and Georgiana's story plausible. Something inside me wanted to write it regardless of the challenge, so I went for it. It wasn't always easy and it took a lot longer than planned, but with the support of my friends and family, I managed to write what was in my head. I just hope others enjoy it as well.

My family is always the first to receive my love and appreciation for their unwavering support. My husband listens to my gripes when a story line frustrates me and is in the process of reading my books. He has never failed to take the children out for a day when I required it to write. For this book, however, he was deployed for the last half of the writing. It made things all the more overwhelming and difficult, but we muddled through as we always do. I love you, Brandon! My children may not read my books, but they think it's cool that I write. They give me advice at times and are very supportive. I couldn't do this without them!

I've had a wonderful group of friends and fans from Meryton.com and DarcyandLizzy.com since I started. They're always good for an ego boost and are a great sounding board for a new story.

I've had a number of betas along the way, but Lisa Toth and Suzan Lauder have stuck with me from the beginning or nearly the beginning. They have become amazing friends and are always a willing ear or eyes when I need an opinion on anything from a book to a blog post. I have learned so much from them both, and I owe them so much.

My editor, Brynn, was a lucky find. Who knew a cup of coffee and discussion on editing would lead here? She adds the multitude of question marks that I forget, fixes my complements, and keeps me consistent. I'm just thrilled she could take the time between diaper changes and feedings to ensure Georgiana and Nathaniel's story was what it should be.

One last thank you to Kathy and Brenna for proofreading! I am terrible about changing things as I read over and over. I really appreciate the help. It saves my sanity.

JAFF is a relatively small and tight-knit community, and I love that. The support of other authors in the genre is lovely as is the support and devotion of our fan base. Huge thanks to everyone who has purchased my books, left me wonderful messages, and followed me after reading one of my stories. I wouldn't be able to have this much fun without your encouragement.

About the Author

L.L. Diamond is more commonly known as Leslie to her friends and Mom to her three kids. A native of Louisiana, she spent the majority of her life living within an hour of New Orleans before following her husband all over as a military wife. Louisiana, Mississippi, California, Texas, New Mexico, Nebraska, and now England have all been called home along the way.

After watching Sense and Sensibility with her mother, Leslie became a fan of Jane Austen, reading her collected works over the next few years. Pride and Prejudice stood out as a favourite and has dominated her writing since finding Jane Austen Fan Fiction.

Aside from mother and writer, Leslie considers herself a perpetual student. She has degrees in biology and studio art, but will devour any subject of interest simply for the knowledge. Her most recent endeavours have included certifications to coach swimming as well as a fitness instructor. As an artist, her concentration is in graphic design, but watercolour is her medium of choice with one of her watercolours featured on the cover of her second book, A Matter of Chance. She is also a member of the Jane Austen Society of North America. Leslie also plays flute and piano, but much like Elizabeth Bennet, she is always in need of practice!

Leslie's books include: *Rain and Retribution, A Matter of Chance, An Unwavering Trust, The Earl's Conquest, Particular Intentions*, and *Particular Attachments*.

Two strangers with no one to turn to but each other...

Fitzwilliam Darcy is in a difficult situation. His father is pressing him to propose marriage to the last woman in the world he would wish to take as his wife. With a fortnight to announce his betrothal, he makes the acquaintance of Elizabeth Bennet, who is in a predicament of her own.

Could Darcy be willing to consider Elizabeth as a solution to his problem and to hers? And can Elizabeth ascertain enough of Darcy's character to trust him upon nothing but a first impression?

"The book is everything touching, full of emotions, funny, sentimental, whatever you need, wish or hope." - Obsessed by Mr. Darcy

"I loved this unique premise! There was desperation, danger, a daring rescue - it was fascinating and gripping!" - Austenesque Reviews

"I found the reason for the arranged marriage in this book to be very different and unique from any I have previously read. Ms. Diamond, your skillful writing made it seem plausible and I loved it." - More Agreeably Engaged

Fascinated upon a first acquaintance, the Earl of Matlock is a determined suitor, but Rebecca Fairchild is not so certain. The earl is kind, yet he is always so frustrating and stubborn! He is not what she had planned or what she ever imagined in a partner. Other ladies have also laid claim to the handsome Lord Matlock despite his preferences. Can he convince Rebecca he is her future or will other forces stand in the way of their happily ever after?

A prequel to An Unwavering Trust!

"All the characters in this tale were well-defined, strong, and memorable. Whenever I put this book down, my head would remain full of them for long periods after." - Austenesque Reviews

"I fell in love with the Earl when Rebecca did." - Obsessed by Mr. Darcy

www.ingramcontent.com/pod-product-compliance
Lightning Source LLC
Chambersburg PA
CBHW070912180626
46817CB00003B/1022